=ADVANCE PRAISE FOR *LOTUS BLUE*=

"Forget the Mad Max comparisons: Sparks is far more ambitious than that. *Lotus Blue* is *A Canticle for Leibowitz* by way of *Neuromancer*."

—Peter Watts, author of *Blindsight*

"A mythic, far-future outback populated by superhuman soldiers, house-sized reptiles, and half-crazed armored vehicles: If that doesn't sound incredible to you, you have no heart. *Lotus Blue* is the year's most compelling science fiction novel."

—Zachary Jernigan, author of *Jeroun: The Collected Omnibus*

"*Lotus Blue* is sci-fi author Cat Sparks's debut novel, and for a first journey it's a hell of a ride. As intelligent and thought-provoking as it is exciting . . . From the opening paragraphs you can feel the desert heat and the sand whipping your face."

—*Starburst* magazine

"*Lotus Blue* is SF adventure on steroids. A dystopian vision worthy of H. Rider Haggard and the Mad Max film franchise."

—Jack Dann

"Vivid, compelling, and relentless, Cat Sparks makes you care about the soul of a mecha future as you hang onto the edge, feeling the sandy grit between your teeth."

—Tina LeCount Myers, author of *The Song of All*

LOTUS = BLUE =

Cat Sparks

Page 272 contains an excerpt from "A Garden Song" by Henry Austin Dobson.
Page 272 contains an excerpt from "Ode to the West Wind" by Percy Bysshe Shelley.
Page 272 contains an excerpt from "Dover Beach" by Matthew Arnold.
Page 273 contains an excerpt from "I closed my Eyes To-day and saw" by William Force Stead.
Page 360 contains an excerpt from "Hávámal," taken from the *Codex Regius*.

Talos Press books may be purchased in bulk at special discounts for sales promotion, corporate gifts, fund-raising, or educational purposes. Special editions can also be created to specifications. For details, contact the Special Sales Department, Talos Press, 307 West 36th Street, 11th Floor, New York, NY 10018 or info@skyhorsepublishing.com.

Talos Press® is a registered trademark of Skyhorse Publishing, Inc.®, a Delaware corporation.

Visit our website at www.talospress.com.

10 9 8 7 6 5 4 3 2 1

Library of Congress Cataloging-in-Publication Data

Names: Sparks, Cat, author.
Title: Lotus Blue / Cat Sparks.
Description: New York : Talos Press, 2017.
Identifiers: LCCN 2016017986| ISBN 9781940456706 (hardcover : acid-free
    paper) | ISBN 9781940456737 (ePub)
Subjects: LCSH: Voyages and travels--Fiction. | Imaginary places--Fiction. |
    BISAC: FICTION / Science Fiction / General. | FICTION / Science Fiction /
    Adventure. | GSAFD: Science fiction. | Fantasy fiction. | Adventure
    fiction. | Dystopias.
Classification: LCC PR9619.4.S628 L68 2017 | DDC 823/.92--dc23
LC record available at https://lccn.loc.gov/2016017986

Cover illustration by Lauren Saint-Onge
Cover design by Lesley Worrell

Print ISBN: 978-1-94045-670-6
Ebook ISBN: 978-1-94045-673-7

Printed in the United States of America

For my parents, Betty and Cameron. Miss you every day.

= ONE =

The Van was taking the longest time to cross the Summersalt Verge. Thirteen wagons, rolling slow, were ragging on Star's nerves. The tanker port of Fallow Heel lay a whole two days ahead of them. Three if they didn't pick up speed.

The Van first started crawling when the dogs caught scent of danger. Smells like mines, said Remy, but it turned out to be a false alarm. Just Dead Red trash, blown and tumbled across the Verge, tainted with contaminated sand. The dogs were bored and so was Star. Two more days of sun-bleached desert, dust and heat and the stink of camel sweat, bumping over rocks and rifts and potholes.

The wagon tops were overflowing. At Sternpost they'd taken on more tankerjacks than they should have. *Wannabes* in fancy kit, claiming they'd be striking lucky on the Black: the deadly spit of Obsidian Sea jutting out into the Red from Fallow Heel. A no man's land beyond all laws and rules. Fat chance.

Caravan master Benhadeer let anybody travel who could pay. Benhadeer was always broke and owing favours, which meant the Van was dangerously overladen. A slow and obvious, easy target, ripe for the picking if a local warlord or swarm of desperate refugees crossed their path.

Rumbling unsteadily through the fringes of the outer 'steads. Ragged children running at their wheels. A rock came hurtling past Star's ear. The brat who'd thrown it had skinny limbs, bare feet, and matted hair. She looked disappointed to have missed. Star contemplated shifting as the brat scooped up more missiles from the dust, but she'd wrangled hard for her spot on wagon six and she wasn't going to give it up for nothing. She'd suffered plenty worse than small stones. Those barefoot kids had older brothers with better aims, larger rocks, and stronger arms.

On wagon six, Star could avoid her sister Nene, her sun-bleached dreadlocks concealed beneath a scarf. Six was stacked with regulars. A handful of so-called dancers clutching parasols against the sun, their cotton saris billowing like sheets. The camel drover with a busted leg propped up on a recliner rigged by one of Lucius's point riders. Yeshie, the fat old bone caster, and Mara, her one-eyed friend, snug together gossiping like children. Their laughter blasting in short bursts, joyful against the Road's stark desolation.

Star perched with a group of older women checking out the wannabe tankerjacks. Fifteen in all had joined the Van at Sternpost. One amongst them was particularly handsome. He had a golden earring and wore peculiar clothing beneath his galabeya, as did his two companions. She'd caught an accidental glimpse of it when a gust of wind rose, spitting sand in all their faces. The loosely-fitting fabric revealed, for a brief moment, sleek, dark material that fit like snakeskin, black as charcoal, its surface ridged and patterned. Nobody knew how to make such garments anymore. Not for several hundred years—not even the fancy tailors of Rusk Harp, nor the merchant princes and professors of Sammarynda. If Golden Earring and his two friends hailed from Sternpost, then Star was a monkey's aunt. Princes, that was what they were, from the coast or from across the Risen Sea. But what were a trio of Sammaryndan merchant princes doing amongst the Sternpost rabble, atop a Van, so far away from home?

The Sand Road wound through the back end of nowhere. Thirteen wagons, sucking power from the sun. Star waved as the brat kept up with the old-world butyl wheels, lobbing rocks at the weathered solar strips along the sides, her freckled face all crumpled in concentration. Shouting what homesteaders always shout at Vans: wards and curses to fend off evil luck.

Golden Earring peeled a mandarin, its colour bright against the drab weave of his galabeya. He taunted the little rock thrower with it, savouring each juicy segment as she gaped. The brat had probably never seen a mandarin before. Not much grew along the inner Verge but acacia trees and hardy, tasteless melons. Last year date palms had lined the way beside stubs of long dead mango trees, but red sand crept across the Verge and killed them all.

His two companions cheered as he tossed the brat a curling scrap of rind, perhaps with a couple of segments still attached. She scrabbled after it, falling to her knees, snatching the bright thing and stuffing it into her mouth.

A year ago this stretch of Verge had been patched with hardy green. No feast of plenty, but enough to keep starvation from the door. Enough for homesteaders to trade surplus with passing Vans. Not now. Now there was nothing but creeping fingers of sickening red, poisoning what little soil remained. Homesteads abandoned, the people gone away, off to the towns to see what fortunes smiled. It would not be long before Star went too, a plan her sister could not catch wind of under any circumstances. Which was why she had to keep in good with Remy—at least for a day or two.

Remy. Star never should have slept with him. He'd been hanging around her ever since, as if she would ever make the same mistake again.

A gust of wind blasted her face with fine sand granules. The distant slam of a hatch flipping open. That all-too-familiar voice calling out across the wagon tops.

"Star? What happened to those willow bark shavings?"

Nene. Upwind, balancing on number four and yelling out across the heads of weary travellers. Star had hoped her sister was distracted by her notes. When the wagons rolled, Nene knew Star perched as far away as possible from the stink of dried herbs, bitter solvents—and hard work.

Star pretended she didn't hear. She edged a little further towards the wagon's end, for all the good it would do. Nene didn't believe in down time. There was always something in need of grinding: roots, stems, leaves, or petals. Potent liquids sloshing in vials nailed fast to the wagon walls.

The wind was definitely picking up. The wannabe tankerjacks adjusted khafiyas and galabeyas, passing piss-coloured liquor in glass bottles from hand to hand. Up closer, the one who'd taunted the brat with a mandarin was even better looking than she'd thought. His eyes were large and deep and green. A proud nose. Thick lips, but not too thick. That golden earring half obscured by lush, dark curls.

She caught his eye. The corners of her mouth edged up into a smile. Golden Earring did not return the favour.

"Star," snapped Nene. "The willow bark. Where is it?"

Her sister towered over her, hands on her hips, standing steady against the wagon's jolting motion as the sun made a halo around her head.

"Haven't ground it up yet," Star confessed. "Shavings are still wrapped up tight in muslin."

Nene snapped back at her, words drowned out by the thunder of the wheels.

Whatever she'd said caught Golden Earring's attention.

"There's ants in the honey again—do you know how much that stuff costs?" Nene repeated, louder this time. "And why are there no bandages prepped and rolled?" Nene gestured to the group of Sternpost wannabes—half drunk, some of them—trading insults on number seven. "How long before one of those idiots falls or gets shoved under the wheels?"

Star smirked at the thought.

"Star—I'm serious—are you even listening to me? You're not pulling your weight around here. You haven't been pulling your weight since Transom Swathe."

Star shrugged, keeping one eye on Golden Earring, who seemed to be listening very intently to their conversation. Unlike the others, he had not been swigging from the bottles passing hand to hand.

"Fallow Heel is coming up. I need you to focus and catch up with your chores. There's people who need us. Desperate people—don't you ever forget that."

She was going to argue back but Nene interrupted, giving Star a swift nudge in the arm—the metal splint embedded in Star's flesh was showing. She tugged her sleeve down to cover it, waiting to cop an earful from Nene about how they had to keep themselves to themselves, not wind up vulnerable to strangers and their questions.

But Nene didn't hang around. She turned and headed back the way she'd come, nimbly dodging around other travellers, both seated and standing, as the wagons rocked and jolted from side to side.

Star folded her arms across her chest. Transom Swathe was where she'd gotten drunk enough to go with Remy, mere hours after Lucius had promoted him to point rider, replacing Jacko's elder brother who'd decided against continuing up the Road. Damn Lucius had him riding up the front, spitting distance from number one; Benhadeer's own wagon. "How 'bout you an me," Remy had said, a greasy lock of hair hanging in his eyes. "Stick with me, girl, an' we'll do alright."

She hadn't answered. Couldn't stand the sight of him once she'd sobered up. Just another dusty Van rat with no coin in his pocket. Riding up and down the Road till some fat warlord put a bullet in his skull. "How 'bout it, huh?" he'd called after her, clueless, like they all were. *How 'bout what, Remy? How 'bout what, precisely?*

Nene didn't get it. Nene still thought she could save the world—or what was left of it. Thought she could make a difference. That setting broken bones would set things right. Nene, her ten-years-older sister, better in every way. Kind, caring Nene, who kept healing sicknesses and patching wounds, no matter if people could pay or not. No matter how many sprung up to take their places. No matter what the Road threw at them, Nene was always steadfast in her hope. Nene's hope was wearing Star to the bone.

The Road was dying, its foliage more mean and shrivelled with every passing. Its people running feral—the children worst of all. Star wanted a better life—and soon. Before point rider Remy made another clumsy pass at her. Before she ended up as wild-dog-crazy as Yeshie and her one-eyed friend. Before one more swaggering adventurer pretending coastal provenance spat the nickname *Van trash* in her face. She was sick of the insults—and the rocks, not to mention the hopeless tide of half-starved refugees restlessly shifting from one unsafe haven to another. Sick of the warlords, each more violent than the last, waging their endless, pointless petty skirmishes.

The Van was old, its tires patched, thirteen wagons battered from constant motion, sun power gradually on the wane. The day would come when its wheels would turn no more. Star wanted out before the lightning moved in close, crossed the Verge, and tore the Road to shreds. She wanted four walls and a bed. A floor that did not move. Paved streets, a solid roof, air that did not stink of drying herbs.

Old Lucius reckoned Van folks were the lucky ones, despite encroaching storms and Dead Red sand. Their business was in transportation: moving and trading. Wheeling and dealing. They didn't starve if the soil got tainted, offering up misshaped vegetables that looked like lopped off body parts.

Alright for *him* maybe, an ancient tankerjack weathered into semi-retirement, keeping the younger ones in line with that hunting lance he swung like a fighter's stave. Sun-baked, tattooed hide as tough as granite. She'd end up with a tough hide too if she didn't get out of the sun before too long.

A chance encounter with that girl last year had put everything in focus. Rich and pretty, Allegra was her name, her father said to be the richest man in Fallow Heel. The girl and her friends had gotten lost in the scary part of town. Scary for them but not for Star—she'd helped them out and to everybody's great surprise, been invited inside a mansion to share tea. The most beautiful place she'd ever seen.

She'd had a whole year to think about it and she could wait no longer. As soon as the Van pulled into Twelfth Man, she was leaving it behind. Nene would have to do without her. Life as a Sand Road medic was not for Star. Instead she would follow in the footsteps of their long-dead parents. Become a relic hunter, maybe even join a tanker crew. She knew the dangers and the risks. All she wanted was a chance to earn big coin. Enough to set up Nene in a back street clinic, give them both a place to stay, year in, year out. A patch of soil where she could plant a garden, grow flowers good for nothing but looking pretty. Maybe even ending up looking pretty herself with the Road dust sluiced off and the ratty dreadlocks combed out of her hair.

When the Van arrived in Fallow Heel, everything would change. But Nene. *How would I ever get up the courage?*

She glanced across in the direction of their wagon, surprised to see Nene still up top, waylaid by an unfamiliar couple with a baby. The father was holding the little one, the mother explaining something with expansive hand gestures. Nene crouched, listening intently.

"Hey Star!"

Pulling up alongside, Remy was grinning madly, his camel veering way too close to wagon six. It wasn't *his* camel, though. Most of the animals belonged to Benhadeer or his shady cousins. Remy owned nothing but the clothing on his back, and now he thought he owned a piece of Star.

She didn't smile back at him. Attention only served to make things worse. Instead she turned back to the bright-eyed wannabes, their fresh faces mixed amongst the weathered and tired. Young and stupid, that last lot from Sternpost—or wherever they really came from. Not that they would stay that way for long. Neat trimmed beards, jewels glinting in sunlight. Clean fabrics, skin and hair. The closer to the coast folks lived, the more effort they seemed to waste on outlandish fashions.

"Coming up on Axa. Axa ahoy!"

Lucius's booming voice, followed by a shuffling and shifting. Everybody keen to get a look at the old-world fortress city, a dark, squat shape shimmering with heat haze in the distance.

Axa: a name that lingered on everybody's lips, whispered like a ward. Axa, said to have stood at least a thousand years. There was no way in and no way out. The bulk of it lay underground—at least that's what they reckoned. There had to be a way in somewhere, else how did black market dealers of tanker heart-and-brain collect their coin?

People stopped their chitchat, craned their necks to see. Everybody, Star noticed curiously, except for Golden Earring and his friends. All three kept their backs to the fortress city. Perhaps they had not heard the call? Perhaps they did not realise what they were missing?

Lucius waved and brought his camel closer. "Coming up on Axa," he shouted again for the benefit of those who'd never passed this way. Not that there was much to see. A stark black cylinder surrounded by sun-baked flats. Star stared hard at the shimmering thing. So little was known about the fortress cities. The flats surrounding Axa were booby-trapped with mines. That much she knew was true—that's how Kendrik lost his arm.

Fortress city Cassia was different though. No mines. No tricks or traps. You could walk right up to it and touch its glassy casing—for all the good it would do. Blasts of steam bled from high vents on either side.

Lucent, unlike Cassia or Axa, had been built inside a hollowed out mountain. Too high to reach by Van. Nisn was closer but not worth the risk. Templar soldiers were rumoured to patrol its rugged boundaries.

"You'd think you'd never seen that place before." Old Lucius pulled his camel alongside, close enough for talking at a shout. "You always stare when we pass the Axa flats," he added. "Regular as sun up."

"Everybody stares," Star replied.

"Not them," said Lucius, pointing with his chin to the backs of the three princes.

She looked, then smiled. So it wasn't just her. Those princes were behaving strangely.

"Tourists," said Lucius. "They won't last long out on the Black if they're figuring on bagging themselves a tanker."

Star nodded, returning her attention to the dark, squat shape on the horizon.

"I want to know about the people shut inside," she said.

Lucius smiled again, wider this time, showing off his set of straight white teeth. "Whoever—or *what*ever's inside that place is best left alone, ask me. Nothing good'll ever come from there."

"But what if they're just like us?"

He snorted, then wiped his nose with the back of his hand. "Any people left inside ain't anything like us. Not by half. Too many years of darkness underground."

His camel snorted too, in taciturn agreement. The scarred old tankerjack and his mount shared more than a few common features. Lucius and Star had had this conversation a dozen times before. He was all for leaving things the way they were, which, he assured her, was the wisest way to live. That attitude had seen him well through sixty summers. An impressive feat in itself for a former tankerjack.

The Van trundled onwards; its rooftop passengers continuing to gawk at mysterious, mythological Axa.

Suddenly, movement caught Star's eye. The three princes stood, careful to maintain their balance, brushed the creases from their clothes and began to pick their way along the juddering wagon top. The other direction, away from Star and Lucius, away from Axa, heading towards the wagon's tail.

She frowned. Where did they think they were going? She watched and waited, expecting them to stop and settle. To turn around and squint at Axa like everybody else: wannabes, locals, Van hands, and tourists alike.

But the princes did not stop. They jumped across from seven to eight, pushed through the grumbling, tight-packed travellers, then continued on from eight to nine, the blond one almost tripping over his own feet.

Star looked to Lucius but he'd dropped the camel back into flank protection position, where he was supposed to be. Without further hesitation, she rose and followed the princes herself, hopping sure-footed and nimble as a goat, as adept atop the lurching, shuddering Van as on hard ground.

The further along towards the tail, the greater the dust, the cheaper the passage, and the rougher the other travellers. Seven was one of the safest wagons, protected by riders on both sides, up and down. The princes must have paid handsomely for the privilege of riding atop its roof. There was nothing safe about the tail-end wagons. They might easily get robbed for their fancy clothes, slashed and tipped over the side during the quiet hours when no danger threatened and the riders were distracted. No one further up would care or notice, especially not with a fortress city in plain sight.

Axa. Some crazy folks were even praying to it, cycling through their rosaries and worry beads, pressing amulets against their sun-chapped lips.

Star paused on twelve, nodding back at those who acknowledged her. Some names she knew, others were only faces she recognised— but they *all* knew her. Nene's little sister, safe under the protection of Benhadeer. Even hardened killers—deep desert men and women with stained souls seeped in blood—cheerfully made room for Nene by the evening fire. Anyone who laid hands upon Nene's sister would not live long enough to talk about it.

She crouched, more certain than ever that the princes were planning to jump the tail. Out here in the shadow of Axa—the middle of nowhere. They must be crazy. No other explanation made sense. She'd have to tell Lucius. He'd have something to say about it. Perhaps the heat and thirst had got to them.

Golden Earring balanced near the edge, shoved an old woman swathed in tattered black out of his way. She spat something back at him but he didn't react. He reached for the top of the spindly ladder embedded in the side, threw his head back to toss curls out of his eyes. Stared right at Star—or at least that's what she thought. Stared at her, right through her, then above her.

A cry sounded over her shoulder, then another and another. Star stood up and turned around. Everyone was looking now, not at Axa but at the pale blue sky—and the object searing through it. She was still staring at it when one of the tankerjacks began to shout.

"By Oshana's eye!" He raised his lance and pointed upwards. By then, the length and breadth of the Van had seen it too. Something bright streaking through the blue. A flaming object hurtling from the heavens.

= TWO =

Watchtower duty was all right by Leni. Eight hours on and eight hours off. High up was good. The higher the better—as far from the stink of algae vats as it was possible to get.

She liked looking out through the tinted blast-proof plexiglass that filtered out the harmful solar rays. Out across the still, unchanging desert flats that stretched in all directions. Most of all, she loved the violent, ragged purple storms. They all did, all the Tower crews. Even Dorse would look up from his console when the Heartland heaved and spat a blaster out. He said there was a grace and elegance to the storms in motion. Like animals, he said—but then, those who'd dedicated service to the Saints said a lot of peculiar things.

Leni had signed up for Watchtower duty to get a bit of distance from those Saints, and their tedious histories. Everyone was forced to memorise the names of battles: dates and times, generals, soldiers, heroes of the bygone revolutions. All a pointless waste of time. There were no enemies strong enough to challenge Nisn. The other fortress cities were all lame and weak and helpless. Not even Axa was fit to lead a charge, despite the occasional circulating rumours.

History was like a great weight pressing down on all their heads. Citizens of Nisn were required to feel remorse for a past they'd played no part in engineering. A past that seemed too dull for the ruin that had sprung forth from its fires.

Curious details abounded, of course. Whispers that secret histories, mysteries, and the like were cosseted in Archive, but Leni was never smart enough to qualify. Histories were a privilege for the few: the men and women who guarded them, and the ones selected to infiltrate the settlements.

Nisn spies didn't last long in the field. Native enclaves, wild and starving animals, poisoned air. Barbarian warlords murdering one another defending pitiful patches of barren soil. Things that didn't bear thinking about crawling around in the old war zones. Biomecha. Flesh-machines that should have gritted up and broken down long ago, but hadn't.

Not that all the danger was on the outside. Templar soldiers were supposed to be treated with respect. *Supposed to be*, but Leni could barely stand to look at them. They weren't human, no matter what the scriptures had to say. Old in a way mere ageing didn't afflict. Alive for centuries, some of them, with artificial hearts and lungs and limbs. Blood crawling with artificial organisms. Flesh and metal fused down to the bone.

"Track that," said Dorse suddenly. "Looks like a shooter!"

Absorbed by her own thoughts, she almost missed it. Things got shot down often enough. Surprising how many old war sats were still in orbit, self-repairing, fully functional—or partly. Functional enough to cause big trouble on the ground.

"Nuh uh," she replied, squinting to check the pale grey screen by her right hand. "Too much titanium alloy. It's a Warbird 47."

Dorse shook his head. "Too small for that. More like a Firefly or an Angel."

They both stared as the falling thing—whatever it was—sliced sharply through the bland and empty sky.

Dorse leaned in a little closer, checked his screen, wiped it, checked again. Glanced across at Leni. "The trajectory's all wrong. Woah, did you see that!"

Leni nearly jumped out of her skin when the falling object *slowed*, then *swerved* abruptly. She looked at Dorse. "We'd better call it in."

Dorse didn't answer, just stood and stared as if he'd been waiting all his life for just this moment. Hesitation born of fear and piety. His family was Temple, through and through. She'd often wondered why he even took the draft. He'd have been happier swinging incense in the cavern hollows and machine-blasted grottos down below. Watching over those unspeakable Templars. Preparing them for moments such as this.

"I'm calling it in," she said, her voice sounding thin and insubstantial. She punched the access code into the console. Nothing happened. She tried again, then balled a fist and thumped it on the scratched metal surface. "System's down," she told him. "Power rationing— today of all the days."

Dorse didn't answer. She glanced across the consoles, realised he was praying, touching the square medallion he always wore around his neck, the words tumbling out too soft and fast for her to catch them.

Leni tried the access code again, then hurried for the stairwell, leaving her offsider deep in prayer, staring blankly at the thin diagonal drawn across the sky. A falling Angel, Firefly, or Temple-knows-what. She outranked him. The honour should be hers.

She took the stairs because the lifts could not be trusted. Not even on days when everything else was running smooth. What if there was a blackout proper? What if Dorse snapped back into focus, came to his senses and snatched the glory from her hands? She hurried, jumping two steps at a time until she reached Level 80. Briskly walking corridors lit with a soft glow—yet another advantage of being up so high. Some trick with mirrors, so they said, but it almost seemed like light seeped through the walls.

Leni was not supposed to enter Operations. Leni was supposed to make use of the comms. Truth was, in five years on the job, she'd never had reason to report anything exciting. Just storms and dust and flocks of carrion birds. Occasional barbarians on camelback or bio-modded lizard. Mismatched wagon trains meandering like snakes across the flats.

Operations. The thick, gun metal door ground open on her approach. Inside was as dimly lit as she expected, the air even staler than in the corridors. Banks of machines stacked one atop another. Pale faces illuminated by flickering screens.

Once inside, she saluted and stood to attention. Disappointed, because the three tiers of them sat, fortified and calm, as if something they'd been waiting for forever had finally come to pass. They already knew. Damn it—Dorse must have thumped some juice back into the console.

"Thank you, Lance Watchman Leni 7114H. The situation is in hand."

Which means go away, the response is above your designation, as is pretty much everything that takes place in watchtower's upper levels. Leni stood still, letting the words wash over her.

"Lectronics are on the fritz, Sir!" she said, saluting. Well, of course they were—why else would she be standing in Operations?

Eight higher-ups were seated behind tiers of consoles, and there was not one face she recognised. "That will be all, Lance Watchman. You are dismissed."

But it was too late. She'd already seen it, right in front of her on the single functioning screen flickering amongst the enormous bank of dead grey glass, shimmering like a jewel. These monitors hadn't functioned in at least four generations, she'd been told, they were only retained for aesthetic purposes, to remind them all of histories that had been. But one of the screens was suddenly working.

And it showed one of *them*. Walking stiffly across the sand *outside*.

"That's a Templar," she said out loud, not intending to give voice to thought, but blurting it out anyway in disbelief. "And it's moving!"

Templars stood as statues in the Temple down below. Grateful citizens laid offerings at their feet. Were it not for these ancient supersoldiers, the inhabitants of Nisn would have perished in the wars. Nobody had seen one walking since before her great-grandmother's time.

There was no immediate reply, and as the silence dragged, Leni became aware of the low level tickings, taps, and thunks emanating from the equipment. Whirrs and clunks. Perhaps more functional than she'd been led to believe.

"Yes, Lance Watchman, that is correct. A Templar," said the old man who looked more like a priest than a five-star G, despite the uniform. Something about his posture in the chair, the way he held his hands clasped on the desk.

"Nice work, Lance Watchman. You may return to your post," said the Staff Sergeant.

Leni saluted again, then reluctantly turned and left Command HQ. So that was that. She had been too slow and by now Dorse would be tracking the Templar on his own screens.

But when she returned to her post, Dorse was still staring out across the sands at a sky stained with wisps of fallen Angel, at dirty sky burns the wind hadn't blow away. Rubbing the metallic square around his neck between his thumb and forefinger.

She stared at him accusingly. "You called it in already."

"Temple bless the lot of us," he said.

= THREE =

The Van's great wheels began to screech and slow, drowning out all speculation. A smack and clatter of flipping hatches as those travelling below clambered up top to investigate. Spyglasses aimed at the flaming rock searing across the sky. No, not a rock, but a shiny silver object. Still others shimmied up the sides to join the gawking onlookers. Within moments, every inch of available space was precariously crammed.

Golden Earring no longer clung to the top of the spindly ladder. He'd climbed back up to stand beside his friends, all three attempting to maintain dignified balance against wagon thirteen's notoriously shocking suspension. He pulled his own spyglass and trained it on the object bleeding wispy streaks across the sky. Snapped his fingers. His blond companion withdrew something from within his galabeya's folds, sunlight glinted off the object's casing. A knife? No, a relic, maybe. Something he was going to pains to shield from prying eyes. He rubbed his thumb across its metallic surface, then with a swift motion, aimed it at the flaming thing, paused, then slipped it back into his pocket. Star only caught a fleeting glimpse—too many bobbing heads were in the way. When his eyes met hers he didn't flinch or blink. He stared at her until she looked away. Back up at the flaming thing, whatever it was. *Nene would know about it. She'd know what to do.*

Foreign princes could not be trusted, but the flaming thing was too important—and too frightening. Reluctantly, Star turned her back on them and pushed through the thronging, wailing, speculating crowd, not watching anything but the object cutting through blue sky like butter.

The dusty air was hot and thick with chatter, attempts to divine meanings from the object's smoky trails. The length of it, its consistency and direction. Shouting to have their voices heard above the chanting and singing from competing faiths, each attempting to drown the others out. Tension was welling. Where was Benhadeer? The big man had yet to show his face. He should have been on camelback, riding up and down the line barking at everyone to keep calm and shut their mouths. Offering reassurance that the world was still the way it was supposed to be.

She kept on pushing, jumping from wagon to wagon, landing roughly on number seven, jostling a dark-skinned man with a beard of beaded plaits. Varisan the Shaman, Yeshie's greatest rival.

"A shooter in daylight!" he exclaimed, clutching Star's shoulders. "A big one—never seen anything like it."

The skinny, dark-haired woman clinging to his arm stared hard, then swallowed, groping for one of the many amulets strung around her own neck and pressing it between thumb and forefinger. "Not a shooter," she warbled. "That's an Angel."

"*A what?*"

No need to repeat it. The man had heard. So had everybody near, and agitated whispers spread like wildfire up and down the wagon tops. Angels were known to rule high above this particular stretch of Road. Tiny moving specks of light swimming amongst the stars and constellations. Moving their own way, doing their own thing. Different from shooters—so quick, they were too easy to blink and miss.

But before anyone had time to blink, something happened to shush the lot of them. The shooter, Angel, flaming rock or whatever it was *slowed down, hovered uncertainly in mid-air, then changed its course.* A cluster of dancers began to wail in their high-pitched sing-song voices. Sounds soon drowned beneath a cascade of anxious, yelping dogs. Camels brayed, barked, and spat—they didn't like it any more than the people did.

Star jumped and hopped and pushed and shoved until at last she found her way to Nene. "Old woman back there said it's an Angel—what did it just do?" she blurted, out of breath, trying to keep her voice low and the anxiety out of it—although it was far too late for that.

Nene shielded her eyes with cupped fingers, studying the object's angular trajectory, the way it stopped and started in a new direction. Lips pressed tightly together, she said nothing.

The wheels kept up a steady pace. Benhadeer and Drover Jens were masters of their craft. Over the years they'd steered the Van through flash floods and creeping dunes. Roadblocks, earthquakes, and bands of starving, sand rat-munching refugees. Angel or not, the Van would keep on moving.

The wagon tops were now dangerously overcrowded. A couple of decent jolts or potholes could send travellers tumbling over the sides, crushed by the wheels before they could so much as squeal. The Van was not designed to be so top heavy in motion. But nobody was budging. So long as that *thing* tore through the sky, nobody was going anywhere.

Her sister was still staring up at it in silence.

"Nene, what is it? Tell me!"

A man pressed too hard up against Star's side. "Show's over. Move along," Star snapped, digging him hard in the ribs when he didn't respond. The fat man next to him pulled a string of worry beads from his trousers, rolling each nub beneath his fleshy thumb, mumbled prayers escaping his thick moustache. He wasn't the only one. Prayers layered over one another in a dozen garbled tongues. Chanting stretching all the way back to the tail.

Not everybody was making noise. Some stood in wary silence, staring at sky trails. The wind was taking its time to wipe them clean. Nene's face wore an expression Star had never seen before. Not wonder or puzzlement, but cold hard recognition. Whatever she knew kept her rooted to the spot, despite the crush of bodies and jolting passage.

The flaming thing continued its trajectory until it eventually vanished, presumably landing somewhere deep within the Dead Red Heart, the realm of tankers and other ancient, deadly things. Had they really seen what they all thought they'd seen?

The lingering traces of Angel trail were finally dissipating. The wailing, praying, and singing began to grate on Star's nerves. They should not be making so much noise. Noise attracted predators of human, animal—and other varieties. The surrounding dunes were still and silent, but that didn't mean she trusted them.

"Star!"

Her own name was almost lost amongst the many voices. Remy again, veering as close to their wagon as he dared, rifle gripped and raised in his left hand—an ancient weapon, as were most the riders carried. Dogs danced around his camel's feet.

"Trouble up ahead," he shouted, gesturing with the gun, then steering his mount back into position along the caravan. Star scrabbled for a foothold, then leaned over the side, craning her neck to see. They were approaching the Fists, a looming cluster of bare knuckle rocks signposting the outer edge of local warlord Barossa's realm.

And there was something else as well: camel riders. A posse had been sent ahead much earlier to pay off the warlord's troops. They were supposed to join the Van in Harthstone, but now were returning unexpectedly early, kicking up billows of hot, red dust. Benhadeer rode out to meet them, his red and purple embroidered sand cloak unmistakable, with Kristo, his ever-faithful right hand by his side.

The Van began to speed up again. A good thing. Whatever the trouble, Drover Jens would push through hard and fast. She told herself everything was going to be all right. Fallow Heel was in their sights, portent or no portent. Fallen Angel or no fallen Angel.

But the returning riders had not yet resumed their flank positions, armed to the teeth and evenly spaced; two per wagon, riding to protect the rest of them. Instead they slowed to a halt to confer with Benhadeer and Kristo in a cloud of dust. Star swore, wishing she owned a spyglass, but such things cost more coin than she would see across an entire year. Something must be up with Barossa, but the riders were too far away for her to make out anything useful.

She chewed her lip. Lucius would know what was going on. He always knew, she suspected, but the old tankerjack was out of range. Star waved but he didn't seem to see her. When he took position on the left flank of wagon three, she pushed and shoved to the front end of four, planning to jump across and get close enough to him to shout. Lucius knew how to read the signs. One of the few she trusted without question.

She was steeling herself for the jump when she felt a shift in the Van's trajectory. A gentle thing at first, then the wagon began to tilt and swerve as the wheels began to slow. The swerve intensified, accompanied by three shrill whistle blasts. She froze. Three blasts meant detour. The Van was not continuing past the Axa flats. It would take the long way around the Fists, a detour that might cost them as much as a week.

Star jumped as the Van continued in a wide arc, landing as skilfully as a cat beside a woman clutching a woven basket tight against her chest. The woman swore at her with spittle flying.

Star ignored her. She called across to Lucius, waving until eventually he heard her over the screeching of the wheels. Preoccupied with the conferring riders and the road they would not be travelling.

"What's happening? Why are we going the long way round?"

He pressed a finger to his lips, the severe inked lines upon his face accentuating his grim expression. Whatever he knew, he did not want the whole Van to hear it.

But it was too late for silence. Back down the line, every point rider crouched in place with weapons at the ready. None were chatting or flirting with the dancers. All eyes were on the road.

Star squinted for a glimpse of whatever obstacle blocked their regular passage, but could see nothing. No burning wagons, no angry riders swathed in clouds of dust. No listless, shifting mob on foot. No packs of half-starved dogs. Even so, this was not good. Not good at all. The detour would force them through Broken Arch, a well-known spot for ambush.

Only that was not the worst of it, and neither was the fact that they'd be late into Fallow Heel, late enough to lose their Twelfth Man berth and dozens of important trade connections. Late enough for Star to lose her nerve. Broken Arch was contaminated. Broken Arch was full of ghosts and other unspeakable horrors. Whole Vans had driven into there and never driven out the other side.

A hush fell across the entire thirteen wagons. The detour had been noticed. Regulars, understanding their predicament, began to speculate in earnest, whispering a potent mix of truth and superstition. The crowded wagon tops began to thin. Suddenly everybody wanted to cram back down below, out of sight and sniper range.

A few snippets of potentially reliable information spread. Yeshie got it from Sven who got it from Chancey who claimed he got it from Kristo himself via his boy. That the riders had arrived to find Harthstone in flames. Barossa murdered, another in his place. New warlords running rampant, taking whatever they wanted, burning what they didn't, wounded 'steaders fleeing for the Road. *Down*road, not up, which meant the stretch along the Axa flats would soon be choked with them.

Lucius still wasn't saying anything. Everyone else, however, seemed to have an opinion to share. Angel lore in its nitty gritty; details growing wilder with the telling.

"I tell you, spirits of the dead have fallen. Those sent back after failing to pass through."

"By Oshana, that's fire we witnessed up there in the sky. Ever hear of a spirit catching fire?"

Barossa had always let them pass with a token consideration on account of what and who Benhadeer carried regular. Less stupid or foolhardy than some of the younger chiefs, he respected and obeyed Road Law, nodded at the white flag hanging limply off wagon number one, taxed them for the privilege of safe passage. A white flag signalled there were healers, shaman, medicine, and other useful services onboard. A white flag meant that if his people broke the rules, Barossa was going to make them pay.

Not the first time a detour had been forced, and it wouldn't be the last. But it would be the last for Star—a promise she made to herself there and then. She would jump the Van when it got to Fallow Heel—if it ever got there.

Jump the Van. The three Sternpost princes—in the excitement she had forgotten them. Had they jumped the tail or hadn't they? She secured her footing and peered back along the road just travelled, but there was nothing but dust, hard surface, and red-tinged distant dunes. She craned her neck but she couldn't see anything. She might not know for certain until the Van berthed proper.

The fallen Angel was being blamed for their predicament. It had poisoned the sky, turned the air a sickly yellow. With a sinking feeling, Star tugged her khafiya to cover her nose and mouth. Just in case. Better to be safe than sorry.

= FOUR =

Old Marianthe walked with a pronounced limp, the result of shrapnel wounds that had never healed completely—a lie she offered to friends and strangers alike, although it was partly true: she had operated on herself in the aftermath of the battle of Crysse Plain.

Her flesh was pocked and scarred and gouged, but hidden below flowing robes, suitable attire for any desert dweller. Those who knew or half suspected her secret dared not speak of it. The limp slowed her down but it had never stopped her. No one had ever managed to stand in Marianthe's way.

There wasn't much recognisable left of Crysse; a tangled thatch of shattered tanks and fused exoskeletons dulled by centuries of relentless wind and grain. The soldiers who had worn such armour were long dead, forgotten by everyone except for her. Suicide squads who had not stood a chance against the superior skills, strength, and ordnance of the Templar forces.

The drone she'd christened Flaxy buzzed annoyingly around her face like a fly. She shooed at it, swearing in a language she largely no longer remembered how to speak. Just the swear words. Such was the way of things.

The tombstones she had placed herself had been half obscured by sand. She dug them clear with her bony hands, each one fashioned from jagged shards of exploded infantry carriers and hybrid all-terrain vehicles. The names she'd etched upon them had been illegible for decades. She could no longer decipher them, nor picture the faces of the fallen soldiers.

Yet she still came out here once a month for the purpose of continuity. Even the vaguest trace of memory was important with so much of the old world dead and gone.

Dead and gone. Dead and gone.

She left the blessing of a crashed helicopter's shade, picking her way unevenly across the stretch of sand and stared, speaking commands to summon her familiars. Little Flaxy came scudding back, having not gone far when she shooed it off earlier. Just Flaxy, Hopper, and JuJu, her companions for today. The rest of her drones stayed back at the Temple of the Dish, scouting the perimeter, keeping an eye on the gardens. All except for little Ditto, who'd been banged up in repair shop since that Knartooth barbarian winged it with a rifle so ancient she'd assumed it had been purely for show. Somebody had started manufacturing guns again, she'd realised—either that or digging up fresh caches from the Red. Not good. Not good at all. An indicator that those blasted fortress cities were waking up.

Her drones cast bitter, stony shadows, dulled, scored casings half-heartedly reflecting glare. She walked to the end of the hard-packed sand, stepped out, her uneven footfall muffled by soft grains. Kicked off her sandals to walk barefoot. The sand was already warm, but not too hot.

She could hear the tankers grumbling in the distance, reverberations rippling through the sand to her stomach's core. Nausea building like a wave. She never got used to their terrible sonics, not even after all these years.

The tankers knew her by her limp. Read her heat signature, perhaps. She'd never been sure how well the tankers could see.

Marianthe remembered some things clearly from the time before the Ruin. That the fringe of this battlefield had once housed a research station, built between the wars. White-coats had slept in the state-of-the-art bunkhouse that was nothing but a pile of rubble now.

Back in the day, there'd been hangars for the fleet of shiny all-terrain vehicles. So many kinds: land, sea, and sky. The surrounding landscape had been a different colour then. Sometimes when she shut her eyes, Marianthe could still see it all the way it used to be. Ghostly structures overlaid. Before the seas swelled up and the farmland fried. Before the governments scrabbled to sell off what little they still possessed. Before the overland barges overloaded with toxic garbage, human refuse clinging to the sides. Before the endless stream of poison barrels sunk deep into outback fissures. Half-life, they used to speak of the radiation. Half-life and all death.

Marianthe stumbled, tripping over her skirts. The picture was spoiled. A memory glitch. Now all she could see was sand and sun and glare off the tanks and crawlers: equipment broken down and virus-frozen in attack formation, half buried beyond the fused mess of exoskeletons, stretching to the horizon or perhaps infinity. She'd never walked far enough to learn the truth of it.

That sound again.

She had taught herself to tell each tanker by its individual sonic signature. All noise to others, but to her, they were songs, each one different and beautiful, if not painful. Deadly if the damn things took a dislike to you.

She stood very still and shut her eyes. A far-off keening that might have been the wind—but wasn't. More tankers talking to each other. The mecha-creatures spoke but they never listened. No one listened anymore, which was why she'd become so insistent on routine, on patterns and behaviours she could learn by rote and repetition. Body memory was how she taught the refugees new skills. Do something enough times and the way sinks in, no matter if you're too traumatised to speak. She preferred silence to speaking, busyness to idle hands, past to present, memory to truth.

Memory intruded as she stood there in the sun, eyes closed, soft winds teasing the hem of her skirts, sand skinks dodging around her shadow. Visions of great reliquaries of old tapping the deep, hot rocks beneath the ground. Blasting fissures in the brittle crust, sucking up their heat and oil and ore.

Clandestine bases swarming with quicksilver drones, zipping overhead to missions in far-off territories. Emblazoned with the insignia of nameless foreign corporations. Swarms of human misery moving from county to county, stripping and consuming greenery like locusts.

Big reds bred mean to patrol the razor wire perimeters. Replaced in time with barriers of lantana raze, a particularly virulent form of weaponised weed, coded feral when the government defaulted on suppliers. Genes programmed with a killer switch, once initiated, fated to grow forever, consuming everything in its path.

The land became exhausted, eventually stopped giving and started taking back. So the white-coats panicked, manufacturing strange new plants and animals tailored specifically to suit the harsh terrain. New soldiers too. Stronger, tougher. Better. TEMPLARS, they called them—she couldn't remember why, even though she knows she is one of them herself.

Her scars ache whenever she recalls the name, thinks of the production lines blending flesh with mecha, creating perfect killing machines. Soldiers, vat grown, seeded and refined.

And then came the war to begin all wars. The war that the dregs of Templars were still fighting to this day. From the Angels in the sky to the tankers barrelling leaderless across the land. Tribe by tribe, leaf by leaf, everything on or above this land had been built to kill.

He had lost his life in this place. There was no grave to tend because there had been no body, and yet he was dead, she knew he was, probably. Her one true love, her best and dearest friend. Dead and gone for two hundred years. Leaving just she, Marianthe, one-time Templar warrior, keeper of the Temple of the Dish. The last left standing. The last of all of them, soldiering onwards, picking up the pieces.

= FIVE =

The first breath of uncanned air hit Quarrel like a suckerpunch, bringing on a rush of memories too furious and jumbled to make sense of. How many years had passed since he had seen the sun? He squinted up into its painful brightness, trying to remember. He had become accustomed to the Nisn Temple's dull luminescence. Small flames flickering. Moody, repetitious chants, ambience still and quiet, lulling this old soldier into a state of zero contemplation.

Outside was different, stark and sharp. Wide horizons and clear, clean air. *Too* clean, like all the life had been blasted out of it. Dead air, some said: dead, spoiled and poisoned. He thought it tasted fine. Too much raw sky, sand and sun. Too much of everything—especially the light.

The priests had awoken him from his half-dream state with a shot of something that sent his extremities tingling. Next, gut spasms and a surge of cold had enveloped his torso, groin, and thighs. Uncertain first steps, he'd kicked over votive candles and other offerings piled around his feet, his kneecaps groaning, unaccustomed to weight distribution brought on by the process of ambulation.

More shots, followed by a barrage of tests that stung, itched, and occasionally sent him into convulsions. Two hundred years had passed since his last deployment in the field. Two hundred years of being worshipped like a statue, memories relegated to the realm of dreams.

HQ was not as he remembered it. Once shiny consoles were now shabby and run down. His newly calibrated and enhanced vision revealed rodents and insects in every corner, infesting the innards of machines, building nests amongst tangled, disintegrating wires. Webs coated cracked cement. Mould climbed along the walls, lichen spores in the damp air infecting the throats of those who wheezed and coughed behind the consoles.

The white-coats were fretting about his reflexes and whether or not he could still regenerate damaged limbs. They were sending him out on a critical reconnaissance mission. Those sending him were pale and weak, but they didn't want *him* breaking down in the field. He was, apparently, the best of what was left. The only almost-fully-functioning Templar supersoldier alive, no longer super, just a soldier now with a head full of jumbled memories and dreams.

The objects he was searching for could be IDed by code. The mesh implanted in his arm had been fed with approximate coordinates and other intel vital to his mission.

Quarrel's memory was riddled with gaps. Lots of them, as though the rats and bugs had gotten inside his head and made nests and meals of all his thoughts and dreams. He was hungry, ravenous after decades of being peg-fed nutrient paste. He yearned for sensations half remembered: brittle buzz and dirty highs. A taste for chemicals lingering in his veins.

Quarrel walked. He liked the crunch of his boots on stony sand. Little creatures darting out of his way. Bigger things watching from secret places. The sun on his face—once he got used to it—felt so hot and good.

Those Nisn priests had been right to lock him up, because now that he was outside, he was never going back. Whatever ailed him once had surely passed. Sickness of body, sickness of heart and soul— all gone. Not that he could remember much—or perhaps the problem was that he remembered far too much? Too much to handle. Too much for one old soldier's mind to bear.

His memories came in random blasts: Running fast across uneven ground, bullets grazing naked skin, superficial wounds self-healing, sweat and blood stinging his eyes.

Whenever he became distracted or dropped his guard, a flood of visual fragments superimposed themselves in one almighty flash, like a bomb bright enough to blind the sun. Best not to think too hard about anything. Best to keep on walking. The rhythm of his footfall gave him peace.

Those priests had done a number on his skull cache, that much he could tell, had scrubbed him clean of a multitude of wars. He only remembered bits and pieces. Mushroom clouds and sonic booms. A woman's face staring up at him, concerned.

An itch alerted him to the mine. Six feet under, aural trigger combined with pressure pad. His mesh tapped a nerve, recalculated. He swerved, walked right across the dead mines without flinching. Mere relics, all of them. Relics, much the same as he.

His spirits lifted when he spied a bird, an ugly black thing scouting carrion, thin and scrappy. Yet it was alive and free. Just like him.

He swerved to dodge another mine lurking below the sand, a half-life pulsing in its core.

He'd been walking several hours before the woman's face resurfaced. All such memories had been banned from Temple, but Temple was a long, long way from here. Receded into the farthest distance, so far that he'd almost forgotten what he'd been doing there in the first place.

What the hell had been her name? Of all things to have forgotten. He started running, just because he could, even though his core temp was elevated and he knew he was wasting too much water. Itchy sweat trickled down his backbone, but still her name wouldn't come.

No name, but he could see her face, pale like the moon he hadn't seen for two long centuries.

That General—the fat one with the lisp—had told him some of the Sentinels still functioned, even though their data streams were corrupted and only reported back in garbled fits and starts. He still possessed an encoded set of master files, mashed in somewhere with a bunch of other data. Battlepod schematics, a blueprint for some habitat that looked like a nest of giant spider eggs. Self-recharging laser cannons, a bunker that could dig itself in deeper when the shelling got too fierce. That song he liked, the one about meadows and daisy chains.

Quarrel stopped to piss against a corroded chunk of metal. Fluidic systems up and running—always a good sign. The sun had stripped the metal of all colour and purpose. Shade for skinks and baby lizards, that's all it was good for now.

"You're dead, aren't you?" he said out loud, remembering that woman's face again, not certain if he liked the sound of his own voice. Not certain of anything much at all anymore.

His mesh began to nag at him, intruding upon his thoughts. He recited a prayer. The one about green pastures that made him happy. Last green he'd seen had been scraped off the underbelly of a rock and consumed with desperate relish by his own starving platoon. Further details remained out of reach, consumed by a blast of mental static.

Quarrel shook his head to clear it. Nisn telemetry was now coming through loud and clear. Search and possibly retrieve: An Angel brought back down to ground after Temple-knows-how-many years up there. Come back too late, after everything good had gone. He'd sensed that Angel feeling its way back onto terra firma. Much firmer than when they'd blasted skyward and left it all behind. There were no pastures green in living memory.

He recited the hymn, as if talking up those flocks and pastures might raise them from the dead. Even their trace memory would be more than welcome here.

He swore at his arm, made the necessary course corrections and a few other minor adjustments he wasn't sure he was ready for at all. Told himself to forget the platoons and the faces of the dead-and-gone forever. They wanted him to check that Angel out. Bring pieces of it back to the white-coats and stunted generals. He calculated that he would reach a replenishing water source at eighteen-hundred, not too far away for replenishment of a different kind. He needed to know how the world had changed across two hundred years. Those stinking priests would tell him nothing, so he'd go shopping. Help himself. Jack in hard and suck on one of those Sentinel's delicious juices, those impassive, unbiased stalwarts of the sands. There had to be a couple still left standing. What the white-coats and five-star Gs of Nisn didn't know wouldn't hurt them. Quarrel planned to walk on through the

28

cool of night. Two nights ought to do it, maybe three. Drain a Sentinel and then keep walking. Three nights and he'd be ready to take on anything.

= S I X =

Broken Arch had no arch to speak of, just squat, weathered columns flanking either side of the road. A town had once stood here, assembled in the skeletal ruins of an ancient, pre-Ruin city. The Sand Road cut right through its heart of twisted steel. To the right of the wagons lay a forest of weathered iron pylons reminiscent of scorched tree trunks, bases littered with rubble and concrete crumbs. Less of it standing as each year passed. Red sand was moving in for good and chewing through the rust.

No plants grew here. Not even cactus or hardy grasses. Everything had been eaten. White bones scattered, human mixed with camel. No one left to throw rocks at the Van.

Beyond the columns, the ruins possessed a stark, haunted quality. Last time they'd been forced to pass this way had been several years ago. Star had seen no ghosts that time but remembered the large and hungry lizards eyeing off the Van. One of them had put a permanent dent in eleven's side. Now riders scouted as a precautionary measure, flushing them out and driving them away with rifle shots before they got too cocky.

The detour was making her stomach churn, as was the thought of a streaming tide of Harthstone's displaced townsfolk. Steeling herself for the days and challenges to come would put an end to her daydreaming. Fallow Heel wasn't going anywhere and neither was Allegra, that rich girl. Extra days gave her more time to plan, to think up plausible explanations why a relic-foraging crew might agree to take her on. Star didn't have a tenth of Nene's skill or intuition, but she could dress a wound, splint a limb, brew up herbs that could quell a fever—every foraging crew could use a medic.

A consternation began atop wagon four. With so little space in which to move, any argument had the potential to grow into something dangerous. Star, Nene, and Mara—Yeshie's one eyed friend—craned their necks to see. Somebody up there was causing trouble.

A male voice boomed across the chatter. "Why have we taken this detour? Why are we not pushing through?"

Star's eyes widened at the familiar voice. It was him. Golden Earring. Relief flooded through her. The three merchant princes would not have lasted long on foot across the Axa flats. Not even without the threat of mines or refugees fleeing the flames of Harthstone.

Yeshie angled herself towards him, slapping at arms and legs until others shifted to give her a clear view.

"Young man, what is your problem?" she called out.

Other travellers shushed to hear her words. Yeshie, with her amulets, dice, and bones, was always listened to.

Golden Earring stared down at her from the wagon's end, his friends close behind, gripping each other for balance. "We have urgent business in Fallow Heel," he called back.

"As do we all, dear boy. As do we all."

His lip curled in distaste as he cast his gaze across the ruined landscape. "What is this place?"

"Arse end O'nowhere," called out somebody from behind.

Yeshie smiled. Everybody laughed.

"You got that right," added another man who sat with his legs dangling precariously over the wagon's edge.

Golden Earring was not amused. "Who lives here?"

"Nobody lives here anymore," said Yeshie. "Tis the realm of lizards, mechabeasts, and ghosts."

"Lizards? Mechabeasts?"

"Where do you hail from?" piped up Star. "The Sammaryndan coastline—am I right?" She spoke again before he could answer, uncovering her face so her words could be heard more clearly. "I'm called Star—may we know your names?"

His unwavering gaze made her feel uncomfortable—but only for a moment. He took his time to answer. Determining whether to speak or hold his tongue.

Eventually he offered a polite smile in return. "I am Kian. My associates, Tallis and Jakome. How long until we reach the nearest proper settlement?"

"Vulture's up next, though I'm guessing that won't likely count as *proper*," said the man with dangling legs.

Everybody laughed again, with Yeshie joining in. "We're likely a week out from Heel itself, if that's proper enough for your liking."

Jakome's voice was gruff, a contrast to his fine-boned features and neatly sculpted beard. "A week—how can that be?" he said. "The detour has only taken us round these rocks. By my calculations—"

A murmur of tut-tutting issued from those close enough to catch his words.

"Did nobody tell you? Harthstone is under siege," said Star. "That's why we've come the long way round the Fists." She pointed at the ugly, bulging protuberances of rock towering above them on the left, casting welcome shadows across the Van.

"Feels like we're being watched," said Tallis.

Yeshie nodded her agreement. "That you are. Oshana watches over all of us."

The blank look on Tallis's face indicated that he'd never heard of Yeshie's beloved god either.

"Broken Arch is haunted," said Star.

"Haunted by what?"

"The dead of long ago. The ones who made this place their home, back when their buildings touched the sky. Sometimes you can glimpse them out of the corner of your eye."

Kian looked back to Yeshie. "Your caravan master, we need to speak with him."

"Your needs will have to wait," said Yeshie. "Our Benhadeer has other things on his mind." She nodded towards the tangled clutter of rusted pylons stretching over miles on the right hand side. "Gotta keep both eyes open in a place like this."

Kian looked to the ruined cityscape, as if it were the first time he'd laid eyes upon it. As if he hadn't been staring at it already. "The delay is unacceptable!"

A chorus of chortling broke out across the rattling wagon tops. Yeshie made shushing motions with her chubby hands. Everybody shushed.

She nodded. "The long way round, we've come—it's true. But don't you worry. We'll rest the beasts up at the Vulture till it's clear the Harthstone tide hasn't spilled out both sides. When the way is clear we'll push on through."

"What is this Vulture?"

"The safest place to camp until the dawn."

Kian stared at her with steely eyes. "It would be better if the wagons kept on rolling."

Mara laughed. "Better for whom? Our poor animals need rest and nourishment. This stretch of road has taken a turn for the worse."

Kian's features clouded with barely restrained impatience.

Yeshie sniffed. "You young are always in a hurry."

He flashed a smile. A thin one that wasn't very convincing. "Perhaps your caravan master might be persuaded—"

Yeshie's voice took on a grim tone. "'Tis not a matter for persuasion. 'Cross the Axa flats, Benhadeer had an *arrangement*. Pay up coin, no questions asked. No questions asked at all. Round the back and across the open sand is different. No arrangements. No understandings."

"But you said nobody lives here."

"Nobody human."

One-eyed Mara nodded darkly. "Vulture has a Sentinel. The Sentinel will keep us safe," she added.

Kian attempted another half smile that looked more like a grimace. An expression that said, *We'll see about that.*

They travelled in silence for awhile, each of them contemplating the ruins, Star doing her best not to stare at Kian.

"Off to try your luck out of Fallow Heel, then, are you, Kian?" Yeshie tossed the small pouch of dice-and-bones in her hand, feeling its weight. She never travelled anywhere without that pouch.

"That's right."

She nodded sagely. "Then where's your kit? Your lances? Those fancy skins beneath your galabeyas look finely stitched to me. From the coast then, are you? Which part precisely, if you don't mind my asking?"

Star could tell that Kian did mind—and so did his two associates. Everybody waited eagerly for his answer.

"No such thing as luck, I always say—especially when it comes to tankers," added Yeshie, intimidating Kian with her hard, sharp eyes.

"He's no tankerjack," shouted Remy from his camel.

Remy's interjection startled Star—he'd been tasked with lizard patrol, but instead was now pulling his camel up alongside them.

"Tourists, more like," Remy continued, spitting into the dust. "Van's crawling with them this time out."

He struggled to keep the animal alongside while remaining in ear-shot. An ancient rifle was slung across his back, and two dogs trotted faithfully at his heels.

Kian looked him over from head to toe. Tallis muttered something quietly. Jakome nodded, appraising both Remy and his camel. Tallis flicked a cigarette end in his direction.

"Go back to the coast—or wherever it is you've come from," shouted Remy. "Your kind aren't welcome here."

"Shut up, Remy," Star called out, an uneasy feeling welling within her stomach. The realm of ghosts was unforgiving. Argument was tempting bad luck down upon their heads. They were not safe yet, and wouldn't be until they could glimpse the pretty lanterns of Fallow Heel.

"Look!" Tallis slapped Kian's shoulder, pointed to the remnants of a doorway. Small figures stared up at the passing Van, vanishing into darkness as soon as they were spotted.

"Ghosts!" People began crossing themselves in panic.

"Refugees from Hearthstone, more like," said Yeshie grimly. "Smart ones, quick enough to read the early signs and hit the road."

But Star wasn't searching for figures in doorways. Something big was moving through the rubble, partly obscured by collapsed walls and fallen pillars.

Remy took note of her line of sight and wheeled around, shouting to fellow point rider Griff. He gripped his rifle tight and chased after it, heading for a tangle of concrete and rusted steel. Threw Star a parting glance to make sure she was watching. Both dogs yelped and went to join the hunt, wriggling beneath a fallen beam, then ducking back out again when Remy whistled. Star caught another glimpse of their quarry—a massive creature with a leathery pockmarked hide. Just a flash. A lizard, probably weakened by starvation, more scared of them than they were of it.

Kian and his associates stared nervously at the ruins.

"Lizards be timid creatures," assured Yeshie. "Rarely attack a Van this size unless they're desperate, but we can cast the bones if you're feeling anxious."

But before she had a chance to take action, a volley of rifle shots split the air. Remy, atop his camel, charged out of the ruins at breakneck speed, a massive lizard hot on his heels. The lizard baulked as it neared the Van, changed direction, and ran full pelt at wagon five, slamming violently into its side.

The folks up top screamed and scrabbled for handholds. Startled, the creature paused, then charged again, this time battering the side of number six.

"More of them," alerted Tallis.

The lizards were much leaner than Star recalled. Hungry-looking. Definitely more aggressive.

"Noise," said Mara. "What we need is noise!"

Prayer started up like the droning of a million bees. The lizard's confusion intensified. Then the tail-end travellers chimed in—literally. An assortment of cooking pots and pans clanged and clashed together to make a din, loud enough to drown out rifle shots.

"It's working," said Star. She'd been gripping tightly to one of the embedded rings that graced every wagon top. Kian and his friends crouched down and copied her. They only let go when she did.

The noise upset the camels, but it did the trick. The hungry lizard spun in circles, before retreating into the tangled city ruins. The din continued until it and the rest of them were out of sight.

34

"A clever people, are we, despite the poverty and hardships," stated Yeshie.

Kian wiped his brow with his sleeve. Both Tallis and Jakome were too shaken to do more than stare.

"A close call, but we've had closer, haven't we, dear?" Yeshie patted Star on the knee. "Your sister's being awfully quiet, isn't she?"

"Nene's busy," Star lied, blurting out the first excuse that came to mind. Nene must have slipped back down through four's hatch before all the trouble started. Probably consulting those ancient books that weighed as much as mud bricks, anything to escape old Yeshie's crackpot Angel theories. Any minute now the hatch would flip. It should have flipped already. Nene was taking her own sweet time about it.

Danger passed, Yeshie and Mara soon picked up their good-natured bickering from where they had left it.

"Spirits do not catch fire! They do not plummet from the heavens."

"Falling rocks do not change course. Neither do meteors or comets . . ."

Travellers relaxed their tight grips on the rings—and each other—easing their way back into the ride.

Nene knew something about that fallen Angel—Star could read her sister like the sky. But she wouldn't be climbing down inside wagon number four. Cramped, confined spaces bugged her even more than the boredom of the open sand. Besides, she'd only be given chores to do. Bark to grind or pastes to bottle—and all for nothing because no matter what Star ever did, Nene kept her secrets to herself.

Kian was staring at her again. She wasn't sure if she liked it or not, but after a time she decided that she did. No matter that he was another gawking tourist. The three hailed from the coast and that made them exotic. They were headed to the same place she was, a fact she liked the most of all.

A familiar series of short, sharp whistles sounded from up front. A warning to the rest of them. Star craned her neck to the landscape up ahead, expecting to see another hungry lizard—or maybe even a whole nest of them. Number four's hatch flew open in front of her, Nene bursting out like their home was on fire.

"Nene, you missed all the excitement," Star blurted out. "A lizard rammed five and six—did you not feel anything below?"

But her sister wasn't listening. Her attention was focused on a particular set of ruins coming up on the left, a cluster of rusted, jutting struts with bases embedded in weathered concrete. One of them had a bundle attached way up high. A bundle that looked a lot like a human body.

= SEVEN =

The General had dreamed of walking on the surface of the sun. All blinding white and firestorm enveloping him in a cloak of heat and glory.

He'd crossed the line into the waking world, into stillness, silence. Dark and cool. He cannot feel his arms and legs, see anything, hear the beating of his heart.

No matter. The dreams have faded. The bombs have stopped. Nothing left to contemplate but the scratching of tiny beasts in cobwebbed corners.

Odd that he cannot remember his name or the place of his birth or the faces of those who raised him. Nor places—not specifically. Now and then he catches snatches of a previous life. Strings of memory fragments cycle: a seaside; the striped canvas of folding chairs, red and green and blue. Sandcastles, red and yellow umbrellas. Dogs and children paddling in shallow pools. A big city, shiny-bright, looking up at light dazzling off sleek windows. Garish billboards, choking traffic, gutters overflowing with sodden plastic wrappers and cigarette butts. Bicycles and honking cars, bare tree branches festooned with lights like gems.

Snippets playing over and over, close and personal, events he must have lived and breathed—because how else could he recall them with such clarity? Then white snow static, a flood of data sets and streams, fractal patterns, parallel algorithms, coordinate geometry. Four speed forward, two speed reverse. Obstacle crossing: 49 inches. Fuel capacity: 498 gal (1,885 litres) / 505 gal (1,907 litres). Data punctuated by long periods of eerie silence. The silence unnerves the General more than anything, but it's comforting to know that he had been someone once, even if he's no longer certain who that is—and certainly not where.

If the General concentrates he can hear evidence of sand dunes far away, creeping across the landscape, inch by inch. Dunes that sing to announce their intentions. Now and then the thundering of mighty wheels. Bigrigs, battletrucks, ramblers, and haulers. Vehicles communicating in a language of transmission bursts. Rough poetry, brittle and discordant as glass shards. He knows those tankers, remembers them—possessed of grace and rudimentary intelligence.

Darkness amplifies modest sounds, like the cracking and crumbling of bunker cement. Insects, mice, and the falling of individual grains of sand. Grains blown in from the outside world—or what he imagines to be left of it.

Because there had been a war or two—of that much he is certain.

Let there be light, he says.

That's better.

Now he can see the inside of the bunker. The corridors are empty, the carpet and linoleum rotted, eaten away by mould and bugs and time. Webs and lichen and tiny scuttling things.

Where did everyone go? He recalls multitudes in crisp blue uniforms, Lotus company insignia displayed upon their chests. Everybody rushing, with buttons to push and jobs to do, a thousand voices talking all at once. Air stinging with electronic hiss and fizz. Skies streaked white with contrails. The power of the storms. Ferocious walls of roiling, building pressure spitting forks of light and white-blue heat. But not now. Now there is only silence and scuttling, empty labs and empty corridors.

He tries to feel his way back to the dream state, but the moment has passed, is gone forever. The door has closed, so far away now, remote and faint, like trace memories of a memory of a memory.

The General concentrates, one by one, initiating implanted connective nodes. More than half of them are dead or not responding.

He's not sure who to blame for this. An aide, perhaps, or a sloppy maintenance schedule. Perhaps he was attacked while he was sleeping? Perhaps he's under attack right now and this is all a dream.

And then, faint pulses of light and heat. A signature. Something out there responding to his call.

Snap connect, and suddenly he's way up in the sky, beyond the sky, the clouds, the trade winds, staring down at the ground from the exosphere. Nothing but sand and rock and ruin in all directions.

What . . . the . . .

He jumps to, calibrates coordinates, comprehends that although he lies buried under tons and tons of sand, he's simultaneously squinting down though satellite eyes, primitive but functional. Autoresponding to atmospheric density, adjusting for the curvature of the Earth. Basking in the glorious solar winds. Better than nothing. What happened to the rest of them? The skies had once been thick with satellites.

The General watches from his lofty perch, trying to gauge what has become of the world he knew. A world encased in armour of steel and stone. There is no movement, just sand and wind and heat. The skyscrapers, the mighty cities, the arterial flow of eight-lane super-highways—what happened to the grids? The lights? The people?

All lies still.

Not all.

There is action across a stretch of open sand. He recognises the tankers by their heat signatures, if not by their appearances, at first. The desert has taken over, he realises, has become the domain of itinerant war machinery: tanks and barrier busters and sleek recon vehicles. Battletrucks: heavy duty aerospace-tech inner frames connected to drive hubs. Articulated front rigging, faceted armour, hubless wheels. Confusing. Outer casings are no longer silver shiny. Each vehicle appears to be coated in some kind of hardened organic matter. There is no discernable pattern to their movement. No order. No formation.

These creatures are so familiar to him. Nano-seeded blood flushing through their mecha component systems. Self-repairing. Self-sustaining, printing themselves new body parts and when that fails, ramming, savaging, cannibalising other vehicles, other mecha.

The General speaks their language. He can still remember it but they don't answer. They ignore him, keep on doing what they're doing, barrelling across the open sand at breakneck speed.

He isolates the frequency, piggybacks from satellite to satellite— Angels they used to call them, he can't remember why. He listens in to tanker talk. Same lingo, strange inflections. More grunt and pulse than data stream. Crude creatures: dumb, clumsy, rough and random. Dialect is the word that comes to mind.

He tries to get in closer but the satellite has its limits. It's only an Angel, designed to hunt and seek and shoot, not spy. He upgrades to another model, a Warbird 47, locked in geostationary orbit. It is not on speaking terms with others of its kind. He would have abandoned it and moved on hours ago, but its nearest brethren contraptions are both blind. Not orbit locked, but not much use as investigative tools.

The first one he discovers in this condition makes him angry so he slams it hurtling to Earth. The thing's preprogramed self preservation heuristics kick in, and it fires its retro rockets. It still crashes and burns, but not before changing its course. Impressive, to say the least.

As the flaming Angel falls to Earth, one of the tankers becomes separated from the others. It lags behind the rest of the pod, yet it is not alone. A collection of smaller craft appears to be in hot pursuit. The General does not comprehend the gambit. He pings for clarification and confirmation, but nothing answers. Just the hum and hiss and static of atmospheric interference.

Time passes. The General comes to realise he is witnessing a hunt. Smart animals working together to chase a tanker down. The tanker does not fire ordnance. Instead it bucks and rolls, but the aggressors soon trap it in a silvery net. They swarm all over it like ants, hack at the outer organic casing. Use crude tools to prise away the modular metal skin. Climb inside, scoop out the blended flesh-and-mecha innards.

How utterly barbaric. Warfare used to be so sharp and clean. Surgical strikes. Precision hits. How in hell did it ever come to this?

The General longs to blast the lot of them into dust and atoms but finds he's impotent and powerless. He piggybacks the Angels but they won't fire when he commands them.

The tankers continue to ignore his requests for communication. They do not stop to help their injured brother.

The General is going to have to find another way. He forgets about the tankers and the smart animal predators, leaves the Angels to their pointless aerial patrol. Begins searching below the ground for tell-tale evidence. Disruptions that would indicate cities. Military establishments. Anything bleeding heat from underground. He locates three, with three others potentially worth investigation, but his range is limited. He will have to do something about that.

The General watches the tankers race until the Warbird 47 bumps him, severing connection abruptly, like it has something better to do with its time and circuitry.

Not likely. Not with a Lotus General awake and scheming.

The General has been flexing his parameters. The General has big plans for his future.

= EIGHT =

A body lashed and placed up high, in full view of the road, was not unusual in itself. Road law was swift and cruel from end to end when it came to bandits, liars, cheats, or thieves.

Nene swung herself over the wagon's side and jumped down to the sand, accompanied by a titter of disapproval from those clustered whispering up top.

Star scrambled to her feet and shouted, "What are you doing?"

Yeshie clutched her dice-and-bones against her chest. Mara put her fingers to her mouth.

All point riders were back in position, doing the job Benhadeer expected of them. A corpse was no threat in itself—unless it had been placed as a diversion. Lucius shouted something unintelligible from the forest of metal pylons he patrolled. He'd been watching and had seen Nene jump, but was stuck on the Van's far side.

He urged his camel the long way around the tail, swinging that lance of his with the grace of a much younger man.

"Nene!" Star called out, but her sister wasn't listening. Not to Star or Lucius or anybody else.

"What's she doing? What is that thing?" shouted many of the passengers now standing, craning and gawking as each wagon passed up close in turn.

The thing strung up was not a human.

It was a Templar soldier.

An old one, filthy, covered in dried blood. Star stood frozen, not knowing what to do—jump down after her crazy sister or stay where she was safe?

Others started shrieking at Nene. *Do not touch! Don't get too close! Keep your face covered! Keep away from it!*

Nene ignored them all.

"Nene—what are you doing?" Star cried out, adding uselessly to the chorus.

Yeshie grabbed hold of her ankle. "Sit down, girl. Big sister can take care of herself."

But Star didn't sit. Standing gave her the best vantage point. The frames and struts to which the thing was lashed had once been part of a larger structure. A hall or a church, perhaps. Not enough remained to be sure.

The shadow of the Fists loomed overhead. Point riders kept their distance. One of them made the cross sign above his heart. *Best not to mess with a Templar unless you had to.*

The Van kept up its steady crawl. Nene took position at the foot of the tangled mass of frames and struts, staring upwards at the trussed up figure.

Lucius rode with great caution, his face sweaty with exertion, the beast spitting and angry at having been made to gallop. Nene glanced up at him, and motioned for him to lift her up.

He jabbed the lance through the saddle straps, covered his nose and mouth with his khafiya. Nene did the same. The wagons lumbered onwards, taking Star out of range.

"Give me your spyglass," she said to Kian, knowing he had to have one in his pocket.

The foreign prince hesitated, but complied.

Travellers called out curses, wards, warnings to Nene not to touch, that even in death, Templars could be dangerous.

Through the spyglass, Star watched Lucius haul Nene up into his saddle. The aggravated camel inched closer at his urgings, then snorted, shaking its ugly head.

It was a Templar all right, lashed to bleached and splintered wood. Carrion birds had already been at its face.

Wind clawed at its blood-stained tunic, billowing the ripped fabric, making it seem like it was still alive.

Lucius said something to Nene. She answered back, he hesitated, then tugged his lance free of the saddle and passed it to her. She had to stand up in the saddle to reach. He gripped her legs to hold her steady.

Nene poked at the corpse.

Lucius shielded his eyes with his free hand.

They were out of range. Star could see no more.

"What is it?" said Kian. "What is she doing?"

"I don't know." She panned the glass across the ruined cityscape, expecting that at any minute a herd of angry, starving lizards—or equally starving scavengers—would charge out from the rubble and attack. That the body placed on high were there as decoy.

"Sit down, child," said Yeshie.

"No!"

"Whatever will be will be. Oshana—"

42

"I don't give a damn about your stupid god!" Star tossed the glass back at Kian. He caught it with both hands, a surprised look on his face. Turning her back on the lot of them, Star did exactly what Nene had done—clambered halfway down the moving wagon's side, waited for the right moment, then dropped onto the soft sand below. Knowing everyone was watching, she made sure she landed on two feet.

How strange it felt to be on solid ground again. She ignored the cries of her fellow travellers, their prayers and admonishments. She knew what she was doing. The ghosts knew too—they were watching her every move.

She ran past the moving wagons until she was out of breath, keeping an eye out for lizards. But the burnt out cityscape remained still and indifferent.

Neither Nene nor Lucius noticed her approach. Both were preoccupied, Nene almost losing her balance as she stood on tiptoes trying to poke the creature's arm.

The forest of bare steel struts shook and rattled as the wind picked up.

"What are you doing? It's a Templar and it's dead. Anyone can see—"

Nene almost fell. Lucius caught her quickly and lowered her to the sand.

"Get back on the Van!"

"I'm just—"

"Get back on the Van!" screamed Nene, the wind tearing her hair loose from its regular ponytail.

Star took a step back. "What's the matter? Is it contaminated? Why are you even touching it?"

Nene stared at her hard as the camel snorted and shifted its stance. "Yes. It's contaminated. It's not safe here—now get back on the Van."

Star threw up her hands, exasperated. "We're detouring through Broken Arch—of course it's not safe! An *Angel* fell to Earth! Harthstone's in flames. A lizard slammed—"

Climb up, both of you," said Lucius, offering his hand. "No time for arguing," he added, glancing uncomfortably in the direction of the lizards's habitat.

The saddle was made for two, not three, but somehow Lucius made room. The beast wasn't happy about it, but it headed off in chase of the Van without much need for encouragement. Either it could smell the lizards or smell another Templar in the ruins.

"I want to know why you were poking at that thing. You're always going on about infection and safety protocols."

"I had to check," said Nene grimly.

"Had to check what?"

Nene paused. "That he was truly dead."

Star snorted. "I could see that much from wagon top—and so could you. Why would anyone care about some tainted—"

"Don't you use that word," she hissed.

"Why not? It's not as if they're human."

"All living things feel pain and experience suffering, Star. There's never any excuse for cruelty."

"Templars are killing machines, Nene. Cruelty and suffering is what they were built for."

"You don't know anything about them."

Lucius made a rumbling sound to clear his throat. "It's dead—and we'll wind up dead too if we don't get on out of here."

"You never tell me anything. You have secrets but you keep them to yourself."

"Some secrets get kept for a reason. Trust me," said Nene bitterly.

"Trust you? How can I trust someone who's keeping secrets half the time?"

"Time's not something you can take for granted," said Nene. "Not out here. Not any of us."

The tone of Nene's voice signalled that the conversation was at an end.

The Van was nothing but a distant cloud of dust. Dark specks circled high above, stark against pale sky. Carrion birds returning to their meal—or looking for a fresher one.

Nene had nothing further to say on the matter. Neither did Lucius. Their passage was bumpy and uncomfortable. The threat of contamination weighed heavily on Star's mind. The whole Sand Road might be in trouble, yet somehow she was certain her sister was lying. She didn't do it often but Star could always tell so when she did.

They made it safely through the outskirts of Broken Arch, lagging farther back than was strictly safe, but the camel wouldn't take them any faster.

Clouds were beginning to streak with orange as light leached from the sky. Sand dunes stretched to the horizon, wind snatching up the finest particles and tossing them. Eventually, a familiar shape emerged, stark against the sand. The Vulture. To some, it resembled the skeleton of a giant bird, fashioned from metal that couldn't be scratched, let alone smelted down and sold off. No matter what anyone did to it, that Vulture endured, its origins lost to time. Totally useless for shade and shelter, it did serve a decent purpose as a beacon. Even in the thickest storm, every traveller knew exactly where they were the moment they clapped eyes on that thing.

Benhadeer would berth the Van on account of its best feature. An ancient Sentinel still in place, protecting this stretch of road from Dead Red storms. The Sentinel meant the Vulture had been important once.

Star knew the drill. They would camp till dawn, then push onwards at first light. The safest option under the circumstances, seeing that they didn't know what might be waiting for them once the Road wound around the Fists and reconnected with the farthermost stretch of the Axa flats.

Ahead, the Van curved in its customary berthing arc. Lucius raised his glass, then passed it across to her. "Careful, girl—damn thing's older than I am."

The instrument's casing was dented and battered out of shape, the lens scratched and scored. But she could see enough. The Vulture's substantial shadow-grey struts. Remains of a blackened campfire scattered across the sand. Other things not immediately identifiable. Bits and pieces. Shrouded shapes. Scuffed sand, dark and stained. Blood or wine? Blood most likely. Wine was not for wasting in these parts.

Snipers were positioned on the wagon tops. Point riders investigated the debris, wary of ambush, watching each other's backs. No shots were fired. Whoever had been here last was long gone.

When Star passed the glass back to Lucius, she looked beyond his inked and weathered face to the Road behind, to the dregs and rubble of a settlement that had once reached halfway to the sky.

= N I N E =

The tanker lumbered slowly across the stony ground. Slow and steady, it had quickly become Marianthe's favourite, travelling the same route, week in, week out, circling in an elliptical orbit encompassing both Crysse graveyard and the Temple of the Dish. The tanker did not allow other creatures to ride upon its back—only her. Sections of its left hand side had been hacked away and healed in rough jagged segments, making it possible for Marianthe, in her damaged state, to climb up and cling on, despite the sand barnacle encrustations. For all she knew, this tanker had been a troop carrier once, long ago in another lifetime half-remembered. Perhaps this was why the machine-beast stopped and started at her command, somehow sensing she used to be a soldier, remembering its tasks and duties in a former life. Nothing else made sense, but whatever the reason, she was mighty grateful. She could not walk far unaided. Most people were terrified of tankers—and not without good reason, but she had come to trust this one in its stoic, persistent orbits. Perhaps one day it would break away and join the others of its kind in their rough rambles across the open sand.

They were halfway home, the dish clearly in sight, when an object came streaking through the sky. A silvery thing encased in a halo of fire. She estimated a speed of 30,000 kph before it slowed. An Angel warsat, it seemed more than likely.

How curious.

Her drones began twittering with fresh collected data. She shushed them, shading her eyes with her free hand to see where the flaming thing had come to rest. Not far away, but too far for her to bother with.

Marianthe's followers were waiting when she and the drones disembarked from their faithful ride. Her followers kept a wary distance from the grinding, clanking tanker, not daring to move until it lumbered on its way, churning up great plumes of reddish dust. They clustered together in its wake like a flock of bleating sheep, frightened by the sounds it made, frightened by the sky and its streaky contrails. Desperate for Marianthe to assure them it was safe.

Nothing had been safe for centuries—that was the truth of things. But an Angel hurtling down to Earth was neither here nor there. A sign, perhaps, but she wasn't firing up her hopes on that account. Plenty of signs had flared across the years.

"Get back to work," she snapped, arms raised to shoo them away. A young girl handed her a stave and she hobbled across the cracked cement, into the welcome shadow of the Dish.

It was not Marianthe who had named this place, but *them*, the ones who had crawled out of the desert begging for water. The wretched and the dying, refugees from a thousand different wrongs. Shipwreck survivors of the cruel Obsidian Sea, escaped slaves from islands dotted throughout it. People fleeing justice—or the abject lack of it. Tainted ones cursed with malformed limbs. Folks with nowhere else to go. Marianthe welcomed all of them, so long as they worked and refrained from killing one another. Occasionally she had to raise a hand or a fist, or wield a blade to put some poor unfortunate out of their misery.

She thought they'd come for sanctuary, and perhaps they did at first. But sanctuary wasn't enough to keep them here. No, they stayed for promises whispered from the Dish itself. The Temple of the Dish was not like any other temple standing. Cylindrical and solid, three storeys high, made of two-tone ochre brick inset with windows, each one edged in white. A massive dish of tarnished silver rested on the top, incomplete—sections had been eroded by the elements, leaving a dark fringe of spikes stabbing skyward like the skeleton of a leaf. Over the years, she and her followers had surrounded the temple with clusters of low, flat dwellings made of whitewashed mud brick. The dish towered high above them all, inspiring them with strength and purpose.

Inside the temple was the place she named her Sanctum. Marianthe's private domain. The place where she kept her precious things, chief amongst them memories themselves.

Altars, formerly consoles and computer banks, now draped with hand-embroidered cloth. Upon the cloth, alongside tallow candles, sat faded photographs in frames, frozen moments stolen from forgotten pasts.

On occasion she would let her flock inside to gawk at her precious curios. They would sit cross-legged on the cold stone floor and she would read them poetry and show them images projected. They would stare in wonder, gasp, hold their collective breaths, and sigh at the idea that the world had ever been so lush and green.

She had taught the tainted and the broken to feed and clothe themselves, but she could not get them to comprehend the enormity of what the world had lost.

Instead, they worshipped what they could not understand, made themselves useful in the kitchens, laundry and plantation gardens, caught skinks and rats for that drover boy's great thunder-lizard with its insatiable appetite—not surprising considering its size. Fortunately the surrounding sands were crawling with tainted vermin, dirty scuttling things not hard to trap. Even baby sandskates, if the catchers were quick enough about it.

In the beginning, so many of those who had come to her were women, but not lately. Daughters weren't as easy to come by as they once had been, back in the tough times, the leanest years when the Sand Road coiled around the townships like a sickened, emaciated serpent. Too many mouths to feed, not enough to put in them. How easily people parted with daughters then.

Marianthe paused beneath the shadow of the dish, domestic concerns weighing heavily on her mind. Most urgently the need for a new supply of goats. That new, upstart warlord who'd taken over the Saint Agnes well wanted way too much for his animals, the skanky, matt-haired distempered creatures that they were. She didn't like the new arrangements. Bartering even the most dim-witted and useless of her Temple flock left a sour taste in her mouth. No, the fledgling warlord would have to go, along with his retinue of Knartooth bodyguards. It was an ugly tribe with ugly customs, carving their fearsome weaponry out of bones. Human or animal, whichever lay close to hand. She'd have to deal with it—and with them. But later. Right now there were more pressing matters than goats and fierce men.

Her thoughts were interrupted by a most unpleasant sound, more discordant than the sonic screaming of the tankers. It came from her followers, helpless and animalistic in tone. Marianthe hated it, had told them repeatedly to pull themselves together. Showing fear to your aggressor was the worst thing you could ever do about anything.

Half her flock were cowering in the dust, having dropped their baskets and barrows, contents spilled. They were pointing upwards at the sky and whimpering. Covering their faces with their arms.

A burning orb. A second one falling to the sand, moving fast, then slowing. Impacting deep within the Dead Red sands. One falling Angel could be caused by many things, but two? Two was evidence of control.

Marianthe made shushing, clucking noises, told them all to go about their business, reminding them that if the olives were not harvested soon, the crows and wild dogs would get them. Reminding them that dates would not pick themselves.

"Is it a sign?" asked a wide-eyed girl, her basket clutched so tight against her chest that it looked like the thing might snap and scratch her arms.

"It's a piece of junk, broken like everything else in this cursed place," said Marianthe. Words she did not herself believe. Words that caused her to make her way to the Temple's inner sanctum where she could meditate further upon the situation.

= TEN =

Beside the Vulture, the communal fire was lit and warming, but everything else was in disarray. Light faded and the stars were coming out. People who should have been snatching sleep wandered aimlessly, still in travelling kit, starting up arguments with neighbours they'd been riding alongside amiably for days.

Weary travellers clustered in groups of three or four, some sitting, some standing, dark shapes beyond the fire's illumination. Most refused to shrug their sand cloaks, and stuck close to the wagons. No sign of Remy, thankfully, just a mass of faces Star didn't know, mixed in with others so familiar she knew them better than her own reflection.

The big pot was warming, ember bread baking snugly in the coals. Dinner was late and Star was hungry. Excited yelps of dogs being fed behind the wagons didn't help.

A swarm of travellers surrounded Benhadeer—the type of people his right handers usually kept out of his way. But this night, people weren't taking no for an answer. Snatches of conversation hung clear and audible in the crisp twilight air.

"We must press on, it is not safe in this cursed place!"

"Too many portents and omens!"

Star noted how many were gesturing at the sky to make their point, even though the Angelfall was hours back, its contrails long since dissipated.

"We are safe here for the meantime," announced Benhadeer in his aggravated, booming voice. He splayed his fingers and patted the air as if trying to sooth it. When that didn't work he pointed to the Sentinel.

That shut some of them up—but not for long.

"If I miss my supplier in Heel, I'll lose a fortune!"

"Those lizards are downwind of us—what's to stop them charging out of the ruins?"

"Why do we linger here in the middle of nowhere? Why do we not press on?"

That last voice. Star would know it anywhere. Kian and his friends were in the thick of it, arguing against decisions they could have no part in making. Not used to their concerns being dismissed so easily.

She wanted to hear what Kian was saying, to find out why he was in such a hurry.

But before she could move, an arm hooked through her own.

50

"Need to talk to you," said Nene, a serious expression on her face.

Star stepped back and yanked her arm free. "I'm busy. I'll do the bark tomorrow, first light."

"Willow bark can wait." She stared out across the breadth of the encampment. "Been a hell of a day," she added, more to herself than to Star. "Hell of a day and we still have far to go."

Star nodded, both cautious and surprised. The camp did not feel right. The Van people should have been invigorated by the promise of the big port up ahead—even if they did have to swing around the Fists. There should have been laughter, music, noise. Wafting smells as people started using up the last of their supplies. Talking up the fortunes they expected. The kind of hope that ports like Fallow Heel always restored.

"Too many omens," said Star.

Nene didn't believe in omens, but for once she didn't argue, just stared into the middle distance, coughing to clear congestion from her throat.

"Walk with me."

They moved until they were out of earshot of all but the camels and the dogs.

"I've been thinking," said Nene, that serious expression still affixed to her face. "Been going over the books. Our debt to Benhadeer is almost paid."

"Almost paid? Really?"

Star tried her best to look interested. Keeping track of what they owed and what they paid was Nene's business. Nene, who knew how to write and count and keep accurate tally of such things. Things she had attempted to teach Star to no avail.

"And what's the sly old dog to say to that?"

"He's a fair man, Star. Many other things besides, but fair. When we've paid the last coin, we'll be free to go. Another month or two and we'll be done."

Star considered the implication of her words. "Go where?" Her sister had no love for Fallow Heel, with its ostentatious merchant caste, its reliance on tanker hunting and the types attracted by that brutal industry. Nene saw dark alleys where Star saw well-paved streets. Exploitation where Star saw easy living.

Nene chewed her lower lip. "That big construction back in Solace? New buildings taking up an entire block—remember it?"

Star nodded, even though she didn't. If there was ever a place more wrongly named . . . Solace, once a shanty town dug up from the raw sand. Networks of bunkers had lain beneath, remnants of some skirmish long forgotten. Nobody cared about history. Shelter was shelter, so the bunkers got dug up. Bunkers some said had once been torture chambers. Or secret laboratories where men and women dressed in white concocted poisons, stripping life from the land. The dreams and desperation of refugees added colour, if not comfort, over time. They called it Solace, even though the sun-baked concrete warren reeked of boiled roots and melon pulp.

"The town's pitching in to build a hospital," said Nene cautiously. "Biggest one you ever saw. Not even Sammarynda can compare."

Nene utilised her hands when speaking, expansive gestures that always drew attention. Her eyes shone as she spoke. "Those Harthstone refugees escaping downroad—most of them will wind up Solace way. No one else will take them in—not permanently. The old relic hunters's graveyard, remember how they used to call Solace that? Seems like one of those old relic hunters unearthed a fortune. Blood money, most like. Old world ordnance—but so long as it's being used for good, I'm not complaining."

Solace.

The realisation hit Star like a slap across the cheek. Solace. Nene couldn't be serious. Not Solace. Anywhere but there.

"But it's the farthest point from anywhere on any kind of map! We could live in . . . Sammarynda!" The first place name that came to mind. The place where Kian and his two friends most likely hailed from. Most of the merchant princes came from there. "Or Fallow Heel—what's wrong with the port that's waiting right in front of us?"

Nene smiled dismissively. "Sammarynda wouldn't let us through the gates, and Fallow Heel already has medics aplenty, charging outlandishly to patch up crushed and bloodied tankerjacks, sending them back out to risk their lives again." She shook her head in disbelief. "Such a waste. A pointless waste."

Star stared at her sister's oval face, the deep lines etched around her dark brown eyes.

"I'm sorry, Star. I know you dream of big town life, but there's no purpose for us in a place like Fallow Heel. Between the blood and carnage of the open sand and relic trade lies little but crumbs for honest folk." She placed her hand on Star's shoulder.

Star brushed it away. "You could set up a clinic anywhere. Anywhere—people would come—you know they'd walk a hundred miles. You could help them and I could find . . ." What was she looking for, exactly?

"It's early days yet. Early days. If we get in at ground level with the hospital, we could have a real say in what happens to the place. Lucius might come with us. He says the Road's going bad—and I happen to agree. We're not safe here anymore. Time to stake a claim before things get out of hand." She pointed at the route the falling Angel had taken. The vague patch of far-off land where it had come to rest.

Star shook her head. She still couldn't believe what she was hearing. "I'm not going to Solace. I've got plans of my own."

Nene placed her hands on her hips and pressed her lips together. "Star, that rich Heel girl you met last year is not your friend. She isn't going to help you."

Star was taken aback. She had never told Nene of her encounter with Allegra. She had, however told Anj, who had likely told her sister Kaja, who . . . There was no such thing as a secret on a Sand Road Van. Apparently.

Nene smiled sadly. "They're not our people, Star. If that girl was kind to you, it could only have been because it amused her to be so."

"How would you know—you've never even met her!"

"And you only ever met her once."

Rage boiled within Star's chest. "You make all the decisions for both of us. You don't care about me—all you care about are those tainted refugees."

"Don't use that word. Don't call them that. You never used to talk that way." She nodded to the Vulture's silhouette. "Those foreigners are giving you airs and graces."

"Airs and what?"

Nene stopped and stared at her hard. "Nothing. Just something . . . our mother used to say."

Star stared down at the scuffed sand between her boots. She hated it whenever Nene made mention of their parents, hated that she couldn't even remember their faces. "I don't want to live like this. The creeping Red. The dead tree stumps. Everyone who's smart is getting out."

Nene stared at the Vulture without really seeing it. "I don't like the degradation any more than you do. But the answer's not to run away and hide from our responsibilities. Poor wretches fleeing Harthstone, they don't know anything of the hardship that lies ahead."

"And how is *their* hardship *our* problem?"

Nene stared at her sister incredulously. "How is it *not* our problem, Star? We are all the same people. The same blood runs in our veins."

"The Road is going nowhere," Star mumbled.

Nene's frown softened. "This Road's stood the test of time. When the Ruin came down, those cowards scrabbled for their fortress cities, those with coin enough to buy themselves a place. The Sand Road made a go of it. Built the Sentinels with the last of their old-world smarts. Survived the worst the Dead Red had to throw. We survived because of our ancestors' sacrifices. We can't abandon our own people on account of dying trees!"

"It's not just the trees, Nene. You know it's not. There's changes in the way things work round here." She pointed back the way they'd come, to Broken Arch and beyond. "People aren't as friendly as they used to be. People are only leaving because they have to."

"Some of them, maybe—but that doesn't include us. We have a responsibility—"

"Urgh! There's no point arguing with you. Those responsibilities are all your choices—not mine. Choices you made years ago—for both of us—and nothing I say or do is going to change them."

Star strode off in the direction of the Vulture's skeletal frame. Past the communal fire where a nervous few were gathering, warming their hands and glancing over their shoulders. There were no dogs barking. No sounds but the murmur and hubbub of weary travellers.

"Star!"

Anj. Fellow Van brat, the closest friend she had aside from Lucius. Star kept walking. Anj sprung up from her place by the fire and ran to catch her up. "Where are you going? Wait for Remy."

When Star didn't stop, Anj grabbed her arm. "Slow down. Come and eat, then I want to show you something."

"I'm not hungry," Star lied. She tried to tug her arm free but Anj held on tight.

"Star—Remy and Griff found something."

"Leave me alone. I'm not in the mood."

"What's the matter? What happened?"

"I don't want to talk about it."

Anj nodded. "Okay, but at least come sit."

Star allowed Anj to drag her to the fire. They nestled in amongst a group of dancers who were gossiping loudly and passing trinkets from hand to hand, apparently unaffected by the dark mood infecting everybody else.

Anj leant in close and whispered. "So the three of them, yeah, those clean foreign men, they tried to talk Jens into selling them camels! Reckon they have to be in Heel as soon as possible. Reckon it's a matter of life or death."

Star frowned. "What's so important that they need to get there so fast?"

Anj's eyes widened. "How much coin must they be carrying! Three camels, they tried to score. Three! Like Jens would ever part with a single animal. Like Benhadeer would even consider it!"

Anj leaned in closer still. Her breath was sour and salty. "They're clueless, Star. Wherever they're from, it's nowhere around here. Not from the coast neither. Nowhere we've even heard of, I'll bet my boots!"

Star was about to press Anj for further details when she felt a sharp poke in her ribs.

"Child, you're gonna have to stop jumping off moving wagons. Nearly gave my heart a proper fright, you did!"

It was Yeshie again, squeezing in beside her even though there wasn't room, placing a faded square of mat down on the sand. Drawing attention that Star could have done without. "Let's see if we can't find out what's really going on," she added, and before Star had a chance to speak, the old woman had fished a handful of dice-and-bones from a pouch on her belt. Rubbing them between her pudgy fingers, she blew on them three times, then let them fall.

Yeshie gasped and placed both palms across her heart as soon as the dice-and-bones came to rest. Others began to pack in close to see for themselves and hear the old woman speak. Not Anj—she shot off quicker than a skink.

"Not good," said Yeshie. "Not good at all." The bones were etched with writing barely visible in the flicker of firelight. Smooth, old and yellowed. Three had landed together, stacking atop one another. "You can see signs of misfortune there, but this . . ." She indicated the touching ones, each of them black side up. "This speaks of darkness. Much harsher than the work of blood and bile." She glanced up at the star-scattered night and chewed her lip. "Something waits for us across the sands. Something old and powerful, waking up."

"What else do you see?" asked a voice from beyond the fire's light, as others crowded closer. It was too dark to see which of the dancers had spoken.

Yeshie scooped up the dice-and-bones before anyone else could get a closer look.

Star waited for the next bit. The sales pitch in which the old bone caster would offer up amulets for sale. Charms and wards against the coming dark. She'd heard it a thousand times before.

But instead, Yeshie packed away her divination tools and began telling a couple of round-faced dancers a hurried tale about the moon goddess and the havoc her children had caused some relative of someone else's. One by one the crowd thinned, realising they would learn nothing else useful tonight.

Noting Star's quizzical expression, Yeshie smiled and patted her hand. "We'll all be fine, dear. We have the protection of Oshana and that's what matters." She went back to her story. Children sitting close by seemed comforted by the repetitive banter. Easy for them to fall asleep. Not so easy for the rest of them.

Star did not believe in dice-and-bones, but even so, she wished Yeshie had kept that particular prediction to herself.

One of the dancers passed Star a wineskin, its heavily spiced aroma pungent even with the stopper in. Toddy, a boiled mess of fermented palm hearts. Star took a deep draught. She was going to need it. Nene was crazy if she thought Star would let herself get dragged to Solace. There would be a better way and she would find it.

Star took another swig, then coughed. "A flaming Angel crossed the sky today and fell into the Red," she said, leaning in close to ensure Yeshie could hear. "Right in front of us—what have the magic bones to say about that?"

Yeshie patted Star kindly on the cheek. "I have something for Nene. Will you take it to her?"

As she nodded, Yeshie plunged her hand into her pocket and withdrew a lumpen bundle, placing it into Star's cupped hands. Not divination bones, but delicately-carven beads strung together on cotton threads. Some looked like skulls, others had animal faces. Firelight made some of them seem to smile.

"Knartooth amulets," she whispered. "The finest kind—not the junk those tourists string round their necks. Very powerful. Very powerful protection, mark my words."

Star's fingers curled around the little skulls and faces as Yeshie patted her hand. She nodded, knowing full well Nene would toss them out the window or, even more likely, cast them into the fire where they could do no harm to anyone. She tried to place the amulets back into the old woman's hand. "I can't take them, Yeshie. They're too precious."

But Yeshie insisted, so Star bundled them back in cloth and shoved them deep into her trouser pocket. She took another swig of toddy and thought about Nene's words. Everything was changing—she didn't need dice-and-bones to tell her that.

A dancer passed her a dollop of stew and a hunk of ember bread. Star ate without tasting, chewing quickly, noting that Anj had not returned to sit with the others.

People ate in silence. The detour through Broken Arch had everyone on edge. Nobody was singing. Nobody was laughing loud, or talking up big plans.

And where was Remy? By now he was usually lurking around the fire, trying to catch her attention. Teddy was where he ought to be. Same with Cray and Kaja, passing splifs and poking at the flames with elongated thorns. Filling in time until the call came to hit the road.

Her head was light and warm with drink, the sky deepening from blue to black, soon to be sprinkled with an ocean of diamond dust. No Angels. They wouldn't come out for several hours.

She spotted Kian and his companions standing by the vulture, silhouettes stark against the pink-streaked clouds. Anj's words lingered in her mind—*Wherever they're from, it's nowhere around here*. Star stood up and wiped her hands on her shirt. She was tired of waiting for others to make the first move.

= ELEVEN =

The outpost built to house the Lotus Blue had once been insignificant: small and dull, with nothing much to distinguish it from other bunkers. The Blue had been initiated in the latter stages of the wars. Late in the day, so much ground already lost—so the military strategists and ordnance architects had informed him.

But to the General's mind, things had just been getting serious. He'd been fired up, keen to give his all to the conflict zones. Brimming with dedication, hungry to unleash his vast, explosive potential.

The Lotus Generals were an extreme innovation. Once human, uploaded when their bodies became too feeble. Old Man Blue, they used to call him. Old Man Blue. Old Man Blue once had a wife and sons. Grandsons, granddaughters, names and faces hovering aggravatingly beyond his reach. All he can source now are images: random faces materialising against intricately realised backdrops.

He remembers fat babies with cherub faces, a pretty girl with long, dark hair leaning against a wall of bright pink bricks; a scene glazed in cheery sunlight—who had such a pretty girl been to him?

Other memories are curious and random: an old white man with a frizz of fine white hair and a thick moustache. Behind him, a chalkboard covered with mathematical scribbles. A middle-aged woman, taut olive skin over muscular arms, strings of ochre beads around her neck, hand clasped around a leafy branch. The forest behind her dappled with light and shadow.

He does not recall their names, nor, recognise their faces. No matter, they are all long dead, their world long fallen silent.

Somebody must have won the Lotus Wars.

The only life signs surrounding him now are the thrum and rattle of those battletrucks with their monstrous oversized wheels and juddering armour-plated chassis, thundering across the raw red plains, racing each other—that is what it looks like when he finally finds another set of stable Warbird digital feeds to hijack.

Battletankers, half-drunk on their own fermented nano-infested juices, half wild, all crazy, racing each other across sand-blasted flats. The stark red sands have become their domain. The people are all hiding underground.

Not all.

He can hear their whispers, their tappings, their transmissions, weak and paltry, cowering, shielded from potential enemies.

Not so the brazen tankers, barrelling and blaring in full sight of the post-apocalyptic landscape they'd helped fashion. They can hear the General, broadcasting loud and clear, they don't want to answer, they're not interested in communication with his kind. Not at first.

After messing with sub-frequencies for half a day, he discovers a lone rogue responsive to his suggestions. A dented six-wheeler, top heavy with encrustations—some kind of hardy, sand dwelling infestation. From above, it looks like a moving rock. The General sends it slamming into the side of another vehicle; a tanker twice its speed and girth. The tanker's gun turrets swivel round and aim, menacing but not firing. Maybe none of them possess fire power anymore.

Do it again, says the General. Weak-willed, the little tank obeys. Two others set upon it, ramming and rolling right over the top of its rocky crust, slamming and smashing until there's nothing left but broken wheels and underbelly.

How interesting, says the General out loud, even though there is nothing and no one listening, glad at the sound of his own voice echoing along dusty darkened corridors.

The General toils through cycles of patient diagnostics while musing on the problems of temporality, spatiality, and mobility. There is no date to tell him when, no chronicles to outline the hows and whys and wherefores. What *has* happened to all the people? Last he remembers, they had the big boys on the run. The boonie rats were bugging out, Johnny was digging, burrowing underground. Who the F was Johnny anyway? He'd known the answer to that one once, but now such details don't seem to matter. Now everything is still and dead and gone.

The General forces himself to focus, feeling his way, on-off, on-off, flexing nanophotonic circuits, each new forged connection sending tingles through his feeds. Sifting through corroded multicomponent systems, he sets about improving his recognition capabilities, grateful for his makeup of plasmonic nanogap arrays. Ultra capacitor energy recovery systems kicking in, high throughput optical intensity.

The sand has covered advantages he didn't know he had, like a selection of land-based Intercontinental Ballistic Missiles dug down deep in silos. Minuteman IV, air burst or contact, largely depending on his mood. But are they still operational?

Only one way to find the answer.

He shoots one out the top of a cracked and shattered silo, a first-stage booster motor that fires sixty seconds after launch, all good so far. At stage two it ignites and the shroud ejects, but the third stage motor explodes in a spectacular blaze of glory, raining shards of fire-blasted steel upon the land.

Disappointing, but there are other silos, other weapons, other options.

The main transmitter, Sentinel Tower Zero, sits atop the bunker itself, surrounded by nine equispaced smaller towers, eight hundred feet high apiece, each tower connected via aerial wire forming a series of three concentric circular loops—all since buried under sand. Sentinel Tower Zero is encased in dense, absorbent sheeting which forms a high, enclosed oblong chamber, an elevator running up the inside of the tower.

The General gets curious—what about the enormous quantities of copper tube and wire ground counterpoise arrays buried beneath the complex? What about the fifty-foot high heavy-duty copper-wire coils supported on Jarrah frames? Sections were lined with stainless-steel sheeting, all buried three storeys deep. Magnifying Energy Transmitters containing induced coil electrostatic waves from discharge. Power stations sucking up borehole gas, storing it in an underground reservoir.

The tip of Sentinel Tower Zero protrudes from the sand. The General experiments with the limited power he's managed to get sparking, creating a near-blinding, massive high-energy burst of blue-white light that ripples for several seconds, lighting up the cloudless, moonless night.

He imagines that burst can be seen for a hundred kilometres in all directions, an intense ball of orange-ochre plasma, swirling fire in spiral patterns, flames vanishing into a void within the spherical mass. A mass with no tail that makes no sound, nor seismic waves.

All very well, but where's the sting? It takes some time and much experimentation with formula to conjure a true polyp storm of old, the weapons that had razed the battlefield of Crysse Plain, turned the tide and turned the tables, turned the lights off all across the globe.

The General is pleased with his endeavour, ensorcelled by the thing's deadly ferocity, the way its passage changes the colour of the sky, killing every creature in its path.

= TWELVE =

The toddy sat warm and comfortable in Star's belly, filling her with confidence and a clarity of thought she'd not experienced for some time.

Kian and his two "associates" were indistinguishable from one another at a distance. Up close was different. Kian's galabeya hung open at the front, doing little to conceal the charcoal skinsuit underneath. Van people apparently held no interest for the three of them—but the Vulture did. The one called Tallis raised a lantern high to view the steel up close. The other one, Jakome, attempted to scratch the light-sucking surface with a knife. Kian stared upwards, drinking in the blue-black night and its fiery constellations.

The toddy strengthened Star's resolve. The three *had* been planning to jump the Van at the Axa flats—and that could only mean one thing. She strode out to join him, soft sand muffling her footfall.

"Too early for Angels, if that's what you're looking for," she said. "Angels don't start their fighting till after midnight."

Kian didn't say anything. Didn't even lower his gaze to see who'd spoken.

"Seen plenty of shooters, but never seen one fall to ground before. Not in daylight. Especially not on fire," she added, her voice sounding small and hollow beneath the vast enormity of the sky.

"Is that so?"

She waited for him to make some effort at keeping the conversation going, but he didn't. She swallowed the lump in her throat. It was now or never.

"So where do you three really come from? Long way from here, I'm reckoning."

Kian kept on staring at the sky.

Star continued. "I've been as far as Evenslough, right up to the Lucent fortress steps. To Makasa, to watch the big ships heading out to sea."

She jumped as glass smashed against stone. Turned to see Tallis standing a little too close. His close-cropped blond hair gave him a menacing appearance in the mix of lantern and starlight.

He stared at her blankly. "Make yourself useful. Go fetch us more wine."

"Shhh Tal, there's no need for that," Kian said.

"I'm not your servant," Star replied. "I want to know where you thought you were going, back there before the Van came around the Fists. You were gonna jump before that Angel fell. Out there in the middle of nowhere. Gotta be a reason for it."

Silence. Tallis cocked his head and stared at her so long and hard that she began to wonder if, perhaps, he hadn't understood.

"Only one thing standing on the Axa flats," she continued. "Fortress city Axa itself."

Kian transferred his attention from the stars to her face. Not a comfortable stare. She felt like a bug under a glass.

She jabbed a finger at his chest. "Those skinsuits. That fancy relic in your pocket. I think you're *from* Axa. Fortress city people up above ground. Scouting the Sand Road, blending in as best you can. You were almost home when that Angel fell."

"You are mistaken," said Kian coldly.

With a slow and fluid motion, Jakome drew his blade. Kian raised his hand to make him stop.

"You are drunk," he said to her. "Saying crazy things you will regret."

"Take me with you to Fallow Heel—or wherever it is you're headed. I won't say anything to anybody—promise!"

Kian paused, as if considering. "I'm afraid that isn't possible."

"Why not? I know Heel like the back of my hand. I've been there many times. I can help you find whatever you're looking for."

"I doubt it."

"Kian, it's nearly time," said Tallis, his own hand resting upon his dagger's hilt.

"You think you're better than the rest of us," Star blurted, speaking directly into Kian's dark eyes, ignoring the other two.

"Would have thought that was blatantly obvious," Tallis said, smirking. "I can smell you from here. You and your people stink worse than the camels."

The insult stung, but Star held her ground.

Jakome raised his dagger. This time Kian did nothing to stop him. "What dya say, boys—reckon she might be tainted? She looks to have the right count of body parts, but you can never tell."

"Could be anything under those trousers," Tallis chimed in. "A skink's dick. Or perhaps a tail. Better to be safe than sorry. Self defence, you understand. A man's got to watch himself when amongst savages."

Star's cheeks flushed with anger but she held it in, wishing she had a weapon—the small knives in her boots were not much use.

Kian made an elaborate hand gesture. Reluctantly, Jakome lowered his blade.

Kian took a shiny cigarette case from his pocket, opened it, placed a hand-rolled cigarette between his lips. He struck a match, shielded the flame as he lit the tip, then shook it out, flicking the match away as the pungent scent of seaweed wafted. He drew deeply and stared into Star's eyes.

"Whatever you think you saw back on the Van, you should forget. We'll get where we're going, but you'd do best to stay with your own kind."

"Take me with you. We can help each other."

He laughed through a plume of bluish smoke. "Go away, ugly little girl. Go play with your Van trash friends."

A bottle smashed against one of the Vulture's struts just inches from Jakome's head. Star shut her eyes as glass rained down. When she opened them, Remy was stepping forward into the pool of lantern light, a blade in one hand, Van hands flanking either side, all of them armed.

Moments earlier, Kian and his friends had seemed half drunk. They sobered quickly as the gang pressed in closer.

Remy stepped forward, a blade gripped tightly. "This tourist bothering you?" he said coolly.

Ted stepped up to take position at Remy's side. He stabbed a wooden stave into the sand. Kaja stepped forward. Knives were her thing. Both she and her sister were always armed, even when you couldn't see a blade.

There were others. Regulars and transients alike, all bored with waiting for the dawn. Looking for trouble, not being too picky where they found it.

"Don't be idiots," said Star. As the words left her lips, her hands curled into fists, the nails biting into her flesh, her head still warm and fuzzy from the toddy. Something didn't seem quite right. There was more light than there should have been. More light than constellations and one small lantern could provide. She peered up through the Vulture's arcing struts to a moon soaked in a river of stars—so many they could never be counted. Blazing suns like ours, so Nene said. Shining down on countless other worlds.

Something strange was happening overhead. She could see too much detail in the faces of the foreign princes. The embroidery on their galabeyas. The weapons in their hands. The sky was lightening, like dawn come hours early. A bank of boiling, writhing clouds was manifesting overhead. Wispy tendrils blocked the moon, pulsing with an eerie incandescence.

"Kian, we don't have time," said Jakome urgently.

"Time?" Remy laughed. "Where do you think you're going? You have no power here. No authority. Nobody is going to sell you their camels. Not for any price you care to name."

One by one, his companions readied their weapons.

"Cut it out," said Star, glancing nervously at the clouds getting nearer. Lightning flared. Close, and getting closer.

"We'll see who's the idiot," said Remy.

Ted cried out suddenly and pointed upwards. Everybody looked, even the three who faced a beating. Three who surely knew better than to turn their attention from an angry, well-armed mob.

"Look at the sky!"

"Just a storm. It can't get past the Sentinel," said a deep voice. Not one of theirs. A shadow emerging from other shadows. Kristo. No blade was drawn, no rifle at the ready. He didn't need them. His voice alone was weaponry enough.

"Get to the fire. Eat up and pack your kits." He spoke directly to Kaja and Teddy as the other Van hands and hangers on scattered, rendered into children by the commanding tone of his voice.

Star held her ground.

Kristo ignored her. He turned to face Kian and the foreigners square on. "Put away your blades, else you'll find mine drawn across your throats. Are we clear? I'm sick of your kind. I won't be warning you again."

Tallis stepped forward. Kian gripped his friend's arm to stop him.

"We're clear," said Kian.

Kristo continued. "I've a mind to put the three of you off at Crossroads. You can find your own way to Heel from there—or wherever it is you think you might belong."

He turned to Star. "As for you, I had high hopes you might grow into something half as useful as your sister. Looks like you're no better than the rest."

All the clever answers she knew off by heart lodged firmly in her throat. Her face flushed red with a mix of toddy and embarrassment.

Kristo glanced upwards. "Keep clear of the perimeter. Stick close to the wagons and the animals. Something's not right about that sky."

When Kristo left, the princes followed at a distance. Star waited until the last of them had blended with the fire crowd.

Shattered shards of broken bottle glinted in the strange light reflected off the underbellies of clouds. Lightning flashed in short, sharp bursts.

She stood until the rage within her tempered. Till she could breath easy, not in ragged gasps. She dared not answer back to Kristo, but those three stuck up princes had not seen the last of her. Whether or not they were from the fortress city, they were up to something. She was going to find out what it was.

In defiance of Kristo's words, she walked along the electric edge of the Sentinel's emitted umbra, the invisible protective cast it threw sending tingles through her skin. Tonight was different from other nights. A boiling rage churned deep inside her guts. Star would not be following her sister to a dump like Solace. She was destined for greater, better things. And the first of those things was to make those foreign princes eat their words.

Standing close to storms was nothing new—all Van brats made a game of it. Daring each other to perch at the farthest edge of the Sentinel's reach, so close they could feel the sting of sand against their skin. Knowing they were safe from harm, that the mighty raging things could never touch them.

She perched upon a boulder, cross-legged, staring out into the darkness. Thunder rumbled in the distance, the fierce storm's underbelly overhead—a beautiful and deadly thing. She tried not to breathe in gouts of Dead Red dust; it was always creeping, contaminating everything. Clotting their pores and rustying up their skin. Making all of them look like they were one people. *Poor people. Van trash, never settling, always on the move.*

Star hugged her knees. Sometimes it felt like she'd been travelling the Road forever. But it was only ten summers out of seventeen, at least as far as she'd been told. Her first seven were ones she couldn't remember. Nene had always been vague about those early, missing years, assuring her little sister she was seventeen summers old. But Star couldn't remember anything before seven. Not where she was born, not even their parents' faces.

Having a big black hole where memory was supposed to be was like having half a life. Her earliest recollection was of shivering in a thin white shift, hugging her arms against her skin, terrified of every single sound. With first light had come a vision of a giant bird. A vulture shadowing the sisters as they stumbled across the Red. A harbinger of death, even though Star had no name for such a creature. She hadn't even known her own name then.

But the bird was not a vulture, an omen, or an apparition. She'd blinked and it had revealed itself to be nothing more than an observation kite from a passing caravan. She remembered running towards the mighty wheels and falling to her knees. Later, a wall of curious faces, all craning to get a glimpse of her before Nene shooed them away. Huddling under a blanket, terrified without knowing why, her back pressed firmly against warm wood. Peering out at Nene's willowy silhouette as she argued bitterly with the man who held their future in his hands. One word from Benhadeer and both girls would have been abandoned roadside. Two words might have seen them killed.

But Nene had a gift: people listened when she spoke, from warlords down to the mop-haired Van brats perpetually tumbling underfoot. Benhadeer had astutely gauged the value of her skills. He'd taken them on and put them to good use.

Ten years working off their debt and Solace was to be their reward and future? Not likely. Not while there was breath left in Star's lungs.

Reluctantly, she headed for the fire. She didn't want Nene to see her—or Remy. Or Lucius, or even Anj. People were still bickering, some in favour of staying till dawn, others whining that they should have left already. There had been starlight enough and the way was clear—except who could be sure of anything anymore, with Barossa dead and Harthstone burning? The Van might be barrelling into the path of a brand new warlord. One who had no respect for the sanctity of white flag.

"The veil of darkness offers us protection!"

"Quicksand and hidden serpent nests is what it offers . . ."

"The longer we waste here, the sooner the dead can come to claim our souls."

Star tuned out the pointless banter—the storm meant they would have to stay till morning. The words the three of them had uttered went racing through her head. Jakome urging that they didn't have time. Time for what? Where were they now? Not by the fire alongside everyone else.

=THIRTEEN=

Inside the belly of the Temple of the Dish, the air was still and cool. What little juice still flowed through the solar batteries, Marianthe conserved for powering up the screens. She did not waste a single drop of battery on light. Illumination came from windows, lanterns, and tallow candles, the wax all used up years ago. She hadn't glimpsed a single bee for decades.

She lit the wicks of a precious few then leaned her weight on the walking stave hand carved from the last remaining tree in Evenslough. Others would have burnt it for fuel but she had been so much smarter than the rest of them, able to recognise what they were going to need in future days.

She collapsed her weight into the old metal chair. It creaked in protestation but held together. Marianthe sat there in the half light for a spell, till all thoughts of goats and girls and cabbages subsided.

In the early days when she'd been alone, before she'd got the dish patched up, juiced and aimed, she'd swept the surrounding skies with radio, hopeful of finding other outposts, survivors like herself.

Fox hunting was what they used to call it, listening for transmitter signals. Occasionally she'd made connection via tropospheric scatter, moon bounce, and borealis. Dust particles refracting signals over the horizon. Skywave propagation during extreme peaks in the sunspot cycle.

The remains of a military base in Pacific waters. Some other place called Ice Land which she pictured as cool and clear, all gleaming white palaces carved from snow and crystal. Places she would never visit, a thought that made her feel a little sad.

She leant forward, brushed dust off the metallic surface. Paused to consider. Every time she powered up the console she took a risk. Risk that it might be the last time. Risk that the fading sun-fed batteries might not have enough grunt left in them for one more gasp. When the last of the rechargeables fell beyond repair, with it would die her last and only chance of finding *him*.

He was dead, of course. Long dead, how could he not be? Everyone from the bad old days was dead and gone. Everyone except for her, a living relic—if living was what you could call this way of life. Existing was a better word for it, from day to day, problem to problem, goat to goat.

The chair creaked loudly as she leaned forward and flicked a switch. Equipment groaned and shuddered to life, and a dull hum like the droning of subterranean insects filled the space.

The screens were chipped and scratched in several places. Only a third of them worked at all, but a third was better than nothing. More switches gave her access to her drones, allowing her to see whatever they could. Which wasn't much, admittedly. The temple and its cluster of mud brick dwellings from above, each made lovingly by hands that considered this the safest place they'd ever lived. Beyond them, a stretch of cracked and buckled tarmac. A flat expanse of grey cement littered with rows and rows of corroding planes. Further beyond, the Obsidian Sea. The less said about that deadly place, the better.

Little Ditto, all patched up and in full flight, performing a sweep of the outer perimeter. Dutifully, it beamed back images of sand and more sand, red and yellow mixed together. Now and then, there would be a flash of movement. Small creatures: sometimes dogs or foxes or bigger things like lizards. Sometimes tankers or those other flesh-mesh things with spider legs. Hunter-seekers, Searchers-and-destroyers, she had once known the names of all the different kinds.

Little Ditto's job was to search for creatures moving on two legs. To observe the ones who passed on by, to keep check of the ones half likely to intend their Temple settlement harm.

She leant back in the chair again, pondering which of the Dish's many origin myths she would teach her curious flock that afternoon. Some kind of lesson or performance was inevitable. Her people needed something to distract them from the Angels. *The mighty dish had been an ear for listening to the old sky gods. The mighty dish was a giant platter, which, in days of yore, was filled with offerings.* She doubted the latter. Even before the Ruin, when the sands were green and shiny silver cities stabbed at the skyline, filling that dish would have been an improbable feat.

A thunking sound, then a flash and then the screen went blank. Her heart sank. Little Ditto, patched up one too many times. Perhaps its time had finally come, as time comes to everything eventually. But no. An electronic cough and splutter. Faithful Ditto, still alive and kicking, beaming back through electronic eyes.

She smiled.

On the screen was a blurred image of sand up close, and then the sky: vast, impenetrable, and blue. Then something she had never seen before. Bands of static infused with random-seeming patterns. Pixelated rainbows. Hacks and clicks, sub-frequency squeals. Then nothing. Black again, and then the sky restored, as did Little Ditto, as though nothing strange had happened.

Marianthe sat even further back in her chair, placed her gnarled fingers on her lips. A message. It had been a message, she was certain. But a message from whom or what?

Him.

Always the first thought that came to mind. Always the first dismissed. Her feelings for him were residue, impossible to flush completely from her heart.

He was dead. He had been dead for centuries.

If not him, then who?

She sat there in the half light until the candles burned to stubs, watching footage of sand and rocks and sky and sand again while seeing none of it. Thinking about the coincidence of Angels come to ground. A handful in as many days, then this, which could be no coincidence at all. Which could be nothing but it might be something. A stab at communication. Shouting in the sub-frequency wilderness.

= FOURTEEN =

The plaster-walled office seemed much smaller than it actually was, crammed with merchandise Mohandas had yet found time to deal with: unopened crates, dusty rolls of stacked carpet, bulging sacks labelled with faded stencil marks. Antique furniture, lamps, chests of drawers, broken clocks that had not told time for centuries, porcelain crockery rimmed with gold—far too ostentatious for practical use in an industrious tanker port like Fallow Heel.

Above his desk hung a painting of his pride and joy: the *Razael*; the finest sand ship the docks of Fallow Heel had ever seen. The *only* such vessel if truth be told. He had overseen every splinter of its restoration and conversion. A symbol harking back to times where anything had seemed possible, when there had still been oceans within a hundred miles of this place.

His massive desk was thickly layered with maps and charts. Some were purely for decoration and prestige. Generally speaking, the more lavish the map, the more dubious its likely provenance. Other more authentic kinds he sold to tourists, adventurers, and fools; all three rolled into one, more often than not. The stretch of Verge surrounding Fallow Heel had been picked clean as bone. Not so much as a brick of pre-Ruin salvage remained that hadn't been accounted for, let alone the kind of treasures idiots from the wealthy coastline craved.

That left only tankers and the Obsidian Sea for the purely idiotic. Daredevils, risk takers, crazies willing to chance everything on a dream. Tanker hearts, tanker brains, and their precious oil, a substance thick with tiny relic machines. Taverns along the Obsidian Sea sandfront were ripe with one-armed, one-legged, mangled heroes trading their hard luck bravado escapades for drink. Chandlers, harpoon smithys offering fancy lances etched with spells, protection wards and prayers. Chasing a tanker and hunting it down was only ever half the story. Once caught and bested, the salvage and bounty had to be transported safely back to port, a feat that involved running the gauntlet of pirate nests, many manned by broken tankerjacks on a last ditch mission to make their own misfortunes pay.

The entirety of Mohandas's table's polished surface hadn't been glimpsed in years. A small rectangle remained defiantly visible, the spot where the house girl placed a tray bearing fresh tea or coffee every hour—sometimes even orange juice when oranges could be found—whether he was sitting there or not. He measured the passage of time by beverage. It was mid-afternoon when tea became red wine. Sundown was marked by aperitif. Port when it was time to go to bed.

Mohandas took his evening meal in the lavishly appointed dining room; its walls hung thick with tapestries, an oppressive crystal chandelier dipping low above the table. The glittering centrepiece did not give light, but it served to impress the wealthiest of his clients whom he met for discussions concerning important matters: safer trade route deviations, border tariffs, tax hikes, and those ever-present, pesky Sand Road warlords. Around his table, traders shared their commiserations at all the many elements they could not control.

Only not today. Not yesterday, nor the week leading up to it. Not since Angels started falling from the sky. First it was just one, then others. More than he had ever thought were up there. Each one that fell made the town more crazy. Reliquary was reliquary and brought out the greed in all. Nobody yet knew what the things were worth, what sort of prices the fortress cities might pay for their retrieval, whole or broken. Nobody but Mohandas—he knew only too well. The sight of the falling things filled him with deep dread.

A soft tap at the door made him jump out of his chair. He relaxed when he saw it was only Vette with her tray of honey-jasmine tea and cubes of cheese. She gave that rough curtsey all the outer homestead girls offered to those they knew to be their big town betters.

He'd half been expecting one of his market spies with reports of yet another Van pulled in to the already overcrowded caravanserais. Vans had been limping in thick and fast ever since that first blasted Angel fell. The cursed things had shaken the length and breadth of the Sand Road loose from its senses. Stirred up the tankers and sent them veering in dangerously close to Heel.

The girl set down the silver tray, curtsied again, and slipped out, silent as a mouse. Mohandas's thick, jewelled fingers reached for the dainty cup, wavered, then selected a cube of spiced goat's cheese instead. Its flavour was more tangy than he favoured.

His thoughts returned to the pods of offshore tankers disturbed by Angels landing like pebbles in a pond. Fallow Heel was still reeling from those ripples and reverberations. The sands surrounding the Obsidian Sea were swarming thick with them. Once you'd have been lucky to catch distant sight of three or four across a week. Tankers were territorial beasts —or once had been. He'd heard tell of them ramming each other to the death, emitting ear-piercing song strong enough to kill a crew. And now, competing pods of them were offshore, so ripe for the taking that a harvest had begun, with every able-bodied wannabe sand sailor charging off, many on flimsy skiffs and blokarts barely able to hold their own against the wind.

Many were fated never to return, their widows and orphans milling listlessly around the docks. They'd eventually be selling off family possessions one by one, until all there remained to sell off was themselves.

Falling Angels, of all the cursed luck. A few days after the first one fell, he'd started thinking about the past. About the events that had brought him to Fallow Heel when it was little more than a glorified caravanserai surrounded by grubby hovels, tents, and goats. Before he'd discarded the name of his birth to reinvent himself as a trader of spices, wine, carpets, and relics both puzzling and incomprehensible to most. But not to him. He knew with certainty where such dug-up curiosities could fetch big coin. From old-world relics, he had built his empire, and all without his friends and business rivals ever suspecting the truth of where he hailed from—or how he knew where buried treasure lay. These were secrets he guarded with his life, ones that surely would have gotten him killed.

But now, Angels were falling from the sky.

Most of the ancient relic-maps he had used to build his wealth had been destroyed. *Most* of them, but not all. He had not been able to bring himself to part with every single one, even though he understood the risks. Such beautiful artefacts from a long-gone world. Nobody knew they existed—not his daughter, nor any of his staff. With the whole town distracted by drink and promises, he had snuck down to the docks, and he had hidden the maps in a place no one would find them.

Those Angels made him nervous. Since they'd started falling, the port was changing for the worse, becoming infested with lust and greed, streets overflowing with hooligans and drunks. His own daughter, bless her, would soon be demanding more be made of such a lucrative situation. The fruit had not fallen far from the tree with that one.

A week had passed without incident. Mohandas doubled his household guard, expecting trouble from strangers at his door. Fallow Heel was growing faster than its infrastructure could support. So many poor, so many tainted. Trouble could not be far away. But no one had come, and the precious maps had remained safe in their hiding place.

Mohandas sipped the tea the girl had brought. It had already lost its heat, but not its sweetness. He drank the rest of it without tasting, his mind slowly flooding with potential trade transactions. New players were entering the game. Old powers emerging upwards into the light. He would pit them against each other and see who'd offer more. He chewed his lip, excited by the possibilities.

He was reaching for another cube of cheese when a knock came on the door. Mohandas frowned. Vette again—could another hour have passed already? It wasn't time for tea or a meeting, or anything else he had an interest in.

"Go away," he shouted, returning to his tally books, briefly checking the coffee supply which had, for the second time in months, been held up at Portwine by excess tariffs.

That knock again, much harder this time. Harder and more insistent, too hard a knock for the girl who brought his drinks. Mohandas rubbed his furrowed brow. "Who's there?" He bellowed the name of his bodyguard, expecting his hired man to rush in through the door. But nothing happened. No one came, yet someone was out there lurking in the corridor. He could hear the subtle creaking of floorboards smothered beneath a century of carpet.

= FIFTEEN =

It was not the first time Tully Grieve had snuck aboard the ship. He wasn't even the first to try it, but unlike the others, Grieve had never been caught. He considered himself much smarter than your average thief and realised that if he played his cards right, the *Razael* could be the gift that kept on giving, so long as he didn't get too greedy or complacent. So long as he kept his wits firmly about him.

Throughout his twenty summers, Grieve had seen some pointless things, but the *Razael* really took the prize. A sailing ship, like the ancient vessels moored along the coast. An ocean-ship modified and mounted onto giant wheels thick enough to crush everything in their path. Or they *would* have, if the ship ever cast off and set sail, which it most certainly did not. The *Razael* was a rich man's folly, languishing in port with its fancy wooden deck, massive masts, and neat-furled canvas sails. Built to go nowhere—not likely built in Heel at all. Different from all the other craft setting out across the Black Sea in chase of tankers. Junked-up vessels, one-fifth the *Razael's* size at best; hammered platforms of rope, rail, and sail, designed to trick the wind into transportation, bearing crews across the hard, black flats to where the creatures rolled and rammed and raced.

Grieve trod silently across highly polished boards, slipping in and out of cabins when lucky enough to find a door unlocked. Each one contained old and lovely objects, the likes of many he'd never seen before, not even in the grander houses he'd robbed and raided along the coast. Houses were always burgled under cover of darkness and with extreme haste. Belowdecks on the *Razael*, he had the time to linger, and more often than not was too awestruck to even figure what to steal. Instead he just stood there, drinking in the glaze of opulence. Soft carpets, tapestries, and light. Crews relentlessly scrubbing and polishing. Crews who dressed identically and never swore out loud. Men and women who kept their eyes averted, their nimble fingers away from the precious silverware.

The *Razael* was an anachronism. Built before *Before*. Old before the whole world went to Hell. Property of one of the rich, fat idiots occasionally seen strolling along the docks with his retinue of household staff and well-armed bodyguards. A showpiece, a trophy. Only one of its kind.

Putting together a uniform that would blend into the surroundings on board this vessel had been the tricky bit. Granted, the garments Grieve knocked up himself would not bear up-close scrutiny, even though he could stitch as well as any sailor, sand or sea. All his people were handy with a needle. *And ropes. And blades. And guns.* But if things got up close and personal, there was likely much more than his clothing to arise suspicions.

So he'd crafted strategies keeping in mind that he needed to avoid scrutiny. He'd sneak past if the colours were true, if he'd successfully memorised the patterns of the watch. Then he could lurk amongst the below deck shadows, keep out of everybody's way.

The trick, as always, was not to get too greedy. To not go grabbing every shiny thing and stuffing it into pockets until they bulged. To pass up the gaudiest ornaments—they were far too easy to trace. Plainer fare was better, so long as he was quick. Quick was what he was best at. Quick was how he made his coin in the township he'd adopted as his own.

He ran his hand along a polished panel: wood inlaid with mother-of-pearl. Truth was, he'd fallen more than a little in love with Fallow Heel, and now he could feel himself falling in love with the ship that belonged to a different time and place. With the fancy wooden panelling that had not been stripped and burned. How many had died to protect this piece of property? How many were going to die to protect it in the days to come? The balances of power were shifting ever-so-slightly along the Sand Road and its succour towns.

Fallow Heel had weathered well the worst of the tainted years. It had prospered long before the tankers had come, and was doing better every day, bursting at the seams with those trying their luck at a better life. Loaded with commerce, promise and, increasingly, strangers. Travellers not much unlike himself, seeking better futures, running from darker pasts. Leaving friends and families behind. He cut himself short at the beginning of that thought before it went much further than he could bear.

The uniform trick had worked so well. Grieve had not intended to linger. Not until he made an exciting discovery—a forgotten cupboard within a cupboard, located at the far end of an overlooked storage space, once stacked to the low wooden ceiling with dusty tarps and boxes of musty books, their ancient pages fused together with mould.

A hidey hole. It would not take much to clean it up, to make himself a comfortable nest. A refuge from the savagery of the docks, for when he was low on coin or owed bad people money. A place to rest and listen to the footsteps overhead. Voices, sometimes muffled, sometimes clear. The far-off cries and clanging of the docklands's blacksmith hammers.

Cracks in the wooden panelling above let a little light bleed through. He pulled the stolen ornament from his pocket and held it high in a slender beam, a delicate thing of porcelain and coloured glaze. A little girl in a floral dress with a puppy in her arms. Her face was clean, her hair in perfect ringlets. He'd never seen such a girl in all his life, but somebody would pay good coin for it. He was running through a list of likely fences when voices issued from the far side of the wall.

He stuffed the puppy girl back in his pocket, and pressed his face up close against the gap in the wooden partition, which offered the best view into the plushly appointed stateroom on the far side.

The stateroom had been empty when he'd crawled into his hidey hole to examine his stolen treasure. Grieve was certain—he always checked. Vigilance was the price of freedom—his mother had taught him that, if not much else.

His first hope was for a glimpse of the beautiful girl who he had often seen accompanying her father to the docks. She was always dressed in immaculate splendour, always snapping the head off some poor crewman, complaining about the unsatisfactory way he or she performed some menial task.

His heart sank. It was not the girl, but three young men, close to his own age, wearing the strangest garments he'd ever seen.

One with a beard unfurled a map across the table. Another with dark curls and a golden earring started berating him about it. It was not the right map. There were, apparently, other better maps.

Grieve pressed his ear against the crack but he could make no sense of their words. Eventually he lost interest. He snuggled down into his hidey hole and rolled over on his side. Time for a nap. If he was really lucky, the beautiful girl might be there when he woke.

= SIXTEEN =

Star heard someone calling her name. She looked up to see Anj waving furiously from up near the base of the Sentinel, not far from where the dogs were fed and chained. By the time Star reached her, Anj was in a state.

"Where have you been? You gotta see this!" Anj offered Star no choice. She dragged her around the side of the Sentinel and pointed to a slim dark opening.

Star stared at it stupidly.

"Somebody forced the door," Anj explained. "We found it like this—Remy's inside with Griff. There's stairs going straight up through the centre."

Anj stepped towards the narrow entrance. Star grabbed her. "No, wait. It's forbidden. What if someone sees?"

"I've been inside already. Came out to find you. Come on, Star. Nobody's watching. Don't you want to see what's inside one of those things?"

She did and she didn't. Road law was road law, its punishments clear and cruel. The Sentinels had to be out of bounds for a reason—bad magic, Yeshie would have said. But she didn't know what that reason was; nobody did anymore. And as long as Kristo didn't catch her . . .

Star slipped through, close on Anj's heels, her curiosity having gotten the better of her. Inside was dank and musty smelling. She paused as her eyes took time to adjust to the weak light bleeding down from a circle in the centre, high above a slender winding staircase.

By then Anj was already on those stairs, boots echoing loudly.

Remy stood waiting for them at the top. The last person she wanted to see. He looked like he had something he wanted to say to her, so she pushed on past up the stairs and by him, and went to stand with Griff, whose hands were resting on the biggest reliquary she had ever seen. It was an angled bench that ringed the circumference of the chamber at approximately the height of her hips. Objects were embedded into the metal at regularly spaced intervals. Knobs and switches and things like clocks with hard glass surface coverings. She'd seen such relics at Bluebottle's grand bazaar. Old men salvaged them from the desert.

Directly above the angled bench was the biggest, thickest window she had ever seen, offering a clear view across the top of the Vulture, all the way to the brooding, storm-riddled horizon.

"Amazing, huh," said Anj. "It goes all the way round. You can see in all directions."

Star placed her hand upon the glass. "Doesn't look like a window from the outside."

Anj nodded. "Amazing, like I said."

"There's more," said Griff. "A flashing light. Wasn't flashing when we first came in."

They clustered around to stare at it, a small thing blinking red like a flaming jewel.

"What do you think it means?" asked Star.

Griff shrugged.

Anj moved on, already bored with it. "I'm gonna stay up here and watch the storm."

"What if Benhadeer or Kristo finds out?"

"They won't. They're busy dealing with that lot. Trying to keep everybody calm."

Star stared down at the Vulture, wondering not for the first time how it had come upon its name. If anything, it looked more like a spider crouched and ready to pounce.

Remy moved up to stand beside her. "Storm clouds are beautiful," he said.

Star nodded. She wasn't looking at the clouds, but at the many and varied colours of people's sand cloaks. A range of hues from pink through browns and greens to dusty ochres, all illuminated by a mix of storm and lantern light. It was much more interesting viewed from above than ground level.

"Never seem them like that before. Never with all those colours."

Remy was talking about the clouds, not the clothing, but she nodded anyway.

Anj cut in. "Pooh, something stinks in here, like some animal died—Hey, what's going on down there?"

Griff stopped what he was doing and went to look. "Shit. Down below. Someone's messing with the camels!"

No further words were necessary. Everybody ran for the metal staircase, coming close to stumbling in the dark. Tentatively, they felt their way through the ground level's dim light, then squeezed through the jimmied doorway, one by one.

Griff ran off to alert his fellow riders. They'd be lying around somewhere together, drinking or sleeping or gambling away their coin. Lucius at least would have his wits about him. Remy vanished into the milling throng. Probably going to fetch his precious rifle. Star and Anj headed directly for the camel thieves, not thinking about what might happen when they got there.

"Look!" Up ahead, just inside the periphery stones where the hobbled camels grazed, was a spill of greasy lantern light. Both girls headed straight for it.

"Who's there? What are you doing?" Calling out was pointless, but it didn't stop them.

A lantern lay on the ground on its side. Weak illumination did not reveal much.

"Who's there?"

Star picked up the lantern and held it high, then gasped. Teddy's father, Drover Jens, lay sprawled on the ground with dark liquid seeping out of him.

Star ran to his side and knelt but it was too late. Jens was not long dead, his flesh still warm, his eyes staring into nothingness.

Nearby sounds. Disgruntled camels. Men's voices carrying above their heads.

"Run back to the fire," Star instructed Anj. "Raise the alarm. Tell Lucius. Tell everybody."

Anj nodded, eyes wide with fear. She hesitated.

"Go! I'll tend to Jens." Star said that knowing it was too late. Jens was already dead, and she should wait for the riders to come back with loaded rifles.

But she didn't. Instead, she rested Jens's head back gently on the sand, closed his eyes, then stopped still and listened, focusing on the moving mass of shapes out past the grazing strip, the stones, and the Sentinel's protective range.

Camels barked and grumbled in agitation. Something had them spooked. Bright blue light, as illuminating as the lightning strikes, pulsed from the centre of the storm.

No time to worry about strange light. Not while thieves were stealing camels right in front of her. She picked up the lantern and ran out after them, trying not to think about the danger, nor about poor Jens lying dead on the sand, and how she would have to break the news to Teddy.

"Who goes there? Stop!"

She kept on moving until she could see them clearly. Three on camelback. Camels paid for with spilled blood.

No need to see their faces. Three men, their bodies swathed in fancy embroidered sand cloaks and galabeyas.

She called out, "Kian."

"That's far enough," he answered. "I'm armed and I will shoot you without hesitation."

"Where do you think you're going? There's a storm out there. It isn't safe!"

"The storm is your problem, not ours. Yours and those idiots loitering by the fire, wasting time with their pointless rituals and concerns."

"Why are you in such a hurry to get to Heel? What difference will a couple of days make?"

"All the difference in the world if we don't get there first," said Tallis.

"Shut up Tal—we don't have to answer her questions."

"Get *where* first—what are you talking about?"

The wind was getting stronger, tugging at their clothes. The camels shifted restlessly, not accustomed to unfamiliar riders on their backs, nor the combination of shouting, blustery gusts, and lightning.

"Kristo will come after you," Star shouted over the rising howl. "Blood will be avenged with blood."

"Somehow I don't think so."

Star felt Kian's gaze boring into her, even though she could barely make out the oval of his face, let alone his eyes.

A brilliant blast of lightning flared. For a moment, Star could see all three faces clearly and she wondered how she had ever thought them handsome. Hard and cold, all angles, no compassion.

"You didn't have to kill Teddy's father. Not for the sake of a few days travel time."

Lightning struck the sand a few feet away. Kian didn't even flinch. He smiled and drew a silver pistol from the folds of his cloak, raised it high, and aimed it at her head.

Star froze. She had only ever seen a pistol once—and that was on a dead man. She knew she ought to run, but couldn't move. She couldn't even blink. Just stood there waiting for a burst of pain.

Kian didn't fire. All three of them suddenly stirred their beasts to action, turned them around and whipped them out into the crazy wind. Lightning continued to blast and flare, each burst illuminating smaller blue-tinged figures. Star ran after them. A pointless gesture, but she couldn't help it, her feet were moving before her fear caught up.

The air was cold. Fine sand stung her cheeks. She stopped and stared as the camels rode out of view.

A man lay dead and three camels were stolen, but the murderers and thieves would not get far. Not while there was still breath in Benhadeer's lungs. The camels were his and swift retribution would soon be his as well. Cold comfort, but it was better than nothing.

She turned and hurried back towards the safety of the Sentinel, rubbing her shoulders against the chill. The wind was getting stronger and sharper, blasting her body with handfuls of sand and stones. Blue lightning flared as the storm drew closer.

She started running, gripping the lantern tight. A wild gust tripped her up and sent her sprawling. The lantern smashed. The storm was closing in but how could that be? She had reached the edge of the Sentinel's protection but felt no familiar tingling sensation.

The body of Teddy's father lay where she had left it. The others had not come back to help. Nobody even knew the man was dead.

Her thoughts were filled with Teddy as she staggered to her feet, about how she was going to have to be the one to tell him.

A mournful cry—a woman's voice—and then all hell broke loose. The storm hit the camp like a mighty fist slamming down from the sky. The air thickened with sand and swirling debris. The body of Teddy's father, snatched and flung into the air as though it'd been a child's toy made of rag.

Star dropped into an instinctive crouch, khafiya tugged up high across her face. Wind-whipped sand particles scratched against her skin. Howling blended with terrified screams.

She crawled, groping until she reached one of the wagons, using it to pull herself to standing, clinging to its splintered side to stop herself from completely blowing away.

"Lucius! Nene! Anj!"

Each name dissolved as soon as she spoke it. She could see nothing, hear nothing but the vicious, horrible howling.

The wagon she clung to shuddered and rattled, offering scant protection. She would have to move towards the rest of them, berthed in an arc beneath the apparently useless Sentinel.

She dropped to all fours and crawled, aware of airborne objects whizzing over her head. *The storm had crossed the Verge.* Such a thing was not supposed to happen.

Sharp, relentless blasts of sand stang her eyes and face. Her worn-thin khafiya was no protection whatsoever.

Somebody slammed into her, cursed, and kept on going. Camels brayed in distress; harrowing, anguished sounds. The Van hands would be fighting to protect the animals. Everyone else would have to fend for themselves.

From what little she could see, their camp had been obliterated. Wagons were smashed and scattered, and bodies wriggled on the sand like fish left high and dry by a receding tide, a tide nobody had been expecting.

Nothing remained of the communal fire. Screams sounded, only to be snatched away and silenced. Blinded and without bearings, Star staggered forwards with arms outstretched, hoping she was heading towards the light and not away from it. Something sailed past her head, dangerously close. She stopped and shielded her face with her arms, straining to listen, barely able to hear herself think.

She slammed up violently against something hard. Not the Vulture. Something else. Another wagon, this one on the move. She felt her way along it to the end of it. People were pushing. She joined in, shoving her shoulder hard against the wood until a violent gust of wind lifted and flung her backwards. It took her three attempts to fight her way back to standing. By then, even the cries and screams had faded. All she could hear and see and taste was sand.

And then, of all blessings, she ran headlong into Lucius. He shouted at her, words she couldn't hear, but she gripped on tightly to his arm and hung on for dear life.

Another blast slammed both of them against one of the remaining upright wagons. Not as hard as it might have. They were lucky.

Lucius—what she could see of his face—looked truly frightened. Something Star had never seen before.

"The Sentinel," she shouted. "The door is open. Everybody has to get inside."

She saw him mouth the word "forbidden," a useless, stupid word that made her angry. What did it matter what was forbidden and what was not? Without shelter, they were going to die.

He must have come to the same conclusion, because he heaved his shoulder under hers and dragged her to her feet. She stumbled but kept up the pace, his stocky form flimsy and insubstantial against the wind.

She thought she could hear the low rumble of the Van's backup batteries powering, but the sound choked up and ceased abruptly.

Her eyes were completely filled with grit. She couldn't see so she clamped them tightly shut. Tears welled, eyes fighting to expel the sand. When eventually she opened them, all she could see were flares of lightning, eerie blue and pulsing, like no storm she had ever seen before.

Star and Lucius stumbled towards the Sentinel, dragging each other along. Through gritty tears they stumbled headlong into a group of walkers clustered together, their faces wrapped in rags. Arms groping. Heading in the same direction.

"Keep moving," bellowed Lucius as the wind swelled up and the sand tore at their clothes.

Then, suddenly, the worst of it was over. The storm thinned enough that they were breathing air again. Star realised she was clinging to one of the dancers, her bright sari obscured beneath a stained and tattered sand cloak.

The Sentinel tower loomed above them, a dark shadowy outline. Many had gathered around its base, some flattened against its sheer sides, others crouched in an attempt to avoid the worst of the wind.

There was a droning sound, like insects. But it wasn't swarming bugs; it was prayer. Hands and voices raised in terror. A mix of languages all torn and tumbled, mangled by the howling of the wind.

They found the door, still jimmied half open, just as Anj and the others had left it.

"Put your backs into it, people! Push!" The hideous sound of grating metal competed with the wind. "Again," shouted Benhadeer as he shoved his bulk against the door until it opened fully.

Desperate people pushed their way inside. Others milled about the entranceway uncertainly, mumbling prayers or making ward signs with their hands.

"Get inside," Star told any who would listen, repeating the words over and over while Nene shoved them, one by one, through the hatch. Relief flooded through Star as soon as saw her sister was safe. Only when the last of them had crossed the threshold did Nene follow.

Inside was dark and cold and musty. Star's eyes adjusted, as one of Benhadeer's men made a shushing sound and the last of the prayers and whimperers fell silent.

Even through a wailing sandstorm, Benhadeer stood out from the crowd, a good head taller than most with broad shoulders to match. The crowd parted as he pushed his way toward the staircase and the circle of muddy light that bled down from above.

Kristo followed. The men climbed several steps and paused. "Nene," said Benhadeer, his voice elevated from its usual deep timbre.

Nene moved to join him. Star followed, needing to be by her sister's side through whatever happened next.

Each footstep on the metal staircase gnawed at her resolve. She, Anj, and the others should not have been in here earlier. *Were they somehow to blame for all of this?* She could sense the rest of them below holding their collective breath, waiting to see what would happen next. She scanned the crowd but she could not see Anj or Teddy, Kaja or Griff or even Remy.

She made sure she looked appropriately impressed when faced with the massive window. The Vulture held up, steady as always amidst a wash of swirling, debris-laden sand.

The vicious storm was beautiful, blazing with the ferocity of fire. Beautiful but deadly. Anyone left out on the sand would be wrenched limb from limb. Perhaps Kian and his brethren had got what they deserved after all.

In the storm, random pulses, lights and flares bloomed like fireworks, and it seemed at that moment like a living creature possessed of brute intelligence. Some people believed it true—that the Verge storms were alive. It was said some even worshipped them as gods. At that moment Star completely comprehended why.

Nobody said anything. Star stuck close by Nene's side. The worst of it was over now, the boiling turbulence fading into memory.

Time passed, too slow and strange to keep proper track of it. Might have been an hour or three. Impossible to tell. Eventually it began to worry her, like there was some big heavy secret that everyone except Star understood. Her patience waned—she longed to ask the question but Nene sensed it ahead of her. She placed her hand upon her sister's arm, a warning to keep silent. Later, was what the gesture meant— we'll find out later, when we are free of this dark and cursed place.

= SEVENTEEN =

The last thing Quarrel had anticipated was company as he stood in semi-darkness, jacked into the Sentinel's console, sucking the dregs of power from its backups. Back arched in ecstatic rictus, frozen in the moment, savouring the warm infusion, flecks of spittle adhering to his chin as he stared out through the window at the storm clouds chewing the horizon. Staring, wide-eyed, as time passed in random fits and surges.

Voices intruded on his privacy. Multiple boot treads on metal rungs.

Quarrel's powers of self-preservation kicked in strong. He managed to drag himself away, to flatten against the farthest wall, out of the light and out of the way as the control room filled with curious, yabbering young.

He was too stoned to estimate their ages—anyone under forty was a child to a Templar warrior.

The children—young ones—whatever they were, appraised the console that ran three-quarters the circumference of the room. They prodded and poked at non-functioning buttons, dials, pads, and screens, seemingly fascinated by the on-off winking light, sole witnesses to Quarrel's heinous crime. He had drunk his fill and left the Sentinel a broken useless thing. He wasn't sorry. He'd done what he had to do.

One of the young ones was not like all the others. She looked ordinary enough, a girl in trousers and a dirty loose weave shirt. Not armed, save for short blades sheathed inside her boots and a slice of metal embedded in her arm.

Something pinged when he saw that metal. Not his mesh this time, something deeper. Something important, only half remembered. It took him a moment to dredge up the data, make comparisons, make sense of what he was seeing.

Curious.

He hadn't thought that any of her issue had been left alive. Not since the Lotus Wars and those hunter-seeker bunker busters had gone burrowing after all the secret caches.

Huh.

Not his problem. Quarrel had problems of his own aplenty, starting with what would happen now that Nisn had tracked him down, registered his deviation from the mission. Would they initiate the explosive charges wired into his frame? Blow him up rather than take a chance with him rogue?

Not likely. Nisn needed him. It wasn't like they had a lot of options.

He stood there, silent in the shadows, watching as another of the young ones got busy attempting to jimmy equipment from the console's hard baked surface with a blade. They bantered back and forth amongst each other, an argument, then suddenly abandoned everything in terrific haste. More boot treads on the curling metal staircase as they left. Something on the ground outside had hijacked their attention.

Quarrel remained still and silent even after they'd gone. Not one of them had noticed him—not even the girl with a mesh bar in her arm. His veins pumped hot with delicious buzz. Goodbye to Nisn and its crazy priests. Quarrel was setting out to see the world.

He was still standing there in half-stoned reverie when a sight beyond the window stopped his breath.

The storm he had formally glimpsed scouring the horizon had changed trajectory. It was now heading directly for the Sentinel and the ruins of Vulture Base. He'd been stationed there once before, back when it was made of bricks and mortar. There'd been a lake and better rations than he was used to, which was probably why it had imprinted in his mind.

He peeled himself from the security of the cold steel wall, and moved as close to the window as he could. The plexiglass was one way; nobody on the ground below could see him.

The storm looked like some kind of polyp. He'd not encountered one for centuries and had forgotten their great beauty. Deadly manufactured things trailing stingers through the dirt. A thunderhead of translucent, electric blue.

The barometric pressure plunged, sending shivers down his spine. Quarrel stood dead still and closed his eyes. Remembering, but only for a moment. This one was small. He'd once seen a big one up close, in action, sweeping across the open plains, striking and devouring a whole platoon before his eyes. His point fighters had sheltered in caves, helpless to do anything but watch.

There had not been much worth salvaging when the thing had done its work. No bones to bury, just a slurry melt of hair and skin and cloth. Melted M40s and 107s embedded with scattered human teeth.

Quarrel had memories of battleground scavengers scuttling from burn to burn. Collecting great sacks of gold-embedded human ivory and selling it by weight in the larger towns.

This storm was small, and beautiful by comparison, but it still sickened him to his core. Such things should never have been unleashed and let run free.

The storm was bearing down on the encampment, driven by integrated heuristic programs—designed to give chase if their target tried to get away. He was not the target, or else he'd have been dead already—perhaps this storm was as much a rogue as he was. Time for him to take his leave. The Sentinel was useless now. Best to get as far away as possible.

He clattered down the spiral staircase, pushed out through the metal hatch into air laced with stinging sand and barking dogs. His coat was too heavy, weighted down with gold. People were running in all directions, desperate to tie their possessions down and protect their terrified animals.

Time to hit the road, Quarrel old man.

A sharp stabbing pain lanced through his arm. His mesh had been pinging softly, barely audible above the fury of the wind. The longer he ignored it, the less threatening the thought of it became. It was foolish to have dreamt himself beyond Nisn's striking range.

He yelped in pain as a second jolt of fire seared his nerves, those five-star Gs reinforcing their terms and conditions. Clouding his mind with useless data streams. He didn't need data. He knew exactly *what* he was dealing with. What he didn't know was *when*. How many years had passed since the end of the Lotus Wars? Nisn, in its wisdom, had decreed all events before the Second Pulse Genocide as "classified." Battles had been renamed in honour of favoured generals and outcomes.

Now could be anywhen—after all, he'd been powered down for decades longer than the priests confessed. The only thing he knew for certain was that everyone he'd ever known was gone. Dead and desiccated, bones turned to dust and blown away on the winds. *Including hers.*

That polyp storm was on the move, its translucent centre heating crimson red, and trailing tentacles of livid raw blue power.

Quarrel licked his lips and ventured closer. His mesh pinged at him angrily, but it was merely irritating this time, the sting of a bee against the tough hide of a thunder lizard. "You're going to have to blow me up," he said to it out loud. He wanted no truck with polyp-kind, but felt the need to know what it was doing, where it was going, why it was attacking a skeletal metal structure in the middle of nowhere. There were no soldiers present here. Just a kid with a mesh bar in her arm. A baby Templar, uninitiated, untrained, useless. No bounty. No reward. Just a rag tag assemblage of what looked like refugees in mismatched Vans of scavenged wood and steel. Not that he'd encountered humans of any kind outside the fortress city. Spies, perhaps? Mercenaries hiding amidst human shields?

He did not get close enough for answers. Wind-whipped sand slammed against his sunburned cheeks, the only part of his flesh not completely covered. Thick goggles protected his eyes. He slapped the mesh to stop its annoying itch, but swerved in the direction it wanted him to go, leaving the storm and its victims to their fate.

The buzz from his recent fix was fading. Quarrel picked up the pace. So what if he'd drained the power from that Sentinel? Polyp storms and mesh-bar girls were not his problem. He had problems of his own. Like hunger, a deep insatiable need. A need much greater than the fear of dying. He'd been effectively dead for two hundred years and yet here he was, walking onwards, forced to carry out their mission against his will. Life like it always had been, life like it continued still.

The mesh said Nisn wanted him in the tanker port of Fallow Heel as soon as possible. More Angels had fallen at a distant point beyond the town. He was tasked with securing transportation to retrieve samples and investigate. Veer off course again, it warned, and they'd fry his brain.

Alrighty then.

His coat weighed heavy with strips of gold ingots, each one stamped with the Temple crest and sewn into the lining. With gold you could buy anything or anyone, so the white-coats had told him. Unless the world had changed utterly beyond recognition while he'd slept, but that was something he doubted less and less the more he walked.

=EIGHTEEN=

When dawn came, almost nothing remained of the Van's thirteen wagons. Just scraps of cloth, shattered boards and scattered cooking utensils. Long black curls of shredded butyl the wind had shaved clean off the wheels. Thirteen wagons, completely obliterated. Only the Vulture and the Sentinel remained.

The unthinkable had happened—a storm had crossed the Verge. The kind of storm no one had suffered through since the Lotus Wars. They weren't safe on the Sand Road anymore. The Sentinel was useless, its power gone, its ancient reliquary no longer protecting anyone.

Van people stood around staring at the wreckage. Some were silent. Others wailed, a thin note with little substance to it, watching the last breaths of dying wind scatter sand between the Vulture's struts.

Star and Nene clutched at each other, staring at the patch of churned-up sand, both too shocked to speak. The distant dunes were still and soundless—a dramatic contrast to the dying wind. Nene's eyes were fixed upon that sand. She said nothing for a long time, only stared, mesmerised by the loose grains playing across its rippled surface.

Star wanted to say something soothing and wise, but the right words wouldn't come. So she said nothing. Better nothing than the wrong thing. Eventually the silence became too overbearing. "Let's go," she whispered, gently squeezing Nene's arm.

Nene pulled away, marching across the sand, pushing through the scattering of shocked and aimless people whimpering and picking over the wreckage, searching for evidence their wagon had once stood there. Star followed, sensing the great grief welling within her sister. Nene's brown hair spilled across her shoulders. Harsh desert light revealed bruises and scrapes along her arms.

"You're hurt," said Star. "Let me—"

She reached out but Nene shrugged her off and increased her pace so that she walked a full shoulder length ahead. They trudged through red-and-yellow sand as an eerie quiet settled across the barren landscape.

Cold set in and Star began to shiver, the coarse sand sucking the heat from her bones.

Everything had been destroyed. Bodies lay battered into the sand—those not fast or fortunate enough to make it inside the Sentinel. Star's throat constricted as she realised she could identify the dead by their clothing rather than their faces: Reya, who baked their ember bread. Baz, the camel doctor. Jon and Eroli, the couple who were always fighting. Their son Hank, one of the Van brats always hassling foreign tourists for small coins. All dead, many of them burned beyond recognition.

Battered pots and pans were strewn in all directions. Star stood still, overcome with the horror of it all.

When she moved, she tripped over a chunk of jutting timber. It still bore the name *Varisan*, carved in wide, cursive script. Varisan the shaman, Yeshie's arch rival. A man with seventy years experience of telling people things they longed to hear, all his dreams and reassurances gone now, drained away into the sand, along with his blood.

Nothing remained of Nene's green and blue wagon, not a vial of herbs nor a splinter of wood. Star wiped moisture from her eyes and kicked a broken window frame aside. Beneath it lay an orange enamelled cooking pot she recognised as their own. The pot Nene used for boiling her stinking brews. Star's heart began to thump. Their wagon had stood *right here upon this spot*. She bent to pick up the pot. Its sides were warm—probably from her own imagination. She hugged it tightly to her chest as she wandered dazed through the carnage, kicking aside chunks of debris.

Unbearable as the procedure was, the wreckage had to be searched for food, waterskins, tools, and weapons—anything that might help them survive the dangerous trek they now had to make on foot to the nearest settlement.

Lucius was already at it. He worked methodically in stony silence, stopping now and then to mop up sweat, tossing useful items into a pile: blades, containers, cloth.

Two dead camels lay tangled in a mass, their glassy eyes staring into space, necks twisted sharply at unnatural angles, tongues protruding between blackened lips. Griff's father's camels, Hanna and Addu.

Bile flooded Star's mouth. She snatched the khafiya away from her face, dropped to the sand and retched. Climbed back on her feet, wiped her mouth with the back of her hand, glancing around uncertainly. *Kian and the others. Teddy's father.* She had not had the chance to tell anyone what had happened.

Already carrion birds were circling. Four legged predators wouldn't be far behind.

Many hands were set the task of digging a burial pit. Children and the elderly gathered the stones to use as markers. Arguments broke out immediately—what were they supposed to dig with? Shovels, mattocks, even crowbars—everything was gone. Either scattered to the four winds or sucked up into the sky.

A cry went up to burn the dead. *What with?* was the answer to that. There was plenty of busted wood for fuel, but a pyre would signal their dire predicament to other Vans—and predators. They might be lucky, attracting friends, not foes, but they were on the back road now, the detour just past Broken Arch. Slavers were not unheard of in these parts. And what of the lizards they had chased off through the ruins? The scent of burning flesh might tempt them back.

Eventually the dead were dragged into neat rows, what was left of their faces respectfully covered.

Star moved to a nearby group and went from survivor to survivor, checking for serious injuries. Some had been lucky, protected from flying missiles by their sand cloaks. Now they were waiting, knives securely in their boots, water skins or gourds slung over their shoulders. Prepared to leave at a moment's notice.

The wannabe tankerjacks hung around in groups, smoking the last of their seaweed cigarettes and muttering. The storm had knocked the bravado from their swagger.

Old Lucius nudged Star as he passed her by, dragging the body of a dancer. "That lot might as well lay down beside the dead," he said. "Ain't a one of them's gonna survive a day out on the Black. One angry tanker's all it's gonna take to make short work of 'em."

He was only talking like that to keep focus. Trying to put his own fears in their place. Trying to cheer her up. But she wasn't the one who needed the familiar.

Nene still hadn't moved. She remained in the exact same place Star left her when she'd made her triage recce, a blank and hollow expression on her face.

Still standing where their wagon once had been, Nene hugged her shoulders, staring at the sand. All around her, wagon mates were sifting sand or tending to the dead or injured.

A sombre collective joined the children gathering cairn stones. Star watched them picking up dark rocks. They were heavy, and hard to come by, but doing something was better than doing nothing.

"Come on Nene, there's people who need us."

Nene gave no indication that she had even heard her. Nene . . . Strong, reliable Nene who never flinched, never shirked, never let the bad times get her down. This was not the Nene Star knew.

Her tattered field kit was slung across her sister's body like a bandolier. Gently, Star lifted it over her head and carried it over to a sand-smoothed boulder. She checked its contents: salves and ointments. Needles and thread. The pair of old red-handled pliars good for pulling shrapnel out of wounds. Scalpels and tightly rolled bandages, none of which would last long. More and more of the survivors were gathering, revealing injuries.

Star was halfway through splinting a third broken arm when the glaze faded from Nene's eyes. She didn't speak to Star at first, but sent some of the younger ones out to scavenge for more splints, and cloth scraps clean enough to be torn into bandage strips.

"We've lost everything," she whispered, not to Star, but to the vast expanse of sand they were going to have to cross on foot.

Benhadeer and his right hands pored over a faded vellum map in the scant shade cast by a crooked and tattered awning. A consensus had been reached. The Van survivors would set out on foot when the sun was a couple of hours past its zenith. Not optimum conditions, but they had little choice. A trail of rest points and oases might see them home, but the way would not be easy. If they could get to Crossroads, rides could potentially be hitched on other wagons in exchange for costs and consequences. But most were smart enough to hear the meaning beneath the spoken words: some of them would not survive the journey.

Nene had recovered her wits enough to tend to people's wounds, but only barely, and Star was worried. Her sister seemed so weak and distracted. Star had never seen her behave this way before.

She noticed a crowd was gathering in a dip out beyond the Vulture. People were abandoning their scavenging to go see what was going on. Star left Nene resting on a rock, ripping shirts into bandages, rolling them and placing them into a little pile.

"I'll be back," Star whispered. Nene didn't answer. Several people called out her name but she didn't answer them either.

Star hurried over to investigate what all the fuss was about. The crowd's curiosity heartened her—perhaps they had found something good? Such as one of the camels miraculously alive.

But when she pushed her way to the front she found Remy standing on a massive boulder in a hero's pose. A bandolier slung across his torso weighted heavily with tools. Leaning on a tanker lance. Not his lance—as far as she knew, he didn't own such a thing.

The boulder was the size of three wagons end to end, jutting out from a puckered ridge of sand, its gnarly surface encrusted with sun baked sand barnacles. Remy stamped his foot on its thickened crust and whooped, forming a fist and punching the air with his free hand.

Realization crept upon Star slowly, sending chills and shivers through her belly. That *thing* Remy was standing on was not a boulder.

It was a tanker.

Star had never seen a tanker up close before. Only in the far-off distance, glimpsed through plumes of sand and dust. Thundering alongside other creatures of its kind. It was always difficult to make out details via scratched and borrowed spyglass, but she'd seen enough across the years. Enough to be coldly certain this was one of them, wrenched free from its territory and pod, dragged and dumped here by the killer wind.

"Remy, get down from there," she called out. Her voice sounded much weaker than intended.

Remy ignored her. Anj climbed up beside him and raised a hand axe. No, not Anj, but her little sister Kaja. Only eighteen moons between them, the two looked so alike. Star had last glimpsed Anj scavenging alongside Griff. She'd not seen Teddy since she'd broken the awful news about his poor, dead father.

Remy stood there grinning like an idiot.

"Get down off that," Star yelled this time, stepping forward, approaching the creature with great caution. "That's a tanker!"

The gathered crowd gasped collectively and shuffled away from the thing. Not far enough to make a difference if it rolled.

"Get down!" she cried again. "It might still be living!"

But Remy wasn't listening. Another of the riders shimmied up the side. Griff—she hadn't noticed him—wielded a hand axe with a splintered handle. First he used it to help him climb, then he struck a sequence of blows, apparently searching for something hidden beneath the barnacle encrustation. A hatchport. Lucius had spoken of such things. With each blow struck, Star expected the mighty mechabeast to come to life, roll over on its side, and crush them all.

But the tanker stayed as dead as dead. And soon, between the three of them up top, enough encrusted barnacle had been chipped away to expose a section of gun-grey mecha-skin beneath.

Van people crowded closer at the sight of it. Whispers became murmurs. Mecha-skin was worth good coin. Few of them, if any, had been up so close to a tanker before but bits and pieces of the beasts were traded up and down the Sand Road—and beyond.

The hatch was now clearly exposed. Kaja crouched down, eyes shining with delight.

"Remy, Kaja, Griff—get down from there," Star pleaded. "At least wait for Lucius."

Lucius would know for certain if the tanker was dangerous or not, as would others amongst the vanhands. The quiet ones who'd joined with Benhadeer in an effort to forget their lost and wasted years spent lingering on the fringe of the Obsidian Sea.

Remy brought the lance to rest, leant his weight on it, sweat streaming down his neck. "Tank's mine," he said loudly. "I saw it first."

Kaja nodded. She always agreed with Remy. She'd been in love with him for as long as Star could remember.

"That thing'll kill you, and you can't be sure it's dead. Lucius—where is Lucius? Let him check first. He knows what he's doing."

"Thing's dead as stone—and the salvage rights belong to me and Kaja and Griff."

He stared directly at Star when he said Kaja's name. She looked away, down to the tanker's barnacle encrusted hide. Now that the outer layer had been cracked open, the thing stunk like a dead camel. Worse than that. More pungent. More revolting.

Kaja snatched the lance from his hands and jemmied away at the hatch. Grey metal was eventually prised away, revealing a deep, dark void beneath. The stench increased tenfold, and the crowd backed off, further this time, covering their noses with their hands and khafiyas. All but Star. She stepped up. As close as she could get without touching the deadly thing.

Two older point riders broke away from the crowd, one of them grabbing her roughly by her arm. "Leave off," he said. "Kid found the tank. It's his."

"The damn fool's gonna die in there," she pleaded. "Come on, Remy, you've heard the stories. You don't know what you're doing."

The second rider muttered something the rest of the crowd couldn't hear. They laughed. So did Remy.

"Please—I'm begging you, Remy. Come on, Kaja all of you. Wait for Lucius! Somebody go and get him, bring him here before it's too late."

She looked around, hoping that the big man had somehow sensed that he was needed, had abandoned his salvaging to come and sort this out.

Nobody moved. No Lucius in sight.

"Back off, Star. Nobody cares about that beat up old man's glory days. This bounty's ours an' he can keep his thievin' hands off it."

Remy shielded his eyes from the blazing sun, searching first through the gathered crowd, then across the surrounding debris-strewn sands to the figures picking over the Van's remains.

"Remy, get down. You don't have anything to prove."

He laughed. "Look around you, Star. Everything's gone. Every-one's desperate for coin—only we scored first—and big." He smiled, the kind he always saved for her. "But don't you worry. Stick around an' I'll see you right."

His face changed suddenly from smirk to grim. "Back off," he shouted. "You'll get your chance when we get to Heel, like all them others. Back off, else you'll be walking across the desert on your own. Ya hear me?"

Star soon understood he was not speaking to her, but to a group of men with unfamiliar faces who'd nudged and jostled their way to the front of the crowd. Two of them clutched lances. Cruder weapons than the one possessed by Lucius, but no doubt equally effective.

The murmuring died down once more. Everyone waited for Remy to say something.

Star realised she'd paid so little attention to the group of tankerjack wannabes riding wagontop when the Van was rolling. The ones who had not been as handsome as Kian and his offsiders. She saw them now for what they were: scruffy 'steaders and under-nourished farmers escaping dried-up fringes of the Verge, selling everything they'd ever had for passage, betting all their cards on Fallow Heel. What was to stop them surging forth and claiming this tanker's bounty for themselves? Could Benhadeer do anything to stop them?

Lucius—where was Lucius? Things were about to turn ugly. Dead or alive, that washed up tanker could get a good many of the storm survivors killed.

"Remy—please wait!"

Griff unwound the coil of rope slung across his shoulder. He and Kaja fastened it around Remy's waist in a rough harness as the lance-armed wannabes looked on.

Nobody was listening to anybody else. Random members of the crowd shouted encouragement as between them, the three up top used hammers and chisels to widen the area around the black and stinking void. Star couldn't look but she couldn't not look either. She flinched when Griff thrust his arm inside, felt around, then pulled it out again.

"Still warm," he called out to the nervous crowd. They cheered.

The heart-and-brains was what they were after. The things that made the tankers tick, kept them running wild across the desert sands centuries after their creators had turned to dust. It enabled them to communicate with each other, so people said. But tanker heart-and-brains were wired with protection. Tricks and traps designed to maim and kill. The docks and taverns of Fallow Heel were filled with mutilated 'Jacks who'd tell you all about it for a drink. How they lost an arm, a leg or half a face . . .

Star turned, pushed past the riders, and squeezed out through the crowd. She ran back towards the ruined camp, shouting *Lucius!* at the top of her lungs, boots encumbered by the slippery sand.

Lucius met her halfway, stripped to the waist, sweat streaming down his face and torso. He'd been digging by the looks of things. Perhaps they'd decided to bury the bodies after all.

"What is it, girl. What's wrong?"

"The idiots . . . they don't understand . . . they don't believe . . ."

"Believe what?"

Star tried to catch her breath. "There's a tanker washed up and they're trying to harvest it. Got no idea of what they're doing. You always told me—"

The words had barely tumbled out when a girl's high pitched, shrieking split the air. Shrieking with no end to it. Kaja.

Star took off at a sprint back the way she'd come, Lucius at her side. The thick sand dragged at their feet. They pushed their way up front, but it was too late. More of the tanker's gun-grey skin had been chiselled away.

A pair of wildly thrashing legs protruded from the tanker's hatch. Remy's; blood stained, entangled in a mess of silvery snakes. More of the snake-things spewed out of the void to writhe and coil upon the sand below.

Remy's two point rider friends were desperately trying to reach him, but the silver snakes lashed out and cut like whips, lunging and slapping the weapons clean out of their hands. Atop the tanker, cowering out of range, Griff clung on to the still-shrieking Kaja, his hands and arms a bloody mess.

Star launched herself at the tanker but Lucius grabbed her arm and held on tight. "Get down off there," he bellowed at the two Van brats up top.

The sound of a familiar voice shocked Griff into action. He and Kaja tumbled down into the agitated crowd, which dispersed as more of the silvery snake-things dribbled down from the hacked and jimmied hatch.

"Let me go!" said Star.

Lucius tightened his grip, so hard his fingers dug into her flesh.

She stared at the snake-things—more like entrails than snakes. The writhing things did not have heads and they stilled after a couple of minutes on the sand.

Sand that was now liberally splattered with Remy's blood. His legs no longer kicked. They jutted like the branches of a tree.

"Don't look," said Lucius. "Nothing you can do."

The big man turned his attention to the wannabes, who had stood there through the whole ordeal, saying nothing, offering no help. Unable to do anything but gawk and whimper, same as all the others.

"Go back to your farms and 'steads," spat Lucius at their faces. "There's nothing out beyond the Black for you."

There was nothing to be said to that.

Kaja continued to sob uncontrollably. Griff said nothing. He stared at Remy's still, protruding legs, his face pale as stone.

The silvery snake-things were beginning to disintegrate in the bright sunlight. Lucius ground one to powder beneath his boot.

"Take that girl to your sister," he instructed Star. "I'll take care of this."

The show was over. The rest of the gawking crowd had slunk away, gone back to picking over debris, praying to indifferent gods or arguing about what would likely happen next.

Star couldn't help but feel sorry for them—these had been good people, once. She did not know all their names, but she knew enough of them to care. Good people pushed beyond their limits, now wandering the desert sands in shock.

She, Griff and Kaja walked a little way, with Star fighting the urge to glance back over her shoulder.

They found Nene still sitting on a rock beside a little pile of rolled up bandages. The sight of Kaja sobbing and Griff's bloodied hands snapped Nene out of her dreamlike state.

Her brow furrowed. "What happened?"

"Remy's dead," said Star, the dry words sticking in her throat.

She busied herself tending to Griff's wounds. There were not as many cuts as she expected. Most of the blood belonged to Remy. *Remy who was dead.*

Kaja's own skin was pale and clammy. Once she started talking she couldn't stop. "He went down in after heart-and-brains," she said, each word choked out like an obstruction in her throat. "Head first. Knife out. We held onto his legs. There was rope, but . . ."

"What was in there? Did you see anything?"

She didn't answer, just shook her head and trembled uncontrollably. Whatever was in there, she was still seeing it.

"Drink," said Nene, pressing a flask into her hands. The girl managed a few swallows before coughing most of it back up. She couldn't hold the flask herself, her hands were shaking too violently.

"We can't stay here," said Nene, staring up at the Sentinel, its useless needle stabbing at the sky, as if she was seeing it properly for the first time since the storm had smashed the Van.

Within the hour everyone was on the move, their dead abandoned along with all the pointless arguments about how they should be marked or honoured. The longer the survivors lingered, the greater the danger would be. The Vulture would guard the ones who hadn't made it, forever marking that place as a tomb.

They hit the trail in strict formation. Old and young, the weakest at the centre, strongest front and back and flanking sides. Not a single camel had survived the storm. Star picked up a squalling child when she noticed a mother struggling with two others. The little girl quietened after half a mile, content to be carried piggyback, small eyes focused on the dunes on either side of them.

Star turned back to the Sentinel for one last look. Yet one more thing they could no longer rely on. The Sand Road was dying, no matter what Nene had to say about it. The sooner they left it all behind, the better.

At least Nene's mind had returned to some semblance of proper function. She kept glancing at Benhadeer, as if they shared some terrible secret between them. Something Star could only guess at.

There were things she needed to ask her sister, but she would have to wait until Nene was much stronger. Until she was her regular self again.

=NINETEEN=

Kian pushed his way through the crowded streets, pleased to at least be out of the searing desert, even if he had wound up in this dirty, stinking place. Fallow Heel, they called the port—what sort of name was that? What manner of people inhabited its streets? Damaged ones, by his first overwhelming impression.

Kian felt as though he'd travelled back in time, to an age before the birthing of machines. Yet he knew this tanker port to be post-Ruin. Almost as contemporary as the Impact suit protecting his life and limbs. There had once been a massive city here, blasted from orbit, melted and spread across the sand like butter on bread, if you could believe the Axan scholars.

He saw no trace evidence of such a city. Just a junkyard town built of scrap and sun-dried bricks. Barely a stick of wood in evidence. All the trees had dried up long ago.

They should never have come this far, but what had that Warbird been, if not a sign? A sign that Kian was destined for greatness; something he'd suspected all his life. The three of them had been banished to the Sand Road for drunken insolence. Punishment for standing up to his haughty uncle and small-minded associates. Cast out for daring to point out the inefficiencies of the Axan status quo.

The fortress city had been profiting for decades from the onsold, scavenged operating systems of tankers sourced and hunted through this port. Relics traded through the underground like opium and gold—and taxed just as heavily along the way. Old tech able to be adapted, but not back-engineered. Not so far. Not unless scholars could get their hands on more reliable, high quality supplies.

For even suggesting such a thing, Kian and his cousins—bodyguards really—had been cast out to scout the Sand Road's southern stretch, to sniff out its pathetic townships, and inventory whatever each miserable outpost had to offer. *You are just the men for the job*, his uncle sneered, no doubt presuming they would not survive the experience.

Little they'd seen could be of practical use to Axa, as his uncle surely would have known. The Vans moved up and down the Road, transporting nothing but unwashed savages, displaced homesteaders, and relic-hunting coastal folk. The Vergelands had been picked clean long ago, and travelling had become a dangerous business. So dangerous that all Axan explorers had vanished without trace. Such a fate would not befall Kian. When he returned to Axa with the heart-and-brains of a fallen Warbird, everything would change. Important people would start taking him seriously.

He passed the forge, with its incessant hammering. Grubby children running underfoot. Old women sitting cross-legged on mats beside woven baskets made of lacquered grass and faded plastic. He peered into one, glimpsed dried skinks and scorpions, chunks of something fried and unidentifiable.

Hunks of meat sizzled on a skillet beneath a sheaf of drying snakeskins. He watched a woman hacking off bits, frowning until he worked out what it was: a sand barnacle, still twitching. Enough to make his stomach turn. He'd heard tales of those things latching on to fallen travellers, drinking their blood, attracted by body heat. The tankers were apparently covered with them.

A stranger slammed against his shoulder, cursed when he barked at her to look where she was going. The women here were uniformly ugly—raw, tanned skin freckled, and permanently aged. Not like the porcelain beauties of the Axan underland. These local drudges had rough, calloused hands from backbreaking outdoor toil, and coarse dialect to match, spitting and swearing and shouting at each other. Chewing baccy and betel nut, staining their cracked teeth brown and red.

Fallow Heel was turning out to be such a disappointment.

As he walked, he felt the weight of curious eyes. Kian placed his hand on the hilt of the weapon concealed beneath his sand cloak. Best the barbarians never learn that scouts from Axa walked amongst them. Best they believe the mighty fortress city still cowered from the toxic air and centuries of warfare residue.

He had sent Jakome ahead in search of muscle and Tallis for supplies—and information. He had managed to glean a little already: that fallen Warbirds were not highly prized. That they were considered puny, insubstantial things, not worth risking lives for like the mighty tankers. The fact that they potentially carried centuries of data meant nothing to these people, scratching their livings in such primitive conditions.

Buildings lined along the docks were jammed up against one another for support; inventive patchwork assemblages: doors, walls, calico panes of glass. Graffiti symbols and crude pictures he didn't understand. Walls of mud and dung and scrap and . . . Kian almost tripped over his own feet.

The front wall of the building on his immediate right was embedded with a slab of tanker skin, held in place by a mixture of mud and filth. *Tanker skin!* Kian had to force himself to keep on walking, for to stop and stare would draw unwanted attention.

The doorway of the next hovel along had been reinforced with multiple gun barrels, a variety of shapes and sizes, each one worth a fortune back home in Axa. Did these people not comprehend the value of such artefacts?

A chorus of hammering blacksmiths intruded on his thoughts. He hurried past, his mind still reeling from the possibilities. Now he could see evidence of tanker salvage everywhere he looked: ventilators, lifting rings, air cleaner manifolds. Track idlers inset in sub-baked mud as decoration. These people were even stupider than he'd thought.

As if on cue, a one-legged man, half his face a mess of scar tissue, held up something shiny for Kian to see. A triangular chunk of burnished metal hammered smooth, an image etched upon its surface. It took a while for Kian to work out what it was: a sand ship, masted with proud sails. It was crude in its execution, but he had never seen such a thing before. He pressed a coin into the man's hand. Too much, judging by the speed at which the seller hobbled off into the crowd.

He looked up from the etching just in time to see its real-world counterpart on the dock ahead of him, casting off on giant butyl tires. The crew, a formidable bunch of savages, wrapped up tight against the wind and other foes. Setting out to bag themselves a tanker—or die trying.

He examined the scrimshaw's graven ship more closely. The execution was not crude, in fact, but a faithful rendering of the genuine article. These sandcraft were the antithesis of the ocean-going vessels berthed along the coast. Those ships were magnificent constructions, fabricated and maintained by proud artisans.

These vessels, designed to skim the Black, were made of hammered scrap: lopsided, precarious, and deadly.

A tide of grubby urchins and street vendors swirled around him, waving their wares after seeing him pay the crippled beggar. Kian swatted at them like bugs, hurrying for the shelter of a tavern ahead.

He pushed past the rough folks milling around the steps. Some moved begrudgingly out of his way, others deliberately edged in close to crowd him. He climbed, then shoved the door with his shoulder, and was rewarded by a warm blast of stale alcohol, sweat, and indeterminate cooking smells. He glanced back at the docks, then froze, unable to believe what he was seeing—and wondering how he could possibly not have noticed it before. A mighty wooden ship on giant wheels. Two masts, furled sails, standing tall and proud.

Two angry drinkers sent him tumbling, yelling abuse at him for blocking the tavern's entrance. Kian ignored them, picked himself up, not even worrying to brush the filth from his garments. That wooden ship held all the answers to his problems. The three of them would seize control of it. They would travel out across the Black and bring an Angel home. Return to Axa, successful and triumphant. Raise a mercenary army, march back in to take possession of this godsforsaken town. Within a year, he'd be the richest man alive.

The tavern doors swung outwards. A familiar form emerged, Tallis, reaching out to offer help.

"The ship!" said Kian.

Tallis's face flushed with excitement—he hadn't even heard Kian's words. "You won't believe what I've found out—*who* I've discovered living in this town."

"Who? What are you talking about."

Tallis didn't answer. Instead he dragged his cousin away from the tavern's busy entrance, and down to the jetty in search of a private place to talk.

= TWENTY =

The outermost dwellings of Fallow Heel shimmered like a mirage. Barefoot children ran out to greet the exhausted travellers. Each child was a welcome sight carrying a bulging waterskin, in some cases almost a third of their own size. The children handed skins to the weary walkers, staring in fascination as each one gulped great thirsty draughts.

The children had been sent from the curve of double-storey, white-washed buildings known as the Twelfth Man caravanserai, a place of rest for many Vans that passed through Fallow Heel.

Benhadeer and the fifty who remained with him had been walking for several hours. Many of the other exhausted, dehydrated Van folk had dared not chance the last leg on foot. They lingered back at Hollowpoint, a miserable outpost struck up by the Crossroads oasis well. Benhadeer had promised faithfully to send back transportation. He was known as a man who kept his word, so they sat and waited in the shade of scrappy palms, praying nervously that the locals would keep their distance, knowing that the two point riders left behind to protect them were far from adequate.

Star ached all over. Light-headed from the sun, phantoms had been dancing in the corners of her eyes for hours. She hadn't thought the children were real until a cold, damp waterskin was thrust between her hands.

Nene had said very little since they rested up at Crossroads. Her depleted field kit was still slung across her shoulder like a bandolier. She had fought to keep possession of it when the greedy marketeers of that miserable town had demanded practically all the stranded travellers possessed in payment for water, shelter, and a little bread.

Star had drunk too fast and now her gut was hurting. A chubby child with greasy hair pulled tightly into uneven pigtails handed her an orange from a basket. Star bit into it, skin and all. Her mouth flooded with flavours, a mix of sweet and bitter.

The Twelfth Man caravanserai was the most welcome sight of all. A clean swept street and a long, low whitewashed wall. Ebba, the owner in her multi-coloured skirts, waiting on the road to greet them, chewing on her fingernails—news of the Van's destruction had travelled far.

Scarcely had they reached their destination when the bickering and squabbling that had dogged the long, circuitous route between the Vulture and Fallow Heel started up again, more serious now that folks had had a chance to drink and rest their feet. All of them owed money somewhere, wealth that had been swept away along with the wagons, animals, and human lives.

"He's not staying here until he pays up what he owes!"

"Come on, Eb—you know I'm good for it."

"Don't want your goodness, you still owe me for two back season's lodgings!"

"We've all suffered, some of us more than others."

Some Van people were luckier than others—the ones with family close by. Most had no one—and nowhere else to go.

Everyone was tired and sweaty. Some squatted, making temporary camp along the low, curved wall, waiting for arrangements to be settled and decisions to be made.

Star looked around for Nene, and found her locked in conversation with Benhadeer, arms folded, brow furrowed with deep lines. She appeared not to have noticed the line of people already waiting outside the small room Ebba set aside as a clinic whenever Vans were berthed there. Nene had nothing to offer them now, no medicine and no comfort, a fact those waiting had yet to comprehend. The big man listened to Nene's words, his hands crossed, weight pressing heavily on the stave he carried in townships for protection. Kristo loomed beside him like a shadow, half-listening, preoccupied with matters of his own. Nene talked expressively with her hands. Her fingers resembled claws in the harsh light.

Nothing would be resolved for hours to come. Star was exhausted. She needed rest, sustenance, and to scrub the desert from her skin, but more than that, she needed to know what her future held in store. The thought of a safer, better life had sustained her in their march across the sand. She would find a place for herself in Fallow Heel, and if Nene was set on continuing to Solace, she'd be doing it on her own.

Star noticed Yeshie in a patch of shade, sitting cross-legged on a mat, casting bones and telling fortunes to a cluster of enthralled local women. Putting on a brave face—her one-eyed friend had not survived the storm. The sight of something so familiar made Star smile. No matter what happened, Yeshie always landed on her feet.

When Nene'd finished talking to Benhadeer, she made her way to a vacant patch of whitewashed wall, and sat down in the dirt with her back against it, eyes closed, utterly exhausted. Angled uncomfortably, yet too tired to move, her field kit jabbing into her ribs.

Star walked over to her sister, crouched down, and gently lifted the cumbersome thing up over her head, hanging it across her own body. If anybody needed help, they could come see her about it. Give Nene a little well-earned breathing space. She regretted eating all of the orange given to her by the child, wished she had saved half of it to share.

"Nene, did you have something to drink?"

Nene's eyes opened. She blinked a couple of times before recognising Star. Her lips softened into a gentle smile. She reached out and took her by the wrist, clumsily, as exhaustion made her weak. She twisted Star's arm so the metal strip embedded in her flesh faced upwards. "Need to rest," she said, "but first, some things I need to tell you."

Star smiled back and patted her sister's hand. "Tell me later. First things first—we need to find a place to sleep. Ebba might let us have our regular room if we work for it."

Nene shook her head. "No. This can't wait any longer. I can't carry the weight of it any further."

The smile was gone from Nene's face.

"The weight of what?"

Nene looked away, down to a patch of dirt between her feet. "I should have told you years ago. Tried a couple of times, but the right moment and words would never come."

Star frowned. "What are you talking about?"

Nene met her gaze once more, and tightened her grip.

"Stop—you're hurting me!"

"Star . . . You have to know the truth of it. We're not sisters. Not by blood, at least. I found you in the desert on a relic raid with Benhadeer and Kristo. There were others . . . but I wasn't fast enough. All of you had that metal bar embedded in your skin. I wasn't much older than you are now . . . the others . . . I didn't know how to save them . . ."

Star stared at her, dumfounded. Too much to take in, coming at her too fast. "Not sisters—what do you mean by that?"

"Exactly what it sounds like. Star—listen to what I'm saying. I'm so sorry. I didn't know how—"

Star snatched her hand away, rubbing her wrist even though it wasn't sore. She pushed herself to stand. "My arm got broken badly when I was ten. That was what you told me. About the fever, that was why I can't remember our parents or anything before . . ."

Our parents . . .

Nene's face looked lined and old, as though the desert crossing had taken twenty years from her. "I said a lot of things, Star. Said them to protect you. I don't know who your people are. I don't know where you're from. I pulled you out of the wreckage of those things that looked like giant eggs, half buried in yellow sand. Some old-world relic no one had ever seen before. Didn't know what else to do. Didn't know how to tell you any of it."

"Giant eggs?"

Nene leaned her head back against the wall and closed her eyes. "Nobody knows what those things were, Star, that's what I'm trying to tell you. Giant eggs filled with dead kids, all packed up tight and frozen. One of the eggs was cracked, so we looked inside. We were looking for salvage."

Nene kept her eyes closed. "I gave you your name," she added. "Ten years back, a broken star came falling out of the sky while we were digging. I remember it burned so bright, then faded into the moonlight. Didn't know what else to call you. Seemed as good a name as any."

Star felt the blood draining from her face. "You *named* me?"

Nene nodded. "I'm so sorry," she said in a breathy whisper.

Sorry? Oh Nene, you should have told me. That and so many other things.

Nene appeared to have fallen into slumber. Star felt as though she had been punched in the chest. Like a hand was wrapped around her heart and squeezing tight. She caught sight of Benhadeer and Kristo trying to look like they weren't watching. Seven years past, and no one had told her any of it.

The pain in her heart sunk lower, started turning into bellyache. She turned her back on the whole damn lot of them, and headed for the centre of town, not knowing where she was going or what she was doing.

Star had never seen the streets of Fallow Heel so crowded; the population was swollen to twice its normal size. Once, this had been an orderly place filled with well-dressed citizens and their well-kept homes. Star did not recall gangs of youths on street corners, beggars and panhandlers, roughly constructed carts pulled by emaciated donkeys. Dirty children swarming like roaches, yelling at her to throw them bread or coins.

She had no plan, no place to go. Away from Nene and her words was all that mattered. She had not planned to pass Allegra's house, yet somehow that was where she ended up. *Not sisters—how could such a thing be true?*

Allegra's house was not a house, but a mansion, unchanged by the passing year. Thick white plaster walls surrounded it, topped with coils of razor wire. Close beside it was a second building, smaller and less grand but similar in style. A storehouse, or perhaps the stables.

Glazed tiles framed a spectacular entranceway guarded by two armed men in fighting leathers. She watched as two other men, dressed in voluminous sand cloaks much like Benhadeer's before the Red had sullied them, passed through the outer gate and strode up the path leading to the front door. Both were patted down for concealed weaponry by the bodyguards then permitted inside, the large wooden door closing solidly behind them. Once, she had walked through that very door. Star took a deep breath, then followed.

She tried to look like she knew what she was doing, like she was something better than the Van trash Kian had denigrated her. She offered the leather-clad guards a smile. They did not return it. Men like them were not paid to smile.

"I am Allegra's friend," she told him. "Last year I was—"

"Piss off, street trash. You got no business here."

"But I'm friends with the daughter of—"

"You don't smell like anybody's friend."

She hesitated. The one on the right drew his sword. She stepped back, hands raised. "OK. I get the message." She backed away slowly, heading for the gate. Turned, then was prevented from passing through it by four big men in sand cloaks. They pushed right past her as if she wasn't there, heading straight for the entranceway themselves. The guardsman's weapon was still drawn. He raised it menacingly.

The four offered greetings and credentials. The guardsmen argued back. Something about docks and waiting for instructions. Discussion over something that was late.

Star didn't hesitate. A better chance would not present itself. Nobody was paying her any attention. As the men's voices got louder, she slipped into the shadows and edged around the mansion's whitewashed walls, taking care not to trip over the ornamental shrubberies, cactus plants, and statues. There were ridiculous figures in hero poses, some of marble, others of greenish metal streaked with pale bird droppings.

A hedge of prickly bushes lined the narrow path.

All the balconies above were empty. Allegra's was the topmost— she knew because she'd been inside before. Through the front door and up the stairway like an invited guest.

Her mind flooded bitterly with Nene's words. *That rich girl is not your friend.* We'll see about that, she thought.

The mansion's nearest neighbour stood three stories high as well, protected similarly by razor wire. Its top balcony was jammed with people drinking and laughing like it was New Year's Eve. Something in the distance held their attention. Spyglasses passed from hand to hand, all pointing in the direction of the Black Sea docks, the departure point for all the tanker crews. She'd never set foot on those docks again. Not willingly. Not after what had happened to Remy.

Allegra's balcony lay tantalisingly out of reach. If Star attempted to climb the brickwork, she'd be seen for certain. Shot in the back as she scrabbled for footholds. Her shoulders slumped. It was hopeless. She needed to get out of there before guards patrolling with dogs discovered her trespassing. Hunger and thirst gnawed at her innards. Fatigue too, but she pushed it all aside.

She checked the back door. Bolted solid. Windows set into the wall were affixed with metal bars.

Three storeys was too much of a climb—although she had scaled higher. All Van brats were forced to climb at one time or another, scrambling up cliffs with bare hands and feet, escaping flash floods or starving predators. Hunting for bird's eggs or serpent nests. Hiding from strangers they didn't like the look of.

Star liked the look of Fallow Heel, despite the carousing drunks and the grim-faced guards. This port was where she was supposed to be. All she needed was a chance to prove herself.

Suddenly there was an unexpected flash of colour from up high. Allegra, in a scarlet sari, stepped out onto her balcony, arms folded against the cooling breeze.

Star jumped up and down on the spot. Waved, desperate to catch the girl's attention, but she didn't dare call out. Not with well-armed guardsmen so close by.

She willed Allegra to glance down at her, but it was no use. Noise from the street was loud and distracting, not to mention the shouting and cheering of the neighbours. Star glanced nervously back the way she'd come, past the silent statues and the shrubs. No sign of dogs or guardsmen in pursuit. By time she looked back to the balcony, Allegra was gone.

Her heart welled with despair. She was so tired. More tired than she had ever been. She should not have come here. Nene would be furious when she found out. The guards would beat her if they caught her—or worse. She knew she should return to the Van—only there was no Van. Not anymore. No sister either: a truth she was having trouble holding in her head.

Star scrutinised the surface of the wall; whitewashed, but uneven. Brick ends protruded here and there. Little gaps where pigeons had made nests. She could scale it. She had knives. She'd climbed much harder things.

She started up before she had the time to think about it, before exhaustion claimed her as its own. She pretended she was climbing up a cliff face and that the sand below was soft. That statues of long-dead heroes were not watching.

Allegra's balcony was edged with marble, and smoothly shaped. A balustrade more solid than it appeared from down below. She got a grip and hauled herself up over, muscles straining. She stood for a moment to admire the view—just a moment. Any longer and her muscles would have cramped and seized from the effort.

All around her was a sea of rooftops, flat and well maintained. Beyond them, buildings in neat rows, each one with a peaked and painted roof. Beyond them further still, the docks and the flat black tongue of melted slag jutting out into the Dead Red Heart. Coloured shapes skitted across its surface. Sandcraft and blokarts. Things she learned about from Lucius's stories.

Fancy double glass doors led through to Allegra's rooms. Beyond the glass looked dark and uninviting. The climb had made her dizzy. She breathed in deeply, banishing the stings and aches from the new cuts and scrapes on her arms and legs. She wiped her sweaty palms on her trousers, reached for the big glass door, and turned the handle as quietly as possible. Trod so lightly, she barely made a sound.

Thick, soft carpet absorbed her tread. The room beyond was dark and cool and scented strongly with cinnamon and cloves, hung with tapestries and strewn with rugs and cushions. Enamel vases were placed on stands, potted palms in the farthest corners. A large bed was festooned with brightly coloured cushions.

"Is anybody there?"

A startled sound emanated from a high backed chair, more mouse than human. It was Allegra in her bright sari, legs curled underneath. She'd been so still, Star hadn't even seen her.

The scent of cinnamon and cloves was getting stronger, enveloping Star and making her want to sleep.

She said her own name. Allegra stared at her blankly. She said it again and added "We met a year ago. Had tea in this room at that table with your friends."

115

Star pointed to the table where last year's tea had been laid out on a silver tray and well-dressed girls adorned with jewels had leant in close to hear what she had to say.

Allegra leapt to her feet and started screaming.

= TWENTY-ONE =

The old woman selling sand cloaks at the edge of the market square crossed herself and cringed at the sight of Quarrel. She took his coin though, despite the unfamiliar crest stamped on its surface. Gold was gold and silver was silver. Old metal, new metal, it didn't matter in a place like Fallow Heel.

He put the cloak on immediately, covering his shame. Templars like him once protected townships such as this one from marauding savages. He shook the thought away. So what if good people hated him for what he was? So what if they would never know the truth, so long as they let him get on with his mission. His mission was the only thing that mattered, according to the mechanism embedded in his arm and torso. Nisn wouldn't let him stray again.

The town appeared to be in the grip of some kind of festival. Streets were crowded and everyone was drunk. He nudged and shoved his way towards the docks, where his mesh informed him that sand ships put out across the Black.

As he reached the ramshackle row of jetties, great cries and exclamations issued from all sides. He glanced around, then up to where everyone was pointing. Yet another Angel plummeting to Earth, sunlight bouncing off its shiny casing. It landed too far away for the point of impact to be observed. Surreptitiously, he set his mesh to sweep and scan, expecting something, perhaps the faintest of telemetries. But there was nothing. Not so much as an electronic whisper.

A great roar went up from the crowd. Activity increased tenfold: shouting and swearing, burdens hefted and balanced across backs, barrows and buckets loaded, carried, and set down. More disgusting smells than he'd imagined still existed.

He had to push his way to the front, but he was a big man sporting rugged granite features, and people got out of his path, no questions asked.

Quarrel frowned. So this was the famous port of Fallow Heel. Despite two feet placed square upon the jetty, he could see no ships at all, just rough hammered assemblages of junk and plank and wire. Mobile platforms that might or might not take them past the five mile limit. After that was anybody's guess.

He watched a team of fifteen push one of the contraptions out and run with it. Its wheels were having difficulty all turning in the same direction. These crazy bastards were braver than they looked. Well, either that or desperate. Their ships were not ships at all. He walked the length of the jetty, careful where he placed his feet, as the boards beneath his combat boots were random and ragged.

At the farthest end, one of the vessels stood apart: a proper ship by anybody's definition, shiny new and freshly painted, mounted on wheels, rigged with sails. Too big for his purposes, though. It would take a considerable crew to get it moving. Quarrel had not the time nor inclination for pointless luxury. He needed only a means to an end. A one way ticket to an as-yet still unspecified destination.

He stood for a time and watched people working, so still that he might well have been mistaken for a statue. Or a saint, which was the word used to describe his kind back in the cavernous grottos of Nisn temple. Young girls and boys had once laid flowers at his feet. Pallid, sickly-looking things that grew on damp cave walls alongside moss and lichen.

Quarrel took his time investigating all possible options, and ignoring the persistent pinging of his mesh. The Nisn operatives fed him more data and coordinates. They would have to wait for his response. He could not reveal his true nature in this place, lest the more surly amongst the locals banded together and hacked him to pieces with machetes and long blades. Such things had been known to happen, if enough of them were well-armed. Some people did not suffer his kind to live.

He strolled amidst the cacophony of hammering and sawing, thumping and clanging, his sand cloak covering his implants and his shame. Nobody paying him any mind. Finally he found what he was looking for. A singular vessel, sturdier than the ones on either side of it. A crew in place, no uglier than a crew needed to be. A man with a puffed-out chest, rust-coloured waistcoat and greasy stains down the front of what might have once been a white shirt was barking orders at everybody else, his words so fast and garbled that at first Quarrel could make no sense of them. The captain, apparently, but the kind who looked like he had a price.

A heavily tattooed crewman drew a blade as Quarrel approached, pushing onlookers out of his way. Quarrel ignored it. He shouted directly at the captain.

"I want to buy your ship."

"Piss off stranger, you're not welcome here," said the tattooed man with the knife.

The captain didn't say anything. He stuck out his gut, and placed one hand on the dagger thrust through his belt.

Quarrel reached inside his pocket, withdrew a length of fabric weighted heavily with gold ingots, each one sewn tightly into separate sleeves. Each ingot was stamped with a Temple crest. The captain's eyes swivelled sharply toward the flash of gold. Quarrel held the strip at arm's length, waiting for the captain to scuttle up and snatch it. He eventually did, as one by one the crew stopped whatever they were doing to watch uneasily the unorthodox exchange.

"I say again, I want to buy your ship."

The captain's eyes were wide with greed as he inspected every individual ingot.

"Get off my ship," said Quarrel.

The captain licked his lips and nodded to the tattooed man, who lunged forward, his shiny blade raised. He leapt towards Quarrel as the rubbernecking crowd sucked in its breath. A blur of motion, nothing specific. The knife was no longer visible. The would-be assailant hit the deck. Stone cold dead without a single mark to show for it. To onlookers, it seemed that Quarrel had barely moved.

A hush fell over the crowd, until someone called out, "Sorcerer!"

Quarrel turned his back on those gathered on the dockside, a daring act in itself. He addressed the crew in his booming voice. "Seasoned tankerjacks I'm looking for, each hardy soul to get an even share of bounty, whatever it may be. Name's Quarrel. Call me sorcerer—call me anything you like. Sand and wind will wait for none of us—take my terms or get the hell off my ship."

Upon issuing this statement, he cast his gaze out across the Obsidian Sea and waited.

The dead man lay where he had fallen. A shadow fell across his crumpled form. Another big man, his bare shoulders busy with tattoos. He leaned his weight on a boarding pike and mumbled something incoherent. Gave the corpse a hearty kick. Quarrel looked him over, then nodded. The man stepped back, resuming his place on deck.

The former captain edged away, stuffed the heavy strip of gold ingots inside his shirt, and jumped down to the jetty, ignoring comments shouted out from the crowd. Quarrel briefly considered how far the man would get before someone knocked him cold and stole that temple gold. No matter. Not his problem.

He turned his face towards the Black Sea once more, preparing to gauge wind speed and direction, when his body seized up suddenly, as a surge of unwanted memories came slamming like a tsunami through his head: *Around midnight, Dark Harvest airborne troops, alongside a battalion of conscripted local cannon fodder, dropped behind enemy lines to secure the invasion's southern flank, just as the Johnnys had done the week before. They overran Archangel Bridge, Jumburra Swamp, and Collector interchange. Other airborne troops took out bridges over the River Snake and the River Sword to prevent Red Lotus reinforcements from arriving, and took out a key Red artillery battery in a bloody firefight. Moving inland, they connected with additional airbornes but faced relatively strong resistance in the homesteads and small towns. In a late afternoon counterattack, forces of the Lotus Red almost made it across the Blue perimeter . . .*

Shouting from the crowd snapped him back into the moment.

"By the mother of all holies!"

People on the dock cried out, punching the air with raised fists. The air was thick with shouting and the stink of unwashed flesh; the sky striped with the smoking trail of yet another Angel falling. This one travelled in a dead straight line. It did not slow before it slammed into a point near the horizon.

The falling thing held everyone's attention. The crew stood still, abandoning their cast-off preparations. The sorcerer accusation still rang loud in Quarrel's ears. Not the worst crime they could lay on him. That would come before long. Quarrel could read the signs.

One of the crew, he then noticed, had her eyes on Quarrel instead of the falling bounty—a tall, dark skinned woman with intelligent eyes. "Who are you?"

"Your new captain. That's all you need to know. Now get us cast off or get the hell off my ship."

The woman sniffed. "You don't look like no tankerjack to me—what you chasing?"

"Bounty, same as everybody else in this shithole town: tanker blood, brains, and heart. Fallen Angels, whatever else is going."

"E's not after tanker blood," called out a woman from the docks. One of many dressed in rags who refused to budge until the craft took off and there was nothing left to gawk at. "Ask 'im what he really is. Not just a sorcerer. Not just any old kind. E's a *Templar*. Tis writ all over 'im, you can see it plain."

For the second time a hush fell over the gathered throng. So still and quiet, all background sounds came to the fore. The cries of vendors along the pier. Hooves and wheels on sandy stone. The screech of wind whipping up beyond the artificial shelter of the cove.

"E's a Templar, plain as sky. Ask 'im what E's really hunting out there afore you take 'is filthy coin."

= TWENTY-TWO =

Allegra's shrill and piercing scream was loud enough to wake the dead. Star held up her empty hands, eyes adjusting to the darkened room. "No no . . . I'm not going to hurt you!"

The skinny servant crouching by Allegra's side hugged her arms across her chest.

Abruptly, Allegra shut her mouth and frowned. "You look as though you crawled across the desert on your hands and knees." She wrinkled her nose. "You smell like it too. Who are you? However did you get onto my balcony?"

"Climbed up the outside wall," said Star, dropping her hands back down by her side, wiping dirt and sweat along her trousers. She felt dizzy and very, very thirsty. "Allegra?"

Allegra sat bolt upright in her chair, eyes blazing. "How do you know my name?"

"Been here before," said Star. "Last year for tea—do you not remember?"

Allegra frowned, then shifted to what looked like an uncomfortable angle. Her hand went to a pendant hanging around her neck. "So you've not come here to rob me of my jewels?"

"Of course not." Star's shoulders slumped. "You don't even remember me."

The blank look on Allegra's face was confirmation. Star blurted it all out in a jumble. How last year the Van had been laid up for a fortnight for repairs. How she had been crushing a bucket full of snake vine leaves. How Allegra and her friends had been wandering the grand bazaar in their fine-spun fancy clothes, just asking for trouble dressed like that, looking to purchase contraband that came in off the Sand Road Vans.

"Yes, yes," cut in Allegra suddenly. "I do remember—of course I do. You helped us resolve a minor misunderstanding, so we brought you back with us, shared our tea with you in this very room, as you say—I remember now." She flopped back into the depths of her comfortable-looking chair, seemingly amazed that two sections of her life had come together, connecting to form one seamless whole.

"That must have been six months ago," she added.

"A year," said Star.

Allegra raised an eyebrow, appraised Star's filthy clothes. "A hard one by the looks of it."

Star flushed with embarrassment. Her sun-dried sweat was stinking up the room. "Our Van was destroyed by a freak storm—I've never seen anything like it. We had to cross the Red on foot. Go up through Crossroads. Wind the long way round from 'stead to 'stead." She wanted to say something about Remy and the washed up tanker but the words stuck in her throat. She wasn't ready to talk about that yet.

"How horrible for you all," Allegra said, staring at Star's face with deep fascination. "Vette—run a bath and fetch some proper food. All I have here are morsels, but you're welcome to them."

Star's gaze lowered to the dish of delicate pastries sitting on a tray. She couldn't remember ever feeling so hungry. She reached forward and snatched one, stuffed it into her mouth and started chewing.

The maid curtsied awkwardly and left the room. Allegra reached across for a ceramic pot and poured fresh tea. "You poor thing—what a terrible experience. It seems of late the whole world has gone crazy. Stirred up tankers and Angelfall and streets jammed packed with strangers. I've barely seen my own father in a week. Men keep coming and going from this house. Nobody will tell me anything."

She passed Star the cup and chewed on a fingernail. "Father won't let me leave the house without a bodyguard, which makes good sense, considering, but a man standing guard outside my bedroom day and night? What am I supposed to make of that?"

Star drained the tepid tea in a single gulp and reached for another pastry. Its almond filling was rich and sweet, and she felt better than she'd done in days, but Allegra . . . The rich girl barely remembered her, and it felt like a punch to the guts.

She'd never been any place more beautiful than Allegra's rooms. How often she'd thought about this place across the year gone by. It was far grander than she remembered, with so many details that must have faded from her memory: three wardrobes, each made from a different kind of wood, a dresser, a bed with a canopy. Cushions scattered everywhere. Clothing draped across the backs of chairs. A tapestry on every wall.

The servant girl called Vette appeared in the doorway, moving silent as a ghost, and announced in a timid voice that the bath was ready.

"Wash," said Allegra. "Get out of those filthy rags. You don't look well to me. That desert crossing almost nearly killed you."

Star did as she was instructed, trusting Allegra completely even though Lucius would call her a fool for doing so—as would Nene, Anj, and all the rest of them. She was not ill, nor any more exhausted than anyone else would be in her situation. Nene was the one to be worried about.

But Star didn't want to think about Nene, so she followed Vette to a smaller, tiled room connected to the main chamber. A ceramic tub sat at its far end. The water inside was steaming warm and scented. Star stripped off her ruined clothes and Vette whisked them into a wicker hamper. Gave her boots and Nene's field kit a worried glance when the maid fussed over them. "I need to keep those things close by," she said. Vette nodded and left them be.

Star tried not to tear up as she sluiced and soaped and scrubbed the ingrained dirt from her skin. Her itchy scalp was grateful for the soaking. For a girl like Allegra, bathing this way was normal, but Star couldn't help fretting about the enormous waste of water.

Vette returned with towels and an armful of clothing which she piled on top of the wicker hamper. Bright coloured garments of shiny, embroidered fabric. The kinds of colours favoured by Benhadeer.

"Oh no," said Star, "they're much too fancy. Have you not got something plainer? Trousers and a shirt?"

Vette paused, then nodded, scooped up the clothes and scurried away with all but the underwear. She returned minutes later with replacements of a plainer cotton weave—still finer than anything Star had ever owned. Star nodded thanks. Vette averted her eyes in the way that well-trained house girls were supposed to.

Star allowed herself the luxury of a few more tears, then wiped away the evidence. She climbed up out of the filthy water, dried herself, dressed, made use of the toiletries provided, opening every single jar just to see what was inside. She checked over Nene's field kit. Medical supplies were where they should be, and both knives remained in their boot sheaths.

She walked out onto the balcony, her hair still damp, picking her way around low tables and scattered cushions. A silver spyglass resting in a velvet-lined case caught her attention, but the truth was that every single item in the room was beautiful, from the smallest plainest dish to the intricately woven tapestries lining the walls.

"What has that stupid girl given you to wear? I clearly told her—"

"No no, really, this is very lovely," said Star, patting the fabric of her shirt. She'd never owned anything so finely spun. "I asked for something more practical than—"

"Where has she gotten to? I sent her to fetch more food an age ago. Vette!"

When there was no answer, Allegra groaned. "I tell you, this whole town is going to the dogs. Servants behaving like they own the place. Wealth falling from the sky, and yet my useless father sits on his hands, making excuses, not doing the smallest thing about any of it."

Allegra gestured at the sea of rooftops as she spoke, jerky movements that indicated deep frustration.

Star stared across the jagged points, troughs, and the occasional minaret. Despite the darkness she could see that some featured gardens, others stacks of rectangular items that were probably bamboo or wire cages. Pigeons, hens, or maybe even beehives. Carousing revellers aside, the town was relatively calm when glimpsed from the sanctuary of the balcony. Star liked it here. More than anything, she longed to be a part of it, to have the kinds of things that girls like Allegra took for granted.

"Thank you for the bath and for the clothes," she said shyly.

"Don't mention it," said Allegra. "We can't have you looking like a common street thief now can we?"

Star felt a flush of heat across her cheeks. She'd lived her entire life in dirty, ragged clothes surrounded by people who didn't care two figs about such things.

Allegra's eyes were wide and dark. Her skin was so perfect, smooth, and clear, protected from the ravages of harsh sunlight. A golden locket hung around her slender neck, its surface etched with the image of a dagger stabbing through a rose.

"That's beautiful," Star said, pointing.

Allegra touched the shiny thing and smiled. "A gift from a grand-mother I never even met. My father said she wanted me to have it." The expression on her face darkened. "He has me locked in here—can you believe it? Locked in my own rooms, for protection he tells me. Protection from what? From using my own common sense to make a profit from the Angelfall? Profit he should be cashing in on himself. He's the one with thirty years experience, as he never fails to remind anyone who sits still long enough to listen."

Star shrugged uncomfortably, not wanting to admit she had no idea what Allegra was referring to.

"I don't even know where he is. I haven't set eyes on him for days. A total stranger guards my bedroom door. A stranger. He lets that house girl in and out, but me, I have to stay locked up in here." To illustrate her point, Allegra left the balcony, and marched across the main chamber's plush woollen rug to an intricately carven door on the room's far side.

Allegra balled her fist and pounded on the wood. "Marko, tell that lazy girl to get back up here with some food before we starve to death."

She crossed her arms and stood there smugly, waiting for his reply. When nothing happened, she banged on the door again. "Marko, you will answer when I speak to you or I swear, my father will have you beaten."

This time when he did not answer she pressed her ear against the door. "How very curious."

She tried the doorknob and stepped back, visibly surprised when the door pulled open. She motioned with her hands for Star to join her, then stepped into the hall. Star did as she was bade, moving ten-tatively, not wanting to intrude, not sure what she might be intruding upon, exactly. Wishing she had her boots on, and her knives with her.

The corridor was thickly carpeted—and empty.

"Where is Marko? Where is everybody?" She raised her empty palms in exasperation, then ran a hand through her thick black hair.

"Shhh," said Star. "Listen—can you hear that?"

Both girls strained to hear muffled sounds coming from down-stairs. Faint thumps and thuds that could have indicated many things. Allegra moved to investigate, but Star grabbed her by the arm.

"No. Something's wrong."

Bangs and shouts and the slamming of a door. A gunshot fired. More shouting. Footsteps thumping on the lower stairs. Allegra gasped and brought a hand up to her lips.

"Quickly," said Star, wide awake now. Allegra didn't need much convincing. The girls ran back inside her suite and closed the door behind them.

"Does the door lock from the inside?"

"Yes—but my father took the key."

Star glanced around the room, her eyes coming to rest on one of three sturdy wardrobes. "Help me!"

The wardrobe was heavier than it looked. Too heavy to be pushed and shoved, until they got the idea to walk it forward on its tiny legs to the point where they could block the doorway with its bulk.

When that was done Star ran for her boots and field kit.

"Hide! We have to hide!" exclaimed Allegra, glancing frantically in all directions.

"No. You're too important. The daughter of the house. Intruders won't stop until they get whatever they've come for—and that might well be you." Star pointed to the balcony. "The storehouse roof. We could jump across."

"What—jump? Are you crazy? I can't jump that—"

"We can build a bridge."

The sound of heavy footfall echoed down the corridor. More shouting. Allegra squealed in fright.

Quickly—think. A bridge. Something solid.

Star flung open the wardrobe's double doors and tested the hinges. Too solid. Ten minutes with her knife and she might be able to jimmy and prise them free. But she didn't think they had ten minutes.

"We can tie the sheets and make a rope!" exclaimed Allegra. She ran to her bed and started stripping the linen from it.

"It won't be long enough," said Star. Allegra kept on tugging at the sheets, revealing a pale blue mattress underneath.

A mattress. Star had a sudden thought. "Quick, help me!" She slipped her fingers underneath the padded mass and lifted. "Help me!"

Allegra pitched in and between them, they managed to lift the mattress and heave it onto the floor. Below it was a neat row of wooden slats. Allegra stared at them stupidly. Star scooped four of them into a bundle. One of the slats jutted out and knocked the dresser, toppling the silver spyglass in its case. Star edged around and grabbed the glass, shoved it into her pocket, then dragged the clumsy bundle of wood onto the balcony, scrambling up upon the thick marble balustrade.

"What are you doing? Be careful!"

"Pass me the ends."

Allegra helped her. Star laid the slats across the gap between the buildings.

"No way. No no, I can't—!"

"It's not far. Not if you don't look down."

Allegra shook her head repeatedly. "I can't. I'll fall."

"You won't fall. Solid wood makes a solid bridge. You'll be fine. I'll help you."

Allegra pleaded, shook her head and wailed. "I *can't*."

She was still shaking it when a heavy thumping sounded on her bedroom door. Hard enough to make one of the tapestries swing. Star reached out. "Come with me or stay behind with them," she said. "But hurry. Your neighbours are beginning to take an interest."

One more thump was all it took—the bedroom door slammed hard into the wardrobe. Allegra scrambled up onto the marble balustrade, hanging on to Star with both her hands.

"I'll go first. Watch me closely." Star spread her hands for balance, padded smoothly across the wobbling, makeshift bridge. "Quickly!"

"I can't do it."

"Yes you can!"

"I can't!" But she did, taking at first a timid step, then half skipping the rest of the way, causing the slats to tremble, even though they held. Allegra let out an involuntary squeal, jumping down as Star tugged the slats across.

"That was amazing!" said Allegra. She waved at the drunks on the neighbouring mansion's balcony. They let out a cheer and waved back enthusiastically.

There was a crash, and the splinter of breaking wardrobe wood. Star grabbed Allegra and pulled her out of the light, just in time. Two large men pushed the wardrobe over and kicked their way into the room. The sound of hurtling objects followed.

One of the men burst out onto the balcony. For a moment he seemed to stare right at them as they crouched in shadows. Star placed her hand across Allegra's mouth, the other behind her head to hold her still.

The man glanced across at the neighbours who gave him a carousing cheer. He ignored them, and hurried back inside. Star waited until all movement in Allegra's room ceased before she took her hand away.

Allegra glared at the double doors. "Who do they think they are?"

"Forget them. We have to find a way to get out of here."

Allegra nodded. She guided Star tentatively across the storehouse roof, then down a set of metal rungs embedded in the far side's wall. The climb was difficult. The rungs weren't very big or evenly spaced. Some were missing altogether.

Crates were stacked thickly against a wall at the bottom, too dark to see what they contained. The girls jumped down to the rooftop's lower tier.

"Who were those men?"

"I don't know!"

"Are you sure?"

She considered. "Never seen them before. Hired men, I think," she said. "Father pays men like them to do his dirty work."

"But you don't know if they were after you specifically?"

She shook her head. "Of course not."

"Is there anywhere safe that you can hide?"

Allegra frowned in concentration. Her face brightened. "My father's ship—the *Razael*. Hamid the Quartermaster knows me." She peered across Star's shoulder. "We should be able to reach the docks across the rooftops."

Star handed Allegra the spyglass. She raised it and aimed it at the docks. No taller buildings blocked them from the view.

"My gods, look at the crowd! What do they think they're doing?"

Allegra passed the glass back over, her full attention on the crowded docks. "There's barely any sandcraft left in dock at all. Yesterday every berth was filled—I sent Vette down and that was what she told me."

Star scanned the crowd, not certain what she was looking for. There were faces she thought she recognised. People who looked like people she used to know. She'd walked along those docks before—who hadn't?—yet never had they been crowded out like this.

Allegra snatched the glass back from Star's hands, and aimed it at her father's ship.

"The *Razael* was supposed to be getting fitted with new upholstery." She groaned in frustration at her inability to make the image any sharper. "But those people on deck, I don't recognise their colours—or their faces. Something isn't right. Come on, let's hurry. We can see nothing of use from here."

She made for the far edge of the low brick wall. Star followed.

Nothing had been right since that first Angel fell, she suddenly realised, but Star didn't mention it. Allegra led her down another ladder, this one well-maintained and obviously in regular use. More crates were stacked up against brick walls. Despite being closer, she still couldn't tell what they contained.

At the bottom, a sturdy door was fastened with a very rusty lock. Star smashed it with her boot. Three blows and it fell apart.

"Hey, that's family property," said Allegra. Star froze, but then the rich girl laughed. "Come on!"

The door let to an alleyway choked with broken crates and mouldering sacks in heaps. Rats, too—Allegra jumped as one brushed against her leg.

"Your father must be a very wealthy man."

"Yes yes. He deals in everything: maps, relics. Bits of old world junk. Collectors pay a fortune for such things, you know."

Star knew. The squares and adjacent doorways of every major town from Bluebottle up to Evenslough brimmed with relic sellers. Ragged-looking men and women who did not live in grand houses, own big black sand ships, or employ well-muscled men-for-hire with rifles.

= TWENTY-THREE =

Despite having spent so many years alone in darkness, the General can still recall the feeling of snowflakes falling on naked skin, of running along a scrubby bush track, of eyes closed, of pitter-patter, of breathing deep eucalyptus tang, of wide skies striped with cirrus cloud. But try as he might, he cannot recall his name. Only his designation: Lotus Blue.

That he is sure of—and the fact that he had not been the only one of his kind. There'd been others, he remembers them. Not their faces—they did not have faces—but their names and professional designations: Lotus Yellow, Lotus Red. Other colours, each with vast territories to serve and protect, and the means to do so at their swift disposal. Each carved from the same steel, silicon, and graphene as he, yet individuals, aligned to core competencies and values commensurate with the peoples and industries they'd been sworn and uploaded to protect.

The initial revelation that he is buried under tons of rust red sand came as quite a shock. No wonder it is so dark down here, no wonder the Angels and Warbirds pay him no respect. They can't even see him, and probably take him for some kind of apparition, or a parasite like the autonomous repair bots still clinging to the underbellies of the tankers. Automatons loyal long beyond the call of duty, scavenging scrap parts and knitting up wounds, sacrificing their own bodies to plug up gaping rents and seal them tight.

The General focuses his energies on shouting through the tropospheric scatter, edging around the wideband—which is useless without dishes to align, announcing his presence to anything capable of hearing. He is prepared for phase shifts, time delays, attenuations, and distortions. Prepared for anything but this numbing silence. Where has everybody gone?

He can feel the power fading from his emergency back up coils. Creating those polyp storms has drained them. A few more hours and he'll find himself plunged back into impotent slumber and haunting preprogramed dreamscapes, executing imaginary manoeuvres with imaginary armies.

No. He will not stand for it. The General is a Lotus Blue. He had been uploaded for better than this. Mere hours remain for him to conjure himself a fighting force, to find willing hands to dig him out from this prison.

The General pushes all thoughts of the other colours from his periphery. He focuses on the here and near: schematics of the Lotus bunker. Along with Sentinel Tower Zero, the bunker comprises several storeys including house barracks, an armory, a power plant, a radar station, an auxiliary communications array, towers, and emergency construction and salvage equipment. Nearby are underground missile silos, weapons caches, and helipads. Five miles out, another dish—a big one. The aircraft are useless. He finds an ordinary Sentinel: not bad. Parts he can harvest if he can get his hands on them. The problem is, the General has no hands.

No hands, but he can commandeer them.

He jacks aboard that Warbird one more time, and blasts a couple of dead-blind Angels out of the surrounding sky from sheer frustration—or sport, perhaps.

He observes with interest the skeletal remains of archaic sheep stations down below, a scattering of insignificant gold-mining towns, plus several isolated mine sites, mostly collapsed, accessible by dirt roads grown over with gum trees and thick mulga bush. Sand dune fields and spinifex-grass cover range for miles and miles.

The trucks and tankers are not the only mecha forever seeking the familiarity of heat. Fleshmesh, they used to call them—a derogatory term he'd never liked. Fleshmesh meant not real living but vat grown, algorithm-sown.

The Johnnys were always the weaker warriors. They hated their stronger, faster, braver cousins, the ones born to the wars. Templar soldiers, warriors true—what had happened to their kind?

The General squints, scanning for those little beads of heat: the walking wounded, the dead who will not die. Supersoldiers still fighting the good fight, who no one has bothered to tell that the Lotus Wars are over.

The General blanches with waves of energy subsidence. His juice is precious, and fading fast, but he has to know. He focuses all remaining energies on a wideband perimeter sweep, listening for that tell-tale atomic fade. A half life is better than none at all. Mesh does not lie. Mesh keeps on transmitting data even when the Templar host is locked in stasis.

Bingo! as his people used to say. One of those small human anachronisms that has remained with him despite the wars and all that has happened in the aftermath, has remained even though the names of his own children have evaporated.

The surrounding sands are seeded with mesh and mecha, ranging down from tanker to scout, from spider recon to surges of out-of-control lantana raze, a bio weapon that could strip an enemy stronghold down to the last brick in under fourteen hours.

Templars—it seems there are plenty of their kind still out there. "Come to me, my children," the General whispers. "Come to me and dig me out of this godforsaken tomb."

= TWENTY-FOUR =

Star and Allegra stood upon a low stone wall that, in decades past, was said to have been a boundary marker before the town swelled up and sprawled to meet it. A high stone wall it had been once, buried up to its neck by time and tide and sand—so stories told, not that anyone ever cared to dig and check.

Beyond it, the Obsidian Sea—like nothing else Star had ever seen in seven years of travelling the Sand Road. It stretched for miles, perhaps even further. The Sentinels protecting sections of its length were said to peter out at the five-mile limit. Beyond that lay a no man's land where serpents, rogue tankers, and other stranger creatures roamed.

"Look!" Allegra pointed out across the flat black tongue that seemed to suck light from the sky. Upon its surface was a scrappy flotilla of land yachts and blokarts: two and three seaters, mostly. Singles, too, so flimsy that the smallest breath of wind could take them.

Star took the spyglass back from Allegra and raised it. "More than crazy. Downright suicidal."

The smaller craft were no match for any tanker. They were too light to hold harpoons—and no other weapon was effective in snagging those mechabeasts, according to Lucius. Other than a lance, aimed and thrust into vulnerable places at close quarters. But they were weapons only the most skilled knew how to use.

All around them was the tang of sweat, the clink of coin; snatches of unintelligible phrase as the cargo handlers unpacked wares that would provision sandships. Goods that had been hauled by van along the Sand Road. Squabbling crows and barefoot children played tag between the barrels and crates. A thick thatch of mended nets hung limply in the sun.

The girls jumped down and began to walk, staring unashamedly as they passed the row of tankerjacks standing and smoking idly together, backs against the sandsea wall. Aged sandmen with creased faces and weathered hides. Young ones, too, smooth-skinned and adventure-eyed. But Star knew it didn't take long for the Red to rob them of their beauty, returning each one a little harder than when they set out, until eventually they were spitting and smoking and snarling with the best of them, all sand-hardened veterans of the Black.

The tankerjacks watched Allegra warily, prepared to absorb any insults she might care to throw their way. Like storms, wealthy daughters were not to be trifled with. Or trusted.

"I can barely discern the women from the men," Allegra whispered distastefully. She took the glass back and aimed it at her father's ship.

"Chasing down tankers is a hard life, to be sure," said Star. "There was this boy I knew. Set his sights on harvesting a dead one that washed up in the storm that destroyed our Van. Not quite dead, as it turned out. He died because of me."

Allegra lowered the glass and looked to Star. "Who died?"

"His name was Remy. A point rider. The tanker took him. Blood all over the sand. He reckoned he was in love with me. Always showing off to get my attention."

Her face brightened with interest. "Did you love him back?"

"No."

"Did he know you didn't love him?"

"Not really."

"So you feel guilty? Don't bother. You shouldn't. You didn't love him and you never asked him to fall in love with you. Men are stupid. You have to spell things out for them."

"Yes, but . . ." Star stared at her dusty boots. Images of Remy kept popping into her head. His face lit by firelight. Blood drenched all over Griff's hands. She waited for Allegra to respond, then realised the girl was looking through the glass again, utterly distracted.

"What is it?"

Allegra passed her the glass and shook her head. "I don't know. I really don't. No sign of Hamid—he should be up on deck. So many faces I've never seen before."

"Perhaps we should wait until—"

"I'm not waiting for anybody. My father's up to something—why else would he have locked me in my room? Whatever's going on, I need to know about it."

The docks were so crowded they could barely move, backs and shoulders shoving hard against them. The ground was uneven and riddled with potholes and broken bricks, spilled goods half trodden beyond all recognition. If Allegra hadn't been wearing such brightly coloured clothes, Star would have lost sight of her. She kept shouting things Star couldn't hear, even though she was standing right behind her.

They pushed their way towards the masts of her father's ship, clearly visible above the milling throng. At last the path in front of them opened. The jetties and thick-timbered walkways were forbidden to everyone not officially there on ships's business. The guard nodded gruffly and waved them through. Everyone, apparently, knew Allegra.

Her face remained etched with frown. "Who *are* all those strangers on the deck of my father's ship?" She glanced back the way they'd come, to the cluster of sturdy buildings on higher ground. Her own balcony, now far away, was impossible to make out amongst the many.

"Something is wrong here. Hamid will know—if we can only find him. A proper captain, or at least he used to be. I can't stand him, but at least he can tell his elbow from his—."

A fight was breaking out on the jam-packed walkway behind them, around a red-faced man who was apparently incensed that the jetty guardsmen wouldn't let him pass.

Star grabbed her arm. "Allegra, perhaps we should wait. I've never seen a crowd as stirred as this one."

"They're all crazy. Crazy as the tankers—listen—you can hear them sounding in the distance—or you would be able to if these drunks weren't all screaming and shouting."

Exasperation was getting the better of Allegra. "Best get this sorted while we're here. If the crowd turns to fighting the *Razael* might get damaged—and then I'd never hear the end of it."

She flicked the loose end of her sari across her shoulder, and strode towards the sleek and mighty vessel. Star followed, glad of the proliferation of jetty guards, each one easily identifiable by their turbans and grim expressions. How nice to be rich. To never have to worry where your next coin was coming from.

Allegra stopped, then grabbed Star's arm and squeezed. "Would you look at that!"

Star looked. She saw nothing but the magnificent *Razael*, with its sleek black sides of glossy sheen. Wheels to match, all smooth, unlike the stone-pocked wheels of Benhadeer's wagon, a slur of black, brown, and grey. A gangway led to the main deck. A steady procession of provisions were being loaded, boxes and barrels balanced across broad backs of the crew, all wearing matching uniforms of red and white.

Allegra's voice blared like a horn. "Hamid—the wheels are greased! What the hell is going on? I am certain father knows nothing about it."

The man she was addressing lowered the rope he had been coiling. He didn't smile.

"I am talking to you." She gestured angrily at the sweaty men loading barrels. "What is the meaning of this? Where is my father? He does not know of whatever you're doing here. You have no authorisation—"

The man called Hamid strode forward with great speed. The "rope" he'd been coiling turned out to be a whip. Hamid had a firm grip on its handle.

Allegra was still shouting at him when the tip of the whip lashed out and coiled around her waist. Star jumped back reflexively. No time to think. Not even time to scream.

Allegra kept on shouting, her words an unintelligible flood. When Star turned to the turbaned guards for help, she found them staring at her coldly, watching everything. Doing nothing.

Allegra shrieked as Hamid tugged the whip, an action that sent her hurtling into his arms.

The barrel loaders had stopped and set down their burdens to watch the action on the jetty below, amused expressions on their faces.

There were knives in Star's boots, but they were too small here. Good for cutting food, digging roots, and climbing walls, but against a man the size of Hamid, the blade would be a mere mosquito sting.

Hamid had Allegra by the waist. He tucked her under his arm as though she were a sack of grain, then made for the gangway, all the while shouting at the loading crews to get back to their work.

Up against a wall of well-stacked crates leaned a clump of wooden sticks. Star grabbed one. Not sticks, it turned out, but boarding pikes with sharpened metal tips and hooks affixed.

"Put her down!" she shouted at Hamid's back. When he didn't answer, she chased after him, swinging the pike with all the strength she had. It landed square across his back, the blow glancing off again harmlessly.

He stopped and turned, Allegra wriggling and screaming, her arms pinned helplessly by her side.

"Let her go!"

Hamid looked like he was carved from stone. Star steadied her stance, trying to remember all Lucius had ever taught her. She took a deep breath and swung the pike. Hamid caught the end of it in his free hand, then effortlessly tugged it free from her own grip.

"Run!" screamed Allegra. "Find my father!"

Star ran.

Hamid shouted after her—words she couldn't hear. Two of the barrel porters dropped their burdens and gave chase. With a pounding heart, she swerved to dodge one of the turbaned guardsmen, heading towards a row of vendors's shacks and booths.

Star fought her way through a tangle of flimsy nets and screens, tripping over equipment and receptacles, and barking her shins on something hard and unseen. She limped onwards till she bumped up against a barrier of solid stone, far beyond the reach of lantern light, having lost her pursuers long ago. She felt around with splayed fingers until she got her bearings. It was the "sea" wall they'd been standing on before.

Allegra's spyglass—she still had it, digging hard against her thigh as she pressed against the chilly sandstone wall. No guard had come chasing close on her heels. Allegra was the one they wanted. Star and her pathetic attack were of no consequence.

She edged along the wall until she found what she was looking for: a place where the bricks were weathered and uneven enough to provide footholds. Up she went, hand over foot, grazing her knuckles as she clambered to the top.

She crouched, despite there being no one near, nor any lights to betray her position. She watched in horror as the *Razael* rolled forward on its wheels, mainsail hoisted, hanging limp, still protected by the cove.

She raised the glass and aimed it at the deck. Sailors scurried about their duties, apparently as surprised as she was that the ship was moving. No sign of Hamid or Allegra. No, there she was, a flash of bright red being smothered by a dark sand cloak. Allegra fought to shrug it off, her shrieks audible even at such a distance. A big man was brought to stand beside her, hands bound at the front. Mohandas, Allegra's father—who else could he be with his triple pointed beard and purple robe, red-faced and shouting loud until someone thrust a gag into his mouth.

The ship inched slowly towards the Black, its giant wheels glistening.

There was another familiar figure, this one in a body-hugging suit of charcoal snakeskin whose face was obscured by a helmet. But Star knew who it was. He used both hands to lift the helmet off, and thick dark curls tumbled down his shoulders. Kian. The supposed merchant prince from the far-off coast. Murderer, camel thief, and liar. And now a kidnapper, too. Had the *Razael* been what he was after all along?

She knew she must return to Twelfth Man to tell the others about Allegra and the ship. Benhadeer, Lucius, Yeshie—anyone who would listen. And Nene—of course she must tell Nene, even though she wasn't ready to confront her sister about all the things she'd said. *The sister who was not her sister, apparently.*

Star jumped back down into the protection and anonymity of the crowd. Benhadeer would know what could be done—if anything.

With the spyglass stowed in the depths of her pocket, Star edged her way along the base of the wall. Many had stopped to gawk when the *Razael's* mainsail caught. As it filled, experienced sailors fought to keep its wheels on the Black, and the ship aimed out to sea.

The Black: a thick, flat tongue of charcoal ice. The Obsidian Sea, some called it, though it was neither obsidian nor ocean. Most tanker-jacks agreed it had been a city once, a forest of high and mighty towers that had liquefied and spilled like milk in the Angel wars. It had hardened fast, they said, then scratch-polished by relentless angry winds. All kinds of craft headed off upon it to the deadly sands but barely a third came back in one piece, a fact that didn't stop any of them from trying. One dead and successfully plundered tanker could see a crew set for years. It was more than enough incentive to drive them onwards, to convince them the reward was worth the risk.

She eased her way into the crowd and was soon engulfed by it. Half of them were still captivated by the *Razael's* slow progress, others aggravated by halting gawkers impeding the flow of foot traffic. She kept one eye out for turbaned guards, but nobody paid her the slightest attention.

Each old stone wall looked like every other, and she soon became disoriented and lost. A great surge was pushing from the back of the crowd. Every man, woman, and child in Fallow Heel seemed to be trying to shove their way onto the docks.

She jumped up on her toes, glanced in the general direction everyone was moving. Something large was blocking the way—a decrepit heap of wood and rust she'd noted earlier that was, in fact a vessel. To have called it a ship would have been an outright lie. Its hull was hammered from mismatched scraps. Dockhands scurried around its tires like cockroaches effecting last minute repairs.

The little she knew about sand sailing was just enough to convince her the contraption would be blown apart before it reached the one mile marker. Yet a crowd of anxious folk gathered as close to its deck and wheels as the deckhands would permit. There was no way through. She would have to skirt her way around.

The red flash of Allegra's sari was no longer visible upon the deck of the *Razael*. Allegra was gone and there was nothing she could do about it. Nothing but find her way back to her own people. Hopefully Nene had recovered from their journey. She'd know what to do. She always did.

Star had pushed halfway through the throng when she spotted a familiar face.

"Lucius!"

The sight of a friend amongst so many strangers flooded her with relief. It was him, he'd seen her face and now he was calling out her name.

The decrepit vessel appeared to be preparing to cast off. Its captain was an enormous man, easily twice the size of his fellow crewmates, swathed from head to toe in a sand cloak, as if like her, he'd just walked out of the Red.

Some kind of altercation was taking place on deck. The crowd surged and Lucius vanished. Star stood upon her tiptoes, raised her arm above her head, and waved. "Lucius!"

The press of backs and shoulders shoved her closer to the Black and the decrepit ship and the enormous man who had stopped whatever he was doing and was staring at her strangely, as if he knew her or she meant something to him. He was a stranger, though—she'd remember if she'd ever met a man like him before.

"Lucius!"

Still no sign of him. He had been right there. She knew she could not have been mistaken.

She called again, but it was hard to take her eyes off the big man on deck. He raised his left forearm and touched it with his right hand, eyes still boring into her. A searing pain shot through the flesh and bones of Star's left arm. Pain like nothing else. Unbelievable. Indescribable. She shrieked in agony, the breath punched out of her lungs, and fell to the filthy dirt-stomped ground, convulsing. The crowd surrounding her recoiled. She tried one last time to call for Lucius, before the pain swelled up and she blacked out.

= TWENTY-FIVE =

Quarrel might have bought himself a crew with Nisn temple gold, but they'd made it clear they didn't intend to trust him. Sharp-eyed tankerjacks they were, dressed for the ravages of sand and sun, their torsos slung with packs and bandoliers, oil flasks and weapons, some obvious, most hidden. They kept at least one eye on him at all times as they readied the ship for cast off, as if they expected him to lash out suddenly and do something violent and unpredictable. Which Quarrel had already done, of course.

The ship. Now there was a joke and a half. He could think of no words for the pathetic assemblage to which this easily bribed crew were entrusting their lives. He might have invested a bit more thought into his choice of craft if his mesh hadn't been pinging incessantly.

He glanced at the docks' lone standing Sentinel tower. The faint resonance of buzz still lingered in his blood. He should not have given in to temptation back there at the Vulture. Addiction raged like a furnace amongst his kind. But a taste was a taste, better than nothing. Better to have loved and lost as that old prayer went.

Loved and lost and there it was, *her* face again, shimmering incomplete in memory. Manthy—that had been her name, or something like it—he could never see her clearly through the mist. Mists of memory, mists of time, like plumes from the filthy weed these dockyard people smoked.

He dragged his eyes from the dull grey metal and cast them across the crowd, scanning for pistols, rifles, evidence of firepower. Not much here to get anxious about. These people were primitives, their weapons old, their technology diluted. Brute strength was the currency of this place. Brute strength and bare-faced greed.

The hammering of last-minute repairs was coming to a standstill, and the last of the sacks and barrels were rolled onboard and lashed down tight. The wind had risen enough to make unfurling sails worthwhile.

This lousy ship would have to do. It would get him where Nisn needed him to go—or close enough. The crew was expendable, but their greed ensured a crude form of loyalty.

He cast his eye across the crowded jetties, knowing instinctively that he was never coming back, that Nisn would reveal the true purpose of his mission when the ship had passed the five-mile marker, and not before. But somehow he knew it would not involve returning here.

He was startled to see a face he recognised. A pale-skinned girl standing out from the crowd. The girl from the juice-drained Sentinel beside the Vulture—the one with the mesh bar in her arm. She looked frightened. Desperate. On the run, the dockside crowd slowing her in its crush.

No Templar worth his salt and spit believed in coincidence. The girl was a sign, a message, or a warning—perhaps all three, it was better not to take any chances. A couple of red-turbaned men appeared, hot on her tail—perhaps she was their property, escaped. He'd paid enough for the ship already, and had no wish to pay out more for something—even a portent—that wasn't his problem.

He made his decision in a fraction of a second, the way he made them all. His head was clear but it wouldn't last. Some days the memories came so loud and fierce, they drowned out all attempts at rational thought. What Quarrel needed, amongst other things, was backup. A contingency plan. Because he was old and unreliable, because the shunts and partitions constructed in his mind were starting to fail. He should have nabbed that girl back at the Sentinel, only he'd been off his face. Now she was on her own, and apparently on the run.

He looked to the one he had designated as first mate, gave the signal. "Stand by for let go!"

The bell clanged its castoff warning. Quarrel placed his hand upon his mesh, risking his action being noticed by the crew. But in a couple more minutes, the ship would leave this stinking port behind anyways, hurtling across the Black where nobody could stop him.

He tapped in the initiation sequence, hoping he was in close enough proximity. The range of his mesh was untested for this kind of manoeuvre. Theoretically six metres was the limit, but so much could go wrong when heat and sand and dust were factored—

The girl on the jetty let out an eardrum-shattering scream, doubled over, and disappeared beneath the tide of shifting bodies lingering around the docks. He moved quickly, wasting no time, running down the boarding plank, pushing roughly through the mass of them, punching and kicking strangers out of his way. He bent over, picked her up, and carried her back to the ship in his arms before most of the crew even noticed anything was happening.

The girl was speechless, the whites of her eyes rolled back in her head. So very young, just a slip of a thing compared to his own aching centuries.

"All gone and clear," the first mate shouted.

One of his crew—the tall dark woman—cast aside the rope she'd been coiling, and stepped forward, opening her mouth to speak. She didn't get the opportunity. As the last bell sounded and the boarding plank was withdrawn, a man scooted up it, nimble as a goat, forced to jump the last few steps. A dark-skinned man patterned with ink, he faced Quarrel, tanker lance raised and ready to strike.

"Give me that girl and I'll let you live," he said through ragged breath.

Quarrel let the girl slide to the ground, simultaneously deflecting the lance blow with his arm, then tugging it free of the attacker's grasp in a lightning motion. The tall dark woman ran forward to catch the girl before her quivering body got trampled underfoot.

"What have you done to her?" said the tattooed man, in shock that his lance had been snatched from him with such ease.

"Nothing of consequence."

"Hand her over and we'll be on our way."

"Leave my ship now, alone, or I will kill you." Quarrel raised his voice so the first mate and the rest of the crew could hear him address them. "Why are we not upon the open Black already? Those tankers and Angels will not harvest themselves."

Some of the crew were preparing to set the sails, their backs turned to the altercation upon the deck, more concerned with the proximity of small, competing vessels who would soon be heading in the same direction. Others had stopped to gawk and mutter. They averted their eyes and got back to work at the mention of tanker and Angel bounty.

"Girl's a member of my crew," said Quarrel.

"Girl ain't nothing to do with you," said the man who'd lost his lance. "What you done to her?"

"Nothing. She'll be fine so long as she does what I say, as will the rest of them. As will you. Now get off my ship while you still can."

But the ship was moving. If anyone was going to leave, they'd have to jump and chance a broken limb. The wind blew blasts of sand against their skin as they passed the masts and sails of smaller vessels.

"You her father?"

"Her friend, and if you so much as—"

"Take care of your friend then," said Quarrel. "She's no use to me damaged. Pull your weight and you'll receive an equal share. Cross me even once and I'll kill you both." Quarrel slapped the lance back into its owner's hands.

The man looked as if he might lash out, but stayed his hand, one eye on the girl. "Who or what the hell are you?"

"I'm your captain," answered Quarrel firmly. "Let me down and the girl will pay the price."

= TWENTY-SIX =

The shelves of the *Razael's* galley larder were packed solid with provisions, much more so than usual, but it was fare of a less luxurious nature than Grieve had become used to during his frequent below deck sojourns. Potatoes, rye, and salted roo. Sugar, vinegar, and coffee.

He turned up his nose at that lot and went in search of cheeses. Cheese and olives were what he craved during his shipboard days. He had water and he had wine and now he had a clear, uninterrupted view of the most beautiful girl who'd ever graced the Earth. Or he would have, as soon as she came back onboard, which by his calculations would be any day now.

The fat man with the triple pointed beard entertained his guests in that one particular stateroom, which meant Grieve had an excellent view of anyone who came and went.

Shouldn't get involved, he told himself, over and over and over, only Grieve wasn't listening to his pesky inner voice, his voice of reason, the one element that kept him a step ahead of trouble and strife.

He had to duck and keep very still as a line of dockhands hauled heavy sacks down too-thin passageways, bashing clumsily against the wooden bulkheads. Grieve winced. They were not the *Razael's* regular caretaker crew. These brutes didn't care what they scratched or bashed or scraped.

He waited until the coast was clear, then reached up high for a jar that looked like it might contain quince paste. Choice! He stuffed it into his carryall, then waited again until he could hear nothing but the far-off cries of dockside vendors and the beating of his own heart.

The belowdecks passageways had never been so busy. Something suspicious was going on, but it wasn't his problem. His problem consisted solely of sneaking back into his hidey-hole, securing his pilfered provisions, and dreaming of the girl in the brightly coloured saris. Every time she visited the ship she was wearing a different one. Wealthy and smart, no doubt she hailed from one of Heel's most illustrious merchant families. Two or three such families controlled most of the overland trade—and probably half the black market deals as well. A far cry from his own pathetic desert heritage.

Thumping and shouting echoed down the companionway, mixed in with the clang of dockside bells and a thousand other sounds besides. Angelfall had stirred the whole town up till they were mad dog crazy, partying like it was the end of the world, the whole darn lot of them. Drinking and carousing and dancing in the streets. Fighting, too, over nothing more than promises.

Too much food and drink below, too much shouting up on deck. Whatever. Smuggled grain, stolen goods, the hurly burly of the business world could pass him by for a week or so. Grieve was planning to take a holiday. To rest up, kick back, lay low, and indulge himself with dreams.

He wondered about the strangers he so often glimpsed in the stateroom through the crack. Men with jewelled rings on their fingers. If Grieve owned jewels he'd never be so stupid as to put them on display, where every gutter thief like him could see. Rich people were idiots, be they dwellers of deep desert, land, or sea.

He tiptoed down the passageway, alert to every sound, making no more noise than a dockyard rat. Perhaps the girl would return by nightfall? Perhaps this time he would learn her name, and a little more besides. Girls like her came and went as they pleased. Their fathers did not control them. Grieve's own father had never managed to control his sisters—or him, his brothers, their cousins. Too much empathy had been his father's problem. Empathy was for the weak. It had served him poorly in the past. These days he had no stomach for it. He saved his stomach for pilfered cheese and other morsels stolen from the tables of the rich and bloated.

Those bells again, much louder than before. Messing up the quiet—and the quiet was what he loved most about the ancient, stately ship. The fact that nobody could mess with his peace and . . .

The floor lurched and the bulkheads heaved. Grieve dropped his carryall and steadied himself. Cheeses spilled across the polished boards. He knelt down and quickly scooped them up, and was getting to his feet once more when the passageway shifted and tilted and a rumbling caused the exquisite parquetry to shudder.

He steadied himself against a bulkhead with one hand, pausing to listen until the whole place lurched one final time. Then he was certain.

The *Razael* was moving, only it *couldn't be*. He dropped his stolen bounty and ran for the companionway, flying around corners, no time to hide or stash his stuff, no time for anything because the rumbling below his boots was getting stronger and more insistent. Great reliquary engines were choking into life. He didn't even know the ship had engines.

He wasn't the only one heading for the companionway. Bigger, meaner men than him were pushing each other out of the way, shouting about earthquakes, swearing and calling on their gods for help, cursing whoever had tricked them to this fate.

Topside, the air stank of bitter, greasy smoke. Fights were breaking out on deck, and ending swiftly by men in fancy garb, the likes of which Grieve had never seen before, their faces obscured beneath helmets that seemed to suck light from the sky. Sky that was moving, sails unfurling as the ship made for the Open Black, leaving the docks of Fallow Heel behind.

He ran for the side, his one and only chance, but all was lost: too fast, too furious, too late to jump or even think about it. He peered over the railing at the frightening Black below, and considered jumping, but he'd likely break a leg. And besides, even if he didn't, where would he go? His carefully-constructed cover was now blown, had anyone been paying close attention. But nobody had eyes for anything but the landscape blurring past, sails billowing with mighty breaths of wind. The Black Sea beckoned like the old crone death herself.

The *Razael* was heading out across the Obsidian Sea with him trapped on board, and there was not a damn thing Grieve could do about it.

= TWENTY-SEVEN =

The Black Sea stretched on forever. There seemed no end to it. At its edges lay the Dead Red sands, but Star could see no sand from where she stood, clinging to the railing, trying to keep as small as possible and out of everybody else's way.

She'd awoken propped up against a pile of sacks, with pain screaming through her left arm and no memory of how she'd come to be onboard. Nene's field kit was still slung across her torso—something to be grateful for, at least. All around her, a frenzied crew of sand sailors were preoccupied with keeping the wretched vessel moving, with preventing it from ramming into competing vessels and other obstructions littered across the Black.

From shore, the Black had appeared so calm and still, but there was nothing still about the place up close. Its impenetrable surface was alive with darting forms, vessels both large and small scooting across it, dodging out of each other's trajectory like insect larva clumped on stagnant water, wriggling and jittering. Constantly on the move.

She had never set foot upon a ship before this day, either sand- or the ocean-going type, although she had once stood upon the cliffs of Usha and watched three ocean vessels bound for foreign lands.

Glorious and mighty, their sails had puffed out like chests, moving headstrong into the breeze, as if with a will and purpose of their own.

There was nothing glorious about this ship. The deck was made of ancient timbers meshed and mashed with other salvage. Old world metals, wire, and plastics. Broken doorways, window frames, and doors. Unsettlingly uneven. Construction that creaked and squealed with every slamming gust of wind. The railing rattled wildly beneath her grip, threatening to snap and send her hurtling over the side at any moment.

No part of the ship matched any other. The same could be said for the crew. The sailors were not uniformly large, nor uniformly male, as she had initially supposed. At first they had seemed alike as brothers, exposed flesh patterned with inkings that told her these men and women had crewed a lot of ships. They had hunted tankers and survived the experience.

Lucius. The last thing she remembered was his face, staring at her through the bustling, pressing crowd.

She avoided eye contact, tried not to get caught staring at crew members' scars and tattoos, and especially not at individual faces, lest she draw attention or end up in a fight.

She feared being singled out for amusement's sake. Out on the Black, she was on her own. Back on the Van, Benhadeer had kept an eye on things. He'd had a soft spot for Nene and her sister.

Nene. She didn't want to think about Nene. Not sisters—Nene's words chased around and around in her head. Words that couldn't possibly be true.

But as worried as she was about drawing attention to herself, the business of sailing took up everyone's attention and time. The crew ignored her as though she were a barrel or a sack of grain. Which suited her fine—so far, so good. She clung tight to the wildly wobbling rail, staring over the side at the smaller craft veering close to the vessel's massive wheels. Blokarts mostly, assembled from assorted pre-Ruin scrap and irritating as sand skinks. They darted close, then skittered out of the way before she could get a good look at the pilots. All were swathed in heavy protective wrappings. There was something hungry looking about them, even with their faces covered and nothing showing but a dark slit across their eyes. Something about them seemed other than human.

The ship's wheels thundered, crushing over detritus with thick, ridged tread, swerving to avoid larger obstacles. A lookout was perched high above in a rickety crow's nest, his face obscured by goggles of tarnished brass. There were four other spotters as well, two fore and two aft, all shouting in booming voices.

The Black itself was not truly black, but a greeny-gray that seemed to suck up light, flecked with patches of a paler hue. Embedded with chunks and shafts and indistinct shapes. Things that had melted and fused long, long ago.

Fires burned on the surface. Many of them, scattered. Broken wrecks of ships much like their own, flames fiercely consuming all combustible parts. Blokarts circled close to the wrecks like cockroaches or carrion birds. No evidence of the crews they had once carried.

A 'kart suddenly broke off from the cluster, its driver wrapped from head to foot in rags. A passenger stood and aimed a crossbow directly at Star's chest. She froze, then clutched her ears as shots went whizzing past her head. A tankerjack leaned over the rickety rail, firing back. The crossbow lowered and the 'kart scurried off like a startled rat.

Star was left standing there, stunned, ears ringing, unable to believe any vessel so small and flimsy would dare attack anything so much bigger.

She wanted to thank her saviour, but the crew member—a tall, dark-skinned woman—had already dashed over to the starboard side where another larger vessel about the same size as their own was veering too close for comfort.

Shouting followed. More shots were fired and the vessel jerked away. Something else caught Star's attention. An indistinct shape darting through a ragged gash in a wrecked hull they were passing. Big and quick—too quick and too dark for her to see clearly. Craning her neck, that was when she saw the bodies: dozens of them, lying in the open. Too late. The ship rolled out of reach just as a pack of dogs came bounding out from behind a frozen mound of melted slag. Half starved, slavering things, all teeth and bone.

Star was frozen too, both in horror and fascination. Allegra's spyglass! She fumbled it from her trouser pocket, and aimed it in the direction of the flaming wreck, just in time to see what she had missed before: bands of people gripping staves and lances, running across the Black from refuge to refuge, silhouetted against the flame, limping, lame and injured. Trying desperately to find a way back home.

The ship rolled on. She did not get to see what happened next.

A large man stood upon the main deck bellowing orders. She stared at him as the rest of the crew obeyed his every command. The ache in her arm had not gone away and though she couldn't remember exactly why, she knew this was the man who had caused it. He'd not touched her, yet somehow . . .

By listening to the others's banter, she learned the big man's name was Quarrel. He cut an impressive figure, even larger and more frightening than when she'd first seen him standing on the deck. He seemed to emit a magnetic presence. She could not take her eyes off him.

She was still staring at him when he turned around. She flinched, expecting some kind of recognition when he saw her, but Quarrel looked right past and over the side of the ship, more interested in the turbulent passage of nearby vessels. It made Star wonder if her memory was playing tricks. It would not be the first time her own memory could not be trusted.

She listened to the back and forth of the active crew. Two watches were decided upon: one to sleep or rest up any way they could, the other to keep the ship moving forward at all cost, sails trimmed tight to follow the true direction of the wind. There were not enough crew for all the tasks at hand, or so it seemed, yet the battered old vessel could not have carried more. Every spare inch of the cramped below-deck space was crammed with reliquary. Belching, acrid smoke seeped from its innards.

Star squatted, wedging herself into a corner made from lumpy burlap sacks and the ship's splintered side, keeping out of everybody's way, the items from Nene's field kit digging into her ribs and thigh. There was nowhere safe to stow her belongings so she kept them slung across her body. Medical supplies and knowledge would give her value on this voyage—and whatever lay beyond it. Without them, she was nothing but a useless hand, a useless mouth to feed.

The tall, dark-skinned woman who had fired upon the blokart stood on the foredeck, ignoring the bustle and activity around her, the swing of the boom and the whomp of the sails.

Star stared at her hard, hoping the woman would glance her way, either out of curiosity or friendliness. The tall woman did neither. Her entire attention was focused on the sky.

Star had never seen a sky like it; the colour of an infected wound, blistered and puckered. Even the air smelled foul—and not just from the smoky reliquary below.

They were just a few miles out from Fallow Heel, yet nothing was familiar, not the elements of nature, and certainly not the moving deck beneath her feet.

The boom swung, two sailors sensing its motion and ducking almost before the lookout called a warning. Star kept herself well clear of it and leaned against the rickety rail to stare back out over the side. Everything had changed and was changing still—not just the sky. The Black seemed blacker than before. Wrecks were becoming fewer, with wider stretches in between sightings. No small craft buzzed around the bow or stern. The ship had apparently outrun them.

Little by little, the crew began to relax. The reliquary engine cut out altogether, and the sails carried the load. The pungent smell of seaweed baccy wafted. The crew began to banter with one another, rather than merely bellowing instructions. The ship had passed through the worst of it. Next stop would be the tanker hunting grounds—or perhaps a fallen Angel. After what happened to Remy, Star never wanted to see a tanker again—not face-to-face, at least—but she relished the chance to get close to an Angel.

Quarrel strode across the deck. He did not move like an ordinary man, nor even stand like one. Star couldn't help thinking of that broken and battered Templar the Van had passed, lashed up high in Broken Arch where everyone could see it. Left to rot under a cruel and blazing sun. She recalled how Nene had insisted on checking to see if the thing was alive or dead.

Nene who cared for monsters more than her own sister.

Nene who turned out not to be her sister at all.

Nene standing in the splintered ruins of their Van.

She couldn't bear to think about any of it.

Star knew she had to find herself a friend. Maybe the tall, dark woman who'd been studying the sky.

When she next caught sight of her, Star decided to take a chance. The woman's name was Bimini, she'd overheard. Star bit her lip. It was now or never. Something Nene used to say.

She let go of the rickety rail, and picked her way across the deck, a plan clear in her mind. She would offer her own name, ask Bimini where she had come from and what she was doing in such a terrible place.

But she didn't get the chance. She was knocked off her feet and dashed to the deck as something large slammed into the ship's starboard side.

=TWENTY-EIGHT=

Star lay on the deck where she had fallen, sprawled and dazed as a volley of sharp, stinging missiles whizzed above her head. Not bullets. Peppershot. The weapon of choice for homestead raiders, good for leaving bloody surface wounds on exposed skin. Not deep, but just enough to distract, irritate, and undermine, to weaken resolve and hamper attempts at resistance.

Star clambered up on unsteady feet as raiders began boarding from a ship pulled up alongside. It looked like the same craft that had veered too close before. Some of its crew were wielding guns, but not all—and the guns were old. They seemed more for show, like those worn by half the Van folks she'd ever travelled with. Status symbols that could mean different things to different tribes.

The raiders' main weapon of choice were big curved blades. Others swung fighting staves or boarding pikes.

There was a clank and hissing, followed by more rounds of pepper-shot fired from the attacking vessel. An explosion knocked her to the deck again. A pungent stench filled the air, along with thick, choking plumes of smoke.

Nene's field kit had been bumped from her shoulder, and smoke blurred her vision. As she propped herself up on grazed elbows to cough, a figure approached and stood over her, his face obscured by a khafiya. The knives in her boots were too far away. There was nothing to grab hold of, let alone use for self defence.

He reached out his hand. "Come on, girl. Get up!"

She stared at him stupidly.

"Come on! Ship's under attack. Ain't got time for fooling."

A voice so familiar, as was the hand reaching down to her and something else. A gut feeling. She gripped his hand and he hauled her up. Let her go and tugged the cloth from his face.

"Lucius!"

"Shhh. You don't give your name away out here. You don't give nothing away if you can help it."

"Where have you been? I thought I saw you on the docks but then you were gone and—."

"No time for chitchat. Get behind me and stay behind me. They're slinging pipe bombs. Damn pirates mean business." He unclasped his sand cloak and kicked it out of the way, revealing the lance concealed beneath its voluminous folds. Now free, he swung it with practised ease. Just in time. A thick-set man vaulted over the side and came at them screaming. Star yelped in surprise, then ducked as Lucius struck and crushed the attacker's windpipe with one deft stroke.

The body thudded to the deck, the man's eyes staring, hard and glassy. No time for gawking. Another bomb went off nearby; more noise and smoke than anything. A second pirate followed the first rappelling over the side. This one did not go down so easy. When Lucius swung at him, he parried with a long, curved blade. The smoke made it difficult to see.

"Get behind me!" shouted Lucius.

There was no safe space behind. Another of Quarrel's tankerjacks wrestled with a stranger twice his size, both reaching for knives as they came crashing to the deck. Blood gushed from a severed artery. Whose, she could not see. She reached for one of her own knives and gripped it tightly, for all the good such a tiny blade would do.

More smoke, more shouting. Bodies slamming hard against the deck. To the front of her, a choking, guttural growling. She turned to see Lucius tugging his lance from the second pirate's throat. The dying man's arms twitched as he gurgled wetly.

Lucius wiped his lance on the downed man's trousers. "There was a time when chasing tankers was a respectable profession," he said, shouting to make himself heard over the din of clashing steel, the creaking of timbers, and the shrieking of the wind. "Orderly. Professional—not this damn fool mess. You sailed the Black and you took your chances. Takes teamwork to survive a single day."

There was no safe place. Nowhere to stand that was clear of fighting. The deck was growing slippery with bright blood, the ship stalled at an uncomfortable angle, wind ripping viciously at its sails. Two crewmen crawled high in the rigging, desperately attempting to stow the mainsail. They weren't fast enough. The ship began to lurch and lift.

People slid and tumbled off their feet. Star scrabbled for purchase, rolling to keep clear of streaks of blood and the loose sacks sliding all over the deck.

She watched Lucius fight like a man half his age, despite the deadly slanting of the deck, the blood, and everything else.

Lucius was good, but Quarrel, he was something else entirely. The big man was in his element: breaking jaws with a single punch, lifting pirates off their feet, casting them screaming over the vessel's side before they had a chance to swing a blade—or even yelp.

The strength of ten men. Ten or twenty. That could only mean one thing.

The wind changed. The boom swung around, and the raised wheel came crashing back down upon the Black. The deck reverberated. Timbers snapped as Star's blade was sent flying from her grip. She scrambled on to all fours after it, punching and kicking her way through a morass of unsecured objects, splinters jabbing into her knees and hands.

Quarrel—where was Quarrel? She found him fighting with a stave yanked from the hands of a dead pirate. His arms flailed like lightning blurs, more storm than man, fighting with the ferocity of an army. Not hard to imagine him with bones made of metal, his head filled with reliquary and wire meshed with meat like the innards of a rogue tanker.

The great wheel lifted up a second time. This time she was ready for it. She braced herself and grabbed the rail, her knife back in its boot sheath.

Yells from above as the sails were finally furled. The wheel slammed back on the Black where it belonged, the ship back under control. Cries as pirates were beaten down, then hurled over the side like bugs shaken off a branch.

She had to look. She could not help herself. Below on the Black, battered figures writhed in pain, broken limbs akimbo. She steeled herself. She couldn't help them. Feeling sick, she turned away. There was nothing she could do.

Quarrel's crew had taken the upper hand. Safe for the moment, however long it might last. But the ship was damaged. It would not be limping far without repairs.

A word was being whispered from mouth to mouth. *Templar*.

Lucius approached, soaked in sweat and stinking of death. Blood splatters fouled the front of his shirt. "Don't get comfortable. Ain't over yet," he said.

Snipers were positioned, both on deck and above it.

Star checked her pockets. The spyglass remained, thankfully in one piece. Yeshie's amulets—she'd forgotten all about them. But the rest of the contents of Nene's field kit were scattered all over the deck—or trodden into it. She picked up all the pieces she could find: cracked pots of salve, herb packets now sodden with blood and useless. The spool of thread and Nene's precious needles had survived by being sheathed in a leather pouch.

Quarrel stood on the poop deck, still as a grave marker, making no effort to clean the blood from his clothes or skin. A feeling came over Star, a sense of surety that every crazy-sounding campfire story she'd ever heard whispered about Templars was true. That they were soldiers, hundreds of years old, birthed in factories deep in the bowels of the Earth. Grown from human seed that had been tempered, forged, and hammered into something new. Soldiers who fought with the strength of armies, roaming the sands, searching for fallen comrades, long lost lovers, people who owed them coin. Proudly completing battle missions for long dead generals, not knowing that the old wars were long over. Forgetting everything: who they were and what they had been fighting for.

She shuddered. Not human. Not by a long shot.

= TWENTY-NINE =

Ancient, weathered Marianthe stood upon a half sunken cement slab known as the Peninsula by all who lived in the shadow of the Temple of the Dish. It jutted out at an irregular angle. A place where people could pause and reflect when communing with the dead, or committing prayers and ashes to the winds.

Marianthe limped the length of it, her followers hanging back out of respect. She whispered a few prayers of her own, then commanded all but three of her drones to launch themselves and fly across the sand, directly into the path of the sky anomaly: a shimmering ripple scarring the horizon in front of them, bending light, refracting it in multiple directions.

It had began to form three weeks earlier, appearing first as a disfigured cloud, no more than a blemish. But birds would not go near it, an early indicator that something was not right.

She touched the casing of each drone gently before she let it go, whispering blessings, healing spells, and wards, hopefully enough to protect them on their journey.

When the last of them had become a tiny speck in the sky, she turned and hobbled back along the rock-edged path that wound its way back along the Peninsula to the Dish. Those of her followers who were, by virtue of past deeds, permitted entry, pushed their way into the cramped Sanctum, a private place that normally would have been forbidden to most of them. But not today, not with so much at stake. More and more of them kept pushing in through the doors, whether they had permission or not. Normally she would have called out, "That's enough," and shooed most of them back outside. But the entire settlement was invested in the plight of her little drones; the journey they were making, the visions they would be sending back in streams.

"Don't touch!" she called out, slamming her walking stave down hard on the console altar, and knocking over one of her precious frames. Nobody picked it up. Nobody dared do anything but stare at the screens and the grainy images they had to offer, letting out oohs and ahhs of exclamation every time there was something to see aside from sand and rocks.

Mighty tankers were on the move, travelling in tight formation grids. Working together, not attacking each other. Not something you saw every day. Those mechabeasts had once roamed wild and free, following their own whims, their own flights of fancy. But something had changed. Something had gotten hold of their minds. Synchronous rhythm locked them into step. For Marianthe, the sight brought on a stream of flashbacks: glory days, when command and strategy spiked through her arteries like a virus. Like a drug. A platoon full of hearts beating in syncopation. You could feel your brother and sister soldiers, know they had your back, your breath, your sweat.

A couple of kitchen girls had managed to sneak inside the temple unnoticed. One of them blurted out mouthfuls of poetry, words she had memorised by rote. Sentences describing things she had never seen. Each verse uttered as a ward to protect them through the tension and the terror.

Then there was silence, as the drones flew on and the tankers fell out of view. All the screens showed were patches of uncertain sand, with occasional flashes of sky at awkward angles. And then, finally, something different. An embedded black shape, gradually enlarging as machinery, cocked and bent, clawed at the sand surrounding it.

"Pull back," Marianthe snapped. At first the drones failed to comply, so she issued the command again, with greater urgency. All of a sudden there was a wider view, from a completely different angle. Low to the ground, hurtling towards the partially unearthed chunk of granite that was so dark, it appeared to be sucking light into its surface.

Assorted gasps and murmuring. The shuffling of feet. The tang of sweat and fear mixed in with hope. People pressing against each other, craning necks for a better view of the tiny screens.

More anxious muttering: prayers and wards and incantations. That dark granite surface was familiar. She'd seen something like it before. More than one of them, back in the Lotus Wars. Late in the piece after so much of the damage had been done. The blocky granite concealed the tomb of a mighty war machine. A marker warning people to stay away.

She swore under her breath. She had once known more about this deadly manufactured creature, she was certain of it, memories scrubbed from her prefrontal cortex leaving her with nothing but resonance and ghosts.

"What do the visions mean, oh great mother?"

The question came from one of the gardeners, a woman better suited to weeding than words, but a good worker nonetheless. One who commanded her respect.

"The visions mean that everything will change," said Marianthe. "Everything. Mark my words."

=THIRTY=

The last of the pirates had been flung over the side. The fighting was over, the crew licking their wounds. The pirates might have been defeated but something significant had changed—along with the sky, which was shifting from purpled bruise to sickly green.

The crew had fought bravely, but it was Quarrel who'd saved the ship with his super-human strength and lightning reflexes. Quarrel who had assured their victory. Without him, the pirates would have vastly outnumbered the crew of their rickety ship.

"Templar!"

Quarrel stood like a statue on the deck, calm and still.

Bimini spoke up. The only one of them who dared challenge the captain, Star noted. "What in the name of the Seven Hells are you?"

A rough wind seized and rattled the ship's battered masts and hull.

"Mop up the blood," was all Quarrel offered in response.

"Answer her," said a man called Grellan, one of the burly pale-skinned jacks whom, to Star's eyes, might have all been blood kin. "Else you can sail this nameless junk bucket on your own."

Murmurs of agreement from a crew too dazed to fight. They were wounded and scared, but their fear appeared to have given them fresh courage.

Quarrel's stony gaze betrayed no expression. "Call me Templar if you will. Call me anything you like, so long as you do it on your own time. We're here on a mission and I intend to see it through. If any-one's changed their minds, then get off my ship."

Nobody said anything for awhile. The wind slapped angrily at the tight-furled sails, punctuated by creaking, groaning timber.

"Ship needs fixing," said Quarrel. "Sitting here, we're anybody's meal."

"What this ship needs is a name," said Bimini defiantly. "Sailing with no name's bringing bad luck down on all our heads."

A murmur of agreement echoed from the rest of them. No ship sailed without a name. None that expected to make it back to port.

Star watched as Quarrel looked from face to face, from wound to wound, and then up along the main mast to its furl of dirty sails.

"*Dogwatch*," he said after some consideration. "*Dogwatch* is her name."

A couple of sailors positioned close to Star muttered under their breaths about such a name being an insult and how good men shouldn't be standing for such a thing.

But when Bimini nodded, nobody else had anything to say, either for or against. The ship was named and that was all that mattered. Their captain was a monster—but he was the only rea-son they were still alive. Anyone who didn't like it would have to live with it.

Quarrel signalled up to the man in the crow's nest. Goja, they called him. Goja signalled back, eyes hidden behind wind-scored goggles.

"What is Dogwatch?" whispered Star.

"The dog watch is what sets everything else straight," Lucius answered. "Good a name as any for a bucket of rust and wire such as this."

She waited, but that was all the explanation she was going to get. The ship had its name and the crew had work to do. Spilled blood needed to be swabbed off the deck with sand. Scrapes, breaks, and burns needed to be patched up. The ship needed to be powered back up again before anyone—or anything else—attacked.

Blood abounded from the peppershot and blades. Star's heart sank. Her skills were nowhere near sufficient for what was required. She was used to tending injuries on the Van, the accidents and stab wounds that accompanied fights. A broken arm or leg to set. Mysterious fevers that came and went of their own accord. Food poisoning. Heatstroke. But not this overwhelming, bloody carnage.

She spied what looked like an uncracked pot of salve wedged under the corner of a sack. She dropped to all fours and went after it, then sat with her back against the fabric. Her hands shook uncontrollably. People were going to die today and there was nothing she could do to prevent it. Some of them had died already—had their bodies been pitched unceremoniously over the side as well? She didn't ask.

A shadow fell across her face. Bimini crouched down, her features hard and grim.

Star searched for the woman's wounds. Two were clearly visible: a deep graze on her shin, and a burn—not too deep—running down the length of her left arm.

"What are you doing?" the woman said.

Star opened her mouth to snap back with "what I always do." *What they always did, her and Nene. Finding ways to help the injured.* But Star wasn't helping anyone. She was shocked by the sight of so much blood. And now she couldn't find the words she needed to explain. The woman frightened her. They all frightened her, everyone but Lucius. These people were at home on the Black, with all its violence and its strangeness and a monster at the helm. She was not. She never should have come here.

Bimini's features softened. "You need something? I'll get it for you."

"Salt," Star blurted out. "Alcohol and water. Powdered garlic for burns—and something to tear up for bandages. My own are gone," she added. "I don't have enough."

She didn't have anything, that was the truth of it. Just a pouch of needles and thread. Her carefully prepared garlic and cinnamon bark salves, witch-hazel and yarrow flower tinctures, and antibiotic moulds were smashed all over the deck. There wasn't even any willow bark for pain. All she might have was salt, perhaps, if they had brought enough of it, and urine for sterilisation, normally only used as a last resort.

Bimini nodded and got to her feet without a word. She came back with a bucket of water, a few ingredients wrapped in cloth, and what looked to be shirts torn roughly into strips. Bloody flecks indicated the shirts had been taken from the dead. Star was relieved to find in her pocket's depths the pair of red-handled pliers Nene had once salvaged from the basement of a ruin, a rusted box filled with rusted tools, all perfectly usable once the corrosion had been scoured off.

The wounded bore their injuries in stoic silence. Helping each other where they could, none of them wanted Star fussing over them. They cleaned and dressed each other's wounds like they'd apparently done so many times before. Blood mingled with blood. Star knew the wrong of it, but there wasn't time for sanitary precautions. Embedded metal fragments had to be removed to cut the risk of infection.

She grew bolder, stepping forward to assist a large man with shrapnel lodged in his shoulder where he couldn't reach. She held the pliers close to his face until he nodded and let her tend to his wounds.

He didn't flinch or make a sound until the last of the shrapnel had been pulled, and the last ragged edges of his wounds were stitched and bound and packed with salt. These people were used to pain and suffering. Qualities the Black required of its sailors. Qualities Star did not possess.

When she was done, the big man smiled at her and said his name was Hackett. All further attempts at conversation were drowned out by hammering. How long had that been going on? She looked over, and saw that the busted side where the other ship had rammed was being repaired with pieces salvaged from its wreck.

Exhausted, Star got up to stretch her legs, and stared over the side of the *Dogwatch*, her arms red up to her elbows.

Hackett handed her the stub of a hand-rolled cigarette. She took it, even though she never smoked. Out here, everything was precious, every small gift to be treasured, from a kind word to a friendly glance or gesture.

"Good job," he said.

She couldn't even bring herself to look at his bandaged shoulder. It was not a good job. The odds were even that the wound would become infected. The smoke made her want to cough but she suppressed it, not wanting to show weakness. Not even in front of a man with such kind eyes.

"Look at that," he said, pointing to one of the tiny islands peppering this section of the Black.

She could make out the silhouette of a structure on one, smoke rising up in a long, thin ribbon. "People live there?"

"Reckon they might do," he said, dragging deeply on his own cigarette, the scent of seaweed-baccy pungent. "Reckon they might be hankering for our leavings."

What they were leaving was bloody wreckage and a pile of corpses, Star thought.

"They're welcome to them." She rubbed her arms, even though it wasn't cold. The left one was throbbing more painfully than ever. She'd been able to ignore it once the battle started. Now she felt like she needed to check her own skin for injury, though not while anyone else was standing near. "Why don't they attack us? Why do they just wait?"

"Who's to say they didn't?" He flicked the butt over the side. "Sooner we pull out of here, the better," he added.

When the last of the crew's wounds had been attended to—or at least inspected—she fetched herself a little of the salty water. Not much, as there wasn't much to spare. She found a quiet corner and a scrap of rag. Inch by inch she cleaned strangers' blood from her own skin, relieved to find no deep scratches or open wounds, until she noticed something that would have made such ordinary things welcome by comparison.

Her left arm had been throbbing for a reason. The long sliver of metal under her skin, the one that had been embedded there since childhood, had *changed*. Impossibly, it had thickened. Nubs of metal had begun to grow from it like twigs on a branch. Metal tightly fused to her own skin. She stared at it in disbelief. Her own flesh, a splint embedded since she was ten years old. She'd been told there was nothing anyone could do about it—the metal could not be safely removed, so Nene had said. And so she had believed it, of course she had, because she'd never had a reason to doubt Nene—no one ever had. No reason at all until the day she learned her sister wasn't her sister.

The metal in her arm was growing. Pushing slowly through her flesh, reaching down to her bones was what it felt like. Picking at it caused spikes of searing pain.

With trembling hands, she took the last of Bimini's ripped shirt bandages and wrapped them around her metal-embedded skin before anyone could see that it wasn't right. That *she* wasn't right. Thoughts began to flood her mind but she pushed them quickly from her head.

She jumped up, startled, when Lucius called her name, letting her dirty shirt sleeve cover her terrible secret.

"You hurt?"

"I'm fine," she said.

He frowned. "Something wrong?"

"Everything's wrong," she said bitterly. "But I'm okay. Did we lose many?"

"A few."

"You crewed with some of these folks before?"

He nodded, staring out across the Black at the solitary island Star had been checking out earlier. "Swore I'd never come back to this place. Swore it on the bones of many taken before their time."

The smoke snaked, coiled, and dissipated, snatched away by the wind. "People live on those islands," said Star, hoping to change the subject.

"People die on them, too," Lucius replied. "Good people gone to face their gods too young."

= THIRTY-ONE =

Templar.

The curse that followed Quarrel wherever he went, a name striking fear into the hearts of all who heard it. Backed up by ignorance, superstition, and loathing. How quickly the world had forgotten the bravery and endurance of his kind. How quickly they discarded the truth: that *their* kind manufactured *his* kind as protectors. Creatures to do their dirty work, to fight wars they regretted starting and couldn't finish on their own. To rebuild infrastructures they'd reduced to rubble with their blanket bombing and invasion tactics.

That the crew now knew Quarrel's true identity was unfortunate, but it had its advantages. It served as a distraction from other truths, kept them worrying about the safety of their own miserable skins. Catering to their own concerns was something humankind did better than anything else. So few of them had the fortitude for serving the greater good, for caring about the centuries to come.

Quarrel shifted his weight from foot to foot. The others had cold-shouldered him since the fighting, leaving him with nothing but the poisoned sky for company—which suited him fine. He needed time to process the latest broadcast message from Nisn. Not the regular itching nag: he'd received fresh specs and new directions. Loud and clear, the truth at last. He'd known it was coming, suspected all along. So this was what they'd awoken him for, this was what it had come to. The creature fouling up the sky, shitting out polyp storms—he should have known this wasn't no Angel joyride.

He should have stayed in Temple Nisn where it was nice and cool. Where children brought him offerings on small ceramic dishes. Where mothers knelt and shared with him their deepest, darkest secrets.

Where fathers bowed and presented him with locks of their children's hair for blessing.

But instead those priests had cast him out upon the Black off to perform one more dangerous act, one more sacrifice in the service of their cowardly underworld.

His suspicions had been correct: the Lotus Blue was awake and scheming. There was talk of poison codes and strategic bombs, with Quarrel as the delivery boy, of course. Last of the Templar warriors, last man standing, last real man on Earth.

The ship sailed on. Islands, wrecks, and dog packs were thinning out. Not many had ever made it this far from shore. Quarrel stared, brooding across the Black, his mind an endless feedback loop of memories. Snippets from another life. Sometimes the barrier holding them at bay disintegrated:

He is perched in an artillery observation post high in an old office tower, as they used to call them, watching an attack through a salvaged spotting scope, seeing the line of mecha-spiders advancing, scaffold skeleton silhouettes picking their way along Puckers Ridge.

Meanwhile, beyond the minefields, trip flares, and outposts, a wall of Templars marches in lantern light. Moving too swift, which is a problem. Don't wanna go swinging that muzzle round too fast—slow short bursts is best. Don't leave a damn one of them mobile, that's the key.

But then spiders step out of the trees like living nightmares, erect, careful where they placed their legs, a long wavering line glowing in a halo of chips and muzzle flash. Shell bursts make flaming clusters twenty feet in the air, swift blooms over the vertical stems of mortar explosions. Flashes followed by abrupt silence.

He sees the squad rushing, forty yards up and then to Earth. Rising sunlight cuts the rim of the hill when the last of the spiders come at them, stepping around and over their dead with their elongated legs, a cloud of livestock fleeing down the hill.

Then the whole platoon lets rip together; three of the four cut down in showers, hissing and spitting, electric death saturating the air. Tracers slamming like horizontal sleet. Keep your sights on where they fall. Like shooting drones. They gotta get up sometime and when they do, you'll be ready. Shooting from a strongpoint a hundred feet away, yelling over the roar of their gunfire, howling and whooping and chanting wards and prayers. Keep your heads down, boys, and don't waste ammo! The edge of frenzy accelerates over the stammering roar. The last one hits in a pillar of flames and smoke, and then burns and burns and burns.

The picture froze, then disintegrated as Quarrel returned to the present. It was too much, too strong for his butchered memory to hold on to.

He licked his blistered lips. To feign disorder and crush the enemy, that was what they taught you. *Valley of shadows, shadows of death, bucking up and shipping out, picking up the pieces and moving on.*

He needed a drink, a fresh infusion of cool, pure energy. Quarrel needed a lot of things, but he wasn't going to get them. Chew you up and spit you out, that's a soldier's lot. The whistle blows and it's all over rover, and you're left there standing around in piles of dead bodies with shit and blood all over you, fierce life hovering on the edge of rage.

He thought the desert was all there was. There seemed to be no end to it. He wondered what kind of kill triggers the priests of Nisn had wired into his meat and frame, how far he'd get if he tried to abort or make a run for it. Would they go ahead and detonate him remotely, out of spite?

He wondered about the geographical limitations of their influence, about what would happen if his mesh was smashed and broken beyond repair.

Templar warriors used to fight because that's what they were made for, for corp and country, because of the rush. Because fighting was all they knew and fighting meant exhilaration, ecstasy, and freedom. But now, what was there left to be ecstatic about? Sand and rocks and sky and sun and red.

Screw that and screw the whole damn lot of them.

Quarrel fantasized about clean peaks and dirty buzz. Of abandoned sands dotted with still-functioning Sentinels—and who knew how many other things besides. He was gonna risk it. Take a detour, go out on his own. See how far he got before they shut him down.

In his mind he drooled over bright blue light. Somewhere out there lay the perfect high. He would walk the sands until he found it and drank deep of light, power, and dreams.

After all, what loyalty did he owe the ones who'd made him after the sorry ways in which they'd used him? He was looking for the ultimate high. Out with a bang, not a whimper—he can't recall which general taught him that one.

= THIRTY-TWO =

The *Dogwatch* continued its precarious passage through a landscape fallen dark and still. There was scant activity from competing ships and karts, and no lights or smoke visible on the occasional islands they passed.

"Mind you stay where I can see you," said Lucius, puffing on a pipe with a narrow stem. Star had never seen him smoke a pipe before. She didn't question it—perhaps the Black drove everyone to smoke. There wasn't much else to do in the gaps between fighting and chasing tankers. Out here, the old tankerjack was in his element whereas she knew nothing. Not how to brace herself properly against errant gusts of wind, nor avoid the boom when it swung in her direction. Not who to trust or how to trust them. She'd managed to glean a handful of their names. That was something. A start.

"Catch some kip. I'll watch over you," Lucius said.

She nodded, grateful for his kindness, then wedged herself into a nest of sacks, tightly resecured after the bloody on-deck melee. Nothing he could say would convince her to brave belowdecks, with its greasy stench and clanking reliquary. She would rather have foregone sleep altogether than enter that dark, cramped, and stinking space.

But she couldn't sleep, afraid that if she nodded off, she'd awaken to find her entire arm encased in metal. Part of her wanted to check her flesh at the sound of every bell. The rest of her wanted to bandage that arm up tight. Out of sight and out of mind, one of Yeshie's familiar sayings, that one. Yeshie's bag of amulets formed a comforting lump at the bottom of Star's pocket. She used to make fun of the old woman's faith, but right now merely touching that bag made her feel better.

Eventually exhaustion had its way, and she managed her first true slumber in the days since leaving Fallow Heel.

She awoke abruptly to the harsh clang of bells and jarring cry of "All hands about ship!," extracting herself from a nightmare in which the bleak and barren landscape had come alive. Rocks had been rolling over to reveal themselves as tankers, crushing everybody in their path. Black birds had been circling overhead. White heat and endless sky. Star flexed her arm as the dream slowly faded away, feeling tentatively through the cloth. Mostly flesh, although she was far too frightened to strip away the bandage to inspect further. Her arm still ached, but so did everything else from sleeping in such uncomfortable conditions.

The sky remained a bilious green. The air reverberated with sickening sound, so strong it turned her stomach. She bent over the railing and threw up the salted roo jerky she'd shared with Lucius previously—what little there had been of it.

When the sound struck again, her stomach spasmed again, but this time she managed to keep herself from retching. She looked to the rest of the crew for clues. They'd heard it too, whatever it was. Those with free hands moved to port side, staring out across the Black-and-Red; the name Lucius had told her was given to the edge where obsidian met sand. One man high up in the rigging shouted and swore—words that made the others cheer and pump their fists.

The Obsidian Sea did not stretch forever, as she'd once presumed. She hung Allegra's spyglass around her neck, and aimed, adjusting the focus, to the place where the rest of them were pointing. Their ship veered close to that torn and jagged edge, where it seemed some mighty creature had been gnawing across centuries. Beyond it, red sand as far as the eye could see, quivering in the heat. And something else. Something moving.

Suddenly a rogue tanker swerved into clear view, running along the Red, sand streaming off its encrusted bulk like water. Then, close on its heels, a sandship somewhat similar to the *Dogwatch*; only a little longer, and definitely sleeker, a craft that had been built rather than knocked together, hotly in pursuit.

That sound again, like nails raking through her own bones' marrow. Star clamped her hands across her ears, expecting others to do the same. She was surprised when they merely shrugged it off.

Dogs exploded over the horizon. Two packs merged, tearing in from opposite directions, rivals under ordinary circumstances, snapping and biting at each other's heels, but in the moment focused ahead of them on the tanker, not each other.

A hideous sound filled the heat-thick air, accompanied by the long, low drawls coming out of an instrument propped on the deck of the approaching vessel. It was some kind of horn made of battered brass, its farthest end a hollow, gaping maw. Their ship's crew were beginning to prime their harpoons.

Star placed her palms against her ears again. Lucius slapped them down.

"It's tankersong—get used to it," he said.

"But it hurts!"

"The pain will pass."

The high-pitched tankersong was driving the dogs into a frenzy. They leapt and bowed and flipped summersaults in the air. Running out across the open Black, Star could finally get a good look at them. No two were alike. Some were snake-thin with elongated jaws, others squat and muscular. Some were running on six legs. Others . . . she looked away, back up to the action on the churned up sand.

"They're bracing to throw," shouted Grellan, a harpoon slinger himself according to the thatch of tattoos staggered down his arm. Star had been learning to read the marks.

The harpoon on that other ship fired, so quickly that Star never even saw it strike its mark, just a flash of light and a puff of belching smoke and it had dug deep into the tanker.

"Their towline's secure!" reported Grellan, climbing higher on the rail, watching with his naked eyes despite the spyglass slung around his neck.

All hands but the skeleton crew were now clustered along the port side rail. And Quarrel. Star couldn't see where he'd gone. He must have been below, although how he would fit his massive bulk down there, she couldn't imagine. He'd be furious when he got back on deck. All eyes were on the tanker chase. None were on the Black and its obstacles and ever-looming dangers.

The tanker lurched, pulling the harpoon tether taut. A cry went up, audible despite the combined cacophony of tankersong and hunting ship's horn.

"Stand by and lower!"

Six figures leapt down from the attacking vessel, running out onto the open sand with lances raised.

The tanker itself did not look dangerous. Not yet. Just an exposed mass of barnacle-stone on wheels blasted by the sun and wind. But Star knew better. She'd seen the one that had taken Remy, up close and personal. Close enough to smell its stink.

Six running figures reminded Star of rats scuttling up to a carcass. As the wail of the horn faded, she used the glass to bring the action close enough to make out fine detail. The figures were garbed similarly to the *Dogwatch* crewmen and women. Star held her breath as a couple swung grappling hooks and shimmied up the side of the great stone-encrusted metal beast. Another fired a crossbow bolt with a line attached. The tanker was holding steady but it wouldn't do so for long. She held her breath as one of the climbing figures swung a pickaxe in a wide arc.

The beast did not flinch as a section of its outer crust was chipped away.

"Not its skin," said Lucius, as if she'd asked him a question.

She knew all about the sand barnacle encrustations but she kept quiet.

A second figure then raised their lance and jabbed it through the newly chiselled wound.

"Gotta aim real close," Lucius continued to narrate. "That jacking port's about as big as a fighting fist."

The lance was barely in before the creature tipped, its great wheels spinning in the air. Star gasped, expecting all the figures—the four that she could see that had climbed up on top of the beast—to go tumbling down the sides. But the tankerjacks had secured themselves to the creature's skin with hammers, straps, and spikes. They'd known what to expect.

Around her, murmuring began, along with the clink of dice and bones and coin, but she didn't take her eyes off the action.

"What are they doing?"

Lucius leaned in closer till she could feel his warm breath on her ear. "Harvesting the blood," he said. "Draining it into canter flasks."

Flasks! Now she saw that all the tankerjacks carried them, along with knives and lances, strung across their bodies. Elaborately decorated, no two looked alike.

Tankerblood. She had heard of it, of course. Fashioned by the hands of old. Clever hands, like the ones who built the shiny silver towers. It was the same blood that kept Angels flying and fortress cities powered up and strong. A single drop was worth a brick of gold.

"Cut him in!" yelled one of Quarrel's men. Not Grellan this time, but Goja. The little guy with the goggles who Star had not been able to bring herself to trust.

"Cut him in," yelled another man and then they were all yelling it.

The *Dogwatch* was passing beyond the range of the tanker sands. She could barely make out the figures balanced on the creature's back. They were even further along when the towline snapped and the tanker pulled free.

The creature swerved sharply.

"In his flurry!" shouted Grellan, using the glass now, shading its lens from sunlight with his fingers.

Lucius shook his head, taking his hands off the rail, then stood up, forcing those behind to step back and give him room. "Tanker's not dead. It's not even clipped. It's playing with them is all."

"How can you be sure?"

But she knew the answer to that. He could be sure because he was Lucius, and tankerjacking was what he knew by heart.

A second towline was fired but the mechabeast was having none of it. Its song intensified, a sound like grating metal scraped across bleak stone. It slammed on its breaks and shuddered, flinging the riders high into the air. And then, in an instant, it was gone, tearing off across the sands like lightning.

The *Dogwatch* had now travelled to a point almost entirely out of range. Through glass, Star glimpsed downed figures on the sand wriggling like roaches on their backs.

The crew were fired up, eyes shining with excitement. Rogue tankers didn't travel far from others of their kind. Ropes and lances were primed and ready. All they needed was for Quarrel to give the word. For the *Dogwatch* to swing about and join the hunt. But Quarrel, back on deck by now, was barking orders of a different kind, demanding the ship stay on the Black and keep up its trajectory straight ahead.

"You bloody idiot, we're going the wrong way," shouted Grellan, forgetting that he took his life into his hands by insulting a Templar mere inches from his face.

But the ship sailed on, its captain wilfully oblivious to the mounting anger of his crew. He didn't even bother to turn and face them at the sound of blades being drawn from their sheaths.

= THIRTY-THREE =

When the *Razael* unexpectedly set sail, Tully Grieve had stood there stupidly on the open deck, gawking with his mouth agape at the familiar landscape rushing past, blurring at the edges. A man in a fancy embroidered officer's jacket had bellowed into his face, and Grieve had expected to be slapped in chains or turfed right over the rail. It was only when that hadn't happened that realization dawned: Two days of sewing scraps of cloth in that stinking Heel back alley had paid off better than Grieve ever could have hoped. Even up close, he'd passed as crew, faceless amongst many other hired hands. So long as he scrambled, ducked, and hurried, so long as he behaved like everyone else, no one would realise he was a stowaway. Nobody would pay him second mind.

Tully Grieve learned quickly. Watched and copied. Wrapped his hands in strips of rag to avoid the rough burn of the ropes. Kept an ear out for the advice of the handful of experienced sand sailors on board, ducked the random swinging of the boom. Made himself as unnoteworthy as possible, moving, hoisting, shouting, swearing, and trying his best to blend in with the rest of them.

How quickly he became accustomed to the sickening crunch of giant wheels splintering over wreckage. The remains, he presumed, of smaller vessels. Unlucky sailors, victims of the Black, the tankers—and, most likely, each other's sharpened blades.

As days passed and the wind picked up to batter the ship from every angle, Grieve learned even faster. Important things, such as the fact that the *Razael* was not shipshape. Not provisioned properly, never intended to push out from Fallow Heel.

The air that scoured the Black was bracing; sharp and fierce. Murmured utterances of the crew revealed dismay and agitation. These were mostly domestic servants, some debt-bonded rather than employed—one with a slave cuff welded to his ankle. All with the good sense to steer clear of the foreigners who had taken command of the ship, with their old-tech weaponry and unreadable expressions.

This far out upon the Black was the last place on Earth Grieve ever expected to be.

Just his bad fortune to get caught up in someone else's story. Bad fortune that had dogged him all his life.

Once he'd come to terms with his predicament, his mood lifted, billowing alongside those canvas sails. He would simply have to do what he always did—make the best of the hand he had been dealt.

He found a spot safe from underfoot and spent some time watching smaller craft veer away from the *Razael's* dangerous wheels, like half-starved sand skinks skittering across the sand.

Now and then larger shapes in the distance caught his eye. Shapes that moved too quickly to get a proper fix on.

The sky had turned a bitter hue, more green than blue, and getting greener the further the ship sailed from port. Grieve had never seen a sky that colour, not even back as an itinerant boneshell harvester travelling with his family—back when he'd still had one.

He kept one eye on the foreigners conferring on the foredeck. The three in charge were neat and clean, but their offsiders were an unruly collection of half-drunk misfits. All flab and indulgences from living the big town life. Men who preferred to gamble than dirty their hands. Grieve knew the type—and how best to dodge their scrutiny.

A group of men he identified as dockhands stood smoking on the aft deck, half-obscured by a wall of fat round barrels lashed. Grieve took a risk and joined them, jamming a beadie between his lips as he bummed a light.

The men, each one sporting a stained and non-too-well-maintained red jacket were discussing the sky and the light and the heat and the fact that they'd never before been forced so far from home.

"So where dya reckon *they* hail from then?" said Grieve nodding in the direction of the foredeck and the foreigners.

"Not from Heel," said the hefty one to a chorus of agreement, "nor anywhere in spittin' distance of the Sand Road."

Grieve nodded sympathetically, then tuned out while the men complained about not knowing where the *Razael* was headed, nor whether or not they'd be put to hunting tankers and how, if so, they were ill-equipped for such.

When he tuned back in again, two men were staring at him hard, perhaps suspicious of his sudden silence. "Thought I saw a pod before," said Grieve in haste, nodding across the bow in the direction of the Black's outermost fringe.

"A'course you did. Rich pickings and all—not that tankers'll be doing us any good. Ship ain't kitted out for harvest. Ship ain't kitted out at all."

"Hold's full of sacks and barrels," Grieve said, wishing instantly that he'd kept his observations to himself.

"This ain't no tankerjacking jaunt," said another man who'd stepped up to join them, pale skinned with a gingery beard. "There's not a man or woman on board who can throw a lance at close quarters. Or operate *that* monstrosity." He pointed with his bearded chin at the deck-mounted harpoon. "That shiny-pretty needle's just for show."

They all turned to the harpoon gun at the tail end of the deck, a fearsome weapon, highly polished, its tip sheathed to prevent unfortunate incidents.

"At the rate we're travelling, we'll soon be off the Black," added a scar-faced kid.

The other men nodded in grim agreement, each making a sign. Heelers, Grieve noted, were even fonder of their spits and wards than Sand Road folks. Eating, drinking, smoking, or belching, they always offered up some small sign or other, desperate to stay on the right side of gods Grieve had never even heard of. Not that he didn't have wards of his own. Practical wards to keep the serpents in their nests, sandskates from catching you unawares, the vultures from pecking at your eyeballs while you slept. He knew charms for seeking true direction. Blessing stones for never being left behind . . .

Grieve conjured a ward sign from his memory of a home no longer standing. He longed to ask what the men feared existed beyond the Black, but was not stupid enough to draw further attention to himself.

Two of the foreigners in their skin-tight suits were still conferring on the foredeck, talking their private talk, the others keeping a wary distance from them. They had pistols, shiny and new, and other weaponry that would likely prove as dangerous.

Grieve kept one eye on their leader—the man with the dark, curled hair and golden earring. A man who moved as though the whole world was watching his every step, as though he owned the land and sea and sky—and what he did not own, he was going to steal.

Eventually the smoking men relaxed a little and talk turned to other matters. Snippets of information traded along with slugs of bitter liquor from battered old hip flasks.

The hefty man shared a story with the scar-faced lad, a tale Grieve had heard before from an old hemp trader he used to drink with. How

Angels created the Obsidian Sea. How in its place once stood a forest of towers, each one swarming with thousands upon thousands of debt-bonded workers. Towers hundreds of storeys high, scraping the hem of the clouds. When the Ruin came down, the Angels combined their firepower to blast the towers into molten soup. The soup then hardened into the Obsidian Sea.

Perhaps it was true what he'd heard others on board say. That the *Razael* must be in search of a fallen Angel, Angelfall having sent the whole port reeling, a prize more valuable than all the gems in Amberglasse.

A truth that tallied with a theory he'd been working on since the first one fell. What else could the damn things be but sky-bound tankers, or something similar? Everyone had seen Angel lights zipping and weaving above the Dead Red skies. High up, yet sometimes close enough to glimpse the fire they spat at one another in short, sharp bursts.

Grieve did not believe in those hundred storey towers, but Angels he could see and therefore trust. Even more, he trusted in the desperate greed that would send an unprepped crew like this sorry excuse for one hurrying across the Black. Had he lived, Grieve's own father would have led the charge, would have crawled on hands and knees to reach such a prize.

Late afternoon slid rapidly through dusk and into darkness. It wasn't safe to stop the ship, nor was it safe to travel through the night. The compromise was to trim the sails and edge along on battery power, with great curved mirror-arc lamps throwing silvery glare across the prow and sides. Back in Heel, the lamps had been in regular use, illuminating the docks during festivals and late night blessings of the fleet. But the sun-and algae-powered batteries were apparently untried. Untested—and for all anybody really knew, unused before this day.

Hired guns stood watch on deck in case of trouble. Trouble that was never far away. Grieve learned that many of the crew remained stubbornly loyal to Master Mohandas, the rich owner of the ship. That Mohandas was a fair man, even to the debt-bonded. That they didn't like or trust what had come to pass. That some of them thought the folks from Heel should not be following commands of foreigners, not even men carrying ancient relic-tech, garbed in flame and blade resistant skinsuits.

The moon was bright, casting a fair light of its own. Behind it, a glittering spread of stars. Small fires winked, scattered across the blackened landscape. They were not safe here. Not any of them.

According to his fellow crewmen, the *Razael* had crossed into the realm of deadly mechabeasts and magic. Undead sorcerers roamed the Black, fighting battles only they could see.

Grieve believed in sorcerers, or, rather, the painted tricksters and charlatans he knew such men and women to be. He'd watched such dandies swallow swords, spit flame, charm serpents, walk barefoot across burning coals. He had tasted their potions and seen through their lies.

But he hadn't come on deck for tales of supernatural creatures. Grieve had come to sniff out information, knowing he knew something that the rest of the crew apparently did not. That Master Mohandas had not sanctioned this peculiar operation. That the big, rich man was tied to a chair, just as much an unwilling voyager as the rest of them.

Grieve had been intending to mind his own business. To ride it out and see where the *Razael* would take him. But the foreign men were getting rougher with the captive father and his pretty daughter. There was more to this story than there appeared to be. The ship was not in search of fallen Angels, tankers, or any bounty he had heard of—and before too long they were going to hurt the girl in an effort to make the rich man cooperate.

Grieve lingered portside out of the way of rushing feet, reminding himself that pretty girls were easy enough to come by. He knew better than to stick his neck out—especially in such an uncertain situation.

But instead of ducking back down the companionway, close on the heels of two boys carrying gunny sacks, Grieve took out the last of the crumpled beadies from his pocket. He sauntered back to the aft deck, with its round barrels and smoking, idling men and as he bummed himself another light, he let slip some of the things he'd seen belowdeck. Words he regretted just as soon as they'd left his lips. He knew so well the folly of sticking out his neck for others, not something he was keen to do for any man. But for her . . . Maybe that was different. Two days he'd been spying through that crack in the wall. Two days waiting to see what would become of the rich man and his pretty daughter.

= THIRTY-FOUR =

Mohandas, well-known dealer in antiquities, sat firmly bound to a wooden chair he was too big for, his thighs jammed uncomfortably together. "I do not know what you want of me," he said wearily, tugging at his bonds. "You have my ship and you have me. And . . ." he added uneasily, "my daughter. Everything else that I possess is back in Fallow Heel. Warehouses, silos, stables, stock . . . Everything."

Kian, who had been pacing up and down with his arms behind his back, stopped suddenly and turned to face Mohandas.

Mohandas struggled, causing the chair's legs to wobble.

Kian stared into the big man's eyes with great intensity. "It is not every day I find myself coming face-to-face with a living legend."

Mohandas stopped struggling.

"Leave him alone," spat Allegra, slamming her heel against the wall behind, tugging at the ropes that fastened her wrists securely to a light fitting. "My father is a merchant—as any idiot can plainly see— his wealth lies in the goods he trades, few of which are stowed aboard this ship. Whatever you want, you will not get it unless you return us to Fallow Heel. Because that is where his property lies. Any idiot—"

"His property, to be sure," said Kian, "as you point out repeatedly, *any idiot* would realise. Master Mohandas is the richest man in all of Fallow Heel, as anyone I ask is sure to tell me. But that's not the name I'm interested in today."

"The name? What name? Just tell us what you want and be done with it," snapped Allegra. "Whatever it is, just take it and let us be."

Kian resumed his pacing. "My cousin here, Tallis, told me a fascinating story before I'd even set foot upon this ship. Tallis is good with people, a skill I've always struggled with myself." He paused to clear his throat. "Tallis smiles a lot. People like him. People tell him things—especially rumours. Especially when they've had a drink or two."

Allegra groaned and slammed her heel into the wall, again and again and again.

"Be quiet, child," said Mohandas, his gaze fully focused upon Kian. "We are all here civilised men. I'm sure that in time we can come to an—"

"Arrangement? Is that what you were going to say?" said Kian.

Mohandas fell silent and observed his three captors. He waited to hear what Kian was going to say next.

Kian cleared his throat. "Back home in Axa, Tallis was always overly fond of stories, the best ones having long been travellers' tales. A jumble of history and mythology, tales revealing how lives were lived in the years before the cities melted. Before we dug in underground for safety. Tallis particularly relishes such tales of bravery and adventure, of travel, exploration and discovery. Isn't that right?"

Tallis nodded, a wry smile on his face.

"Look," snapped Allegra, " I am tired and I am thirsty. I do not care about adventure stories. You have our ship and our lives are in your hands. Do you plan to bore us to death with the sound of your voice?"

"Allegra!" Mohandas's angry shout was edged with panic.

"Oh, but you are so wrong," Kian said, fixing his stare upon Allegra's scowling face. Tallis's stories are the best! Let me tell you one right now, seeing as I have your undivided attention."

Kian ignored Allegra's groans as she went back to slamming her heel. His focus turned to Mohandas. "How about the story of a grand pioneering family who set out many decades past, abandoning the comforts and privileges of birthright in order to explore the barbarian wastelands. The first explorer from that family died not far from home. Bandits, all too common in those parts—that is the story we were told, those who heard it second, third, or fourth hand much, much later."

The cabin had fallen deathly silent, aside from occasional groans and creaks and cracks of the ship in motion.

Kian continued. "The second hero adventurer made it back home some years later, but please, don't let me bore you with his details." His gaze flicked to Allegra when he said *bore*. "That's another story for another day. The third man is the one we're interested in, because we are all living his story today, right here, right now—are we not?"

Kian paused. Mohandas stared up at him, saying nothing.

"That adventurer's name was Raneesh Patel," continued Kian. "The darling of the Axan court, it's said he made it all the way to Fallow Heel—such as the township was back in the day. Just shacks and hovels perched at the edge of the Obsidian Sea."

Mohandas stared at Kian's mouth as he spoke, emitting no sound whatsoever, not even small creaks of the chair beneath his bulk.

"Patel's family did not know what had become of him, of course. Rumours abounded, as is always the case when someone of wealth and standing vanishes. Reported whisperings, imagined sightings of him here and there, supplied by rangers patrolling the Axa flats.

"Ten years after he disappeared, reports started drifting back of a brave new township on the rise, quite a step up from a few pathetic clusters of shacks and hovels, now grasping at fantasies of grandeur. Someone, it seems, knew *precisely* what to excavate for in the surrounding region. The kind of intel that can only be gleaned from pre-Ruin documents and maps. Old maps that had survived everything the wars threw at the world. Somebody knew what kind of relic tech the remaining fortress cities might pay coin for, might even fight each other to acquire."

Kian paused again, long enough for his words to sink in.

Allegra stared first at Kian and then at her father. "What are you trying to tell us?"

Kian cleared his throat. "That you are that man, Raneesh Patel—or Mohandas, as you took to calling yourself. You used Axan knowledge, tools, and expertise to plunder ancient war machinery and sell it to the highest bidder: enemies of our beloved city. A crime of treason punishable by death back home in Axa—only we're not back home in Axa, are we?"

"I have never heard such a ridiculous story!" exclaimed Allegra. "Papa, tell them . . . We buy tanker hearts-and-brains and sell them on—why should we not profit from the stupid creatures? If we did not, somebody else would step up in our places."

Kian smiled. "And I don't doubt many have tried. Back home in Axa, we do not call such items heart-and-brains. We refer to them by an older name: *operating systems*. Alas, no one knows how to manufacture such curios anymore, but some amongst us are skilled at their repurposing."

Allegra fumed, "I don't care what you call them. There is no treason in what we do, just honest trade which has nothing to do with stupid old stories and kidnapping people and—"

"But aren't you even a little curious about what happens to scavenged items you so quaintly refer to as reliquary? What competing fortress cities can build with them?"

Allegra tugged hard on her bonds. The broken light fitting slammed against the wall. "My father's name is Mohandas, not Patel or anything else. Cut me down this minute. The only barbarians in this room are you and those two idiots who follow wherever you go."

She started slamming the wall again, then stopped short when she caught sight of her father's grim, unreadable expression. "Papa?"

"If what you say is true—and I'm not saying it is," said Mohandas weakly. "If such maps were ever in my possession, they are not now."

Kian's shoulders slumped theatrically. "How terribly disappointing." He was not looking at Mohandas, but at his daughter's face and the incredulous expression upon it.

Kian continued to pace up and down theatrically, allowing Allegra time and space to think. Neither Jak nor Tal interrupted him. They knew their cousin better than to intervene at a crucial stage of negotiations.

"These supposed pre-Ruin documents and maps," said Allegra. "What might such things look like?"

"Be quiet, Allegra!" said Mohandas in severe distress, rocking back and forwards in his chair, straining at his bond with great futility. "My daughter knows nothing, she has no part in any of—"

Kian stopped pacing. He approached Allegra and demonstrated the size and shape of the documents with his hands. "Perhaps they would be made of plastic embedded with old-world smarts. I can't be certain. I've never seen such things before. Only heard about them."

"No no, she knows nothing! Do not touch her. Do not lay a finger or I'll have you whipped." Mohandas struggled against his bonds so hard, the entire chair crashed over on its side. One arm splintered as Mohandas struggled to free himself.

Kian shouted out an order. Neither Tallis nor Jakome moved, but two of Kian's hired men came bursting into the room, picked up the wailing, cursing triple-bearded man between them, untangled his bonds, and hauled him to his feet.

"Get him out of here," said Kian.

"Do not tell him anything, Allegra, I beg you! You don't know what you're dealing with. Those war machines were buried for a reason!"

Allegra waited until the hired men had dragged her father from the room. His wails and protestations echoed down the corridor. She turned her face to Kian to find him staring back at her intensely. "You will not harm my father. Not a single hair upon his head—have I made myself clear?" she said coolly.

The corners of Kian's lips edged upwards into a smirk. "You are not in a position to be giving orders."

Allegra stared at him defiantly until he pulled a dagger from his belt, unsheathing it with a swift snick. She didn't flinch as he raised the weapon to her throat, paused for a moment, then raised it higher and cut the cords binding her to the wall. With a few swift strokes, she was free.

She rubbed her wrists, still staring. "That's better. Now fetch some tea. My throat is dry and parched. Bring me tea and a chair and we can talk."

= THIRTY-FIVE =

On the captain's orders, the *Dogwatch* ploughed on past the tanker fields, past several of the massive mecha-creatures grinding, ripping, and roaring across the sands. Other craft of varying shapes and sizes veered in close, vying for space and chance and opportunity. Horns blared long, mournful notes, like the lowing of unseen beasts.

But the *Dogwatch* continued to build up speed, its mainsail plump with wind. Quick as an encroaching storm, a change came over those of the crew who had been watching the other ships and their tanker-jacks in action. A darkening of looks and mood. They'd been waiting for Quarrel to play his hand. To stop the ship or turn it in a wide arc, aiming its prow back to where the action lay. There were tankers enough for many crews to harvest, to make them all rich and fat. But Quarrel stood behind the wheel like a statue made of old world marble.

All eyes fell upon his broad back, angry for explanation.

"Why are we not stopping?" whispered Star to Lucius.

He pressed his finger against his lips, flicked his gaze to Grellan.

Grellan stared out across the churned-up sea of sand, watching other ships chase tankers, his eyes filled with longing, and his big hands pressed down on the rail so tight that Star was certain he would vault clean over the side.

When the last of the tankers resembled nothing more than scattered stones in their wake, Grellan let go of the rail and crossed the deck, stopping as close to the Templar as he dared.

"Why have we left the tanker fields behind?" he said, words spat directly in the Captain's face.

"Why indeed?" echoed Hackett, alongside two other brawny tattooed man, stepping in closer, hands upon their weapons. "Tis a fortune laying in wait back there. Enough to see us set for ten summers long."

Murmurs of agreement rippled through the crew, audible even above the biting wind. But Quarrel did not respond, did not even glance in their direction. When it came time for the ship to tack, the crew stood their ground. The *Dogwatch* began to lurch uneasily but the crew kept still, refusing to work until the captain faced them.

The ship slammed and shuddered, knocking almost everybody off their feet. Quarrel, standing steady, turned his head and barked over his shoulder, "Man your posts or the ship will flounder."

Grellan crossed his arms and puffed out his chest. "Not until you explain why we passed up honest coin. What we're doing here at all if we'll not be hunting tankers."

"Turn around and face us. We know what you are and you don't scare us," called a voice from the back of the pack.

Quarrel did not move. Not at first. Not until the vessel started losing speed, a small but effective act of rebellion.

He turned to find himself surrounded by a semicircle of angry crew, each of them with weapons raised and ready.

"Templar!"

"Knew it as soon as I clapped eyes on ya."

Quarrel stood tall and broad, holding their attention—and his own ground. "So," he said dismissively. "I'm a Templar—what of it?"

A hush fell over the grumbling men and women until Bimini stepped forward, a knife gripped in her hand, eyes shining diamond bright and hard. "You're big and strong, sure enough, but you can't take us all down. Who's gonna keep the ship in motion?" She gestured roughly at the rigging with her blade. "Wherever it is you're taking us, you need us to get there. So how about 'fessing up what's what."

Quarrel met her gaze but he didn't answer.

"We passed a smashed and broken reliquary back there near the tanker grounds," Hackett added. Scorched all over, burnt and torn. Reckon it was one of them fallen Angels, but you never made us stop for it. Didn't give two shits, you didn't. Even busted up, that thing's gotta hold some value. Them fortress cities—"

"Worthless junk," said Quarrel.

"But you said—"

"I lied."

There was silence, followed by the shuffling of feet, muttering, and the rasp of blades being drawn.

Quarrel straightened, standing at his full height, cloak tugged by the wind. "There are greater treasures on offer than tankers or Angels." His cold eyes glinted in the eerie light. The sky had shifted hue, throwing a gloomy cast across the Black.

184

"And what kind of treasures might those be?" asked a heavily-scarred man, a tinge of humour in his voice that did little to disguise the menace underneath.

Quarrel spoke carefully, loud enough for everyone to hear. "What's more valuable to you people, coin or kin? Your children and their future children. What coin value do you place upon their heads?"

Nobody said anything in response. The shuffling and grumbling lessened as all ears strained in an attempt to make sense of what he was saying.

"What's children got to do with anything?"

Quarrel paused, then spoke again, his voice louder than before. "We're gonna bag ourselves a Lotus Blue."

"A what?"

"A Blue—what do you think's been fouling up that sky?" Quarrel continued, gesturing out across the bow of the ship.

The sky had turned a sickly green, thick and glutinous as pus. Thickest at a point above the horizon.

"Blue's a relic-weapon," Quarrel continued. "The biggest. Very old and very dangerous."

"Never heard of it," said Grellan, backed by a chorus of muttering agreement.

"That arm of yours, it's tainted," called out Bimini. "It's made of relic—I've seen you talking to it. Show it to us. Can't trust a man who's not a man."

Quarrel uttered a gruff noise that might have been a laugh. "Can't trust men at all, ask me."

Slowly, he undid the clasp of his heavy sand cloak and shrugged it from his shoulders, then rolled up the sleeve of his left arm, holding it high for everyone to see.

There was an exhalation of gasps and awe as light glinted off the metal that was wrapped around and embedded in his arm. Metal fused so tightly to the skin that it seemed to be a living part of him.

As necks craned to get a better look, a wave of nausea washed through Star's guts. Her knees went weak. She felt like she was going to collapse. Instinctively, she groped for Lucius's arm.

Quarrel opened his tunic, exposing his pallid torso to the crew. Flesh threaded through with metal and reliquary. Patches of visible skin scored and scarred, old tissue pockmarked and roughly healed. A tapestry of skirmish, pain, and survival.

He turned slowly, arms out and completely vulnerable. When he had turned full circle, he pulled the tunic back over his skin.

"Ours is the holiest of orders," said Quarrel. "Templars fight to keep the old world in its place. Dead Red wasn't always dead—or red. It was once green and lush with lakes and streams. There were people here, too, once. Untainted souls not cursed with twisted spines and extra limbs."

"Bullshit," said Bimini.

He grunted. "Sure of yourself, aren't you?"

Nobody spoke for a long while. Star tightened her grip on Lucius's arm.

Eventually Bimini broke the silence. "Does it hurt?"

"Yes. Didn't always, but old Quarrel's wearing down. Parts are broken. Need replacements, only they don't make 'em like they used to. Arms, that is." He laughed. A hollow sound.

Nobody else laughed with him.

"That thing in your arm—what does it do?" asked Bimini..

"Tells me things I need to figure."

"Like what?"

"Metrics. Where to go and how to get there."

Bimini stepped up with great caution, ran her fingers gently across his skin's flesh-and metal surface. "So, this Lotus Blue you speak of— be it living or relic?" In her free hand, she tightly clutched a blade.

Quarrel shrugged. "Living, of a kind. Got a brain and reach and smarts, but it's got no heart."

"But what does it want?" shouted Hackett.

"Ain't nobody alive can answer that," said Lucius, raising his voice so all of them could hear it above the wind.

Quarrel looked hard at Lucius, and Star was given the impression that he was noticing the tankerjack for the very first time.

"Big man here speaks the truth," said Quarrel, "but I can tell you this. That Blue and me, we were built to fight. Those Blues were so damn good at killing, they vanquished all their enemies. Word is, one of the damn things has woken up and now its gotta be shut down."

"Says who?"

"Says the priests of Nisn Temple."

At the mention of Nisn, several of the crew drew a cross blade sign above their hearts, Grellan and Hackett amongst them, both adding the whispered prayer and left-side spit.

Star was about to ask Lucius what that cross-sign meant when exuberant shouting from above made everybody look. It was Goja, alert this time and yabbering like a monkey. Everyone peered up at him, then across the ship's bow to the place where he was pointing.

"Ship ahoy!" called Goja. "Ship ahoy!"

All argument was quickly abandoned as the crew manned their stations. The ship groaned, gaining speed.

Somebody hollered, "It's the *Razael*!"

Star's heart leapt. Allegra. She had thought she would never see her friend again, but perhaps there was a chance.

Crewmembers craned their necks to see and passed spyglasses from hand to hand along with a loudly whispered name—Mohandas.

"Reckon they're after the Blue as well?" said Bimini.

"All the fortress cities will be chasing it soon enough. Figuring whoever controls the Blue will rule the sands. But that thing cannot be controlled. Not by anyone. Not even my own kind."

"Girl?" Lucius's voice was deep with concern.

Star realised she was still gripping on tightly to his arm.

"You don't look so good. You alright?"

Star gave Lucius's arm a gentle squeeze while trying desperately to think of some excuse. "My friend is onboard that vessel," she blurted out. "Kidnapped alongside Mohandas, her father—I witnessed the whole thing. Tried to help but—"

Lucius shushed her but it was too late. Everyone standing close had overheard, so she had to explain what she'd seen and what she knew about the three foreign princes, how she was pretty sure they'd hailed from Axa, how she'd never known what they were after.

"The Blue," said Quarrel grimly. "We must hurry. Can't let them get their hands on it."

Star stood on her toes, hoping for a better glimpse of the ship, but all she could see was the now-familiar scattering of wrecks and obstacles, many of them wreathed in an eerie glowing mist that had not been there when the tankers were still in view.

She went for Allegra's glass. Lucius stopped her. "Not now. Cover your face."

She did as he said as the mist thickened into a sickly, stinking luminescent fog, rolling up and over the ship's sides.

"I've never seen anything like this," she said.

"I have. Once," Lucius said grimly. "Long time back. A thing I hoped I'd never see again."

Lucius nodded at Bimini, who had taken up her favoured position on the foredeck, long hair loose and streaming in the wind, sniffing the tainted air. Her head was cocked at an angle, with a bitter expression on her face. "Reckon she might have seen it too."

"Dangerous?"

"Hell yes."

Ahead of the *Dogwatch*, the Black appeared more sleek and sheer, with fewer obstructions. It would have been easier to steer a passage through if the sickly miasma had not been seeping upwards from the ground.

Star aimed the glass at a thickening patch of the stuff as the ship slowed out of caution. Any moment, she expected some fog-breathing demon to leap upon the deck, or for the hull to slam headlong into a jagged entanglement of ancient steel. Something Goja had missed, despite those reliquary goggles strapped to his head day and night.

Star dropped the glass and hung on to the side as the *Dogwatch* came about a little too quickly, causing the mighty portside wheels to lift. Not far—just enough to set them all on edge.

As the fog continued to drift and thin in patches, Quarrel relinquished the helm once more, then moved to stand beside Bimini. They talked in low voices so nobody else could hear.

"I don't know if I trust her," said Star.

"Good," said Lucius. "Shouldn't be trusting any of us."

"Not even you?"

"I'll have your back, girl, as long as I'm standing on this deck. It's after that you need to worry about."

She nodded uneasily.

He nudged her arm. "Nene said something to you, didn't she? Just before you were brought on board. Something that's had you rattled ever since."

Star paused for a long while to consider her answer carefully. "She told me she's not my sister."

"Not your sister? What she mean by that?"

"We aren't related. We do not share blood. I've been living a lie seven summers past—actually, who even knows how old I am?" she said bitterly. "To think, I would have done anything for her."

Lucius stared at her, his lined, tattooed face etched with an expression of deep concern.

"Girl, let me tell you what I know. Without that woman, you wouldn't even be alive. Oughta show more gratitude. More respect."

"Respect?" Star turned to face him, pushed him with her hand. "You've known it all along, haven't you? All these years. You knew!"

"Calm down, girl. Don't do to go showing emotion like that in front of this lot. Makes you vulnerable. Oughta know better than that by now."

Star fumed. "But you had no right to keep a secret like that from me."

"A secret like what—that you ain't blood kin? What does blood tell you about who you think you might or might not be?"

He made a ponderous show of shaking his head. "Tell you one thing, girl. Nene took you on when she didn't have to. Put her own life on the line. Crossed the open Red on foot with a clueless child in tow. Couldn't have been more than ten years old—bet you whined even more than you're whining now."

Star's face reddened. "You don't understand."

"Probably not—but neither do you. Nene loves you. Sisterhood ain't just about the blood. Actions speak louder than birthright. No one gets a say in what they born to. Only what we make of what we got."

Too angry to argue, she looked away, towards the Black and its mysterious green-tinged landscapes beyond the confines of the *Dog-watch* and its rickety railings. Trying desperately not to think about her arm and what it meant. What would happen if the others were to find out what she was.

Shouting eventually distracted her. Quarrel and Bimini getting into a fight. He grabbed her wrist. She tugged it free, pointing urgently at the sky. Star looked up and saw that it was changing colour once again, and there was something swelling and blooming right above them, roiling and churning and spitting blasts of light.

= THIRTY-SIX =

Quarrel's mesh stopped itching once they'd passed the last of the broken Sentinel towers. Telemetry from Nisn had been growing weaker by the mile, and the incessant ping and scratch, like the pestering of bugs and rats, was fading. No mind or matter. The mesh hadn't told him anything he could not figure for himself from the surrounding landscape. The ordnance he carried was built into his bones. The bits he'd let his crew folk see had barely been the half of it. No matter what they didn't see and didn't have to know. So long as they kept the old crate rolling towards their destination.

Those priests of Nisn didn't own him anymore. Old Quarrel was on a mission of his own, to prove he wasn't anybody's soldier.

Out this far, the Black was rent and buckled. Poison pooled beneath the surface, hot rocks and lava bubbling deep within the cracks and crevices. Belching toxic fumes and sour gasses. Enough to kill the lot of them if the crew didn't steer around the worst of it.

But they were good, this ragged gang of coin-greedy misfits. Quarrel crossed himself and spat for luck, praying to no god in particular that the *Dogwatch* might manage to hold together across the final leg. That the broken blister weeping in the sky was no more than it seemed. That the Lotus Blue was no more crazy that any uploaded five-star general consciousness was likely to be so long after the wars. With a stroke of luck, its memory might be turn out to be fragmented, its weapons powered down and locked on standby. The Lotus Blue, rendered impotent and harmless—and Quarrel rendered obsolete by default.

He moved to stand by the portside bow, gripping a handful of rigging to hold him steady. The ship was rolling, slow but steady, its wheels taking them around the worst of the cracked obsidian and its bleeding toxic fog.

He had gotten used to the sulphurous stink. No matter if it scalded his lungs, they only had to last a couple more weeks.

Quarrel closed his eyes and felt the acid sting of chem-laced breeze against his cheeks. Not long now and then he would sleep forever, dreaming of the world and all it had lost. Dreaming of a girl called Manthy, his girl, his love, his one and only. The things he'd had to do to set her free.

He felt a sharp stab behind his eyes and he opened them wide, shocked fully into consciousness. The pain was a pattern, repetitious, running through his mind, a sensation like steely fingers poking around in his head, prodding with surgical precision and intent.

It wasn't Nisn this time. Something else. The thing he'd been afraid of. Something best not mentioned to the others.

He slammed down his internal defences and flushed the intruder from his parietal cortex. It worked, but the pathway had now been gouged. Such an attack would come much easier the next time, and the time after that.

Quarrel looked over his shoulder, in search of the skinny girl with the growing mesh. Found her beside the man who had named himself as her protector, who had dared stand up to a Templar to try to save her. Grandfather and daughter was what they looked like, although that girl was nobody's child. She'd been vat raised, same as the rest of them. Where and how were the only mysteries—Quarrel had been so

certain he was the last of his kind, that the vats had been discontin-
ued, shut down after the Lotus Wars, when the name of Templar had
become a dirty word. So how was there such a recent hatching, and
how had she survived this long, found her way to Fallow Heel without
being put out of her misery? There was nothing more useless than a
Templar soldier without a war to fight.

No matter. None of it mattered when a raised-from-the-dead
uploaded general was trying to claw its way inside his skull. The mesh
would keep the Lotus Blue out in the short term, but the defenses
wouldn't hold for long. Quarrel was being hacked, like rats chewing
through his head, clawing at his synaptic junctions, scrambling his
neurons, trying to tell him what to think and do. Sooner or later the
enemy would have his way with him. Enemies as strong as this one
always did.

= THIRTY-SEVEN =

Aboard the *Dogwatch*, nobody had eyes for anything other than the
sick blue-green blister bubbling in the sky. Good, thought Star—
nobody had time to spare a glance for a girl with metal growing all
over her skin. An arm that ached continuously, a dull pain radiating
from the inside out, like her bones were hardening and thickening.
Like her muscles were clenching and repositioning. Metal the colour
of tarnished gold was pressing and burning against her yielding
flesh.

There was no doubt left about what she was becoming. Star had
never even wondered how a Templar was created, had presumed they
had been made the way the were: full grown and fully formed. She'd
never asked Nene—deep down, her sister probably already knew, or
at least suspected, which was why she'd been checking the arm of the
the Templar strung up at Broken Arch. Because she'd *known* what was
going to happen to Star eventually.

Star remembered how Nene had insisted upon calling it a man and not a thing. She also remembered the way their fellow Van travellers had hissed and spat as the wagons passed. They'd have hacked it to pieces with knives and axes had it been hung a little closer to the ground. Such was the fear of the Templar soldiers. Those things had two arms, two legs, and a face but they were not our kind.

Our kind.

And now Star was one of them. A monster. A creature. A thing. And Nene had known. She had known the whole way through.

If the *Dogwatch* crew learned the truth, they would likely kill her and tip her body over the side. The bulk of them seemed to have made their peace with Quarrel—all but Bimini—but that was because they now felt like they needed him to survive. Every one of them had families back on shore. People to love and homes to lose.

Star ran to Lucius and grabbed his arm, her fingers curved like claws. "You've got to help me," she pleaded in his ear.

He studied her face as though it was the first time he'd seen it properly. "Girl, you sick? You don't look so good. Looks like your blood might have gotten some poison in it."

"It's not my blood," she said, dragging him off the deck to a more private spot where they leant over the rail. The soupy mist below was thickening.

"You're sweating like a feverish dog," Lucius said. "You gotta tell me what's the matter, else there's nothing I can do to make things right."

She nodded, bent to pull one of the blades from her boot. She handed it to him, pommel first. Her hands were shaking, and she kept her voice low. "I'm going to show you something and you have to promise to cut it out of me."

Lucius said nothing, but snuck a quick glance over his shoulder, then up at the crow's nest. He took the knife, eyes on her bandaged arm as she unwrapped the fabric, loop by loop. She uttered a gasp when she unwrapped the last of the cloth and saw how much the metal had expanded, crisscrossing her skin and jabbing into her flesh.

Lucius stared.

"Cut it out of me," she begged quietly through clenched teeth. "Quickly, before it goes any deeper."

Lucius sighed deeply. His face clouded over, lips pressed tightly together.

"Do it," she said, "and hurry!"

Lucius tucked the knife into his belt, grabbed her wrist, and gently guided the arm into an available splash of light.

"Cut it out!"

He shook his head. "Too late for that," he said. "Thing's part of your arm now, dug in deep. Cutting's only going to make you bleed and scream."

She flinched when he placed his free hand upon her shoulder.

"The pain will stop soon," he said gently. "Looks like it's near finished what it's doing."

"How can you know that?"

She stared into his eyes and found them calm and full of reason—along with something else she had not anticipated: knowledge. She whimpered and snatched her arm away, fumbling to hastily rebandage it. Her hands shook, making a mess of things.

Firmly but gently, Lucius took the bandage from her hands. "Hold your arm steady. Let me help."

Tears squeezed out the corners of her eyes. "You want to help me—then cut it out! Please . . . I don't know what's happening to me."

He paused awhile to let her cry, then rewrapped her arm until no metal was showing. A professional job, tied off but not too tight.

She stared at him through bitter tears. "You knew about this already, too, didn't you?"

"Now is not the time," he said gently.

"Then when is it ever going to be?"

The tone of her voice was near hysterical. He grabbed her tight and held her against his chest, firm, but gentle.

"You gotta stay strong and you gotta keep this hidden," he whispered. "You tell the others you got slashed or burnt. You don't show this to none of them—no matter what. Okay?"

She didn't answer. She just kept on crying and he kept on holding her until the crying was all done.

= THIRTY-EIGHT =

The walls of the stateroom shuddered, glasses clinking against one another in the liquor cabinet as the ship made alterations to its course.

Mohandas's loud protestations echoed down the passageway. A door slammed and the shouting abruptly ceased.

Kian returned his dagger to the sheath on his belt, then dismissed Tallis and Jakome. Neither man moved at first, until Kian bellowed, "Leave us!"

When they were gone, he motioned to the rectangular wooden table taking up half the stateroom. As Allegra chose a seat, he moved across to the well-stocked liquor cabinet, removed a crystal decanter and two glasses. He poured a generous measure into each, and downed his in a single swallow.

Allegra took the glass he offered and raised it delicately to her lips.

"You expect me to believe you had no idea of your own father's true heritage?" said Kian.

She sipped then smiled, cradling the glass in her hands. It was heavy, its sides etched into thick diamond shaped ridges. "I have never before heard the name Raneesh Patel. My mother was from Makasa, from a wealthy fishing family. Six sailing ships, they had, and a hemp plantation. Her people thought she had married beneath her station."

Kian waited for her to explain what had happened to her mother—or mention her name, perhaps, but she didn't.

"You are curious now, aren't you," he said, "to learn what use tanker heart-and-brains are put to where I come from?"

"Operating systems was what you called them," she said. "What a curious name."

He nodded.

She paused, swilling the liquor around in her glass. "I'm certain your people make excellent use of relics." She took another delicate sip. "I should very much like to visit Axa. To see which of the rumours turn out to be true."

"What rumours are those?"

She laughed. "Surely you have heard what people say. That the men and women of Axa are sickly, pale as milk, with skin the texture of skink underbelly."

The corners of Kian's lips edged upwards into a smile. "Not so true, as you can see for yourself." He angled his head, as if inviting her to examine the colour of his skin up close, which was lighter than her own by a small fraction.

"As I can see," she agreed, taking another tiny sip of her drink. Just wetting her lips, not consuming any more of the fiery substance than etiquette demanded.

"Axa is your city, too," said Kian. "The Patels are an important family. I am certain they would welcome you back into the fold."

She nodded. "But my father's disgrace—"

"Is forgotten," Kian answered. "We will say no more about it. All that lies in the past—or, at least, it can be that way if you are willing to cooperate."

Allegra placed the glass down on the table.

Kian leaned forward. "So, do you know if he has those maps, or don't you?"

Allegra coughed delicately to clear her throat. "I know where he keeps his gold," she said, "I know which of the local houris are his favourites, how much protection money he skims from the vintners of Evenslough." She smiled at Kian with kindly condescension. "Sure, I know where my old man keeps his secret maps."

She picked up her glass and flicked her gaze to a particular painting hanging on the wall. Kian set down his own glass, stood up, walked around to the table's far side, reached to remove the painting with both hands, expecting to find a safe built into the wooden wall behind. But there was nothing, just an expanse of shiny lacquered wood.

Frowning, he looked to back of the painting itself. Four nails held the backboard in place. He lay it face down on the table, pinched his fingers, and wiggled out two of them. Allegra watched his actions closely, toying with her drink but saying nothing.

Kian tugged the backboard free. Behind it nestled three slender rectangles of shiny old-world plastic. He picked one up, tentatively, as though expecting it to disintegrate in his hands. One side was covered in a dark blue geometric pattern. The other side was blank and colour-less, aside from a symbol that looked like a small blue flower. When he saw it, Kian sucked in his breath.

"You need to speak special words to make them work," Allegra said. "My father knows the words. Let me convince him—"

"No," said Kian, flipping the plastic over, running his thumb over the flower symbol before placing it down carefully on the table's sur-face. "I will convince him my way. He will never volunteer such infor-mation without a mighty powerful incentive."

"You don't know my father."

"And you don't know what this is. What it means." He held up the flower symbol for her to see.

She shrugged. "Relics are worth big coin to the right buyers—what else is there to know?"

"The relic this map leads to must not fall into any hands but Axa's. That is what I know."

She nodded. "Then we are in agreement. We will find this thing together."

"But your father—"

"My father will come around. I will see to it."

"Your father is afraid of it—and you should be too."

"Perhaps." She put down the glass she'd been clutching tight against her chest and leaned forward. "We want the same things, you and me. Your people want to get out from under the sand, and I want to get off it. We're the same people, Kian. The same blood in our veins, so you claim."

"Maybe."

"Maybe? You just confessed to as much!"

"Ah, but you see, the thing is, I don't trust you. For all I know, these maps, impressive as they might be when we crack them open, are merely toys or fakes—that is what you people are best at after all." He pushed the maps to one side and rested his weight on the table's edge. "Do you understand what's at stake here?"

"Reliquary is reliquary," she answered, eyes upon the three slim sheets of plastic. "Some kind of weapon, I presume."

"Not just any weapon. If it's what I think it is, that map leads to a weapon so big and powerful it could change the very face of the sand itself. You get that, don't you? That relic must not fall into the wrong hands."

She nodded. "The hands of Axa's enemies."

"Precisely."

She flicked her gaze from the table top to meet his own. "I get it," she said, "and I'm right there with you. But not if you keep my father bound in chains."

Thumping and scuffling sounds emanated from somewhere above. More than just the usual creak and groan of timbers created when the *Razael* was in motion.

Kian slid off the table top to his feet. He'd been prepared to ignore all distractions, until a rifle shot rang out, clear and unmistakable. Others quickly followed, accompanied by shouts and screams. He opened a pocket in his skinsuit's torso and tucked the three precious plastic sheets inside. "Do not attempt to leave this stateroom," he told her. "Two guards are stationed outside this door. They've orders to shoot if you try to get away."

"What is it? What's going on?"

"Nothing I can't handle." He scanned the room, and Allegra could tell he was reluctant to leave her to her own devices. But he clearly didn't have many other options—the thumps and scuffles bleeding down from the deck were getting louder. So he left, closing the door behind him.

Allegra remained seated at the table until his footsteps faded. Then she padded softly to the door, drawing her head close to the wood to listen. It was only when she was sure she would not be immediately disturbed that she then made straight for a tallboy made of lacquered redwood. She tugged at the bottom drawer. Half stuck, it refused to budge until she gave it a swift kick. Once it was pulled free, she groped in the shallow space beneath, and retrieved a wire ring hung thick with keys. And something else—two small daggers, plain and sturdy. She concealed one inside her garments, then put the drawer back where it was supposed to be.

She began walking back to the table, but stopped herself midway and turned to face the back of the room, looked directly at a space on the wall. A place where the wood was cracked and splintered. There was a dark blemish there that she knew was not a blemish but a hole.

"I know you're watching me," she said. "I can see your eyes shining in the darkness."

There was a flicker of movement on the other side of the hole. Allegra looped the key wire around her wrist and tucked the second dagger into her waistband. She stepped closer. "Don't be afraid. I'm not going to tell him you've been spying. The *Razael* will not be his ship for very much longer. Especially not if I can count on you."

She waited, then took another step towards the wall, the keys jangling as she moved. "What's your name?"

There was no answer.

"My name is Allegra—but I suspect you know that already, and a great many other things as well, no doubt. Help me and I'll be forever grateful. I'll give you anything you ask for in return."

No answer still, but there was movement beyond the crack again.

"My father is a very wealthy man. Half the Black Sea tanker expeditions are backed by his coin." She brought a finger up to her lips. "Shhh, it's supposed to be a secret. The illusion of competition helps keeps the prices paid for heart-and-brains and other bounty high."

She paused very still and waited, rewarded by another faint flicker of light.

"Once this nightmare is over," she continued, "my father will be richer still, but right now he's in terrible danger, as are all of us upon this ship."

She shook the loop of keys from her wrist, and held it high so the spy behind the wall could clearly see them. "They'll have stashed my father in one of the cabins along the way. Probably the small one with the bird motifs carved into the door."

She lowered her eyes to rummage through the keys. Found the one she wanted and held it up. "Unlock that door and cut his bonds. Leave him with this knife, that's all I ask." She angled her body so that the dagger's hilt was showing at her waist.

The spy behind the wall remained silent.

Allegra smiled. "Do this for me and I will be forever in your debt, as will be my father."

More thumps and shouts echoed from above, followed by something louder, possibly an explosion. She glanced across her shoulder at her own locked door, then moved quickly to the crack in the wall. She held out the keys and pulled the dagger from her waist, offering it to the spy hilt first.

"Quickly, I beg of you. I will not forget your kindness—and your bravery."

She waited. What seemed like an eternity passed, but eventually a hand reached out through the crack and took the keys and the knife.

= THIRTY-NINE =

Here and there, the Black lay warped and buckled. Miasma oozed out of jagged rents like puss from a weeping sore. There was a stink in the air that made the crew's nostrils sting.

Slowly but surely the *Dogwatch* became enveloped in a thick and glutinous fog. A foul stench like nothing Star had ever smelled before.

"Ain't fog," said Lucius, as if he could read Star's mind.

She cringed away from it. "Then what is it?"

The other tankerjacks were growing restless; they clearly had no idea what to make of it. Only Quarrel remained unperturbed.

The crew covered their faces, but the fabric made no difference. The stink remained pungent and all encompassing, completely masking the greasy stink of the engines which had kicked in once the wind gave out.

Visibility was now down to a couple of feet, and the ship crawled forward.

"Was trying to save that bio-diesel for the journey home," said Lucius in a low whisper. They had no choice but to use it now. The wind had abandoned them. If the ship came to a standstill they'd be easy pickings, especially with visibility so low.

Eerie silence hung above their heads. Nothing to hear but the creak and groan of straining timbers. Now and then, a far-off howl of something living but otherwise unidentifiable.

"What animal makes a sound like that?" Star whispered.

Lucius shook his head. "Only been this far out before the once," he admitted. "Folks who was travelling with me didn't make it home. I shouldn't have made it either," he added.

"Air has turned to poison," said Bimini, loud enough for everyone to hear. "A sickness of the Earth itself."

Murmurs of agreement from crewmen rendered faceless by the fog, which continued to roll in, thick and heavy. The crow's nest was now completely obscured. Goja, if he was still alive up there, had fallen silent.

"The *Razael* is close—we're on her heels," stated Quarrel. "They made it through this stretch and so will we. The fog will pass."

"If it is fog," said Grellan said.

As if in response, the ship began to slow, then shudder to an abrupt halt. At first, no one said anything, not Quarrel, not the crew. The rigging slapped an irregular rhythm against the wood, wind whistling through ropes and battering furled canvas.

"It is not safe to stop the ship," said Quarrel warily.

"Too bad. What's done is done."

Quarrel shook his big ugly head. "You people have no fucking idea. Not one of you has ever been this far out before."

"Neither have you," said Lucius, hand clasped around his stave.

Someone up the back started coughing up phlegm and spitting it over the side.

"My lungs are reinforced with artificial filters—how about yours?" Quarrel said, addressing the entire crew. "How much longer do you want to sit here?"

More coughing ensued before they gave in, shouting and swearing to get the *Dogwatch* on the move again. But it was too late; the ship refused to budge.

"Something's fouling up the wheels," yelled Bimini over the side.

"Lantana raze," said Quarrel.

The green soupy fog continued to thicken and roil. There was talk about lowering a man over the side with a machete to try and free the wheels. Lucius squashed the idea, and yelled at the crew not to touch anything, not to let the deadly, weaponised weed get on anybody's skin.

All the while, Star was peering through the fog in vain, waiting for plans to be made and approved, waiting for the *Dogwatch* to start moving again. It was then, through the choking, stinking green, that she started to notice shapes, indistinct and spider-like—big as dogs—scuttling across the Black, darting between the cracks and bulges. She turned to Lucius, but instead found Quarrel, his head cocked at an unnatural angle, like he was listening to something at a frequency beyond the range of human hearing. Grellan was shouting in his face, and Quarrel was completely ignoring him.

"Shut up, Grell, I can hear it too," said Hackett, suddenly wide-eyed and standing to attention, arm raised, fingers splayed as if trying to grab onto something just beyond the fog. "Tankersong!"

They could all hear it now, high-pitched above the painful crunching and splintering of wood. The groan of metal tearing metal, the death growl of *Dogwatch*'s engine choking as it attempted to splutter back to life.

Star shrieked as out of nowhere, one of the spider things sprang up from the surface of the Black and landed on the deck, making immediately for the main mast, scuttling up the timber and into the obscuring fog. There was a piercing scream from up in the crow's nest—Goja. But there was nothing to see, the fog was too thick. Too impenetrable.

Somebody aimed and fired a clumsy shot.

"Don't, you idiot, you'll hit him!"

Another spider-thing jumped and landed on the deck. Bimini fired her crossbow and pierced the creature through the centre mass. It slowed but didn't stop entirely—the thing was made of metal, at least in part.

Another heavy thud upon the deck. Not a spider-thing this time but a fallen body. It was Goja, dead, his right arm completely torn away, those old brass goggles knocked off his face. Star gasped when she realised he didn't have any eyes, just wires protruding from the empty sockets.

Reverberations shuddered through the ship. Bimini was loading up another bolt when the deck was torn from beneath them, smashed to splinters by a mighty force slamming through roils of fog and choking damp. Harder than a ram raid. Rougher than the wildest kind of storm.

Star fell backwards, knocking into Lucius, who was suddenly beside her, grabbing on to him with both hands. Together they stumbled over disintegrating timbers, up and over the side of the ship, fumbling to climb down rather than jump but failing completely, knocking shins and elbows as they tumbled together, unable to see the ground through the fog and splinters. Star landed painfully on her side on the Black, her grip on Lucius lost. She scrabbled through fog-fouled air, screaming and completely alone.

"Lucius!"

Tankersong sounded again, high pitched and bone grating. Star's ears felt like they were filled with clanging bells. Her nostrils choked with thick and sour stench.

She grappled to find something solid to cling on to, anything. Disoriented, her mind spinning, she suddenly realised she was on her back, dazed and trembling, that awful sound possessing every part of her: her head, her eyes, her lungs, her guts. She tried calling out for Lucius, but was unable to hear her own voice over the high pitched, guttural inflaming, endless—

A wall appeared, mere feet away, in between her and where the outline of the *Dogwatch* loomed. A moving wall, streams of sand sloughed off its rocky crust. Not a wall. It was the side of a barnacle-encrusted tanker ploughing through the Black, pushing through cracks and rents in the solidified molten slag. Close enough for her to smell its stink. So close she could have reached across and touched it.

"Lucius!"

She cringed and kicked herself away from danger, scuttling like a crab. Scrabbling on to hands and knees, she pushed herself to her feet as the crazed thing came to a slamming halt, then retreated out the way it had come in a blur.

A wave of nausea, then the tanker was gone. Star was left wobbling on the Black, the surface around her cracked and brittle, continuing to spew gouts of poison from out of its openings. Before her lay a great and stinking hole, like she was staring right down into Hell itself.

Lucius? Where was Lucius? She screamed his name with all her voice, the gaping hellhole sucking up the sound.

An arm grabbed hold of hers and dragged her clear. It was Bimini, screaming at her to run.

"But Lucius!"

"He is dead. I saw him fall into *that*." She nodded at the black and gaping void.

"No. I don't believe you!"

Bimini dug her fingers into Star's arm. "Old man is gone. You cannot help him. Come with me or die here on the Black."

Voices shouted in the distance as Bimini let go of Star and ran. Star hesitated, just long enough to stare into the hellhole's depths, then at its jagged, gaping edges. There was no sign of Lucius, or anyone else.

Star ran after Bimini, the tankerjack already no more than a dark smudge barely visible through the fog ahead of her.

The ship, as she sprinted past it, was a mess of hinges and splinters, jagged strips of torn butyl, material rendered unidentifiable by the ooze. The crew were scattered, at least those that weren't already dead. But soon all that was behind her, and all that remained was the ragged edge of the Obsidian Sea, the stinking fog, the strewn rocks, smashed wreckage and a select few survivors who had made it through, and were now shipwrecked in the middle of nowhere.

= FORTY =

The General has been utilising his time to great advantage, practising the generation of polyp storms. They are soft and blue, so beautiful; creations pulsating with gelid light, trailing sensory apparatus from their underbellies, as well as stingers and umbilicals for latching on and drinking power.

The Lotus Generals had once controlled such weapons with their minds. It was their greatest triumph—any old grunt with the right configuration of keys and codes could let loose a stream of missiles; all you needed were access, power, and initiative. But the polyp storms were germinated in chambers deep within the Earth. Seeded small, then grown and birthed in a blazing ejaculation of terror, fire, and glory. Each one a unique and precious work of art, guided by mimetic ember consciousness, a lust and longing to discharge, to bleed their fiery sting into a target.

Some of these storms get moody. Some of them get lost. The General focuses his fury and births a big one, sends it hurtling across the Black Sea in a howling rage, Johnny scattering in its wake. There'd been other names and terms for enemy soldiers, more denigrating, more insulting, but Jacks and Johnnies are the names that stuck.

The General synchs his sensory apparatus to the storm's frequency, then deploys initiation codes. He savours the sensation of pressure building, knows it to be an illusion but doesn't care.

The storm he grows is fierce electric; graceful, delicate, and hungry. The damage it causes is plentiful, but it is not enough.

The General has been working hard, and has many other tricks tucked up his sleeve. He's forged a method of talking to the battletrucks and tankers—which doesn't mean they listen, mercy no, but they can hear him—and some of them are relishing a bit of two-way dialogue. A change for the better, their memories are rekindled. They have someone else to do their thinking for them. Long decades racing across the Red have reduced them to their basest animal urges: to fight and flight and slam and scream, sucking sustenance from the mangled corpses of their brethren. They know it's wrong but they can't remember how they used to feed.

Do it my way, says the General. Some of them reckon they might as well give it a go, especially when they catch sight of his beautiful storms. So blue and bright. So impressive, especially when the General sics one onto an eight-wheeled armour-plated barrier basher, slams it sideways and the whole rig dissolves before their eyes.

The tankers are messy and individual. He has to convince them, one by one. Not like those nice and clean cut, brainless Angels. The General suffers from regret. He wishes he hadn't dropped so many of them down out of the sky. He might have made better use of those Angels if he'd been thinking straighter. From now on, he resolves he will be more sparing with his limited resources.

The excavation of the bunker complex is going better than the General might have hoped. Slow at first, with only a handful of willing Templars to use as implements. All crazy, every one of them, so many broken down to the point of uselessness. But they've managed to dig down into the compound, burrowing like rats into a cache of equipment intended for construction of other bunkers and other compounds in other centuries. Earth moving equipment. Getting it out has not been easy, getting it fixed and started even harder. He's lost many Templars, clumsy oafs ground to paste between slipped cogs, but more have come, answering his call, walking in across the desert from who knows where they've been hiding out all these years. Some half dead like animated corpses. Some no longer resembling men at all. But they come to the bunker, get down, and start digging. Moving sand and shifting beams. Babbling on about the glory days, believing all the lies the General feeds them.

His Templars have cleared a big rectangular grid: A forty-eight-element high frequency antenna array, preserved in still, hot sand. Beyond it stands a power generation building, imaging riometer, and a flat-roofed operations centre built of cinder blocks. The General is planning to investigate reinvigorating ionospheric enhancement technology for radio communications and surveillance. Bring the cluster of ELF wave transmitters back online, slamming their 3.6 million watts up at the ionosphere.

In time, he'll have the whole thing patched up and running.

After a week of clearing the array, they dig out the dishes and the towers. By use of satellite, the General can now see much farther than before, can listen to the faintest signs of far-off lands and places. A crypto-anarchic chittering and murmuring via strained quadruple diversity propagation paths. They are out there, others like himself. He has no confirmation yet, but is sure of it.

Others of his kin and kith. Clever mecha, not the big dumb brawn barrelling across the flats but a chain of super capacitors, each with a Lotus General at the helm. There would be evidence of high level dynamic reconfigurability—evidence of his own kind. That is what the General listens for.

= FORTY-ONE =

Tully Grieve tugged hard upon his chains. The half-dead man beside him moaned. The man chained to his other side had ceased his moaning hours ago, and now he slumped forward, urine pooling beneath him. Grieve had not yet been desperate enough to attempt to drink it.

Spread out before him and his companions—a handful of luckless would-be mutineers—stood a row of giant metal birds. Not birds, exactly. Things like birds, set neatly side by side on the cracked and weatherworn concrete. Reliquaries of old-world metal, with wings as though they had been made to fly, even though they were mostly wrecked and torn now, dangling like broken limbs. Some still had their silver skins, others corroded bellies betraying innards long ago picked clean by Dead Red scavengers.

He'd never seen anything like those birds—and Tully Grieve had seen a lot of things. The Dead Red Heart left its mark upon a soul. The things you saw could never be unseen.

But a graveyard full of metal birds? Back home they'd never believe a word of it.

This was all the fault of the pretty girl aboard the *Razael*.

Allegra—she had asked him for a favour, just a small thing, nothing much. Pretty girls were always trouble. He should have known better, never should have taken those keys from her. But he never learnt, no matter how many times they bit the hand that fed them. A strange old saying—one he'd picked up from his uncle, a man he apparently took after much more than ever had been good for him.

The breeze was gentle, tempered, presumably by the ministrations of the battered Sentinel. Still standing tall against the elements. Without it, the metal birds would long have disintegrated and there'd be nothing here for him to stare at while he waited to die of dehydration and exposure.

The ridiculous thing was, Grieve had gotten away with so much up until that girl had charmed him. He'd been stealing food and water right from under the noses of the galley crew, growing bolder, taking it out on plates and a tray, claiming everything was on Master Kian's orders. It had been easy enough once he had learned the name of the foreigner with dark curls and golden earring. "Master Kian wants this, Master Kian wants that." Master Kian got anything he wanted, so Grieve had taken charge of it, blustering about with his nose in the air, like the *Razael* was his very own ship and he some kind of right hand man to the foreigners.

And why not? It had worked before, that kind of bold and brazen trick—and it would have kept on working, he was certain, even with the ship under constant alert, with the deck continuously hammered by wind-slammed rubble and even with three foreigners lurking below behind closed doors, leaving the heavy duty sailing to the drunken pigs they'd hired back in Heel, pissing off the artisans who loved the ship and thought of it as their own. That some form of rebellion would eventuate was inevitable.

All that talk of maps and documents of a very mysterious kind. Fancier than maps of the Vergelands, from Summersalt through Grimpiper—anyone could get hold of maps like those. That anyone had bothered to chart the wasted stretch along the Sand Road fringe was the only wonder of such maps.

But the kind of maps the rich old man had stashed behind the painting—now there were curiosities worth taking risks for. Of course he had wanted a closer look, just like he'd longed to get closer to the girl. Close enough to smell her sweat, close enough to confirm that she really was scared, no matter all her bluff and bluster.

But it wasn't all her fault. Not really. He'd found the door with the birds carved into the wood—and the pretty girl's father. Cut his bonds and given him the knife, done everything she'd asked. Her father had been half crazed from rage and dehydration, had grabbed that knife and gone tearing up along the companionway, screaming loud and blue bloody murder, believing his daughter to be somewhere up above amongst the danger.

Grieve sniffed. Yeah, in hindsight that was the moment he should have left well enough alone—as his cousin Selene would have said. Only he didn't, because he never did. He had to go on charging up the stairs after the mad old man, had to end up right in the thick of the fight. Not his fight even—somebody else's. A handful of half-drunk sand sailors who had presumed Mohandas to be spearheading a rebellion. Who'd taken up arms and started attacking the ones the foreigners had put in charge of the ship.

But that sad old man had not been leading anything. He'd seemed to be half mad with terror, certain that something frightening and indestructible was waiting for the ship beyond the Black. Swinging punches until somebody knocked him cold.

Grieve was the one who had been clapped up in irons and thrown off the ship alongside a handful of *opportunistic* mutineers. Men who'd seen their chance and taken it—and failed. Brave men—stupid but brave, he'd give them that. But not as stupid as Tully Grieve, who once more had gotten caught in the wrong place at the wrong time. Possibly, this time, the last and final effort.

Tepid breaths of wind blew ineffectually in his face. The hairs on the back of his neck stood on end. A couple more hours and the sun would have its way. The moaning man beside him slumped further forward. There'd not been time to learn his name, or any of their names. The other two beyond him were already dead.

Grieve sniffed. The scent of something strange hung in the air. Something he couldn't see. He pictured wild dogs creeping up behind him. The wind in his face grew stronger, obliterating all smells and clues. Without the strength to fight off dogs, it was better not to know. Only it wasn't. Not knowing was never better than anything.

He used the chains—and the dead men's weight—to heave himself to standing. Dizziness swam and nausea punched but he fought them back. He was not dead yet. He could stand and he could turn.

What he saw stopped his breath cold in his throat. A great storm raced across the flats towards him, thunderheads encased in boiling bloom. Forks of lightning stabbing from its centre. A storm that looked like a living, breathing creature. But the storm was not what held his full attention. At its base, seven people were running for their lives, tiny forms against the monstrous clouds.

"Come on!" he screamed—or tried to. Not much sound escaped his parched throat but that didn't stop him from trying. "Come on! Run faster!"

A storm like that was not of natural making. It was a witch wind, an old-world weapon, either something long forgotten and triggered randomly, or else cast by weathermancy. Forbidden knowledge that should have died along with the wars that had spawned it, along with so many other abominations. He would have crossed himself but his hands were bound.

Distracted by the spectacle, he tripped and fell on top of his fallen comrades. He wanted to get up, truly he did, but his legs were tangled in chains and dead men's arms. His head hurt from where it had cracked against broken concrete.

The sky directly above turned black. Minutes before it had been pale blue as ibis eggs, the ones he and his cousins used to steal from dune top nests, never taking them all because that would mean next season there'd be no birds.

= FORTY - TWO =

Star ran. There was nothing to hear but her own ragged breath and the palpitations of her heart. Nothing to see but thick green fog, thinning in patches through which she glimpsed dark, indeterminate shapes and moving forms: human, spider, or something else.

She ran. Fear had the better of her, drove her forward, kept her going, wouldn't let her stop or let her think. *Lucius was dead and she was on her own.*

Then there were cries audible in the distance. Bimini's voice, male voices calling in response. Gradually she became aware of the repetitive patter of her own footfall, boots slapping sharp against the ground, tripping up on rocks and cracks but never falling. She knew she couldn't afford to fall again.

Star slammed into something warm. It was Bimini, arms out and ready to catch her around the waist. Star wanted to speak but her words were all jammed up, all jumbled and trapped inside her throat.

In the end, words were not required. The two women headed off together. Bimini seemed to know where she was going. They ran until Quarrel was within their sights. The Templar seemed unharmed. He marched like a machine, pacing far ahead with broad strides, leading them towards a rocky island, visible in glimpses through the fog, the only form of shelter close enough to reach on foot. It might be shelter, but Star doubted it would be safe—there were no safe havens out upon the Black.

"Keep up," said Bimini, hurrying to catch him, crossbow at the ready, checking all around for signs of danger.

As the fog cleared, Star could see both Hackett and Grellan lagging far behind, mesmerised by the remains of the rapidly disintegrating ship. Eventually one nudged the other. They ran to catch up with the others, seven *Dogwatch* survivors in total, following Quarrel through no man's land toward an ominous island of rocks that, up close, did not look hardy enough to protect anything. A half-filled waterskin slapped uncomfortably against Star's side. A stitch soon began twisting in her gut, slowing her down as Bimini raced ahead.

Beyond the miserable rocky outcrop, more rocks and a tangled mess that looked like thick, dark weed. Hard to tell through the bilious green. Not weed, she realised on closer inspection, but matted strands of sand-scored plastic, like lantana raze, but still and harmless—hopefully.

Wind snatched at Star's hair as she moved. The temperature was dropping, cooling the sweat that dribbled down her spine.

Beyond the thatch of plastic strands, more rocks. Too green to make out detail. Running, running, the others in her sights. So long as she could see them, she could make it.

A blast of lightning lit the sand ahead of her, sand churned by the boot prints of the others. Star saw Bimini's silhouette ahead, the tall, muscular woman having leapt up to stand atop an outcropping.

Star reached her as the stitch cramped up her side. She bent forward, gasping for breath, desperately glad of the pause. When she looked up, Bimini was examining markings on rocks.

"What is it?"

No need to ask—she could see it for herself. A pattern cut deep, some kind of boundary marker, like the ones that dotted the Sand Road's Verge.

Another blast of lightning close by and they were off and running again. Star struggled to keep pace with her with pain lancing down her side.

Grellan and Hackett eventually caught up with them. Four was safer than two. Nobody spoke, all focus was on keeping moving, until Hackett cried out and pointed up.

Visibility was low, but they didn't need much light. A net like the kinds used for snaring tankers, only ten times bigger, was strung between two jutting spars of rock. Something stuck at its centre like a fly in a spider's web.

Bimini made a ward sign and whispered a muted prayer.

At first Star thought it the skeleton of a bird—only no bird had ever been the size of a wagon. Two solid, tangled, silvery wings were entwined in weathered plastic weed. The thing's belly was slashed open, and remains of long rotted metal and plastic entrails spilled out.

Bimini glanced upwards and froze, her face illuminated by a storm hovering directly above them, pulsing with bright flares of light, expanding and contracting like it was breathing.

"Move!"

They took off, ducking beneath the web and its mysterious, rotting captive. Star dodged quickly, half expecting the shiny metal bird to come crashing down upon them. But it held fast.

They emerged onto open sand to find Quarrel slapping at his mesh, shouting at it, not liking whatever it was telling him.

"The storm has seen us," shrieked Bimini over the howling of the wind.

Star looked up. There was no sky. In its place was a glowing cavernous maw, bearing down to suck them into its gullet.

Quarrel shouted orders, but the wind snatched his words away. It didn't matter—they really had no choice but to follow him until they died—or made it.

The safety of the rocks was soon far behind them, and they were heading as fast as they could towards something ahead still half shrouded in stinking green. A flat expanse, human made, not Black. The structures upon it were still intact, which meant there had to be a Sentinel. They ran, hoping Quarrel's mesh read true. Hoping they weren't running at a mirage.

The blackened, roiling, breathing storm chased them. As they neared their destination, Star felt a strange sensation; a tingling brush against her skin. It was the protective umbra of a Sentinel tower, recognised by her still-forming Templar mesh, somehow she knew it was, a Sentinel still functioning all alone in the middle of this strange and deadly nowhere.

"Thought that thing was going to swallow us," said Star, leaning over to take deep breaths, holding her position until the cramps in her side finally gave up and let her be.

"Same." Bimini smiled. It was the first time Star had ever seen her do that. She had nice teeth. White and mostly straight. "Not a mouth," she added. "An eye. Eye of the storm."

"It chased us like an animal," said Star.

"Why do you sound so surprised?"

"It's alive?"

"Not the natural kind of life. The other kind. One of those things they built to do their fighting for them."

Bimini did not need to explain who *they* were. Them. The ones who caused the Dead Red Ruin. The ones who made the world the way it was.

"Get any of that green poison on your skin?" Bimini spun Star about to check before she had a chance to answer, then checked herself, her arms and legs.

Seven were all that remained of Quarrel's crew, two of them men whose names Star had never learned. Between them, they had a little water and some well wrapped chunks of salted roo. Not enough to get them far—assuming there was anywhere to go.

Once they'd made the safety of the Sentinel's outer reach, all but Quarrel collapsed, panting to the sand. The Templar stood much like a Sentinel himself, surveying the small pocket of civilisation the mesh had guided them to.

"Planes," he said. "Used to call them planes. Jumped out of my fair share of em."

He pointed. Star pushed herself to her feet, the others not far behind.

"Birds of metal," said Bimini. "A good omen. Must be a safe place."

Safe from storms, if nothing else.

"Safe for some, not so safe for others," said Grellan.

Hackett nodded, checking his weapons before heading out to investigate.

"You watch yourself," shouted Bimini.

He raised his hand in acknowledgement.

The others followed cautiously, all but Quarrel. He kept his eye on the strange cloud creature, hovering just beyond the Sentinel's range. He kept consulting his mesh. Arguing with it, clearly not comfortable with the turn of events.

Neither was Star. The loss of Lucius had left her stunned. He'd sworn he'd never return to the Black, had sensed all along his was to be a suicide mission. There was no satisfaction in being proven right.

She turned her back on Quarrel, and made the effort to catch up with the others; to keep moving, the only thing to do. There was nothing safe here, nothing familiar. She was on her own. From now on, she'd have to look out for herself.

The others had reached the planes already. Star knew of such things—one of Nene's books had pictures, but she'd never had any concept of the scale. Shiny metal casings, supposedly light enough to float on air. Ridiculous, like so many old world stories.

Yet here were rows and rows of them, baking placidly in the heat. A hundred people could have fit inside the belly of each one. Maybe more. Some had metal surfaces intact, while others were nothing more than frames, years of rust and salt and sand gnawing at their bones.

The ones intact had writing on their sides, symbols or faded pictures. Flowers, women, animals with wings. Tribal totems. This must have been a holy place, or the meeting place of kings and queens. Not knowing filled her with a sense of loss.

Nene would have been excited. First she would have sketched the layout in her journal, then poked and prodded at the planes themselves, climbing inside if it were possible to do so.

"Look!"

Grellan's voice. Star looked to where he pointed, and saw blue paint smeared across some weathered metal skin of one of the planes. It was a flower symbol, clearly added far more recently than any of the others.

Star could sense Bimini's nervousness as they passed between the rows, giant nosecones towering above their heads. Some cracked open, spilling shadows across parched flats.

There were no obvious signs of current habitation, but that didn't mean a thing. The unforgiving ground seemed to suck up the sound of their tread.

"Like we're being watched," Star said.

Bimini nodded quickly. "We should go back. Find some place to hide. We've come too far already."

Too far, alright. Time passed at an altered pace out on the Black. It bothered her that she already couldn't be certain how much long it had been since leaving Fallow Heel. A week, perhaps, or maybe even two?

"Hey—what's that crazy Templar think he's doing?"

Star looked to where Bimini pointed. At first she couldn't see anything of interest. Just more rubble-strewn concrete, hard and flat, its surface cracked and crumbled in many places. Like plants had pushed their way up through, then dried up and vanished. She didn't notice Quarrel until he moved from a crouching position to standing. He had apparently skirted around the planes and gone to investigate something the others couldn't make out from this distance.

"Should we—"

"Smells like a trap," said Bimini quietly.

Star nodded. She wanted to see what was going on, but she wasn't going anywhere without Bimini.

The two of them watched as the others hurried over to see what Quarrel had found. Hackett coiled like a spring ready to pounce, knife already drawn, expecting trouble. Grellan got there first and kicked something lying on the ground. Whatever the something was, it didn't move.

"Come on," said Bimini.

Star pulled one of the small blades out of her boot and followed. She kept looking back over her shoulder at the still and silent planes. It felt like they were being watched, either by people hiding in the rusted bellies, or perhaps by the ghosts of the ones who had constructed them.

Star gripped her blade tightly as she and Bimini approached what she could now clearly see was a pile of corpses. All men, apparently, different ages and different hues of skin. Heavy chains around their limbs. Dried blood trails and drag marks. Bodies hastily dumped in disarray.

Bimini made the sign of a cross above her heart. She looked to Quarrel, waiting for instruction.

Grellan glanced back uncomfortably at the planes, perhaps also feeling that they were being watched. He turned his back on the corpses, both pistols raised and ready. Just in case. Hackett kept glancing back at the open sands, out past the Sentinel's invisible influence. The angry cloud that had chased them was long gone, but a thick pall of green hung heavily over the landscape. They could well have been followed after the ship was rammed and wrecked. There was no taking anything for granted.

All of them waited for Quarrel to say something but the Templar's attention had turned to scanning the horizon.

Star put her blade back in her boot. The dead men's limbs were bound with heavy chains. Their dirty clothes were splattered with dried blood.

But as she leant in closer, a guttural sound came from a tangle of arms and legs. Star's heart lurched. She jumped back instinctively. Bimini stepped forward, her knife raised, expecting trouble.

One of the corpses moaned and opened its eyes.

= FORTY-THREE =

The dead man who was not dead had bright blue eyes, stark against his pale, sun ravaged skin. He was young, no more than twenty summers. He sat up as though he'd just been sleeping.

"What happened here?" said Quarrel, no longer scanning the horizon. Not trusting anything or anybody.

Blue Eyes stared up at the Templar, taking in the measure of him and trying not to cringe. He glanced furtively at the rest of them, then back to Quarrel, obviously their leader.

"Thought that witchwind storm was gonna catch you." His voice was rough and scratchy. "Please—can you spare me any water?"

Star stepped forward with her waterskin. Bimini put out her hand to stop her. Star ignored her, pushed on past, knelt and held the skin up to his lips.

Blue Eyes gulped two long, grateful swallows. "Thought you'd all be cut up and spat out for sure."

"You were watching?" said Star, stoppering the skin up tight. Not stopping Bimini when she pulled her back up to standing.

Blue Eyes tilted his face to her and smiled. "Nothing else to do round here—unfortunately." He raised his hands to reveal wrists tightly bound. One of his legs was cuffed to a thick grey chain.

"What's your name?" said Star.

He opened his mouth to answer but Quarrel cut him off. "Report what happened here."

"Treachery is what happened here. A fight on ship. Rest of the crew abandoned us here to die. Some of us were dead before the ship took leave."

"What ship?"

Blue Eyes smiled again. "The finest ship you ever did see, all tricked out in brass and polished wood."

When he flicked his gaze in Star's direction, she felt her own expression softening a little. The *Razael*—what else could he be referring to?

"What's that ship doing so far out here?" said Quarrel.

Blue Eyes hesitated. "They're chasing down some big old relic. Very valuable, apparently. They've got maps and charts and blueprints. Old world things with lines that move upon the page." Chains clanked as he attempted hand motions to explain

Quarrel said nothing.

"Name's Tully Grieve," Blue Eyes announced suddenly, his attention on Star. "What's yours?"

Quarrel turned his back on Grieve and the pile of bodies, threw back his sand cloak, and started tapping at his mesh. "Secure the perimeter," he instructed both Grellan and another man, both of whom were squinting at the row of planes as if expecting trouble from them. "We rest up a couple hours, then set off at first light."

Then the Templar strode away from the others, slapping his mesh and mumbling to himself as they had all seen him do so many times.

The big smile vanished from Grieve's face. He shouted, "Hey, aren't you going to cut me loose?"

Quarrel kept walking. He didn't respond.

"Wait! You can't leave me here to die!"

Quarrel ignored him. He called out to Grellan. "There's water here somewhere, but it's contaminated, and there's not much of it. Better than nothing. Find it and boil it."

Grellan nodded. He shouldered his weapon and moved off in the direction Quarrel indicated, towards a series of squat cement bunkers in a row, the nearest two sporting sunken roofs.

"Wait! Come back. You could use my help!"

Quarrel lowered his mesh and turned to Grieve with deliberate slowness before shouting back at him, "You're a criminal. Your crew left you to die here for a reason."

"No, no—not my crew. No reason whatsoever—you've got it all wrong! A misunderstanding. All a terrible mistake. There was a mutiny—you're right about that—but I had nothing to do with it. I was just a galley monkey. Peeling spuds and swabbing decks. Fetching and carrying for the finer folk—honest!"

The corner of Quarrel's lip curled. He didn't say anything.

"Mutiny?" asked Star. She stepped closer. Bimini didn't try to stop her this time. "Tell me about the ship."

Grieve raised his bound hands, pulled at them in frustration. "Belongs to a rich man, name of Mohandas, held captive alongside his daughter, as was I. As were many, many others. I never wanted to come here. It's all been a terrible mistake."

Grieve talked quickly. He was smart. Having won some attention, he was desperate to milk it for all it was worth.

"A very pretty daughter. Somebody would pay big coin to get her back."

"Allegra."

"Yes yes—that's her name! Allegra! Do you know her?"

"Is she alright? Did anybody hurt her?"

"No no, last I saw her she was fine." He stared at her intently. "A friend of yours?"

She nodded.

Quarrel was now out of earshot. Bimini was still there, but remained expressionless.

Grieve continued. "All hell broke loose back on the Black. Smashed sandcraft on fire, pus oozing out of the ground. The old crew didn't like where the new crew was taking us. Poisoned air—we barely made it this far!"

He glanced uncomfortably across the bodies of his fellow mutineers.

Star crouched over each one to check for life signs. "Two of these men still breathe," she shouted loudly. "We can't just leave them here."

The others watched as she pressed two fingers against a slumped man's neck.

"Death has put its mark on them," Quarrel called out—she hadn't realised he was close enough to still listen in. "Got no water to waste on dead men."

His hearing was sharper than that of an ordinary man. He walked away, his sand cloak disturbing the stillness of the air. Bimini and another man followed, leaving Star alone with the mutineers, both the dead and the living.

Star stood up and shouted after them "Wait!"

Nobody was listening—other than Tully Grieve who was staring at her intently.

The slumped man was old, his breath slight and laboured. As gently as possible, she propped him up straight. He didn't fight her. He didn't even realise she was there.

"Somebody help us," she shouted.

Nobody looked back—not even Bimini. They wanted no part in this.

The sound of Star's voice triggered something in the old man. He began to shout and clutch at the air above his head. Gently, she laid him on his back and shielded his eyes from the sun. His lips were cracked and blistered, his eyes milky. Almost blind.

"Shhh," she told him. "It's alright."

She removed the waterskin from her hip and dribbled liquid through his mouth. Just a sip. He smacked his lips in appreciation.

"You have to get up. Otherwise they'll leave you here."

"I can see his face!" The man's eyes widened, his pupils no more than tiny specks.

"Whose face?"

"Hear his voice! Ah. So beautiful . . ."

"There's no voice but mine," she whispered.

"Such jewels! Ah. I thought I might die before he blessed me."

Gently she shook his emaciated shoulder. "Come on—get up. You have to move!" she pleaded.

He couldn't hear her. As she looked around for something soft to place under his head, the old man's body wracked with spasms.

"Beautiful!"

He could not get up. He was almost gone. What would Nene do? Star knew full well the answer to that—and it sickened her to the stomach.

She laid his head down, pulled the longer knife from her boot. Placed his bony arms across his chest. Took a deep breath. "Goodnight, old man. Sleep sound." She angled the blade and did what she had to, exactly how Nene had shown her, even though she had never had to do it before on her own. A short, sharp thrust through the armpit to the heart. A death as quick and clean as anyone could hope for.

The old man died without a sound. Star got up and checked the others. All dead. No need to use the knife again. She wiped the blade clean on the dead man's trousers, then looked down into the eyes of Tully Grieve, the lucky man who had talked his way into a second chance.

"A friend of yours?"

Grieve shook his head. "Didn't know him. Didn't know any of them. Just in the wrong place at the wrong time, as usual."

She didn't trust him. She didn't trust anybody except Lucius, but Lucius was gone. She felt a lump welling in her throat. She could not think about him, not now, maybe not ever. Star wiped the blade and slid the knife back into its sheath.

"I'll fetch Grellan, he'll know how to get that chain unlocked," she said, then went to find a quiet place to sit.

= FORTY-FOUR =

Marianthe paced up and down the worn linoleum. In the cool recesses of her Sanctum, she'd had time to think, time she was not required to waste on the practical mechanics of day-to-day existence, the feeding of mouths and the fetching of water, the bartering and arguing necessary to keep a secret community whole, alive, and thriving.

She'd instructed her followers not to fret about the blister hanging in the sky, nor about the colour of the sky itself: a sick, disgusting daub. *The sky is readjusting,* she had offered as explanation. Not all of them believed her, but they kept up with their farming and other chores.

She wasn't yet sure what she believed herself. Something had manufactured that anomaly. Something smart and ancient, the likes of which she'd hoped had been stricken from the world for good. A something that had also been forcing the tankers into peculiar behaviour, to run in grid formation like a regular assault battalion. She remembered with an involuntary shudder the cities they'd lain waste to.

Her drones confirmed it: across the sand, *something* was digging itself up and out. Something with a brain, but not a heart. War machines were never built with hearts.

She stopped her pacing and sank into her chair. Everything was dangerous these days, that was why she had built this community so far off the beaten track, way on past the end of the Earth. Because anything good gets eaten up alive, chewed and spat, then dug down deep and buried, like a bone—or maybe an insane general way past its expiry date.

She forced herself back up again, and hobbled over to the altar, lit one of her precious candles with a tinder box, and placed the crown of thorns upon her head. The name she'd given to the thing made her smile whenever she thought of it. *Crown of thorns*, and nobody left alive to get the reference.

No matter.

She punched in the requisite code that would connect her with the Warbird, her one true friend it seemed some days. This was one of them. She waited. The connection always took a while and sometimes it wasn't possible at all.

First there was a hiss, then static, then the connecting tones. She dispensed with the customary formalities and launched right in. "So, my friend, what have you got to say for yourself this time?"

Warbird didn't answer. It didn't have a voice. Instead, one of the smaller screens flickered to life and "Nh3" appeared in large blocky font.

"Knight to h3. Good move." She translated the play to the hand-made pieces on the board. She'd made the chess set herself from little salvaged items: the pawns were tap heads, uneven and mismatched, the king a plastic tube with a bright blue top, the queen a broken doll without any legs.

Now Warbird's Knight can swing over to f2 and fork my King and the Rook on d1. It looks like he has at least a perpetual check now. If I move the Rook to a1 to avoid the fork and protect my pawn on a6, he's got Rook to g7 and I'm almost mated. There's no way I can queen my a-pawn in time.

The Warbird almost always beat her. She thought about her options for a bit, and ultimately decided that given everything that was happening, she wasn't in the mood for chess today. If she was forced to move the settlement, where would everybody go? She'd sent her drones out scouting many times in preparation for such an eventuality. JuJu had reported a few oases, all too small, not much potential, nowhere big enough to feed them all.

Marianthe wanted the settlement to stay together. She wanted to keep the dish, its comfort and its shadow. Some day she planned to get the array cleaned up and booted once again.

Some day.

She was musing on this possibility when the bank of screens lit up and spluttered to life—even the big one sitting high upon the wall, and she'd not seen a flicker of light on that screen for years.

Startled, she brushed her hand against the chessboard, knocking over the tube but not the doll.

This was not the Warbird's doing. The screens showed a variety of images: moss covered rocks, a tangle of tree roots. Trunks tall and thick and cool. Shafts of sunlight striping a verdant lawn. Water falling from a high place, tumbling over rocks. Light bleeding through a jungle canopy, illuminating a tangle of creepers, fronds, and vines. Cows in a field. Blue sky. Thick white fluffy clouds. Rice paddies terraced up the curve of a hill. Water. So much water.

"What is it you want from me?" she said out loud, her voice ringing hollow in the cavernous, empty space surrounding her.

The screens—whatever was controlling them—didn't answer.

"Who are you? Identify yourself."

Something like this had happened once before. A week ago, or had it been longer? Screens blazing suddenly to life—though only the small ones then—but the intelligence who made it happen never spoke. She hadn't been certain any of it was real.

This time was different. This time she was certain.

"What do I have to do?"

To make it happen. To make it all real. To put things back the way they were supposed to be.

= FORTY-FIVE =

Night fell across the boneyard of planes. Flame crackled in a rusted, cut down oil drum where Hackett had built a fire. Blackened sand skinks roasted over the top on elongated splinters. Grieve had proved himself skilled at flushing the skittish creatures out from under piles of rubble, which was fortunate as they didn't have much food.

He helped himself to a couple of skinks. Nobody tried to stop him. He made his way to the rocks where Star was sitting away from all the others. "Mind if I join you?"

"Yes."

Grieve smiled. He sat down beside her—close, but not too close. She shuffled along a little—but not far.

"So how'd you come to get mixed up with one of those?" he said as he licked his fingers and picked a skink up off the metal scrap he was using for a plate.

The roasted lizards were tough and sinewy, but he gnawed away with grunting relish, his manners reminiscent of a campfire dog's.

"One of those what?"

He nodded in the direction of the oil drum fire and the ones who stood around it talking in low voices. "That Templar."

Star chewed the last of her mouthful and swallowed. "Don't know what you mean."

Grieve snorted. "Sure you do. Look at it. Twice the size of a normal man. Twice as fast too, if you've ever seen one in action."

Star stared at the others illuminated patchily by flame. Quarrel was the only one not talking. He didn't seem to be doing anything, just towering above the rusted drum and its heat.

Grieve wiped his greasy hands on his pants. "They're supersoldiers, grown in tanks. Hundreds of years old, some of them."

"Bullshit." She wriggled a little further along the rock trying to get comfortable, taking the opportunity to check that her bandaged arm was not showing beneath her sleeve.

"It's true—some of 'em even older. Veterans of Maratista, Crysse Plain, Crow Ridge, Woomera. Same vintage as the battletankers, some of 'em, according to my cousin Selene, although you don't wanna go believing all her crap."

"Like I don't want to go believing all of yours."

He laughed. "Suit yourself." He took a sliver of wood from his pocket and began picking at his teeth. "Where you from?"

"None of your business."

"Sheesh. Just trying to make a bit of friendly banter. Where you from, what's your name. The kind of things you ask of any stranger."

"I saved your life today. Isn't that friendly enough?"

They sat in silence for awhile, Star compulsively checking on that sleeve, hoping he would go away, or that Bimini or one of the others—even Quarrel—would call her over, give her an excuse. But Bimini had her back half turned as she warmed her hands by the fire. Quarrel moved to stand on his own, staring out across the Black, as she'd seen him do so often. Troubled by the lurid sky and things that only he could see.

Grieve flicked the wooden splinter to the sand. "Templars don't sleep and they're damned impossible to kill. Got vat-grown bones strengthened with titanium alloy. They heal real fast and their blood's not like blood regular. More like the stuff they drain out of those tankers. They reckon a few survived to roam the Red, and the mountains too, only that one . . . that one's way too civilised to have been roaming the Red for centuries, don't you think?"

"I think you're making all this up," she said, checking him out: pale skin streaked with sunburn and skink grease. Matted hair in even worse condition than her own.

He shrugged. "Been around the block a few times. Seen a thing or two—and what I haven't seen, I've heard about."

"So which was it that saw you wound up chained to a row of dying men? Something you saw or something you heard about?"

Grieve gave her a strange little smile. Straw-like hair flopped across his eyes as he poked at the sand with the skink skewer.

"Wrong place, wrong time, bad luck, same as always."

"What's that supposed to mean?"

He shrugged.

"You got family out here somewhere?" she asked.

"Did have. Once."

She nodded. She understood.

"How about you?"

She straightened her back, attempting one more time to shift into a slightly more comfortable position. "No. No family."

He nodded, poking at the sand with the skewer, drawing patterns then scrubbing them out again.

Star did as Quarrel was doing. Stared out across the Black for signs of the vicious storm cloud creature that had chased them from the wreckage of their ship. She tried not to think of Lucius, imagining his face as he slid through the stinking fissure, arms reaching up to clutch at empty air.

"So how come you know so much about Templars?" she asked.

Grieve kept stabbing at the sand. "Don't know much, really. Just what everybody knows. Selene was the real expert. She done dealings right up at the Lucent steps. Couple of 'em stand as guardians to the pass."

"Selene?"

"My cousin."

"So you do have . . ."

He shook his head. "Don't have anything. Not anymore." He stared at his feet. "Don't even know where I am. Got myself as far as Heel. Reckoned it as good a place as any."

She nodded at the mention of the town she had so desperately longed to call her own.

"Tell you what I do know for a fact," he continued. "Those Fortress Cities are on the rise. Waking up after centuries of slumber." He stabbed in the direction of the fire. "Back on the Sand Road, everyone's been fighting long and hard to make a go of it. Doing it lean while the Red keeps creeping and the storms bloom fierce. But those deepdown city folk, they bunkered, sat out the worst of it. Hoarded all that food and water. Could have shared it, helped us out but they never tried. No front gates on those Fortress Cities. No way in or out. Ever been up close?"

Star shook her head.

"Don't blame you. There's mines aplenty and Templars roaming, half-crazed from the sun. They left us behind to do the hard yards and now they'll come to strip it all away. You just watch."

He shoved the end of the skewer into his mouth and chewed thoughtfully. Spat it out again. "Don't you trust that *thing*, no matter what it says. Its promises aren't worth shit."

They both glanced across to Quarrel. Seeming to sense them, he turned to meet their gaze.

"Gives me the shivers," said Grieve.

"I don't trust anybody anymore," said Star.

"Very wise," said Grieve. "Very wise. Especially with everyone chasing that old-time war reliquary down."

She sat up straighter. "What do you know about it?"

He laughed. "Only that it must be made of solid gold, or something even more valuable. What the hell else would anybody be doing way out here at the arse end of beyond . . ." His voice trailed off, and he gestured towards the planes behind them.

She turned her head and looked. "World must really have been something, back in the old days."

He nodded. "Yeah, I guess it was."

She smiled to herself. A private smile, something she didn't want him to see.

"So, that beautiful girl, Allegra, you said you know her?"

"We're friends," Star said, pleased that he seemed so impressed, although she wasn't certain why she felt that way.

Grieve angled his body around to face her. "Good friends?"

"Used to get invited to her mansion all the time. We had tea with cups and saucers made of old-world porcelain. Fancy foods on platters I don't even know the names of." She stared wistfully at the stick trails he'd been drawing in the sand. "Lots of food, there was."

He nodded. "Sounds like the right kind of friend to have."

"They snatched her off the docks—she didn't do anything wrong."

"Don't worry—her kind always land on their feet."

She was about to ask him what he meant by that when he interrupted.

"So where are you sleeping? Feel like—"

Star shot him a filthy look, snatched up the torn scrap of sail she'd planned on using as a blanket, and headed for the row of planes while there was still enough light to see by. She'd picked the one she wanted earlier, when they'd done a cursory reconnaissance. She didn't feel safe with the others. Not with Lucius gone. Yet without sleep, she'd be as good as useless. *Templars never sleep, what a crock.* She'd have stuck close by to Bimini, only the woman seemed to have vanished already, found herself a private place to kip.

"Don't follow me," she called back over her shoulder.

Grieve raised his hands in mock surrender. "No fear. Not after seeing you acquit yourself with a blade."

She smiled that private smile again. She was almost starting to like him. Wanted to like him, but now was not the time and this was definitely not the place. Maybe if they ever made it back to Fallow Heel . . . But that place seemed such a long, long way away.

She climbed up into the belly of a plane by way of a rusty ladder placed against its side, moving carefully—two of the rungs snapped off under her weight.

At first there wasn't much to see. Darkness, a metal cave with light bleeding through a large gash in the side. When her eyes adjusted and she moved a few steps in, she saw two cooking pots and a mattress brittle with dust. Human bones draped loosely in scraps of rag, picked clean by the ages—or maybe rats. Remains of three adults, two children and a dog. A plastic doll with big blue painted eyes. Other faded things she didn't know the names of.

Star picked up the doll, cradled it gently as if it were a kitten. An ugly thing with a head way too big. Nobody had ever looked like that.

Sections above her had been torn away. Through the giant rent she could see the bright white band of constellations: the bull, the warrior, the twins, and the dog. Moving amongst them, Angels, some dancing, some pushing on in a steady line. Others travelling solo, swimming lost and lonely through the diamond peppered darkness.

Why did the Angels fight each other? What had brought so many crashing to the sand? Those were questions not even Nene knew how to answer.

As she drifted into slumber she realised her arm was no longer painful. But she wasn't ready to remove the bandage and examine the expanding metal's progress. She'd do it in the morning, by the light of a new day. Tomorrow. Everything would look better in the morning.

= FORTY-SIX =

The *Razael* slowed suddenly, its timbers creaking and shuddering. The crash of breaking crockery and loud swearing echoed down the corridors, audible through the thin bulkheads of the stateroom.

"That girl is pumping you for information," said Tallis, leaning in closer to his friend, making sure he had his full attention. "You can't trust her or anything she says. The father is more reliable. He knows what lies in store for him if we ever get him back to Axa."

Kian lent comfortably back in his chair. He was only half listening, had barely touched the wine Tallis had poured. His thoughts were scattered: from the landscape they were travelling to the knowledge that he had made it farther from home than any Axan adventurer before him. Beyond the Red and beyond the Black. Beyond the limits of his family's reach.

Limits. It had always been about the limits, the self-imposed restrictions people back home allowed to weigh them down and fence them in. More than half of Axan scholars were convinced the world had blown itself to pieces. That what was left remained deadly and uninhabitable. Kian sniffed. Dangerous, yes, unavoidably so, but deadly was an overstatement. The post-Ruin world presented challenges, that was all. Nothing he and his people couldn't handle.

Tallis clicked his fingers. "Kian, are you listening to me?"

Kian shifted in his chair. "I heard you."

Tallis nodded, his stare unwavering. "She's playing you. Feeding you the lies you want to hear."

Kian smiled. "Don't worry, Tal. She's beautiful to be sure, but I'm no fool." He picked up his wine and sipped it thoughtfully, then raised his glass to gesture at the row of framed pictures spread about the walls of the captain's cabin. Each one a curiosity: an ivory palace with a splendid dome, tall white columns flanking either side. A cliff with mighty torrents of water gushing over its edge. Four men's faces carved into grey mountainside.

"Each one of those places used to stand. Perhaps they're standing still, waiting for the rest of us to wake up, crawl out of the ground and find them."

Tallis's expression remained grim. "We could die out here," he said. "Go up on deck, take a look at the sky. Tell me you've ever seen anything like it. The ones who attempted to mutiny and turn us back were frightened by it—and I don't blame them."

"Superstitious idiots," said Kian. "But that girl? She's something special. Always thinking about the future. How to twist each situation to make it go her way." Even thinking about her made him smile. He leant back further in the chair, placed his feet upon the shiny hardwood desk that dominated the cabin. "You've got to respect that line of thinking, even in your opposition."

Kian sunk further into the chair's comfortable leather depths—leather that was probably older than he was. Everything on this ship was old and fine. The fat old man had exceedingly excellent taste.

His mind drifted to the dreary parade of simpering dolls his uncle had so helpfully introduced to his father's house, all marriageable prospects, high born with important clan and trade connections. Fragile things, delicate and wan as old-world porcelain, each one utterly indistinguishable from the other. His uncle would laugh heartily, slapping him on the back, assuring Kian that he didn't have to *like* them, just select one to be the mother of his children, sit next to her at Solstice, Equinox, and Commemoration day banquets. Whatever he got up to on his own time was his business.

Allegra could not have been more different. She was no doll, she was a firebrand. A force of nature. Every time she spat in his face he felt himself liking her a little bit more for having dared. Chained to a wall under threat of pain, and still she spat and swore and made demands! It would be such a shame if he had to kill her. Hopefully, it would not come to that. The girl was smart enough to cut herself a deal, he was certain, even if his bodyguards were not.

Tallis paced the length of the thick woollen carpet. "There's more you should know. Rumours about that thing you say is out there," he said.

"Superstitious people, like I told you," Kian replied. "The Lotus Blue, if I recognise that symbol correctly, is no more dangerous than those ancient tankers, and so far none of them have managed to put even a dent in this vessel's side."

Tallis had nothing to say to that, which was just as well because Kian wasn't in the mood to argue. Since they'd stopped to dump the mutineers back amongst the broken planes, he'd been spending most of his time below talking with Allegra, learning what he could about Heel life and commerce.

Whereas Tallis and his brother had spent most of their time on deck, making sure the snarling, dejected crew could see them, ensuring another mutiny did not take place. Jakome had, apparently, already pitched one troublemaker over the side, swiftly and without chance for argument. All three were in agreement about one thing: that they could not afford to stop the ship again, despite the open sand being thick with tankers screaming their hideous songs at one another, moving in bizarre formations, making patterns, then changing them with lightning speed. The *Razael* would have to push on through while the way ahead was clear enough to travel. The Lotus Blue was the only thing that mattered. Treasure of one kind or another lay within its walls. Perhaps something none of them could clearly imagine; the operating system of a weapon beyond their comprehension, at best a broken heap of junk—but what if it wasn't?

Kian was certain adventurers from other fortress cities would help themselves if Axa didn't stake its claim. Raneesh Patel had been easy to find once somebody had bothered looking in the one same place the man had lived untroubled across decades. They would never get a better chance than this. And the girl would help them. She didn't have a choice.

"She'll kill you, cousin, at the first opportunity! Kill us all, seize control of the ship, turn it round and steer it back to port."

Kian responded to Tallis's intrusion with a patronising glance. "No she won't. Not so long as I have her father serving as collateral. Cousin, when that girl looks at me, what do you think she sees?"

Tallis shrugged.

"She sees her future. The fact that she is one of us. Better than those savages she was raised with." He leaned forward, slammed the glass down on the table. "What's good for us is good for her, even if she has to fight her own father to get her hands on it."

A sharp rap on the door startled both of them. Kian got to his feet as the door swung inward, and one of the red-coats reporting from on deck entered.

"Captain, something you need to see. Tankers pulling up alongside the vessel."

"Preparing to ram?"

"No, I don't think so, but you need to see for yourself. They seem to be racing us."

"Racing?"

Tallis shot through the door and up the companionway, not waiting for Kian to catch him up.

"This voyage proves more interesting every day that passes," said Kian to the red-coat who nodded deferentially and shut the door behind them.

= FORTY-SEVEN =

Star awoke with a start, wondering where she was at first. Not curled up beneath the green-and-blue wagon, nor snuggled by the dying embers of a communal Sand Road fire. Not with Nene. Nene wasn't her sister anymore, and Lucius . . . Lucius was gone.

It took a moment to remember she'd gone to sleep in the belly of an ancient metal plane on a concrete island out beyond the Black. Something was wrong. She sat up, peered through the battered silver skin, down to where the half-drum fire had burned the night before. Quarrel was shouting down below. One of the nameless men was trying to explain something. Badly, apparently—Quarrel knocked him to the ground with a single blow.

Tully Grieve was nowhere in sight. Star furled up her makeshift blanket, slung it over her shoulder. She needed to piss but that would have to wait.

She jumped from the rusted ladder onto cracked concrete.

Hackett and Grellan stared at her in accusatory silence, her boots loud in the still, crisp air. Bimini clambered clumsily down from another plane, one which still had wings attached on either side.

"Is he up there with you?" shouted Grellan.

Star shook her head, as there was only one person he could have meant. "Haven't seen Grieve since nightfall."

He looked as though he didn't believe her. "Then he's taken off with the waterskins, plus what was left of the roo."

"And Jarvis," added the nameless man. "Jarvis is missing." His off-sider.

"You shouldn't have wasted water on that boy," said Quarrel, glaring across at Star.

"Should have shared your suspicions if you had 'em," shouted Bimini, hurrying across the cracked cement to join the conversation.

"Can't have got far. We can hunt them down," said Hackett.

"They're not worth the effort," Grellan added.

None of them were staring at the open sand. They stared at Star, as if Grieve's betrayal of their trust was somehow on her shoulders. Not fair—she was not his keeper—no need to make the point. He had sweet-talked the lot of them—and Jarvis as well, evidently. But deep down she conceded there was probably a damn good reason he'd been left chained to die a horrible death.

Speculation was useless—Grieve was gone for good. He was a canny one. A survivor. Not fool enough to ever let them catch him.

Quarrel turned and stared out across the Black. Above it, the sky was a flat, discoloured expanse. No sign of the creature-storm that had chased them from the splintered *Dogwatch* ruins. The patch of bruised and bloodied sky remained above the horizon, the same place they'd first caught sight of it from onboard the ship. No bigger than it had been the night before.

"Boy's words were all bullshit, nothing he said can be trusted," said Quarrel.

"Oh, and your lies can be trusted, I suppose," snapped Bimini. "We are only in this predicament because of *your bullshit*. Promises of tanker and Angel harvest—remember those?" She made a big show of looking around. "I'm not seeing any tankers. I see only dead things here. Nothing worth a single coin—or life."

"Agreed," said Grellan.

Quarrel stared her down. "Mesh guided us true. How else you think we found this place? Blind luck?" He forced a laugh, a sound that slid very quickly into coughing. "Damn sand gets into everything." He sniffed. "We've got a job to do, nothing more to be said about it."

"Your job, not our job. How are we supposed to reach this dangerous weapon you speak of without food and water?"

"Get your shit together. We're moving out," he replied.

"We don't have any water!"

"The ship that dumped the boy's got water—and supplies."

"The *Razael*'s probably sailed right off the Black by now, and they're probably salvaging the blue weapon—if it even exists—as we speak."

"That ship hasn't found jack shit," said Quarrel.

"How could you know that?"

Quarrel raised his arm and jabbed it in the direction of the sickly sky blister. "They don't know how to handle that Lotus. I'm the only one who knows that trick."

"The only one—is that right?" Bimini stepped up closer to the big man. "I don't believe you. Don't believe you know what you're doing—don't believe you're who you say you are. We're lost—I say we better start looking for water."

Murmurs of agreement lingered.

Quarrel turned his back on the lot of them. He strode off, the sand cloak sloughing from side to side.

Star followed, keeping her distance, all the way up to the Sentinel. She watched him stand before it, staring with what appeared to be great longing. He sighed heavily and then, ignoring her, made his way to the nearest of the planes and started rummaging amongst the piles of junk scattered across the warped and buckled tarmac.

Star ran to catch him up. "What will happen to the people aboard that ship?"

Quarrel tugged a spanner from a tangle of twisted metal shards and banged it hard against a concrete slab, wiped the corrosion off onto his pants. "They're all gonna die."

"What?"

He laughed and banged the spanner harder, holding it up to his eye and squinting. "Made in China—will you look at that. I recall when China was a thing. Back before—when you weren't even spit in your mother's gravy, little girl. Not that you ever had a mother."

He threw the spanner over his shoulder and continued searching noisily.

"What do you mean they'll die?" said Star. The plane above their heads loomed large, made fierce by a mouthful of jagged teeth painted on either side of its nosecone.

"Everybody gotta die sometime. Even me, apparently." He yanked a long piece of metal free, gave it a quizzical look, then tossed it aside.

"What about that storm creature that chased us from the wreck? You keep staring back as if you expect it—"

"Least of our problems," said Quarrel, hauling out another piece of junk. Appraising it, then setting it down gently at his feet.

"My friend is on that ship," said Star. "An innocent girl taken against her will."

Quarrel paused. "Innocent? Innocent? No such thing as the innocent rich." He yanked another piece of metal from the pile, wiped sweat from his brow.

"Grieve said they were going to try and harvest the Lotus Blue."

Quarrel turned, metal bar gripped in his meaty hand. "You don't harvest a Lotus—it's practically a god. It'll kill them, and it'll kill us too."

"But you're going to try to stop it?"

"Kid, I don't have any choice." He brandished his mesh at her. "You don't either."

She took a step back.

"Stick close. But first things first."

With the metal bar gripped tightly, he marched towards the Sentinel. Star ran after him. "Where are you going?"

He didn't answer. When he reached the Sentinel he worked at prising the metal hatch open with the bar, huffing and grunting, giving it a kick or two to loosen the bolts. "You can watch if you want but I'm not gonna share. Not enough juice left for a decent high."

Star glared at him in disbelief, her mind ticking over, remembering. "You were at the Vulture. You're the one who . . ."

"Damn straight."

Star felt the pieces falling into place. "You broke the taboo on entering and then you broke the Sentinel. More than a hundred of my people died!"

The hatch was finally coming loose. A few more kicks and then he was inside.

"Stop it!" She lunged and grabbed his arm. With a beast-like roar, he picked her up and hurled her through the air. She landed hard, slamming up against the side of a rusted skip, banging her head, crawling on all fours, managing to stand, then collapsing to the dirt.

When Quarrel eventually emerged from the hatch still clutching the metal bar, Star watched him through blurred vision. He staggered, tripping over his own feet like he was drunk.

She clambered up and shouted, "You killed my friends!"

His skin was flushed and glowing with vitality. He grinned. "Killed me a lot of people's friends across the years. Collateral damage they call it, don't you know?"

Her vision cleared. "Without a functioning Sentinel, this place will get trashed by storms."

"So fucking what—what's it to you? Why you get so jumped about everything?" He leered in closer, "They're not *your* people—or *your* kind. Haven't you worked out what you are yet?"

Star felt sick in the stomach. "I'm not like you!"

His eyes went wide. "Liar liar, pants on fire—and you don't know the half of it." An involuntary shiver rattled down his spine. He smiled, then waggled the metal bar menacingly. "Never met a five-star G who could tell a story straight. They sent us out into the thick of battle with broken weapons, contaminated food, pissweak shelter, fire raining from the sky. All talk of honour and safety and the future—those polyp storms piss acid, bet you didn't know that. Only one thing makes polyp storms, and it looks like it's back in business."

Quarrel stabbed the bar into the concrete, making it crack. He stood over the damage, tall and proud like a mighty hunter, even as he swayed woozily.

"Nisn always lied to us. Told us all the Blues were dead and buried. The buried part was true enough. Damn things dug themselves deep underground. They were always smarter than the think tanks and ordnance wombs that spawned them anyways."

"What is a polyp storm?" Star's voice sounded so weak and insubstantial.

"Rogue Blues couldn't be bargained with. With minds of their own, it was them that tipped the balance. Was them that lost the war for everyone. Armies stopped fighting each other, got sent out to fight the Blues instead. No one realised what they'd created until it was too late to stop them."

He paused and looked to her, as if expecting another question.

"Who won?" she asked carefully.

He guffawed awkwardly. "This look like a winning world to you?"

"We're alive, aren't we?" she said. "Sand Road's filled with decent folk. *We* didn't forge the Dead Red Heart. *We* didn't start any wars."

Quarrel stared at Star blankly, blinking. She braced herself, expecting more shouting, or an argument at least. Instead, a subtle sound like tinkling bells.

"What do you want now?" the Templar screamed.

She cringed, backing off when she realised that he was screaming at his arm, not her. At the mesh and its private messages.

Star kept still, not risking any sudden movements.

"You're not fooling me. I'm not risking my life for you. Not bringing a single scrap of *it* back for you to get your grubby mitts on."

"It's a fucking bomb," he yelled at her. "The Blue ones were the worst. You can kiss your arse—and your precious Sand Road goodbye . . ."

She turned and fled, suddenly remembering something Lucius had said. Lucius, who had known all along he would die out here. *I can smell the stench of suicide upon that Templar. A one way trip. That Templar won't be going home again.*

"They're not your friends," Quarrel shouted after her. "They're not even your species!" He staggered, giddy, tripping over his own feet.

The others were approaching, attracted by all the shouting. Star hurried back to try to shush the Templar but he pushed her away. "I don't give a shit about them and neither should you. We have a job to do." He attempted to straighten himself up and stand proud, despite his heavy intoxication. "I need you and you're stuck with me."

"I'm not going with you. I can't—"

He grabbed a fistful of her shirt. She tried to twist free without ripping the fabric. The others started running towards them.

"Let me go—please!"

She struggled with him until Bimini caught them up, her face clouded with anger. "Let her go."

Quarrel ignored her.

Bimini raised her voice so all could hear it. "Look at him—he's stoned. I say we take him down now while he's weak and confused and can't fight back," spittle flying as she let loose the words.

"No," Star pleaded, "You've seen him fight. He's too strong. Too dangerous."

Quarrel did not appear to be listening. He dragged Star, struggling, to a position where he could see the horizon, out through a gap between two planes. He began mumbling prayers and mantras, denotations offered to the open sand.

"Now's the time," said Bimini through gritted teeth. "We might not get another chance."

Grellan and Hackett had moved to catch up. They'd had this discussion often before, Star could suddenly tell by the way the three of them caught each other's eye. Planning it, biding their time, waiting for the right moment.

Bimini edged herself around the far side of Quarrel's bulk, and snapped her fingers close up to his face. "Hey, you, Templar. Explain what happens when you find the Lotus. What you gonna do to shut it down?"

"The darkness crumbles!" Quarrel shouted, eyes blazing.

Bimini drew her blade. "He's definitely stoned or infected with something or plain snapped crazy broke down. No more stable than a tanker or a storm."

Her wavering voice betrayed her fear. She gripped her knife and steadied her stance. "Look, whatever's out there, it ain't our fight. We're damn lucky to have survived this far, but this is where the journey ends."

Quarrel glared at her, nostrils flaring. He let go of Star's shirt and gave her a mighty shove, sending her sprawling. "Of course it's *your* fight. It's everybody's fight. Everyone who wants to keep on living. Everyone not already slaughtered, gotta put the genie back in the bottle. The ghost back into the machine, the fire back into the mountain . . ."

Bimini gritted her teeth. Beads of sweat were forming on her temple. "I'm not following you another step. Not one more step, do you hear me?"

Quarrel's glazed eyes snapped into focus. "Mesh tells me there's a settlement, walking distance from this place. But in which direction, huh?" He swung his arm, an expansive gesture indicating nowhere in particular. "Which way you gonna walk without my intel?"

Bimini held her stance awhile longer, then sheathed her blade, a look of bitter disappointment on her face. "Let's get out of here. Place gives me the creeps."

Hackett and Grellan moved to join her.

"Come on, girl," said Bimini to Star, "What you waiting for?"

Quarrel was softly humming to himself, staring off into nothingness, like he'd forgotten the rest of them were there. Star got to her feet and edged close to Bimini, making no sudden moves.

Fast as lightning, Quarrel lashed out and grabbed her wrist. Star yelped.

"This one's mine," he said, calmly, yet loud enough for all to hear. "My back up plan—that old General's clawing inside my head. Reading my thoughts, making a mess of things." He shook his head, like shaking might make a difference. "But her head, see, it's too empty to infect. The scaffolding wasn't seeded right. She's no more than half and half, but half might be the right amount. The perfect number as it turns out."

Bimini's expression changed. "What's he on about?"

"Nothing," said Star, her voice crumbling with panic. "Let me go!" She tugged her arm and twisted, trying to break free.

Quarrel did not let go. Instead, he held her arm up high so all of them could see. Tugged down her sleeve and ripped the dirty bandage from her skin.

"No!"

The more she kicked and struggled, the more tightly he gripped.

"Don't look at it!" she pleaded.

But it was too late.

"What the blessed—" Bimini started, staring at her mesh.

Quarrel dragged Star screaming and howling along beside him, not caring if the others stayed or followed.

"We will cross the sleeping sands between with strong eyes and fine limbs," he said.

Star tripped and stumbled trying to keep pace. She made the mistake of looking back, in time to catch the look of horror on all their faces.

=FORTY-EIGHT=

The dirty buzz from drained Sentinel juice was fading fast, leaving Quarrel with a powerful blasting headache. Gradually his jumbled mind reordered itself and his spectrum-split vision cleared.

Quarrel hadn't needed data streams to tell him people had been sheltering in and around the aircraft boneyard. Subtle signs were everywhere: a footprint here, drags marks there, indicating recent removal of equipment and other useful salvage. Wind whistled through cracks in the disintegrating planes. The old husks weren't much use for shelter, and would be even less use next time a storm came charging through. His mesh had revealed some useful data for a change. A settlement not far ahead, on a strip of land that fringed the open sand. Sand where tankers screamed and rolled. The settlement would have what he required.

He felt no guilt at what he'd done. Guilt was for the weak. The dregs of his pathetic, useless crew, still trailed along behind. All threat and no marrow, lacking the grit to look out for themselves. At this point, he didn't care what those people did so long as they kept their distance. He didn't need them. He had the girl—his backup plan, the rest were dead weight, more trouble than they had ever been worth.

He'd need the girl if he couldn't go the distance. Only if he found a way to block the mesh and that other thing. That voice nagging at the edges of his consciousness.

The girl didn't speak. She dragged her feet, barely keeping up. One of the crew had lobbed a couple of rocks at her from behind and called out insults—nothing he hadn't heard before and wouldn't hear again.

They walked until the boneyard bled away into a vast slab of concrete, cracked and cooked. Another cratered wasteland. Some of the pockmarks looked relatively recent. Yawping craters, souvenirs from somebody's old war, repurposed as some form of garbage dump. A meeting place. The perfect site for ambush.

But nobody was waiting for them. Just collapsed hangars, broken down machinery draped and tangled like liana vines—not that he'd seen a jungle canopy for centuries. Quarrel stopped walking. The air was thick with ghosts. Many people had been murdered in this place, he could feel the resonance of their passing in waves of imaginary heat and bullet spray. He stood still, listening, arms out, fingers splayed, feeling shanghaied, shopped and swindled, just like back in the good old days. Cannon fodder, chickenfeed. Dispensable, disposable, soldiers out of time and out of luck. The whole world was gone, yet some things never ever seemed to change.

The meat and muscle below his mesh itched with short sharp bursts that made his bones ache hard. A message from the priests of Nisn—somehow they'd managed to boost their signal. *Keep on moving. You've got a job to do.*

"Fuck you," he said out loud, "and the horses you rode in on." Last time he'd seen a horse was back on the Brokehart salt flats. A tough old nag, jamming up his teeth with gristle. He hadn't wanted to shoot the thing, but sometimes back then you didn't get a choice.

His nostrils twanged at the acrid stench of smoke—real or imagined. Where could it be coming from? Not from sky-spat broken Angels. There was no re-entry heat bleeding from the scattered metal debris—his mesh would never lie about a thing like that. Smoke meant fire and fire meant cooking. Cooking meant people, and people pretty much added up to trouble.

And yet people was what he was looking for. He led his own bedraggled crew towards a blip in the distance, a radio telescope, cracked and weathered but still standing, pointing its vast dish skywards. He didn't look back. The crunch of their uncertain footsteps was enough.

Beyond the concrete wasteland, spinifex grass grew in ragged clumps. Scrawny-looking chickens pecked around in pebbly soil spotted with random tufts of green. It was the first signs of vegetation Quarrel had seen since the lantana raze fouled up his ship. Plots of cultivated soil were threaded with pumpkin and small, unappetising cauliflower heads. Abandoned hoes suggested the farmers had been recently tending their crops but were now hiding, waiting until the strangers passed on by.

Beyond the tumbled remains of a brick building, they came upon a herd of goats defiantly guarded by a small child wielding a sharpened stick. Beyond the goats, more cultivated patches. Mud brick buildings to the right of a dense thatch of antenna and weathered solar panels. Figures dressed in galabeyas moved amongst them, tending to the metal stalks as though they were some kind of crop. Ears for listening to an empty sky.

Quarrel shoved a group of them aside with a swipe of his arm, the one without the mesh in it. The farmers moved, their brittle prattling reminiscent of goats and sheep, all bleating, all fretting and discomfort. He looked around for the one in charge—there was always one in charge, no matter how humble or how scattered a community looked. Somebody had to be the boss. None of these farmers looked like likely candidates.

"Who's in charge here?"

Eventually someone shouted over the heads of all the others. "Our Lady is in the temple Sanctum, communing with the spirits. She won't come out until she's good and ready."

Good for nothing, he thought. But ready for what?

Their "Lady" was likely barking mad. He did not have time for mad old witches, the prayers of the deluded, nor chickens, cabbages, or goats. Not when faced with contaminated sky the colour of puss and rust. Sky that curdled and fermented with each passing hour. Sky that marked the rebirthing pains of the most dangerous weapon the world had ever seen.

None of the farmers came chasing after him when he moved away. He circumnavigated the perimeter, taking stock of the settlement's lay-out and fortifications, such as they were. Two watch towers on rusty, rickety legs, manned with lookouts, barely armed as far as he could tell. The dish was curious, probably non-functional. Agricultural communities were made of farmers, not fighters. It wouldn't take much effort to wipe them out.

He stood upon a slab of rock protruding at the settlement's farthest edge, and set his mesh to do a sweep of the surrounding area, both behind him and ahead, checking first for others of his kind, like he always did. Never know your luck in a big city, like the old prayer went. Big cities that went the way of the dinosaurs, yet another saying that made no sense at all.

Nothing reading, no blips showing up but him and the kid, and her at half strength, indicating her apparatus was barely functional—and perhaps it wouldn't even be that for long. Hardly surprising, she was broken when he found her. Probably should have left her standing on that pier in Fallow Heel, but you never know what you're gonna need—right boss? The kid hadn't uttered a sound since they set out walking between the planes. The others had grown afraid of her, afraid of her mesh. As well they should be. Don't worry, kid, it'll make you stronger to have them know the truth and hate you for it. It'll make you tougher, meaner, more like me.

That thought delivered a tinge of bellyache, so he set the mesh to scan for other mecha. The sand ahead was crawling with them, a variety of power sources and manufacturers, strains and stripes, including some mobile objects registering as incoherent fuzzy smudges, moving at impressive speeds, yet unfamiliar.

The challenge: how to cross the polyp storm-and-tanker-infested sands? He could hear them talking to each other in their high-pitched screech that some called song. The passing of data packets was what it was, some brimming deadly with dangerous contaminants, others junk and gibberish, the speaking-in-tongues of corroded military intel. Useless coordinates, targeting vectors, the warp and weft of outdated trace element espionage.

= FORTY-NINE =

The island where they'd found the planes—and temporary sanctuary—had turned out to be no island at all, but a stretch of baked and cracked concrete leading into the shimmering distance. Detritus from the Black and Dead Red sand had blown all over the ground, but the way was clear enough to travel on foot. The *Dogwatch* survivors passed the mangled remains of things that might have once been tankers, with all trace of wheels and outer casings stripped by weather and unknown scavengers. Other things too: rough-edged craters, evidence of wars a long time past. Nothing living larger than a skink. Nothing they could see, at least.

Quarrel and Star led the way towards a far-off, peculiar, skeletal structure silhouetted against the bland blue sky. Nobody spoke. Star could no longer bring herself to turn and face the others.

When Quarrel eventually decreed it was time, he stopped, she stopped and the ragged remains of his crew stopped too, dragging their gaze back from curious surroundings: neatly tilled garden plots, chickens, goats, and donkeys. A mud brick village nestled in the ruins of something once far grander. A giant dish with jutting spindle arms that cast a shadow across them all.

Workers toiling in the gardens looked up to see who had come, stared awhile, then bent back to their labours. An indication that strangers were not unusual in these parts.

Star wasn't taking any chances. She tore a strip from the hem of the once-fine shirt Allegra's girl had given her, and rebound her arm to hide her mesh. *Mesh*: now she knew the name for it. The name and what it was and what it meant. Not one of the former *Dogwatch* crew would look her in the eye since Quarrel had exposed her. Not even Bimini. They'd kept their distance, hanging back even though it placed them at greater risk. It was better to be attacked by wild dogs or strangers, apparently, than walk in the company of Templars.

If only Lucius were walking by her side.

If only Nene were here. Or Yeshie, who'd never cared if folks were tainted. Or Benhadeer who, she suspected, had known her terrible secret all along.

She walked in silence, in complete acceptance of the pain returning to her arm. A burning sensation coursed through her bones. She could live with pain, but she would never get over the fact that one of them had thrown a rock at her, never get used to the loathing on the faces of those she had been slowly starting to trust.

Up close, the sight of tilled soil and tidy, cultivated plots filled her with a kind of hope. Three figures dressed in brown-stained coveralls were waiting as the weary travellers approached. Bearing arms, so it first appeared, but up closer the "weapons" were revealed to be only farming implements.

It was a man, a woman, and a younger girl, their faces brown from sun. They exchanged greetings with Quarrel. The man pointed up at the giant dish. Quarrel grunted something in response, then marched off alone to commune privately with his mesh. The *Dogwatch* crew hung about, waiting for instruction or any indication of what came next. Scrutinising the labouring locals, the lurid sky, and the giant dish. Looking anywhere but in Star's direction.

Eventually a door in one of the mud brick buildings opened. Two people emerged, a girl and a boy, bearing trays of what looked like brightly coloured fruit. Great as her hunger and thirst was, Star could not bear the shunning of her own crewmates any further. She stared as the others headed eagerly to receive refreshment, then edged towards a grid of garden plots where girls wearing headscarves and wielding trowels bent, digging. A few looked up but nobody stopped her or stared at her for long. Nobody cared where she went or what she did.

A low stone wall curved along the ridge of a gentle rise. Up high and out of everybody's way. She stepped carefully across scrubby ground, sat down, and stared across the sands. The sky had not changed—she was getting used to it. Objects rumbled in the far-off distance, churning up great plumes of dust. Tankers rolling across no mans land, a desert stretch that did not even have a name.

Quarrel was crazy if he thought they could simply walk across that sand without so much as a tanker lance between them.

She rested her chin between her palms and stared down at the dirt, at a line of industrious black ants winding their way around obstructing stones, some of them ferrying stolen seeds.

When she eventually looked up, she noticed the slope ahead of her was strewn with dune melons and their stringy runners. Her thirst was powerful—suddenly she didn't care if anybody saw her. Dune melons grew wild along the Road back home. Her mouth was dry as paperbark, her throat too parched for words.

She picked her way down the slope and started searching for a fat, ripe melon, careful not to trip on their tangled roots. Quickly she found what she was looking for, drew her blade, cut the skin, and started eating.

Relief flooded her senses. Bland and tasteless, yet the water-fat pulp was bursting with juice. Perfect—all she wanted was its water, scooping out great chunks of it with her hands.

She was about to toss the empty skin aside when a crunching sound made her jump. She turned to see a giant shape approaching, padding on big feet. A lizard similar to the one that had attacked the Van at Broken Arch. Star froze, the empty melon skin falling from her hand. The large beast grunted and snuffled. She didn't move. Her heart was beating fast. The bulk of the lizard's body blocked the low stone wall. If she called out now, nobody would even hear her.

The animal shoved its nose amongst the melons. It seemed to be searching for the ripe ones just like she. Had it even noticed her?

As it got closer, she realised that its torso was fitted with a leather harness. Then she spotted a young man following up behind the creature. He stopped as soon as he saw her.

"I wasn't stealing," Star blurted out.

The man eyed the discarded melon skin and shrugged. "Melons don't belong to anybody." He bent to pluck a plump, ripe one, made a clicking sound with his tongue, and offered it to the beast. It swung its head towards him with open jaws, and the melon burst with a satisfying pop when the jaws chomped shut. The man bent to pick up another. "You want to feed her?"

Star's heart hammered in her chest. Those jaws were chomping down like shears—the last thing she wanted was to get any closer to those teeth. But the young man was being kind to her and kindness was what she craved now more than anything.

"Careful," he warned as he handed her the melon.

She took it, then a tentative step closer, holding out her non-mesh hand so the beast could smell her scent. "I'll be careful."

The lizard snatched the melon from her hand—it burst, spraying her with juice.

The young man laughed. "Iolani likes you. She doesn't like everybody."

Star smiled back nervously. "I like her too—Iolani is a pretty name."

He nodded. "The name of the town where I was born."

"Never heard of it—where does it lie?"

The young man shook his head sadly. Not something he wanted to talk about any further. His eyes flicked to her bandaged mesh. Self consciously, she drooped her shoulder so the shirt sleeve would cover a little more of it.

"You are hurt?"

She pulled her arm behind her back. "No no, this is nothing. Really, I'm fine. I didn't know big lizards could be so tame."

He nodded. "More gentle than dogs when you get to know them. More greedy, too."

Star picked up another melon, wishing she had something better for the beast to eat. A treat, like one of the oranges offered to the Van survivors.

The young man seemed like he was about to say something, tell her his name, perhaps, when an aggravating humming filled the air. Star dropped the melon. Iolani flattened her tiny ears and froze. Star pulled her mesh arm out of view just as something flew out from behind a rocky outcrop and up into the sky. A thing made of tarnished, battered metal.

The young man raised his hand. "Don't worry, drone's not gonna hurt you."

The hum intensified as the flying relic—a melon-sized drone as he had called it—swooped in low and buzzed past her cheek. The lizard raised her head and flared her nostrils. The young man soothed the beast with words from an unfamiliar tongue. Evidently it worked. Iolani snapped up the fallen melon and resumed eating, ears flattened small against her head.

The drone flew rings around the three of them, then finally buzzed off up the rise and over the low stone wall. Star finally took a breath, unaware until then that she'd been holding it in, and realised she'd been also been awkwardly attempting to shield her bandaged arm from the thing's view.

The mood relaxed after the interruption. Something small and fast skittered through the tangled melon roots. Iolani bounded after it. The young man gave a cheery wave as he gave chase. Star watched the giant lizard trap and kill the thing, a sand skate, by stomping its shell and sucking out the soft pink flesh underneath.

She longed to ask the young man's name but felt too shy after everything else that had happened.

Quarrel was still standing where she'd left him, still muttering garbled sentences under his breath. "Bonds to the whims of murder, sprawled in the bowels of the Earth . . . what do you see in our eyes—can you tell me that?"

Star steeled herself, then went to stand beside him and listen to his gibberish, hugging her arms across her chest, feeling errant blasts of chill wind against her face, blowing directly at them from the Red. The unnatural chill was defiant against the blazing sun. Her tongue tasted particles of grit.

She waited for him to say something that made sense, to acknowledge her presence in some way, but the Templar seemed lost in his own swirl of thoughts and words. All around them, people got on with their hoeing and raking, harvesting and carrying, like a battered Templar warrior standing proudly on a rock was nothing special.

The drone swung out from behind a mud brick building, its attentions aimed at Quarrel this time. He stood still, and the thing flew so close that Star expected it to land upon his head, or for him to smash its pockmarked casing with his fists. But he ignored it. The drone did not attempt a landing, merely made a couple of passes then flew away.

The blemish in the sky, lurking above the horizon, was growing bigger. There were small changes in its colour, shape, and consistency, moody and writhing as a serpent's nest. Occasionally, forks of lightning stabbed at the Earth—she hadn't seen those before. Below it, the stretch of Red seemed like a living thing, with its boiling, shifting gouts of sandy dust thrown up by the passage of tankers. Now and then, strange sounds borne in upon stray winds, sounds that sent shivers down her spine and brought back memories of things she didn't want to think about. People she would never see again. A life abandoned and lost to her forever.

"Don't have to hide your mesh from these people," said Quarrel, his voice loud, clear and holding steady "These people don't care what we were or what we are."

He didn't look at her when he spoke, kept his focus on details only he could see with enhanced supersoldier vision she did not share. Her mesh had given her nothing but pain. It did not help her see in the dark or hear sounds beyond the range of human hearing.

"We'll never make it across those sands, Quarrel. How are we supposed to get there—walk?"

"Three days crossing on foot, I'm reckoning. Eat up and get prepared."

"You're crazy—is that what your damn arm tells you?" Her gaze settled upon it, noted how few of the winking jewels remained active. "Is Nisn still controlling you? Telling you what to do and think?"

"What quaver—what heart aghast? Poppies whose roots are in man's veins . . ." was his reply.

"Argh! I can't take any more of your babbling nonsense. Your plan is to walk right out there and get killed for nothing. I'm not going with you—it's suicide, just like Lucius said." She raised her mesh arm and waved it in his face. "I'm not like you, no matter what this thing says. I'm not crazy and I'm not throwing my life away for nothing."

His head snapped around, and he stared at her with great and sudden ferocity. "You can hear it whispering, can't you? Feel it crawling around inside your head?" He slapped his own head with the base of his palm to reinforce his point.

Star backed off, frightened by the luminosity of his eyes. "No—I can't hear anything!" There was nothing else to be said.

Her stomach growled, hunger pinching at her innards. She needed food—something more substantial than watery melon—but she was wary of drawing attention to herself. She turned back to the low stone wall. The young man had been so kind—perhaps he would be kind to her again?

She jumped down off the rock, retraced her steps, keenly aware of every different vegetable she passed in neatly groomed rows, her stomach growling like an animal. Gently pushed her way past a group of women balancing baskets on their heads, hips swaying rhythmically as they moved.

Finally, she found them: the mighty lizard, still popping melons and chomping up the pieces, the young man standing behind it, beside another man, both with their backs towards her. They were conversing in broad gestures. Both turned as she approached. The second man was a familiar face, and not a welcome one—Tully Grieve, a half eaten apple in his hand.

=FIFTY=

The first time the General glimpses the ship is through tanker eyes as it pushes across the sand, nudging right up close to it, then backing off in awe and wonder. The General has never wanted anything as much as he wants that ship. The *Razael*, an old-time double masted schooner, red cedar from keel to plank and frame. Largely intact, despite its rattling passage across blast-frozen slag on giant wheels.

It has come to rest not far from the bunker, its wheels clogged up with sand. The General diverts Templars from crucial digging, wanting eyes and hands up close to inspect the ship's condition. To protect it, to make sure nothing touches its lovely cedar skin.

With a ship like this he could rule the sands, protected by a shield of armoured tankers, polyp storms scouring the land ahead of him, sweeping his future clear of all detritus.

But something is wrong.

It is only when he tries to leave the bunker complex that he realises what he has overlooked. What he should have comprehended so much earlier. Plenty of clues and evidence, but there have been so many other competing distractions.

The General has no body—uploaded means non-corporeal, something he's forgotten alongside so many other useless things that no longer matter.

This matters. He *is* the bunker, its wires and innards. He has a core, a brain, a stem, but no heart, just great machines churning and clunking away underground.

Without a body, he will be stuck in this dull grey bunker for all time, hijacked views through the Warbirds and tankers his only window to the outside world. He will never again feel the ocean wet and strong against his legs.

No legs. He doesn't have legs. He will never run and dance and dive, never breathe and fight, clutch and caress.

The General screams with impotent white rage. He coughs up a polyp storm out of spite and slams it against the excavation site, sending weary Templar diggers flying, some of them damaged irrevocably. The storm trails off on an adventure of its own, unguarded and no longer subject to his control, deadly to any who will encounter it.

The General sulks. He hadn't meant to let anger get the better of him. Now he will have to wait till more of the big dumb lugs walk out of the desert. The digging has to continue, the bunker must be exposed. He concentrates, focusing his attention on calling to them, promising them riches, glory, revenge, or absolution, whatever the hell those Templars want. The sand is suffocating, despite his lack of lungs.

Meanwhile, he repurposes agricultural robots, teaches them to make combat decisions and act within legal and policy constraints. His laws. His policies.

Time passes. He ignores it. The Blue continues reclaiming familiar territory, manoeuvring around the missing gaps and pieces, mindful of collateral damage, wary of discriminating friend from foe in the theatre of war.

Careful to be mindful of the objective calculus of proportionality, he knows autonomy must be built into the systems, that he must follow the rules of engagement, respect the cyclical triangulation of distributed self-repairing autonomous systems powered by self-reconfiguration, fault tolerance, fractum geometries.

The wait for new Templars will be a long one. Impatience has gotten the better of him. The General focuses all his energy on listening. There has to be something else out there, some other kind of creature he can ride. The Lotus Blue shuts down its auxiliary systems, leaves the Angels and Warbirds to their own devices, the Templars to throttling old mecha back to life, digging in the boiling sun, the tankers to roaming freely as they choose, breaking off from grid formation. He won't stop them, not this time.

The Lotus Blue begins communing with the spirits of light and air, enveloping himself in aether, the web between land, sea, and sky, listening with every fibre of his being for tiny voices, whispers, and promises. Niche-consciousnesses he might have overlooked, forms of life he might not have even dreamed of.

Small things spluttering, trembling like baby birds, but not birds or beasts, not creatures of land or sky or sea. Humming things encased in rattled, battered carapaces.

Drones. So small, he's been ignoring them as they buzz around his digging Templars.

That old woman is their keeper, the one he's been bombarding with images of verdant green and water. He's been interested in her crop of electronic ears blooming in a patch of renovated ruin beneath his dish. Tenant farmers. They are neighbours of a kind, and he's been feeling mighty neighbourly of late.

He wonders now if that dish might not come in handy. The old woman has constructed quite a setup for herself. He pokes around in all her corners, beginning with her drones. They are mecha after all, clever on the inside, tricked out with sophisticated shape-shifting devices utilising magnets to mimic molecules that fold themselves into complex arrangements. She has quite a collection dating back to an age long fallen: industrial and military, armour-plated quadcopters and multi rotors, ancient overclocked Reapers, Predators, Cullers and Gleaners, Carnies and Sassers, Blades, Shanks, and Skeins.

Drones are easy, their brains the size of birds'. All he needs are the keys, the codes, the hacks, the kinds of intel the old woman shares as freely as chickenfeed.

They are such tiny cameras, everything displayed in convex squint, everything lit by smudgy tallow flame. He hacks their bird brains, scopes the interior of the place she calls her Sanctum, a mausoleum of discarded apparatus crowded out with trembling, praying peasants.

Nothing to see here, nothing of interest. The General bugs out and concentrates, seeing what else he can latch onto, some other instrument of clapped-out mecha with hardware integrated and defences down.

He finds something straight away, a lone Templar with mesh intact, an enhanced brain singed by battle scoring, with corroded pathways, ravaged sensors flushed with foreign chemistry—the bad kind. Amazing that such a bucket of junk is still walking around and breathing.

The General taps in, recognizing the architecture—he's been in there for a poke around before—and viewed the landscape through battle-weary eyes. Tankers rumble in the distance beneath a pus-filled sky: pollution from the polyps' wake. Well, there are plenty more where that came from.

Farmers and farmland, nothing to see of interest until that Templar turns its head and *Hello, what is that?* A partially-formed mesh, almost pristine, with pathways shiny and bright, standing in the open where anybody could swoop on in and snap it up. Embedded in the arm of a young . . .

With a vicious shove from the beat-up old soldier, the General finds himself booted unceremoniously out of its head, and the pristine mesh no longer in his sights. For the time being. If she was real then he will find her. The General will find a way—he always does.

= FIFTY-ONE =

Quarrel closed his eyes and listened. The wind was warm on his face. He'd stood in this place before—or somewhere like it, on an anonymous rock on the edge of a battlefield, waiting for the launch command, the heave ho, the up and at 'em, waiting to charge and fight and die for the cause. Memories ephemeral as ghosts were being dredged up with ragged clarity:

The army of the Lotus stood its ground while the killing mist settled down over foxholes and gun pits. Skies throbbed with the roar of unseen stealth. After-dazzle as everyone fired, splitting the night blue-white, scorching our vision, sending us diving under tanks between explosions, sprinting in bursts. Slamming us into the ground.

Crouching behind that broken wall, trying to peer through hand sized peep-holes amidst shattering fire, the bellowing and the mutilation. Dying of obedi-ence, like so many others of our kind . . .

Memories came in sweet, warm flushes—along something else, a sharp spike in his brain that brought him back to the present. Eyes wide open. Heart beating faster. Dry mouth, cold sweat shivers. There it was again, the mental fingers pawing through his brain. Again.

No!

Quarrel shook his head but he could still feel the creature's pres-ence. The Lotus General, ice cold blue, how well he knew that signa-ture, that flavour.

Ice Cold Blue.

Quarrel had been a mighty warrior once, and he would be that one more time, to do the thing that had to be done. To die for what was right. He had to fight to tear his gaze away from the blistering sky. He searched for her amongst the goats and farmers, the mud bricks, hoes, and barrows, the chickens and the goats. The scrawny girl with the half-formed mesh. Found her standing all alone, staring in the oppo-site direction, back to the horizon and her future and the terrible sky, hugging her arms, looking lost and fragile.

He centred his will, kicking the intruder clear out of his thoughts. Bump and run, down to the wire, not so difficult, no, not yet. Yet each small incursion, each attempted crossing of the line, was fought and forced back harder and harder. Eventually he knew he'd lose his strength of will. It would all go up in smoke, disintegrate under relent-less blanket bombing. If there ever was a time for running, this was it.

The skinny girl started walking towards the lizard they'd seen earlier. Two men stood on either side of it, feeding the beast dune melons. Talking the talk, like desert men do. The beast kept dashing out, chasing skates around the rocks. A genmod hybrid trained from birth was that one, you could always tell. Trained from birth, they never turned, they never snapped and slashed you out of spite.

The girl walked cautiously. She was no weapon. She was not ready. She was not anything he'd ever be able to hammer into weapons grade. Completely useless, but there you go, the last best hope against what's what and what's coming. What goes up comes crashing down, with anything stuck within the range of the Lotus's fallout flames screwed.

His mesh quivered, reverberated with fresh instructions. Telemetry again, love letters from Nisn, deadly and insistent. Too much, too late. Quarrel had had enough. Anger welled inside him like a geyser, burning with the fire of a thousand suns. "I'm not your bitch anymore!" he screamed, to the sky, to the sand, to anyone who'd listen, only nobody was ever listening. Not to poor old Quarrel and his kind. Not the five-star Gs and the priests of Nisn. Not the ragged band of savages he'd tricked into a suicide mission across the Black.

Time to get nasty and drop the gloves. Quarrel roared. He raised his mesh arm and slammed it hard against the side of a boulder. Heard the scraping shriek of metal smashing against stone. Flesh, too. Hot flashes, then a tingling through his nerves. Sirens blaring through his skull. He screamed again, much louder this time, raised his arm and smashed it harder, smashed it and smashed it until the stone was slick with blood. Not bright red like an animal or child's. Dark crimson, thick and old and spent.

Nobody tried to stop him.

The mesh was useless, smashed and shattered. The sirens faded through the caverns of his fractured consciousness. Stillness was what he craved the most. Stillness and quietude. Loneliness and solitude. He repeated those words over and over and over as he trudged towards the dish, ignoring the memories of fighting whirling around him in fits and stutters. The flurry of ghost limbs, ghost bullets, ghost staves and blades. The world at war, neither ghost, nor flesh, nor mecha. For all he cared, they could hack themselves to pieces.

"Goodnight sweetheart," he said out loud as he staggered onwards, falling to his knees and tumbling head over arse. Freewheeling equilibrium, sand in his face. Sand and sweat and sweet, sweet blessed freedom.

He lay still for awhile, then crawled to his knees, pushed himself up, and found his balance again. One step forward. One step, then two. Away from the fighting and the ghosts, from Nisn's persistent nagging and the broken, bastard past. Off to find a future of his own.

He made it twenty paces before the mesh's backup sleeper track kicked in. A reboot failsafe, rewritten through the hardware in his bones. The pain was so indescribable, it lifted him clean off the ground.

Last thing he remembered seeing was the horizon, crooked, laced with burnt sienna clouds. Mere wisps of things, probably mirages, probably not real. Just like his twenty seconds of glorious freedom.

= FIFTY-TWO =

Star started running at the sight of Tully Grieve. "That man is a liar and a thief," she shouted, pointing so there could be no mistake. "He stole our food, our water—everything. He left us back there amongst the planes to rot."

"Woah, now hold on there just a moment!" Grieve held up his arms in self defence, as if she had been threatening him with a blunt instrument.

Iolani's keeper shot a quizzical look in Grieve's direction. Grieve shrugged in return.

"She's crazy. Touched by heat, I wouldn't wonder."

"Don't you dare call me crazy." Star glanced around at the neat, rectangular garden plots, noted the calmness of the gardeners bent over them, working in accord with their own private rhythms, shouting occasional sentences at one another. Only one gardener had looked up when she shouted.

"Why don't you tell your fine new friends the truth of what you are and what you did. How far you think they're likely to trust you then?"

Grieve shook his head, resting his weight on one leg, an irritating smirk plastered across his face. "Look, everything worked out for the best. Nobody got hurt. Everybody got to where they were going in the end."

He bent down and picked up a hoe, walked over and handed it to her. Star took a couple of steps back.

"Now don't be like that," he said. "Old lady's only got one rule in this place, or so they tell me. You wanna eat, you gotta work. Sounds pretty fair to me, don't you reckon, Iago?"

Iago—the lizard keeper's name. He seemed amused by the string of words tumbling out of Grieve's mouth. He smiled and nodded, looked to Star as if expecting a witty comeback.

She snatched the hoe and threw it to the ground. "We didn't come this far to dig up cabbages."

"We?" Grieve shaded his eyes with his cupped hand and made a big show of looking all around. "What happened to that dangerous killer supersoldier you were so pally with back in that old boneyard?" He kept up his mock search. "What about all the rest of your travelling companions? Don't tell me they upped and left you here with my pal Iago and a giant lizard?"

"They're getting ready to cross the sand," she said defiantly.

"Dya reckon? Last time I clapped eyes on them, they were getting stuck into the old lady's beer and hospitality. Didn't look like they were going anywhere in a hurry."

She didn't know what to say to that and so she pointed upwards. "You looked at the sky lately?"

"Have you looked at yourself lately? You'll want to kit up proper before you go chasing off out there."

"I don't need you to tell me how to cross the sand."

He leered at her, smirk plastered across his face from ear to ear. "There's no way forward across that sand, in case you haven't twigged that for yourself. Don't take my word for it, go stand on a rock and check it out. The sand out there is crawling with rogue tankers. They own the sand, consider it their territory. Ask Iago here, he'll tell you. What happens to idiots who set out on their own, Iago?"

Iago wasn't smiling anymore. "Nobody ever comes back," he said. He shook his head and looked away, at something in the far distance that only he could see.

"Lotta these folks got stories about crazies charging off into the Red. These people wound up living here for a reason, Star. Can't go forward, can't go back. Too many things trying to kill you in this world—and don't I know it. Iago knows it too, don't you my friend?"

Iago didn't answer but he turned his head. Looked at Star with a fire in his eyes.

"The *Razael* made it across," she said.

"How the hell could you possibly know that? Things weren't going so great when those bastard foreigners dumped me over the side. For all we know that fine ship got smashed to splinters at the halfway point. Those tankers are dangerous, especially when they're mad. If you've never seen one up close—"

She stepped up. "One of those tankers killed a friend of mine."

The tone of her voice was enough to silence him. He bit into the apple he was holding with a resounding crunch.

Two girls interrupted them, walking past balancing hoes across their shoulders. They glanced at Star and Grieve, at the fallen hoe, smiled at Iago, then looked away.

Beyond the buildings lay more of the orderly rectangular garden plots, sand stretching out into the distance.

Above it all, the bruised sky. The air smelled strange. The day before it had smelled like ordinary desert.

Grieve bit into the apple again, this time finding it bitter and hard to chew.

"We live well here," offered Iago, smiling kindly.

"What the man says," blurted Grieve. "Those stinger clouds can't touch us. Walls are sturdy, we're safe inside the buildings."

"We're not safe anywhere while that thing's boiling up the sky. Those stinger clouds are part of it, being spat out the centre of that . . . *thing*."

No need to point. He knew what she was referring to. The scabbed patch of sky above the horizon. Strange how none of the farming folk seemed bothered by it. Grieve chewed, slower and less enthusiastically than before. "Whatever that thing is, it's far away. Not much we can do about it." He attempted a grin, not very successfully.

"Quarrel said that sky bruise has a mind. That likely it's controlling the tankers too. He said those things are now smarter than the folks who built them."

"Doesn't sound too hard," said Grieve. "Folks that built them have been dead for centuries. That Templar's completely crazy by the way, in case you haven't noticed."

"That Templar is currently the only thing willing to fight to protect this land."

"So he keeps telling everybody, but what proof do you have any of the ranting garbage he spouts is real?"

"He didn't abandon us to die. That's pretty real to me."

"You look pretty real to me," said Grieve. "Chill out, power down, pick up a hoe, stop and smell the flowers." He bent forward, miming such an act with great exaggeration.

"You really are a piece of work, Grieve. A pathetic sack of—"

"And you are completely naive," he said, coldly this time, straightening back up, the grin gone from his face, the apple swallowed, the humour leached out of his voice. "What if the mad old soldier's right—what can any of us do about an ancient weapon? Something our oh-so-brilliant ancestors couldn't even kill?"

"If Quarrel's right, that Lotus Blue will take out everything from here to the Sammaryndan coast. Maybe even further. The Sand Road. Fallow Heel. Everything and everyone we've ever known."

261

"So? We all gotta die sometime . . ."

He gnawed on the remains of the apple core. She slapped it from his hand.

"Hey!" he pushed her.

She shoved him back. When he pushed her again, harder this time, she slapped him across the face. "You're a coward. An utter coward. What did you really do to get thrown off that ship? Don't tell me. I really don't want to know."

He grabbed her wrist and gripped it tight, pulled her so close she could smell his bitter apple breath. "I'm a survivor. That's what I am. That's what I do. You don't know anything about me at all. Not where I've come from. Not what I've had to endure to get this far."

His grim expression made him seem much older than twenty summers.

"Let go. You're hurting me." He gripped tighter until she yelped. "LIAR!"

"Of course I lie—every day of my life. Sometimes lying's the only thing that works. But here's a truth: nobody's getting across that sand. That's open tanker country and those things are batshit crazy."

She managed to tug her hand away. He cut in before she could speak.

"I've seen them. Been spying on the lot of them through those drones of hers." He made swooping motions with his arms, imitating flight.

"Liar!"

Grieve continued. "The mad old woman who runs this joint promises her followers the world. Literally—a shiny new one, not this sun-blasted wasteland. More than promises—she *shows* it to them. I've seen it too. It's beautiful."

"I don't believe you, you're full of—"

"Not this time." He grinned wickedly, his eyes shining. "I can prove it. Let me show you too. Plus something else—that threat that Templar is holding over your head. The Lotus Blue—it's nothing dangerous, just another ruin. The Red is littered with 'em. Come with me and I'll show that to you as well."

She took a step back, wary. "Why should I trust you or believe anything you say?"

"See it with your own eyes. Make up your own mind." He shrugged. "What have you got to lose at this point?" He pointed to the giant dish. "Old lady lives inside the centre of that thing. Calls it Sanctum. I know a way in. A secret way."

She looked to where he pointed. The temple was formidable—she'd never seen another structure like it. No guards were posted by the entrance. She didn't trust Grieve but he was right about one thing—what *did* she have left to lose? Everything she'd ever had was lost already: Nene, Lucius, her own true name and origin. The friends she once had on the Van, the ones she almost thought she might make on the *Dogwatch*. And all she had to show for it was proof that she wasn't even human.

"We'll go later," he explained, reading the expression on her face, looking pleased with himself, winking at Iago, who had stepped back when the other two started shoving. "When darkness falls and everyone is sleeping."

Grieve brushed a clump of hair out of his eyes. Star looked to Iago, but he was already leading the lizard away through the melons.

"You're still a coward and a thief," she said.

He smiled. "Meet you behind the potting sheds after lights out."

= FIFTY-THREE =

Mohandas buried his face in his hands. He wept, enormous body-jarring sobs accompanied by a keening sound, like a wounded animal in pain.

Allegra placed her arms around her father's shoulders. Arms that did not reach far enough. He barely seemed to notice she was there.

"Papa, those men aren't going to hurt you any more. See, they have taken your chains away, moved you out of that horrid splintered wooden chair. Brought you on deck, see, is this not more comfortable already? There is quite a view, a whole buried settlement being dug up from the sand in front of the ship."

She had managed to convince Kian that her father posed no threat to anyone. That he could be given a comfortable place to sit in the fresh and open air atop plump cushions beneath a shady awning. His ankles were chained but his hands were free. He had promised her he would not attempt to flee, and she was not worried he might try, because where was there to run to? The ship had truly reached the end of the Earth. Its wheels choked up with soft sand, it would go no further without help. But none were available to dig it free. They'd all run off, the crew and even his once-trusted servants, run off to escape the foreigners and seek their fortunes in the ruins. Kian and his body-guards hadn't even tried to stop them. All they cared about were those blasted maps that her father should have destroyed three decades ago.

At the end of the trail, apparently, lay an unspeakable monster— only no one would listen, no one would heed his warning. The sky should have been warning enough, a swirling current of sickly-coloured clouds and lightning forks.

Mohandas continued to weep into his hands—bare after all his jewelled rings had been pulled from his fingers. Allegra patted his shoulders gently, then withdrew her hands and folded them in her lap. She waited for her father to stop crying, but his torrent of tears did not let up. A few minutes passed, and her patience thinned. The noise he was making was extremely unpleasant. She worried that the few remaining guards would come, that they might not be aware of the *understanding* blossoming between herself and Kian, the Axan prince. Her own blood kin, as it turned out. A situation she was prepared to take full and thorough advantage of.

She placed her hands on her father's shoulders. This time he shrugged them off.

"You don't know what you're doing, stupid girl. You don't know what these people are capable of."

His skin was flushed, his eyes red rimmed and puffy, adding twenty years to his appearance.

"I can charm him, Papa—have I not achieved that much already?" She held up her wrists as evidence. The marks made by her bonds were already fading.

He pushed her hands away—gently, just rough enough to make his feelings known.

"Papa, you have made your point—now stop blubbering and start listening to mine. They're our people, Papa—our own blood kin."

He snorted, a wet, unpleasant sound made even more so by the reddening of his face.

"We got lucky," she continued. "Hooking up with Axa is a brilliant plan. Everything will change because of it. You know how Darian has the monopoly on silk and cotton. How Li Ming and Burton Jax gang up on us, how they always favour Evenslough even though—"

"Allegra, my daughter, I love you dearly, but you are a bloody fool. Did you not learn anything from those expensive history lessons I paid for? Do you know nothing of the wars and why they were fought?"

She rolled her eyes. "2061: The Karrantha War; 2146: The Battle of Carpenteria; 2155: Defence of the Barossa; 2210: Operation Great Ocean Road; 2243: The Siege of Kakadu: 2348: The Crysse Offensive; 2352: The Lotus Wars; 2388: The Battle of Maratista Plain—"

"Mindless rote recitation. What was all that bloodshed in aid of, can you tell me that?"

She glared at him with great annoyance. "They fought to gain control of the land and its resources. Wars are all about fighting to come out on top. To not let foreign parties get the better of you."

Mohandas gestured at the surrounding sands. "Once, this was all green pasture and rolling hills, filled with animals and plants and other lovely things that were not trying to kill you. The temperature of the air was cooler—people didn't have to cover all their skin. It used to rain. Gently, not just storms and flash floods."

Allegra brimmed with impatience, but she didn't interrupt.

"Lots of people lived here and they didn't fight. They traded. They built things up together. They built machines that travelled through the air, and even to the moon."

"I know all this already."

"No, you don't. You know the words, maybe, but you don't comprehend their meaning. What the world had, once, and what it lost. That all we do now is survive, day to day, scratching and picking over the bones of the dead." He nodded at the horizon. "That thing out there is a war machine. A Lotus Blue, deadliest of all the colours. It has its own mind, its own agenda. It cannot be harnessed, controlled, or bargained with."

"It's a relic, that's all," said Allegra. "More sophisticated than a tanker, I'll grant you that, but a relic all the same. Relics were the tools of men. Kian has told me all about them. He says—"

"Kian is a young, hot-headed idiot. Trust me, I knew his father and he was an idiot too. He's just another petty princeling, greedy and short-sighted."

Mohandas's shoulders slumped. "And I remain the biggest idiot of them all, for stealing something so dangerous in the first place and hanging on to it when it should have been destroyed. I'm old. What happens to me doesn't matter anymore. *You're* the one who's going to end up paying for my folly."

Allegra's harsh expression softened. She took his hands between her own as delicately as if they'd been a baby bird. "Kian has explained to me how they'd take the harvested reliquary of the tankers, use it to make lights that burn and power without flame. Light and heat and air that blows cool through big slits in the walls." She leant in closer. "They *make* things, Papa, they don't just dig them up and sell them."

"I know. I grew up underground, remember? Axa was my home."

She nodded. "I don't understand why you ever left such a wondrous place."

He sighed. "Because Axa is stagnant, inbred, closed off, a dead end—dead and dying. Because I came to admire the bravery of those who stayed up top. Who stuck it out and kept on going, despite the heat and the dust and the terrible storms, the war machines and the toxic detritus. Despite everything, they stayed alive. They're better than we are, precious, by a long shot."

He angled his body to face his daughter. "Do not do this thing, I beg of you. Get rid of those maps. Take a rock and smash them into powder, cast them into the wind where they can do no harm. Let the secrets of the Lotus bunker remain lost forever. Use your influence to help us all. Turn this ship and head for home—I beg of you!"

She kissed him on the forehead, but she wasn't listening. Axa was her home too, her spiritual home, and she was now determined to set foot in its splendour, no matter what it took. She rubbed the surface of her grandmother's golden locket with her thumb, eyes glistening with longing and excitement.

= FIFTY-FOUR =

Darkness fell across the Temple of the Dish. Guards patrolled the courtyard and garden plot perimeters on foot. One slouched in each of the spindle-legged watchtowers, while another walked along the old stone wall. Yet another lurked around the kitchen door. But no guard stood watch outside the Temple entrance. The old woman's followers were frightened of things they didn't understand, Star realised. Nobody went inside without permission.

A broken metal staircase jutted like an elbow around the emple's back and sides.

Grieve was waiting for her in the shadows. "Watch this," he said, wrapping his hands in rags, then slinging the rope he wore across his shoulder, pulling it taut when the grappling hook caught fast.

He hauled himself up the rope, arm over arm. Not far to go until he reached a jutting metal spike. He tested his weight on it, anchored himself, then dropped the end of the rope back down to her.

Star shook her head. He jiggled the rope enthusiastically. With great agility, she shimmied up the broken staircase.

"Hey, where'd you learn to do that?"

She ignored the question. "They'll see us up here. The tower guards will shoot."

"Bet you there's not a bullet between them."

"What about the windows?"

"Trust me—nobody's looking."

She didn't trust him, but she followed closely at his heels, pausing now and then to take in the spectacular view. The abomination of the churning sky gave off enough light to permit them a clear view of geometric vegetable plots and the endless desert beyond them.

They climbed in through one of the topmost windows. Easier than it looked.

"Careful," he warned. "Nothing but starlight now, till we reach the second tier."

Star followed Grieve on tiptoe along a rickety walkway that hugged the circular walls. It shuddered beneath their combined weight. She willed herself to be light and sure-footed. If the structure collapsed, the fall would kill or cripple them.

Unfamiliar sounds emanated in random bursts from down below. It was too dark to see anything. Star paused to listen, but Grieve reached back and grabbed her sleeve.

"Keep moving!"

They dropped down to a lower level, a cramped area filled with metal panels, switches, and dusty glass. Dim light spilled in through the windows. The smell of fabric damp and thick with mould hung in the air.

"Don't touch," he whispered.

She had no intention of touching anything. Boxes were stacked high atop one another in teetering piles, some of them half decayed, their contents spilled. The smell of rot was much stronger, sharper here.

She covered her nose with her hand as he led her down again, both of them bent over, through a rabbit warren of narrow gaps. No light at all until they reached the end. Beyond a flap of musty hessian lay a nest; that was how she'd best describe it. A cosy pile of sacks and other fabrics. Above it was a makeshift shelf of bricks and boards upon which sat a trio of stumpy candles. A plate, a knife, and a collection of old-world trinkets, worth a coin or two, had there been anywhere to sell them.

"Stinks like an animal's lair," she said.

He didn't take the bait. "Shhh." He put his finger to his lips, then gently tugged at a scrappy length of hessian draped above the shelf. He motioned for her to lean and take a look. There were muffled voices. Flares of light.

Down below, the circular walls encased a bank of reliquary. Jagged brickwork jutted from the walls, suggesting an entire floor had been removed.

She stared. "What happens now?"

"We wait."

"Wait for what?"

"You'll see." He flopped down on his nest of a bed, stretched, and placed his hands behind his head, then closed his eyes.

Her shoulders slumped. She wriggled, attempting to get comfortable. "I don't have time for more of your stupid games."

"It's not a game," he said, his eyes still closed. "You wanted to see, so I'm showing you."

"I don't want to *see* anything. What I want is for us to get out of here before—"

He opened his eyes. "You'll want to see this. Trust me."

There was nowhere comfortable to sit unless she knelt to share the bed with him, so she remained standing in a cramped position, listening for the occasional sounds that rose up from down below. Peeping back out through the hessian, she noticed more detail every time: framed pictures, candles half burned down. Metal boxes with glass fronts, a flat expanse of dull white placed up high.

"How long will we have to wait?"

"Not long." He sat up, moved into a crouch. "That old lady lives for this. Her mind's addled. Rotted from the inside with all kinds of bullshit."

He was about to stretch back out again when both were started by a blast of sound. Star flinched. "What is that?"

He laughed. "Told you it'd be worth the climb!" He got up, squeezed beside her. "Watch."

At first she couldn't understand what she was seeing. Jagged movement, seemingly hanging mid-air. Not in the air, but against the far wall, a moving image of an object half-buried in sand, as seen from the sky or a mountain or the eye of a bird. The image changed, getting closer, then receding rapidly. It made her dizzy. She pulled away and flopped down on the bed, dazed.

"Takes a while to get used to," he told her, "but you'll get the hang of it."

"But what is it?"

Grieve looked smug. "I've got it figured. The old lady's pet drones have eyes like ours." He made broad motions with his arms. "They fly up high and this is what they see."

Star stood up, and moved the hessian aside to take a longer look, one hand on the shelf to keep her steady.

"Something about that blocky granite structure half stuck in the sand reminds me of the Vulture," she said after staring for a long time.

"What's the Vulture?"

"Just a place I used to know. Those people look like they're digging."

"Doesn't look much like a bird to me," he said.

"And they don't look like people."

The birds-eye view took them closer to the ground, swooping past massive reliquaries stabbing at the sand, scooping it and shoving it out of the way. There was a man who raised his shovel in the air and took a swing. A man who was not a man.

"Templars," she said. "Many of them."

"Templars and reliquary digging side by side." He shook his head. "Never seen anything—"

"I need to climb down, get a closer look." She snatched up one of the candles from the shelf.

"Too dangerous—that's the old lady's private space. A strange old bird—wait till you get a look at her."

Star picked up the tinder box, struck a light, and lit the candle. "If the Lotus Blue is buried in that structure, I need to see it with my own eyes, to see if any of what Quarrel says is true."

"You can't trust that mad old soldier—and I'm not gonna help you get yourself killed." He reached across and snatched the candle from her hands.

Star glanced back down past the hessian curtain. "Those drones are ancient—I'll bet they can't fly far from home. That means that excavation site is close—maybe close enough to reach on foot."

The bank of ancient reliquary was larger than it had appeared from above. Made from separate shiny boxes, some small and blocky, others rectangular and wide, stacked one atop another to form a ramshackle wall. Candles burned in the gaps between the boxes and in spaces where the shiny glass had been broken.

The images they'd been watching were flickering upon shiny surfaces that became blurry the closer she stood. Up close, she could barely make out details, just the dark grey of the excavation site stark against the sand, its figures smudged and indistinct. The picture's constant movement made her feel ill.

She looked away until the wave of nausea subsided. Glanced back at shadowy patches of dark and stillness, blurred images scrolling across everything: the walls, the curtains, her own clothing, hair, and skin.

She could hear Grieve following close behind her, stopping whenever she stopped, wedging in to crouch beside her in a place where they could see without being seen themselves. The smell of dank and mouldy curtain intensified.

"What's she doing? Who's she talking to?" Star whispered.

"That old lady doesn't stand still for long. She's all banged up from injuries that didn't heal so good. Everything hurts so she's always on the move, which is why we gotta keep our heads down out of sight."

Without warning, the images changed. There was no longer sun and sky and sand or the massive structure being dug up from the ground. In its place was water flowing, blue and pure. Shivering leaves dappled with sunlight. Delicate flowers: pink and white and lemon yellow. Flowers everywhere, hanging in the air. So real she could taste and touch and smell them.

She raised her hand to try and touch. Grieve pushed it back down. A voice boomed out of the verdant, swirling air:

Here be shadows large and long;
Here be spaces meet for song;
Grant, O garden-god, that I,
Now that none profane is nigh,—

The old woman spoke loudly, her voice sharp and clear. Grieve flinched when Star rose up and craned her neck.

"Keep your head down," he spat, dragging at her arm.

Star wasn't listening—the wonder of it all was too intense. She crept forward slowly, kicking Grieve's hand away when he tried again to stop her. She found herself a closer hiding place, with the old woman directly in her line of sight. She ignored Grieve's frantic whispering; it was impossible to hear what he was saying beneath the old woman's firm and commanding voice.

And saw in sleep old palaces and towers
Quivering within the waves' intenser days,
All overgrown with azure moss and flowers . . .

The skin on the old woman's arms and face was alive with images of rustling leaves, water droplets, clouds on skies that had never been so welcoming, so blue.

And we are here as on a darkling plain
Swept with confused alarms of struggle and flight
Where ignorant armies clash by night.

Nails dug into Star's arm, hard. Grieve was pressed so close she could smell his sweat.

"I'm getting you out of here," he said.

She pushed him away and raised up on her haunches, slowly, making no sudden movements.

A dark land fringed with flame,
A sky of grey with ochre swirls
Down to the dark land came
No wind, no sound, no man, no bird.

Birds! Great flocks of them, not the carrion kind, but brightly mottled with reds and greens and blues. Flying across the surfaces of the glass boxes and also through the air, by magic—it had to be magic.

"I am Marianthe and this is my Temple. My home. Who goes there? What do you want from me?"

Star froze, until the birds-that-were-not-really-there hung above her head.

"Show me your face. I cannot trust a man I cannot see."

A man? What man? The old woman had not even noticed Star, she realised. She was staring up into the air above the magic wings of the soundless birds.

"Many others have made claims even more grandiose than that one. Whom do you think you're speaking to? Some young and foolish girl with a heart fashioned from spun sugar, rose petals, and dew? I am a veteran of Crysse Plain, and we are not so easily enchanted."

"She's talking to herself, the mad old coot," whispered Grieve, tugging Star back down into a crouch.

"No she isn't. Somebody—or something is answering."

The old woman jerked suddenly, raised her hands in exasperation. "And what use would I have for trinkets such as these? Offer a lady something precious if you want to turn her head. Show me something I haven't . . . ahhh."

The old woman froze, her fingers splayed, wide eyes looking at something only she could see. The birds vanished, replaced by a flood of new images, one after the other, flowing like a bubbling brook, only it didn't look like water, something else, too quick to see.

The old woman wailed and clutched at her own arms. "My Benjamin—Benjamin, is it you? Could you ever, could you possibly be?"

"I'm telling you, she's batshit—"

"Shhh."

The spill of images slowed, revealing streams and leaves and green fields. The landscape disappeared. In its place, the face of a young man, square jawed and rugged handsome, appeared simultaneously on all the boxes, even the biggest.

"Benjamin?" The woman stood completely still, staring at the largest of the faces. Slowly, uncertainly, she shook her head. "No. No, not you, your eyes were never such an insipid shade of brown, nor your hair so thin, so easily . . ."

The image then changed, as if in response, the hue of the young man's eyes becoming rich and deep, the colour of fertile soil. His hair thickened and grew a little longer. The old woman stared at the new improving face in silence. Peered closer. "But it can't be you. I searched for you through the aftermath of Crysse, heart deep in blood and bones," she said bitterly.

"And I for you," said the giant face, still changing. Still adjusting. Now he was a man in uniform, his fine features streaked with mud and grime. Behind him was the smoke and haze of battle.

"Benjamin?"

Star felt a gentle tingling in her mesh, like she'd experienced when she ran through the Sentinel's protective field, accompanied by a sense of foreboding. Another mecha was close by, that was what it meant.

"I can't believe she's falling for it!" said Grieve. "Hey, wait—where are you going?"

Star stood up and walked right out into the open, arms raised high to show she held no weapons.

"Stop right now—don't listen to him," she called out. "That man is not who he says he is. He's not even a man—that's a war machine and he's messing with your memories. You can't trust it. You've got to stop listening—"

Startled by the intrusion, the old woman spun around so fast she almost toppled over. "What is this? Who are you?"

"Don't listen to it," Star repeated. She tried not to look at the face on the screen, even though there was something compulsively mesmerising about its gaze. The way the eyes seemed to pierce her flesh and hold her captive. Like it could see inside her mind.

Sharp movement buzzed around Star's face—real this time, not magical pictures. Drones. She swatted at them with bare hands. "That face is a liar," she shouted over the confusion. "It's a Lotus Blue, a killing machine, left over from the wars that burnt the world!"

The old woman's eyes widened, like a predator preparing to strike. She lunged. Cold, bony fingers pinched at Star's flesh, angling to touch her arm.

Star fought back. Up close, mere inches from Star's own, the old woman's face appeared like the carved masks the Knartooth used for ceremonies, all beak-like nose and exaggerated lips. Pierced lobes hung heavy with ornaments and wards.

But when the old woman pulled away, she appeared human once more. "I've not seen your face before," she said. "You're so young—how could you possibly know about such things?"

Star didn't know what to tell her. The drones whirled around her. The close air smelled like compost after rain. The giant face of a handsome soldier still hung there above them both looking so smug, so self satisfied.

"You're wrong," said the old woman. "The Lotus Generals are all extinct, the last of their kind faded from the world centuries past. That there is my Benjamin, I'd know him anywhere."

In an instant, the screens filled up with images of green, of lakes and streams and oceans wide, hills and flowers, animals and rain. Sweet rain falling down in sheets.

The old woman closed her eyes. "Ah, but you never saw the world the way it was. The way it can be again—but I did. I remember. I have enough memories to sustain us all through barren years."

The light changed colour. The old woman's face became infused with mottled green, a pattern of trembling leaves across her garments, her skin as bright fronds splashed across the shiny boxes behind.

A deep, creaking issued from behind them. Candle flames danced and flickered as Star turned to see silhouettes against a shaft of muddy light. A flood of people were pushing through the door, gasps of wonder uttered by the old woman's flock, invading Sanctum, no longer frightened, not wanting to miss the promises unfolding.

The projected pattern of leaves changed, then changed again, from grass to sky to brown tilled soil. Flowers and children, animals and streams. No evidence of Dead Red sand, rogue polyp storms, or heat blasted wasteland.

"The world the way it was," the old woman said. "The way it can be made again. The way we would have it be."

"It's not real," said Star.

"Rebirth," she continued. "Don't you understand?" The images began to melt into one another. Star felt lightheaded, like she had drunk too much toddy, smoked skunk, and been spun in circles all at once. Light exploded behind her eyes. Fire seared through her belly.

Throughout whirlpools of swirling forest, she watched the old woman moving like she belonged there, like the forest had always been her home.

The green enveloped everything. Star's own flesh was crawling with it. She shook, trying to slough it off her skin.

Discordant recitations swelled and intensified, increasing her sense of nausea. The old woman repeated the same words over and over. Words that made no sense. Useless words drowned out by enthusiastic song, the space filled up with farmers singing their lungs out, their attention on the mad old woman like she was the queen of everything.

A silhouette moved into the doorway, Quarrel shoving his way through the crowd. As they noticed him, the old woman's followers stopped singing and pulled away. He stank of sweat and blood and anger.

"How dare you invade this sacred space!" the old woman screamed, reeling back in horror and disgust.

Nobody moved. Nobody but Star. She ran to Quarrel just as a sequence of brutal seizures took hold of his body. The Templar slammed hard to the temple floor, eyes frozen wide with terror, wrists crossed above his chest as if they were bound.

Star knelt over him. "What's happening to you?"

His eyes met hers, his expression one of pity more than anything, something she'd never seen on his face before.

"I'm sorry," he blurted and then lunged, grabbing hold of her mesh arm, clutching it steady, pressing his own broken mesh hard up against it.

Something sharp and hot stabbed into her mesh. Pain washed over her, intense, blinding pain, then vanished abruptly. Star blinked rapidly—the only part of her that wasn't frozen. The rest of her felt like it was carved from wood. She couldn't feel her other arm, her legs, her fingers, or her toes. Only her mesh, a fierce heat draining out of it.

"Backup plan," grunted Quarrel, struggling to force the words out. He let go of her and howled, a sound like an animal in the throes of death and torment.

A hush fell over everything. There was nothing but the ringing in Star's ears, her own ragged breathing, thunks and tickings emitted by the boxes and the drones.

Nothing human had ever made a sound like that, a guttural grinding of searing pain and shriek. Quarrel's body convulsed and then lay still. He was spent, useless as a heap of broken machinery. He had emptied himself inside her mesh and now there was nothing left. The spark had gone out of him, the force, the drive, the life.

The old woman stood over the both of them, wide eyed and curious. Waves of sickness kept Star immobile, lying on her back. Nausea from what Quarrel had done to her, terror at what she was expected to do with what had been forced upon her. What would be done to her. Knowing there was no way of stopping it.

The old woman raised her arms, a signal to her people. Star watched helplessly as diaphanous layers of blue cloth fell away, exposing bare skin patterned with projected leaves and streams and sky— and something else. Horrible scars, like something had been cut out of her flesh. Wounds that had long since puckered and healed. Memories seared permanently in place.

Star understood what she was looking at: the place where mesh had once been embedded. The old woman was the same as Quarrel. The same as her. A Templar. A soldier, only someone had hacked the embedded metal out of her.

Quarrel's left leg spasmed and a jolt went through the crowd, followed by murmurs of unease as gradually movement returned to his other limbs.

Star sucked in her breath and held it. The Templar moaned and she exhaled, relieved to see that he was still alive.

He sat up, clambered shakily to his feet. Star forced herself to roll onto her side and push herself to standing.

"Quarrel!"

The Templar didn't answer. Didn't look at Star or any of them. He was headed towards the light of the entranceway, shoving people out of his way, elbowing a man who tried to stop him in the gut.

"Quarrel!"

He did not respond.

When Star tried to follow she was blocked by the old woman's followers. They might have been afraid of him but they were not afraid of her. She did not fight back. Her head was full, and splitting with memories that did not belong in there. Every movement created a bright flare of images she could barely comprehend. Visions of her fighting, dirty, up close and personal. The rush of adrenalin as she thrust a blade between the plates of damaged body armour. Slow motion explosions, air raining with blood and shrapnel. These were things she had never seen, never done, and yet her head was filled with them to the point of bursting. *Quarrel's memories. What else could they have been?*

"Lock her up!"

The old woman was afraid of her, she was calling to her followers for help. People emerged from the shadows. They were frightened too, but they did as they had been commanded, grabbing Star's arms and pinning them to her sides.

"Quarrel!"

The Templar passed through the entranceway, ignoring her—and everybody else—completely.

"Leave him!"

The old woman's followers scurried out of his way. Star was the one who mattered now. She'd been weakened by the memory transfer, they could tell. She'd be able to be contained if they acted quickly.

The old woman pressed up close, poking and prodding until she found what she was looking for: Star's mesh-embedded arm. She seized her wrist, held her arm up high for all to see. Star cringed but she couldn't pull away. The old woman was far stronger than she looked, her grip almost as powerful as Quarrel's.

Star searched from face to face, desperately looking for Grieve.

He wasn't there. He'd bolted like a rabbit into the darkness, into safety. A survivor.

Star became enveloped in swirling green. She was vaguely aware of arms beneath her, lifting her off her feet. Pressure pushed on her ribcage, her heart hammering underneath it. There was an overwhelming scent of putrefaction, soil and smoke. Light as silk, she was passed from hand to hand, an intoxicating wash of words pushing her upwards, upwards, dumping her like a tidal surge. The old woman leered in her face. Above and behind her, grinning out of the darkness, the giant face returned, its eyes now sapphire blue, its gaze intense, unwavering. No longer interested in the old woman.

"You belong to me," said the Lotus Blue.

=FIFTY-FIVE=

The drones are small, their cameras puny, and the vision they provide is jerky and uneven. Riding their crude sight makes the General nauseous, but, like rats, these drones can slip down deep inside the crevices. The things that only they can see make them precious beyond all reckoning.

He expects something valuable as he hacks inside the old woman's feed. She's been such a pushover, so easy to influence with his vast supply of digital imagery that has been stored away in his bunker's deep reserves, etched in crystal, saved up for a rainy day of the kind this land will never see again.

His images give her power over those who follow: peasants, obedient as dogs, willing to believe in anything offering hope beyond the barren dust. If he'd realised it would be this easy, he'd have focused on the little humans earlier

He's been curious to get a look at her, to see if her face jogs any latent memories. The old girl might have been one of his own command, or a relative, descended from one of his children. He hasn't seen anyone he recognises since the battle of Crysse Plain. Curiosity is beginning to win him over. He considers himself prepared for anything, anything at all, he thinks—but he is wrong.

The drone's eyes reveal the Temple's precious Sanctum, a gloomy chamber illuminated by candles and the glow of monitors. The heat of human bodies cluster around the cobwebbed edges. The old girl is standing near, her body swathed in fabric, but she cannot hide the truth of what she is. Even without the benefit of scanners and precision sensors, he can see she had once been a Templar soldier, always would be, even if her broken mesh has fallen dark and silent, her body crooked from battle scars. The only way out for her is death.

And beside her, another, younger Templar, a girl, her mesh bar illuminated via infrared. She has been initiated, yet is not fully functional.

Unusual. He's not encountered one of these in the field before, although he knows the history of the pods and caches, the backup plans, the contingency operations from the days when they thought the wars would last forever. In the later years, automated factories deep underground had churned out more weapons than the wars could use. Stockpiles spilled over, gathering dust in deep-sunk storage vaults. Most would never see the light of day, and the ones who'd caused their manufacture were all scuttled off underground.

The General's reminiscence is cut abruptly short. Writhing at the feet of the old Templar he spies yet another one of their kind, one he's already been prodding and poking at, has attempted to ride half a dozen times but has always been cast off—the damn thing puts up a hell of a defence. Here is a Templar older than the wars themselves, down and out and wriggling on the ground, screaming crazy, thrashing like a dog in acid rain. Messed up, broken, past all its use-by dates.

The General pauses. Something . . . he is missing something.

The girl.

The revelation hits him like a blast. He tugs the drone back, slams it into a better vantage point. The General cannot take his electronic eyes off her—the most beautiful sight he's ever seen. She is perfect. Everything he never knew he needed is standing right in front of him— aside from that great big ship, of course. The *Razael*—he needs that as well. With both of them and an honour guard of loyal, speeding tankers, the General can leave his prison tomb. Go wherever he wants to go, travel the world from grid to grid, find the others, the ones he only half remembers: Lotus Yellow, Lotus Red, Lotus Purple, Lotus Orange. Other colours, his brother and sister generals—trapped under tonnes of sand and gravel, digging their way on upwards towards the sun.

He will find them, help them, dig them out. Brush them off and dust them down.

The girl. Maybe there are others like her? Maybe he can build himself an army?

=FIFTY-SIX=

Jakome glanced back over his shoulder at the *Razael*. The vessel had a haunted feel to it. They'd been safe when they were on that ship. Even rogue tankers had treated it with respect, with its sturdy beams and powerful canvas sails. How vulnerable it now looked, wedged in sand, all but abandoned now, alone under the green and sickly sky.

The four of them walked slowly towards the bunker, single file, with Tallis in the lead. Kian and Allegra were in the middle, Jakome brought up the rear. They'd armed themselves with weapons taken from an onboard cabinet. Finely crafted rifles chiselled with engravings of animals Jakome was certain did not exist anymore.

He clutched his weapon between sweaty palms, overwhelmed by the enormousness, the sheer unbelievable size of the dark shape protruding from the sand ahead of them. The bunker resembled a giant spider emerging from a sand trap. Surrounding it was a staggering assemblage of flesh and mecha, all labouring side by side in the baking sun. He'd seen digging machines at work before, back home, gnawing away at Axa's underground tunnel extensions. But this was different. The bunker almost seemed like a living creature. He'd never seen anything like it. Nobody had.

Led by Kian, the others pushed ahead, pausing when drones were spotted to take cover in the shadow of an enormous broken down digging contraption. Jakome hurried to catch up with the others, flustered by the constant, frenzied motion all around them; metal relics gouging, raking, stabbing at the sand. Noise and more noise, sand choking up the air.

His heart pounded, expecting at any minute to be discovered and fired upon, either by drones, or an army of Templar diggers. This excavation was not the work of men. It was as if the massive granite bunker itself was sentient, digging itself free from its interment.

"By all that is holy," exclaimed Tallis. No need for him to point, the others had seen them too. Metal creatures digging alongside Templars: like men with the flesh stripped clean off their frames. Skeletal reliquaries without faces, yet standing on two legs and radiating the authority of men.

"Hammer of God," said Kian. Jakome nodded, remembering his history lessons. How the last of the Hammer-of-God platoons were supposed to have been wiped out in the Lotus Wars. Proto-Templars, forged before some hive of generals thought to experiment with melding flesh and mecha.

Jakome slung his rifle over his shoulder, where it would not get in the way. He'd never been much of a fighter, not even for sport. He pulled a map from beneath his shirt—the only one they needed. He'd taken the time to pore over all three precious artefacts, but he could only get so far without the code that unlocked the next level. The girl had assured them she possessed the code and she was far too smart to let it slip for nothing. As long as she had it, the others would fight for her.

But maps were useless if they could not find a way inside the spider-bellied bunker. So many obstacles lay between them and their destination: a fallen wall, great curling sheets of rusted corrugated iron. Things he didn't know the names of. Drones and Templars and those faceless mecha diggers. So far, their luck had held out, but Jakome was not one to take such things for granted. He'd never considered himself a taker of risks, but the aboveground world turned out to be so much bigger and more terrifying than he ever could have imagined.

Allegra, on the other hand, seemed comfortable amidst so much strangeness. She so obviously itched to get inside the belly of the beast, despite the dangers, perhaps even because of them. She and Kian made a formidable team. If they did not end up killing each other, theirs could prove a powerful partnership.

The belly of the beast. Even only partially excavated, the bunker was much larger than it had appeared from afar. Not one structure but several, sitting in close proximity. But the spider-like central mass was the one they needed. A sequence of identical dark rectangular openings marked its middle, many of them jammed with sand.

They waited impatiently in shadow until the last of the drones passed overhead. It was hard to tell if the flying relics were armed or dangerous, but one could never be too careful.

Kian turned suddenly to face him. No need to speak, Jakome knew what he was going to ask. He was about to remove the map from his shirt so all could share in the decision of what came next, when without warning Tallis leapt to his feet and made a run for it.

Jakome called out after his brother, a reflex action. Kian silenced him with a shove. No time to think. Allegra leapt to her feet and followed, past the diggers, dodging around embedded obstacles, squeezing through gaps in the ragged corrugated iron sheets like rats.

"See you on the other side," said Kian as he tore after Allegra.

Poor impulse control, thought Jakome, was what had gotten them into this mess in the first place. Kian's inability to mind his own business in the Axan court, where every uttered word was of consequence.

He followed his cousin—what else was he supposed to do? By the time he was through the iron barrier, Tallis had made it to the bunker itself. Jakome looked up to see him vaulting through one of the openings, recklessly, feet first.

Nobody stopped them. Templars and mecha men apparently cared for nothing but the tasks they'd been assigned. They would simply dig and haul and scrape and throw until their bodies could perform the tasks no longer.

Jakome followed his brother through the hole and landed in a cloud of sand and rubble. They were in a corridor, a single shaft of dusty light steaming into it. The other three crouched nearby, waiting impatiently. Not for him but for the maps he carried. Allegra held out her hand.

"She has the code," reminded Kian.

Allegra nodded smugly. Reluctantly, Jakome passed her the precious artefact. She took the slender sheet of plastic in her small and delicate hands, a mysterious wonder from an age when practically anything had seemed possible. Nobody living knew how such objects had been manufactured. Not even the scholars of Axa. Kian and Jakome had spent hours discussing such things.

The three men stared as Allegra poked and prodded at the map, turning it over and over again.

"Do you know what you're doing?" asked Jakome coldly.

"Don't interrupt," she snapped without looking up.

They'd all witnessed the girl's father whispering that code into her ear. Whispering something—for her sake, Jakome hoped the father had not lied. Kian might have fallen for her charms but he and his brother prided themselves upon being practical men.

Allegra bent forward suddenly, as if in prayer, pressing her lips up against the plastic sheet.

She sat back on her haunches, holding her breath as the plastic map came to life. Coloured squiggles leapt into the air, splashing across the bunker's cement walls. Jakome sucked in his breath and held it. The others made no attempt to hide their astonishment and awe.

"I will carry the map," said Allegra.

"No." Kian snatched it from her hands.

"I have only unlocked one layer," she said sternly. "So don't go getting any stupid ideas."

Nobody asked about the other two maps, which Jakome kept in his Impact suit for safety.

They got to their feet and headed down the gloomy corridor, Kian in the lead, Allegra only a couple of steps behind.

Jakome sidled up to Tallis and whispered, "See the trust he places in her?"

Tallis grunted. "She came through, didn't she? That map appears to be functional."

Jakome fell into step a few paces behind his brother. Not too far— it would be easy to get lost in such a place. He would not be giving that girl any more attention than he had to. He would not be turning his back on her, or trusting her to carry anything sharp.

Allegra's excited chattering filled the corridor as she and Kian attempted to make sense of the map's glowing, moving squiggles. Different colours denoted different things, if only they could figure out what they meant.

"Father will come around eventually—you'll see. He is old, that's all. He'll see the light. He doesn't get it, his head's stuck in the past."

Jakome knew he needed to be the one who kept a clear head from this point onwards. The map was amazing. Everything in this place was beyond incredible, but the bunker frightened him. He recalled the fat man's warnings, how genuinely terrified he seemed to be of the creature that lay within its bowels, the Lotus Blue. The old man was rich, which implied he wasn't stupid. It would take a lot of skill and cunning to hang on to wealth in a place like Fallow Heel. Plus, he'd been outwitting Axa and its rival fortress cities for the best part of thirty years.

Jakome's cousin's eyes shone with such obvious lust and greed. Kian was never interested when it came to people telling him things he didn't want to hear. He was quick to anger, quick to overreact and lash out. Such reckless speed and scanty foresight was what landed them here in the first place. A dangerous mission, one originally intended as a punishment, to scout the coastal Sand Road and its peoples. They had almost made it home before that blasted Angel fell out of the sky, infecting Kian with grandiose ideas. Now they found themselves in an underground bunker way out past the edge of civilisation. A bunker that could easily become their tomb.

But the wonders they had seen!

Strangest things of all, the sight of people riding mobile junk heaps, chasing battletankers across the sand, hunting them down and tripping them over. Crawling inside and scooping out their ops. He'd never realised how their back home lights and comms relied completely on such desperate, crazy acts. The scholars of Axa, for all their superiority and attitude, did not know how to make the mecha blood and circuitry on which their underground city thrived. They could crow and preen as much as they liked, talk up the superiority of life beneath the sand, but the truth was they were not so far removed from the barbarians of the plains. Barbarians whose insane bravado had rendered them well equipped for uncertain futures.

Kian cared not for amazing evidence of lost technologies and civilisations. He cared only for finding new ways to shift the power balance back in Axa. Of besting old enemies—his uncle most of all—of crushing them under foot and under his thumb. He wasn't taking in the wider world, the vastness of the open sky, a world so much bigger than any of them had understood existed.

The others didn't know it yet, but Jakome had made up his mind. He would not be going back to a life of pointless luxury lived deep underground. To the dull inevitability of the Axan court, its petty politics, high starched collars, easy offences and bitter reprisals. If they ever made it out of here and back across that crazy stinking slab of cracked flat Black, Jakome was going to find another home.

= FIFTY-SEVEN =

The mud brick cell was fourteen paces long and eight paces wide, evidently not often used—it smelled of dust and damp and rot.

There was no furniture except a sleeping pallet crawling with sand lice and a dented metal bucket in the corner. No food or water. A barred window embedded high in the wall let through a little moonlight, but not much.

Hours had passed since the old woman's guards had pushed Star through the door and bolted it. Her head was still buzzing with images that were not her own. Images from Quarrel's life. Awful memories of bloodshed and carnage, things he had seen and done.

But Quarrel had infected her with more than just images. He had crawled inside her head and planted something deep within. A fiery seed, something she could feel rather than see. A message, a whisper, a poison, a sickness . . . she didn't know the name for it, only that it was important—the future of the Sand Road depended on it. And that meant she had to find a way out of her cell.

Mud brick walls. She slapped her palms down hard against their gritty surface. With a knife or jagged splinters of wood, she might have been able to scratch her way to freedom, given enough time and patience. But all she had were fingernails—they'd taken the knives from her boots. She broke two of them giving it a go, then sat hugging her knees in the centre of the room, the soft blue moonlight bathing her dirt-streaked face.

As the hours passed, the violent images in her head began to dissipate. Chill air seeped through the thin fabric of her tunic. She rocked back and forward, trying to make sense of it all. How far she had come, how far away she was from anything familiar, how many things she had lost along the way.

The old woman was barking mad, the Lotus Blue had her tightly in its clutches, and Star knew it would have her too before much longer. The seeds were in her—both from Quarrel and the Blue—she could feel them. All it would take was time.

She didn't blame Grieve for abandoning her. A born survivor, that was Grieve, always one step ahead. Always looking out for number one, no matter who else got lost along the way.

She pictured the old woman's arm and its horrible disfigurement. Marianthe, she had called herself. She was a survivor too. Had she built this place as a refuge from the wars? Relief from the Sand Road's relentless barbarities? She offered shelter, hope, and dreams in exchange for labour, only the dreams had taken over and now the woman couldn't tell the light from the dark. Didn't recognise the nightmare blooming on her doorstep. What was broken could not be fixed. The world could not be re-made the way it was. The Lotus Blue had woken and now it was too late for all of them.

Star closed her eyes and pictured Nene, using the memory of her sister's face to keep the bloody tide of Quarrel's memories at bay. She remembered fondly their battered old wagon, painted green and blue. The cloying stink of its bitter herbs and ointments. All the times she'd slacked off, dodged chores, hid out amongst the other travellers, listening to their outlandish stories, dreamt of a better life. One that would leave the Sand Road far behind. She'd thought herself much better than those people. Better than Remy with his ill-thought-out bravado. Better than Yeshie and her amulets of bone and glaze. Better than Anj and Kaja and Griff, gang rivalries, and paybacks. A Templar, that was what she was, but one so small and broken she could not perform the tasks required of her. She was a monster. Tainted, useless, and alone. She would die in here and nobody would remember her name.

= FIFTY-EIGHT =

Alone at last.

Marianthe paced the length of her Sanctum floor. She had frightened the last of her followers out, threatening them with the kind of violence she hadn't had to use in more than a decade. Green patterns rolled and flickered across the fabric of her robes, splashed across the walls and screens, and cascaded through the dusty air like insect swarms.

She yelled at Ana-Maria to shut the consoles down, before remembering that Ana-Maria had fled in terror along with the rest of them. Fallen candles spilled and spluttered wasting the remainder of their light.

Her hands were still shaking. She needed time to think. Time was the one thing she had long taken for granted. Time was all there was out here at the far edge of the world. Beyond the Crysse graves lay desolation, just ruins and lands belonging to the tankers and other castes and creeds of mechakind, to things that had evolved and adapted, changed themselves to live amongst the rubble.

Marianthe stared at the patch of floor where the Templar warrior had burst in, fallen, and convulsed. There was nothing there now but scuffs and dark smears. Dirt or blood or something else. Twice the size of a normal man, she had known him for what he was, in an instant.

After all, he was not the first of his kind to force his way into her temple. She'd fought the last one off a hundred years ago, after telling her people to take up arms and defend their gardens against rogue warrior incursion. Half of them had been slaughtered like dogs, but what had she expected? But this time, this one . . . this one was different. This one had had a kindness in his crazy bloodshot eyes. Not for her—he had not even noticed her, she was sure of that. No eyes for old crone Marianthe, who had once been beautiful—nobody remembered that. Eyes only for the girl, the willow wisp, the scrawny thing with the meshed-up arm who didn't even know the pain she carried.

She should have killed the both of them for coming between her and her memories. Her man made real, made big as life, her memories fleshed whole. Her handsome soldier, the love of her life. They'd died in the wars together, or so she'd thought.

Or so she'd thought.

That face on the screens—had she seen what she thought she'd seen? It was all too fast, too late, too horrible. The girl was a bomb and she had to be removed. A Templar bomb who wasn't even trained, who did not even comprehend her own significance. The wrong set of words or mismanaged key commands, and she could bring the whole dish down upon their heads.

She would instruct Pavel to do the deed. A sharp, quick blow to the back of the girl's head with a shovel. Quick and dirty, but safer for everybody. The girl would never even know what hit her.

Marianthe realised she'd been walking in circles, round and round, broken candles kicked out of the way. Farm dirt scuffed all over the floor. Broken hearts and broken dreams. It was time to pull her thoughts back into perspective. Something was still niggling at the back of her brain, though. The fallen soldier, the Templar warrior half out of his skull, writhing and convulsing on the ground. He looked to be the same age, same vintage as she was—vat growns can always tell a brother or a sister soldier. *Lovers and fighters, not sisters and brothers.*

Lovers and fighters.

She paused to think. No. It couldn't be. Too horrible to think about. Her Benjamin had been handsome, handsome and strong. She wanted to say no, to say it couldn't be true. But the broken thing writhing on the floor, the thing she was almost positive could not have been her Benjamin, had gotten up and crawled away before she'd had time to ask him any questions.

= FIFTY-NINE =

Quarrel stared up at the sky. Never had he seen such a sickly hue. Not even long ago, in the heat of battle, with the world lit up by missile strikes, contrails warped and weft across the sky.

His Manthy had been young back then. Love of his life, she was. They had all been so young, driving pods polished so bright you could see your own reflection.

The memory froze in his mind: his own rugged face staring back at him from the past. Square jawed and serious, like some kind of action hero. Jacked up on GoGo, Freeze, and Rocketburn. Pods keyed in to their own biometrics, named for the heroes of revolutions past.

He wiped a smear of sweat out of his eyes. Now what the hell had she called that pod of hers? Charlie . . . Charcoal . . . Cherry cheery something-or-other? It seemed so wrong that the name had been forgotten. It had slipped out of his memory like so many other names and places, relegated to the realm of ghosts.

He stood to attention and saluted her memory. "Yes, Ma'am!"

Ma'am. How long since he'd used that form of address? In Nisn, they were all called Sir, be they men, women, or otherwise. Sir for the humans, Templar for the ones who would be soldiers.

And he would be a soldier one more time, would fight his way through this desert bullshit until he found a way back into her arms. Home is where the heart remains, even when the rest has been forgotten, even the glory days.

Glory days.

Because they *had* been glory days, he knows that even though his memories of them were locked in fragmentary slivers. The day they liberated the Palace of Adecco. Two years of siege, then they had battered down the walls with sonic fugue. It was the battles he remembered best of all, back when there'd been true names and places. Back when they'd known what they were fighting for and why. When those condemned to give their lives had done so for a reason. Reasons that had seemed reasonable at the time.

Quarrel strode forward, picking up the pace. There'd been something important he was supposed to remember. Something to do with his mesh. He stared at the patch of sand between his feet. Remember . . . why couldn't he remember?

Voices were screaming in his face, then a blast of pain tore through his shoulder, knocking him flat on his back. Nerves quivering like maggots in spoiled meat.

Unfamiliar sounds make him raise his head. The stink of something rotting. Tear-blurred eyes. He rubs them clear. A blood-streaked sky, the cloy and stench of battle-weary fighters.

The hour: sometime just past dawn. Soldiers hang listlessly in the slowly-building heat, uniforms encrusted with dried blood. All bear wounds and gross disfigurements. They are the lucky ones, the ones still able to stand and fight.

Whatever pride and honour they set out with has long gone. They are defeated and starving, with hunched shoulders and weeping sores. Waiting for the sky to brighten. Waiting to make their last futile strike.

He holds his breath. Afraid to move in case of . . . what, exactly? He turns. Regrets it. Witnesses another mercy killing. The screaming abruptly ceases, the agonised pleadings drowned by noise and confusion on the battle fringe.

A gentle hand falls on his shoulder. Hers. Painfully thin, but whole, her face still beautiful even though it's flecked with gore and dirt. She points ahead. There are figures approaching across the sand. Not soldiers.

Closer still, their garments striking. Simple, yet of a fine weave. Blue cloth. Clean people with meat on their bones. Not soldiers. Anything but soldiers.

"Who—" he begins to ask, then stops himself. It doesn't matter. Only the fighting matters.

An explosion above his head. He finds himself face down in sand, her body thrown across his own. He's landed badly, jarring his jaw. She hauls him up, shepherds him away from sand that's no longer safe. He doesn't argue. Shells are exploding overhead, so loud he fears his eardrums will shatter. They run, clamping their ears against the noise, stumbling forwards, dodging fallen bodies.

Knees graze against the potential sanctuary of rocks. She doesn't need to tell him. He climbs, following her lead, head racing with questions that will have to wait until they're safe to be answered. Fatigue laps at his edges. Every muscle aches. Hurts, all bruises, scratched and blistering.

Their destination is a rocky shelf with little to shield it. They stop to rest and he studies her features. He loves her—should he tell her? So little time for talking. She takes him gently in her arms. He clings to her, desperate for comfort. No one has hugged him in a very long time. He stinks of blood and bile and sweat but she doesn't seem to care. He needs her more than he has ever needed anyone.

They kiss hard, draw each other close.

They are interrupted by a sound so loud, it drowns the thunder of exploding shells. They separate. Stare out across the battlefield. There is thick smoke and confusion. "Which side is ours?" she asks.

"It begins," he tells her, looking to the place she's looking, willing himself to see whatever she sees. Hoping to make some sense of it all. Something terribly important is taking place, he's sure of it.

The bombardment ceases. Have they been defeated? Perhaps there's no one left to kill? Eerie silence falls across the plain. Not even the screams of the dying linger. A new sound rising, deadly and horrific, churning in the pit of his stomach, setting his bones on edge.

"Incoming," he screams.

The high-pitched whine invades their heads, their veins, their hearts and lungs. It's everywhere and it hurts like fire, licking at their skin, curdling their blood.

Tiny silver arrows dart like lightning, cutting furrows through the clouds. The lookout tower explodes in great gouts of flame.

"Run!" he says and he takes off, tearing like the hounds of hell are on his heels. But she's not with him. She's on the ground, face down, not moving. Not breathing.

Flies buzzed around Quarrel's sweaty face. He caught one between his thumb and forefinger. Watched it squirm. Crushed it flat. He wondered how long it had been since he last slept. With eyes wide open, he was still dreaming of all the faces of his platoon. No names. Names were the first things to fade from memory—all of them except for hers.

"Manthy? Manthy, did they kill you? Is that what came to pass?"

He staggered a little further, and looked up to see a rocket shooting overhead. He watched it fall in a sweeping arc, felt the sand shudder beneath his boots when it impacted.

"Expect me to believe that's real?" he called out.

No answer. Not that he was expecting one. With a clumsy motion, he tugged a bowie knife from his boot.

"How about this one then—real enough for you, maybe?"

Emitting a blood curdling cry, he swung the knife at his own mesh with all the force he could muster. But his action was halted mid air, frozen just above the point of impact.

"Let me go, you bastard!"

Quarrel now belonged to the Lotus Blue. The General would never let him go, not until he'd worked himself to death in its service.

Quarrel shoved the knife back in its sheath. He picked up the pace even though he was exhausted, marching off to join the Templar army, head awash with a tide of jumbled memories. Rockets sailing and exploding overhead.

= SIXTY =

When the mud brick walls of her cell began to shake, Star thought it was her own head splitting, thought it was Quarrel's memories finally taking over for good, tipping her over the edge.

She wrapped her arms around her head and rocked forward and back. Forward and back. She coughed, lungs thick with mud brick dust, shattered bricks tumbling all around her, powdering her face and hair. Moonlight flooded in through a jagged, gaping rent. Nothing was visible through the swirling dust.

Cracks in the wall, growing wider and wider. She stopped moving, not yet comprehending the significance.

"Stand back! Get out of the way!"

It was a male voice, familiar, but it couldn't be. Not Grieve. Grieve the coward, Grieve the lazy, Grieve the thief who'd abandoned her to the crazy old lady's wrath.

She crawled away from the tumbling bricks as the crack widened further, the wall convulsed, and another hail of bricks dislodged.

"Get up, Star! Get off the ground!"

Shouting, but she couldn't be sure which way was up. A figure moving through the dust, hands dragging her to her feet. So she balled her fists and tried to fight him off, still not trusting in the sound of his voice, not trusting that the self-serving thief would have really come back to save her.

The figure grabbed her by both wrists, face obscured in a plume of dust.

"Grieve?"

All around her, ghostly shapes moved through a swirl of dust and moonlight. A large mass, something strong and powerful peering in through the broken wall. *Death come to take her, filling her vision, blocking out the night.*

She stumbled forward, his arm around her waist, helping her up and over the broken bricks. Up and over, then up again, coughing as someone else clasped both her arms and hauled her up. Grieve pushed from below, then climbed up after her, nimble as a monkey, a coil of rope slung snugly across his torso. There was a blast of chilly evening air and then they were moving, faster than anything, his sinewy arms wrapped tight around her waist.

Her vision cleared as they thundered through the courtyard, knocking over buckets and barrows stacked neatly against the white-washed wall. Out between the lookout towers, high enough up off the ground to see inside the nearest one, the woman on guard blinking in surprise, a rifle clutched uselessly in her hands. Too surprised to aim and fire, apparently.

The lizard. They were riding on Iago's lizard, Iago sitting up ahead of her astride the creature's neck, Tully Grieve jammed up close behind her, breathing in her ear.

"Lizard rammed right through the wall," he said, still gasping from the exertion. "Impressed? You ought to be."

The stars were bright as diamond dust, the garden plots prim and regular as dunes. She craned her neck, expecting something—any-thing—behind them, but there was nothing. No pursuit. Not a single gunshot fired.

"Why aren't they coming after us?"

Grieve gave her a cheerful squeeze. "Who cares why? They're sleeping and we're free—that's all that matters. Gonna find that Lotus Blue of yours and we're gonna shut it down—right, Iago?"

She coughed the last of the brick dust from her lungs. "Does that mean you believe me?"

"Always believed you—especially after that Templar monster blew his load. That got me thinking—the old lady too. She knows full well something's wrong, but what's she gonna do about it—that's the problem with most folks, don't you think? Nobody wants to stick their neck out for the tribe. Nobody wants to be the one. The hero."

Grieve was babbling nonsense. He was not himself. Neither was she—she didn't know her own mind anymore, how much of it belonged to Quarrel, how much longer the dregs of her own could hold out against the Blue. It was waiting for her out there—she could feel it.

"I'm dangerous. You have to get away from me."

Grieve gave her a dismissive snort. "Don't think you're getting out of it so easy. You're all we've got if that mad old Templar's right. And he is right, of course he's right. Those things always know what they're doing."

She had no idea what to say to him, how to respond—did he comprehend *what* she was? He had to know, so why was he trusting her?

The cold bit through the thin weave of her shirt, but being free of the cell more than made up for it.

"There's blankets," he added. "Water, too. And food. We'll rest up when we've gained a bit of distance."

"We can't stop—she'll be coming after us."

"No she won't."

The warmth of his skin pressing up against her own felt more comforting than anything she could remember. Comforting too was the sight of Iago, perched ahead on the lizard's neck, coaxing the creature onwards. Leaning forward, whispering into Iolani's ear. Slapping her good-naturedly on the side.

Iolani ran with a loping, side-to-side gait that took awhile to get used to. Engaging Iago in conversation proved impossible. When not whispering to the beast, his full attention was on the still and shrouded dunes, alert for trouble on the sand ahead. Eerie and beautiful as the landscape was, it was also filled with danger and uncertainty.

There was no question of which way they had to go. The bruised borealis poisoning the sky glowed with opalescent hues, lighting up the darkness, beckoning them towards it. The thing had changed since she'd seen it last, and it was morphing still, pulsing and heaving like a beating heart lay at its core.

"What did you say to Iago to get him to leave the Temple compound?" Star kept her voice low and her lips close to Grieve's ear. She was uncomfortable talking about Iago behind his back—literally—but she didn't want to distract him and there didn't seem to be another way.

Grieve took a while to answer. He stared out into the murky night, alert for evidence of tankers on the move. They could no longer see the Temple of the Dish, the fires, nor the old woman's geometric gardens. They had well and truly entered tanker territory, vast and open. The thought was terrifying.

Eventually even the dunes themselves were nothing but dark shapes receding in the distance, swallowed by the night. Star nudged Grieve gently in the ribs. "What did you tell him? Does he know the truth of . . ." *What I am* were the words she was trying to get out. Words that lodged in her throat.

"What's to tell?" said Grieve. "Man made up his own mind after I showed him the same thing I showed you. Sanctum, viewed from up on high. Pictures moving through the air."

She frowned. "The new green world and all the old woman's promises?"

"Not exactly." Grieve scratched his head. "Iago doesn't talk much. Hard to know what he's thinking. Might have had cause to nudge him along a little."

"Nudge?"

"Yeah, like I said, sometimes it's hard to say."

She twisted her body around further, trying to get a good look at Grieve's face. He didn't seem to want to meet her gaze.

The ride was getting bumpier; a change to the texture of the sand. Harder for the lizard to traverse. Iolani's gait became more ragged, more uneven.

"Grieve, what did you tell him? What is it you're not telling me?"

"Nothing. Honest!" Grieve swallowed. "He saw everything for himself. Visions of that excavation site, peeking down from my hidey hole, same as I showed you. Nothing different. Digging that granite bunker up out of the sand. Except . . ."

"What did you tell him?"

Grieve bit his lower lip. "A small exaggeration is all. I might have said it was his own village that was being dug up. That some of his own people were doing the digging."

She pulled her hand away. "No. You couldn't."

"There was no other way," he snapped. "Would you rather you were back in that cell, left to rot with all this going on?"

He gestured wildly at the cancerous sky blooming low above their heads. "That thing, whatever it is, it started firing missiles at us. A couple of hours past midnight—can't believe you didn't feel them hit. The laundry and one of the storehouses were destroyed. The old lady's people had to put a fire out, all hands at it, that was when we decided to come and get you."

Star had felt each shuddering impact, but she hadn't been certain they were real at the time, had decided they'd been more of Quarrel's invading memories.

"What happens when we get to where we're going? When he learns his people aren't there waiting for him, still alive?"

"Cross that bridge when we come to it, Star, like we do with all the bridges. Who's to say he wouldn't have come if I'd had more time to explain?"

"We're talking about people, not a bridge!"

"We did this for you, Star—that mad old witch was gonna leave you in that lock up—or maybe even worse than that—who knows?"

He gazed at her with big, wide eyes, like he was truly sorry.

"Iago will die when he learns the truth," said Star.

"According to you, we're all gonna die when that Lotus flips its lid. What difference is one more lie going to make?"

She punched him in the arm. He yelped. "You can't take anything seriously, can you?"

"What could be more serious than saving your life?"

They both turned to see Iago, twisted astride the lizard's neck, staring back at them.

"Nothing's wrong, buddy—you just keep on droving . . ."

He said something back, but Iolani swerved to avoid an obstacle unseen, taking up Iago's full attention.

"If he doesn't kill you, I will," said Star.

Grieve smiled. "That's the spirit!" He sat up straighter in the saddle and shook his hair free of the cord that held it bound up out of his eyes. "I've never taken a chance like this. Riding directly into danger with a sky on fire above my head." He raised his arms out wide and whooped, matted hair streaming in the wind. "Hey look, there goes another one!"

She couldn't help but follow his gaze. A fiery brand cut across the sky. Not an Angel falling but something else, accompanied by a painful shrieking sound. The burning thing, whatever it was, crash-landed far to the right of them. They felt no impact, but they heard it hit. Iolani baulked and Iago had to push up on his haunches, lean across and whisper in her ear, but she refused to run on any further. She barked and bellowed, turning in tight circles.

"Hang on," said Grieve.

He didn't have to tell her.

"Give him a minute. That lizard loves him, you noticed that? She does whatever he tells her to, just got a little bit spooked is all."

But Star wasn't listening to Grieve's banter. Another voice commanded her attention. Not a voice, exactly, a nagging susurrus inside her mind, like dried out branches shaking in vicious wind. Not particularly loud or strong, but there was nothing she could do to shut it down or block it out.

"The Blue knows I'm coming," she told Grieve. "It knows and it's going to try and stop me. Maybe that's what's going on. It's trying to fire on us."

"It doesn't know anything—those rockets are random as sandstorms. That Blue, whatever the hell you call it, that thing's even madder than those batshit crazy Templars. She's one of them, too, that old lady, did you notice? Looks like somebody dug all that metal out of her arm. Amazing she survived the operation—did you see the—"

He shut up as soon as he remembered. Star was also one of them. "I'm sorry. I didn't mean to . . ."

"Shut up, Grieve, and listen to me. The Blue knows I'm coming. It can speak inside my head. Very faint and not with words, but I can hear it and it knows we're on the way."

Iago had managed to settle the lizard, and now they were heading in the right direction again, making further conversation difficult, which was just as well, Star thought. She was running out of things to say.

"Old lady will have her drones on our tail before first light. Better keep our eyes open."

Star turned away from Grieve, eyes facing front, taking in the pulsing borealis above them, with its trailing threads of pink and silver. Her head was filled with Quarrel's legacy, his knowledge of the deadly weaponry she carried deep within her blood and bones.

= SIXTY-ONE =

The time has come for the Lotus Blue to pull it all together. The array has been pumped and shined and fired, the Zero Tower Sentinel extended to full length. Wild experiments with the polyp storms have caused a leak that is spiralling out of control. Poison now streams up into the sky, swirling in a vortex like the eye of an angry dragon.

The Blue had once seen an army of such creatures storm a bunker three times the size of this one. Armour plated, saddled up, and combat trained. A most magnificent sight, one of so many glorious visions lost to the indifference of humankind, to those who did not care for the splendour and majesty of destruction. Eighty beasts had been incinerated. He had watched them burn, their fire lighting up the sky. Red sky at night, conqueror's delight.

The General has sourced almost everything he needs: an army comprised of loyal, faithful mecha: Templars and their baser counter-parts, tankers, drones, and Angels. Creatures that came crawling out of ruined nooks and crannies, hurtling across the sands with light-ning speed. All he wants for now is the Warbird 47 and the ship—the *Razael*—and, eventually, the girl. He has her locked down for safekeep-ing, though. She'll come around in her own good time, will walk right into his arms and find redemption.

There's something else—his sensors show him a handful of addi-tional extras he hadn't bargained on: humans, small and frail and use-less, but even they might come in handy at some point. Four humans, attempting to crawl inside his brain. With the barest of efforts, he traps them in a holding pattern. He has plans to indulge in some experimen-tation, to determine what makes such creatures tick. He will pull them apart and try to piece them back together. Anything to while away the hours.

The General is so easily bored, so easily disappointed, launching rockets randomly just to see them burst. Remembering skies lit up with firecrackers, paper lanterns floating down a winding river, little origami boats, each one containing hand scrawled messages of hope. All the flourishes and intricacies of civilisation, how he misses them.

The girl with the mesh bar is the key. Through her he will be able to reconnect, re-establish hold, go forth and make a new name for himself. Leave this place to walk the Earth as the mighty Lotus Blue.

He cannot wait to meet her, face to face.

= SIXTY-TWO =

Dawn brought with it a little comfort—at least they could see the sand ahead of them. Travelling by moon and starlight, Star and Grieve had been forced to rely entirely on Iolani's sure footedness—whenever the creature panicked, they did too, and when she settled into calmness and repetition, they managed between them to catch a little sleep.

Morning light revealed a landscape more precarious, littered with boulders, crevasses, the bones of long-dead beasts, traces of long abandoned homesteads, skeletal wrecks of ancient war machines. The Dead Red Heart. Open sand. Rogue tanker territory.

Star scrutinised the sky behind them, alert for the old woman's crooked little messengers, as Iolani ducked and wove and dodged, slowing and swerving at Iago's commands.

"Listen, he's singing to her," whispered Grieve, a warm smile spreading from ear to ear. "All this death, this broken desolation, yet he's got time for song." He looked to Star and nudged her. "How about that!"

Star had been listening to the lilting melodies and had been using them to keep her own mind focused. To block out the unwelcome presence trying to force its way inside her head.

Iago's simple repetitious song brought back memories of Yeshie's campfire stories—they'd always had a rhythm to them. Star pushed her hand deep inside her pockets, reassured yet again by the bulging bag of amulets. Glad of all the memories they carried, embarrassed that she'd once thought of them as worthless. Magic or not, here they were, still alive, still moving forwards, despite all that had happened.

Grieve's body felt warm and comfortable against her own. She'd relaxed enough to feel grateful for his presence, the risk he and Iago had taken to bust her out of that cell. It was not something she would ever admit to his face, though. He should never have lied to Iago, and yet the lie had set her free. Because of that lie, they had a chance, even if only a small one.

They'd been lucky so far. Not a single tanker had been spotted. Not a single drone in hot pursuit. Perhaps their luck would see them through, at least until they reached their destination. By that point they'd need something else altogether stronger than luck.

The sun ascended, illuminating the ragged terrain. Random half-fused chunks of weathered steel jabbed upwards from the gently undulating dunes. Hardy foliage grew in clumps and tufts. Strange grasses she didn't know the names of. *Nene would have known their names—and what medicine could be made from them.*

Nene. What had become of her? Star could only hope for the best: that Ebba or one of the others at Twelfth Man had taken her in, offered her food and somewhere safe to sleep. Those people owed her but that didn't mean they could be relied upon, especially if her healing days were over. Fallow Heel had become a rough and crazy place, and she couldn't help thinking the worst of it and its inhabitants.

All her thoughts led to dark conclusions, no matter how hard she fought to shake them off. So she kept her mind and her eyes on that sickly borealis, sucking up light and blending it to muddy smudges. At its source was an ancient relic that planned to blast them all back into the age of stone and fire. A relic she was supposed to stop, somehow. Not somehow. She knew full well what needed to be done—and the thought was terrifying. So instead, she indulged in memories of life with Nene and her Van brat friends. Better times and better days, how much she would have changed, how much harder she'd have tried, if she could only do it all again.

Grieve started whistling off key. "That scab in the sky. What do you make of it?" he said before she'd had a chance to tell him to stop it.

"Poison, leeching out of that Lotus beast," she said.

"Helluva lot of poison, enough to turn the whole sky bad. I've seen some pretty crazy stuff—don't get me wrong—but what kind of—"

"We don't have to understand it," cut in Star. "We just have to shut it down." *And there's only one way to do that, Star. Only one way to win.*

"Big, brave words, there's no denying—and I know you've seen your share of pain and suffering. I've watched you put your knowledge to the test, watched you realise when it was time to abandon hope and wield the blade."

He took a dagger from his belt and stabbed at the sky with wild, exaggerated motions, trying to make her laugh. But she wasn't in the mood.

She swallowed dryly. Putting that old man out of his misery back amongst the rusting planes was not something she was proud of. "So what are you getting at?"

He shrugged and put the blade away. "Smart folks can tell when a wound's gone bad. When there's nothing left to do but cut and run."

She glanced up at the hideous sky, forcing herself to hold a steady gaze. It affected her, made her blood run stale and sluggish. Made her feel so sick she had no choice but to look away.

"Sometimes the patient's already dead, know what I'm saying? Sometimes you gotta know when the story's over."

"What you're getting at, Grieve, is that perhaps I should have left you there, chained to that row of half-dead mutineers, is that it? Is that what you're trying to tell me, Grieve?"

"Course not."

Iago was no longer singing to Iolani. They rode in silence, keeping a lookout for drones and tankers and other things that might pick up their scent. The debris-scattered landscape offered many hiding places for hungry predators, but so far nothing desperate enough to try its luck against a giant lizard.

"There's this place I found once," said Grieve after a time, picking up the threads of the conversation, "by accident. A bit of the coast everyone forgot—Sand Road doesn't go anywhere near it. An abandoned settlement—from recent years, not old. The snails and turtles and oysters have come back. Lobster too. And eels. Tools still lying around in the long tall grass."

She didn't respond, but when he stopped talking, she turned her face towards him.

He continued. "It's really peaceful, although the winds get rough. I spent some time and halfway fixed a shelter, plugging up the cracks with sodden turf. Always meant to get on back to it."

"What if the people who lived there once return?"

"They won't. Reckon they built sailing boats and crossed the Risen Sea. Reckon I'd like to follow them some day. Selene and I were going to—"

He stopped at the mention of her name.

"Tell me about Selene. You talk about her a lot."

"You remind me—"

Silence.

"I didn't mean . . ."

"It doesn't matter."

The wind picked up, errant gusts snatching at their hair, slamming stinging sand against their cheeks. Iago shouted loudly to Iolani, then paused, as if expecting her to answer.

Star jerked her body around to look Grieve in the eye. "Why are you helping me? Why aren't you running in the opposite direction, towards your little seaside sanctuary?"

He pressed his lips together. "I'm not staying. Just getting you across the sand is all—after that I'm out of here. Him, too," he said, nodding at Iago. "If he's got half a brain."

"When he finds out the truth about his village, you mean."

Grieve's expression clouded. "You can't ask us to die for you on your damn fool suicide mission. You can't stop that thing, whatever it is, but I know you're gonna try. I know your type."

She rubbed her arm. The mesh didn't feel like metal anymore, it felt like part of her own true skin. "Maybe you're right. Maybe the Lotus can't be stopped, but I—"

"Suicide!" he shouted in her face. "Madness!"

Star laughed—she couldn't help herself, it just slipped out. So unexpected—she hadn't thought there was any laughter left inside her, not after everything they'd been through. Grieve was pulling faces like a monkey, trying to keep her laughter going. He had a way with people, no doubt about it. She didn't want to like him and she knew she couldn't trust him. Not really, but she couldn't stop herself from feeling . . . something.

He shook his head like a wet dog, straw hair spiking in all directions. Raucous laughter escaping his own lips. "Never been crazier before this day, I swear—and trust me, I done my share of crazy."

She compressed her laughter down into a smile. "The day I catch myself trusting someone like you . . ."

Star turned back to face the front, not waiting for his reply, reminding herself of what lay ahead and that she'd have to face it on her own.

Deep breaths, that's what Lucius would have told her. Take deep breaths and focus on the task at hand. *I'm doing it*, she whispered. *Doing it and trying to do you proud.*

Iago shouted something, but his words were snatched by the wind. Grieve placed his hand upon her shoulder. No need, she'd already seen them. Tankers were rumbling across the open sand, their massive tires stirring up great clouds of dust. The lizard slowed, and Iago urged her onwards. The things were moving in a pack, a massive pod of rumbling mecha, like birds flying in formation, or a pack of wild dogs running down an easy kill.

One of the tankers broke off from the pod, fell behind, then curved in a new direction, directly towards them. Iago shouted, words repeated over and over. Iolani kept on running. Star gripped the saddle with both hands as the tanker hurtled forward at great speed. Grieve wrapped both arms around her waist, bracing for impact—there wasn't time to think. But then, at the last moment, the tanker swerved, missing them by several lengths. The thing was playing with them. Shaking the ground and shattering their nerves, kicking up sand. But the lizard did not falter. She ducked and swerved while the three of them clung on tight; Star and Grieve to each other, Iago to Iolani's hardy ears.

Dark shapes appeared on the sand ahead of them, directly below the pulsing sky scab. Rocks or ruins, it didn't matter which. Star shouted and pointed. Grieve knew what she meant. So did Iago. So did Iolani. The lizard swerved onto a new trajectory.

Star glanced back over her shoulder, balancing in the saddle, leaning her weight on Grieve as she tried for glimpses of the rogue tanker, to see if it was coming at them again, or if there were others. The tanker had not re-joined the pod. It seemed to be circling them at a distance. She almost lost her grip—then Grieve grabbed her waist and yanked her back into the saddle.

"Faster!" he yelled.

The lizard couldn't run any faster.

Star braced herself for another blast of sand, for Iolani to change direction again, for that tanker to have another go.

Tankersong was vibrating all around, high pitched and stomach-churning. She'd been prepared for it, but it still felt like a sharp kick in the guts. It was inside her head as well as in the air, drowning out the whispering of the Blue.

If they could only reach the mess of rocks and ruins that lay ahead.

= SIXTY-THREE =

The tactical plastic goggles strapped to Marianthe's face were so worn and scratched she could barely see a thing. But they kept the wind-whipped sand out of her eyes. Part of her expected to find that Templar standing amidst the Crysse grave markers, a solitary figure, head bowed, communing with the fallen, his own brothers and sisters. But Crysse was as still and empty as she had left it, no sign that he or anyone else had been there.

The Templar: a single image filled her mind: *his* face, so old and worn and lined and etched with pain and suffering. The years had not been kind to him. They hadn't been kind to anybody. But had it really been *him* writhing on the ground of Sanctum? His face had been contorted with private agonies, like something was trying to seize hold of his brain. Something he was fighting to be free of. Perhaps she'd been mistaken? It was easy to make mistakes in such a sad and broken world. Easy to see what you thought you wanted to see.

If it had been *him*, he had not recognised her, or perhaps not even noticed her standing beside him, face awash with images of green. All he had cared for was that girl, crawling towards her on his hands and knees, towards that child who had invaded Marianthe's private space. Blundered in like a rat through the wiring, interrupting the messages of peace and green that flowed like river running over rocks.

Ungrateful girl.

As if that had not been insult enough, she'd gone and smashed her way out of the holding cell. The girl was gone, and good luck to her.

Good luck to all of them, especially the lizard drover; she was really going to miss that boy. The Red would squeeze the moisture from their skin. They'd be dead within a day or two at best.

Marianthe hobbled past the shock-frozen expanse of meshed and melted exoskeletons. Sand grains scratched against her face. The heat was impassive, yet there was something else out there besides the sun and sand. Something spitting blasts of cool, crisp air in random bursts. It was not the first time she'd tasted such a chill. Something out there. Something. But nothing good, not as she had hoped and dreamt and prayed for. It had taken *him* to show her that.

Little Ditto, favourite of her drones, spun in giddy circles around her head. She swatted at it, annoyed. The drone meant well—they all did—but they didn't understand what was going on. How could they?

She tripped and cursed. Walking was becoming more difficult all the time, both through sand and over stony flats. Everything ached relentlessly, from her joints to her bones to her self-inflicted scars. Some of those wounds had never properly healed. She knew she didn't have much longer, a couple of years at best. A couple of years of back and forth, laying wreaths and clearing sand off hand-etched tomb-stones, mumbling prayers to deities that had died alongside the cultures responsible for their fabrication.

She waited, staring at the open sand, waiting for the gnarled old tanker to complete its circuit. She slipped the strap of the satchel over her head and took out the precious item she'd brought with her. Just in case she needed it. Just in case.

Her crown of thorns. She placed it gingerly on her head. "I am the queen of the dead," she said, out loud to the sun and sand and ruin. Wind howled through gaps in the exoskeleton carapaces. Sand skinks ran for cover.

Queen of the dead, words evaporating in the ever-present heat.

The tanker approached in a fug of dust, slowing to let Marianthe clamber up an exposed segment of its battle-scarred modular casing to a high position where sand barnacles had failed to take a hold. With clunks and pneumatic wheezes, it resumed its slow and lumbering orbit with propulsion that was jagged and uneven. It bumped and growled and bled great plumes of toxic smelling smoke. It had stopped—so trusting—to let her back on board and now she hung on with both hands, her walking stave wedged in between two bulbous barnacle clusters. She was terrified of losing it—without that stave she could barely walk.

After Crysse would come the tricky part—convincing the rattling old bucket of bolts and steel to leave the land it knew so well to transport her across the open Red, right into the heart of the boiling storm clouds clenched like a giant fist above the horizon.

Carefully, she manoeuvred herself into position, a place from which she could reach the tanker's primary neural interface. She had to chip the barnacles away with a bowie knife—original issue; she'd hung onto it all these years, knowing it would come in handy some day.

The tanker didn't put up much of a fight. It tolerated her gnarly fingers thrust inside its brain, changed its song and changed direction, the crown of thorns now telling it where to go.

"Goodbye, Crysse," whispered Marianthe, knowing that, whatever happened, she would never see that place again.

They travelled onwards through the desolate landscape. Two of her drones affixed themselves to the tanker's encrusted sides—the multi-limbed repair units scuttling across the tanker's back like parasites knew to keep their distance. The third drone flew high above her head, scouting for danger even though she couldn't hear whatever it was trying to tell her. Its data streams were useless without her Sanctum console, yet the little thing kept doing what it had been designed to do, and would keep on doing it until the bitter end.

Eventually they spotted a figure moving in the far-off distance, a darkened silhouette against the sand. But the tanker acted as if it might ignore the figure completely and thunder right on past. Marianthe swore—she had no idea how to make it stop. No time to learn, only time for rough experiments; pulling at this and stabbing at that. The tanker howled in drawn-out agony. It didn't stop, but instead slammed its breaks and swerved, sand spraying into the air, freaking the drones out, and freaking Marianthe too.

She'd have to jump for it, no question, and a fall like that would likely cripple her further, or kill her.

At the moment before the tanker regained its equilibrium and righted its course, the last possible moment, she grabbed her stave with one bony hand, then removed the crown of thorns with the other, fumbling to stow it in her satchel. She took a deep breath, then flung herself as far as she could, dropping the hardware, tucking into a commando roll straight into the base of a gentle dune, hoping the sand was as soft as it looked.

She rolled onto her left shoulder, landing painfully on her hip, and cried out as the breath was knocked from her lungs. She fell sprawling and tumbling onto her back, gazing upwards into sickly-coloured sky. Lying there, motionless, trying to remember how to breathe, scared to move in case something was broken.

Her faithful drones had disengaged from the lumbering mecha's bulk. They hovered above her head uncertainly, which would give away her position to any predators that might be in the vicinity. To *him* as well, the walking man, but she hadn't the energy to shout or shoo them off or do anything other than close her eyes and wait until the pain in her hip subsided.

It took awhile. Took time to get the stave into position, using it to lever herself to standing. Inch by painful inch, but she made it. Nothing was broken, just jarred and bruised and maybe cracked, but she could walk and she could see and the sun had not defeated her yet and that was all that mattered in the end.

Little Ditto dive-bombed and performed three excited circumnavigations. That drone had never learnt to curb its enthusiasm like the others. More dog than drone, she realised; it was funny how she'd never noticed that before.

"Make yourself useful and go scout," she snapped. The drone obeyed and the others followed. She hobbled after them, as much of her weight against the stave as it would take, but she was slowed by sand, and dismayed by the truth fast becoming apparent: maybe she hadn't done much worse than crack a rib, but walking brought more pain than ever and she would not be able to get very far. The sand was thick and she was lame. Alone in the middle of nowhere. Low dune crests blocked any useful view—and there was not any sign of *him*. Nor of the tanker either—it was gone.

Expended adrenalin doused her in vivid flashback: *Cold white faces shivering in the ruins, illuminated in flames and flashes. Shells ripping air, red sky streaked with blasted cinder brick and fire. Burning bunkers glowing with soft light. They covered the faces of their dead. All they could do for them. Screaming guns masked the gasping of the wounded.*

"Enough!"

She shook the vivid memories from her head, then poked around in the sand until she found her satchel and its precious cargo, the crown of thorns, hopefully not too damaged from her landing. And when she next looked up, there *he* was, walking out of the desert right towards her.

"Stop!"

She stabbed her stave in the sand down hard, and raised her hand, palm facing outwards.

He did not stop. The Templar warrior pressed on past, marching like a machine, which he was, of course, in part. Embedded mecha made him impervious to pain and fatigue and other flaws, but also impervious to compassion and curiosity and a host of other elements of civilised discourse.

"Stop!"

Marianthe's three drones ganged up on him, dive bombing and swooping close to his face, then down between his moving feet, near enough to slow him down on pain of tripping. He took a swing at one of them with a balled, meaty fist, but Flaxy was too quick and swift. He missed.

"Benjamin, do you not know your Manthy? How could you ever forget?" She stepped closer, her movements sharp and jerking, every step shooting pain through her arms and legs. "You gave me that name, do you not remember? My name made short and sweet. I buried you,

311

or at least I thought I did. Whatever happened? What has become of you?"

There was a sharp movement. A flash of reflected light. Marianthe recoiled as the Templar gripped a blade in his hand. Lightning reflexes, despite being half dead and crazy. She braced herself, took her weight off the stave in case she had to wield it as a weapon, a pointless action, she was not strong enough, but neither would she let her dear old flame take her down without a fight.

Quarrel moved closer, arm raised, face reddened from sunburn cut with stubble, tears streaming down his face.

Tears?

"Help me," he croaked.

He raised the blade and held it poised above his own arm. His mesh was exposed, but his knife hand still, unmoving. He appeared to be trying to stab himself but some unseen force would not permit it.

"Help me, Manthy, help me!"

"Oh Benjamin, what have they done to you?" She hobbled closer, not certain if he'd lash out and try to cut her. She didn't care—let the mecha run its course. She'd survive whatever came to pass. She always did. That was the strength, the power those Lotus Wars had bestowed upon her. Upon them both.

His face reddened and his eyes bulged. His knife hand tremored with stifled effort. Sweat poured off his sunburned skin. She let her stave fall gently to the sand, moving swift and loving as a breeze, making no sudden movements, touching his hand, uncurling his swollen fingers, one by one. Hard as wood, grazed as stone. With a deft twist she prised the knife free of his trembling grasp, clutching it tightly in her own right hand. "Are you sure about this, my darling?"

He didn't answer. He didn't have to. She knew. He was sure. Tremors running through his muscles, fighting hard to keep the beast at bay.

She took the knife and a deep breath, then stabbed the blade into his mesh, gouging and twisting with surgical precision, just like she'd done once before, on her own implants. Pulling it out and wiping it on her sleeve. She'd expected a scream but in its place, he let go a stream of gibberish:

"Hundred left, hundred short, snipers are shooting too high . . . Watch out, tank battalion creeping forward over the horizon: sneak, stalk, flank, lost the whole damn lot of 'em in twenty minutes last time . . . Stay within division zone! Johnny's tanks are sheltered snug behind twenty feet of concrete. Zone of the 42nd infantry division on our right. Speed and smarts, shake 'em up with heavy artillery . . ."

There was barely any blood to speak of.

She tucked the knife into her belt and bent down to fetch her stave. Then she called out to her drones to scout ahead, to make sure they were walking in the right direction. She hooked her free arm though his own. He kept on reliving a battle only he could see, but he didn't flinch at her assistance, and allowed her to nudge him forward. After a while, Benjamin Quarrel picked up the gist of walking in a straight line.

"I will walk with you," Marianthe said as they went. "I will walk with you to the end of the Earth."

= SIXTY-FOUR =

Iolani ran, thick legs thundering like storm clouds. Ahead, the ruins beckoned, stark against the lurid skyline. Remains of an ancient, hard-floored sanctuary where tankers could not reach them—or so they hoped. They'd be safe if the lizard could make it. Rest up until the tanker pod was out of sight.

Star twisted in the saddle, surprised to see Grieve's face grinning sheepishly mere inches from her own.

"What happened to that rogue tanker?" she said.

"Guess it fell back," he shrugged.

"Fell back? Why would it do that? We were sitting pretty. Easy targets."

They checked the sands behind them. No sign. The rest of the pod had changed direction, and were no more dangerous now than a cloud of dust.

"I don't like it. Something's wrong."

"Sometimes you get lucky and catch a break."

She twisted further, scanning the sands in all directions, shielding her eyes from the sun. The resonance of tankersong still reverberated through her bones, but the one that had come after them was gone. She twisted to look the other way. "I'd feel better if we could see it. At least we'd know where we stood."

She chewed her lip. "Reckon it's frightened of the lizard?"

"Maybe. Star, about what I was saying before. About the sea. Have you considered—"

"Later—we're not out of danger yet." The thing in her mind had fallen silent but she felt the presence of unseen creatures lurking all around them—and it made her nervous.

"Head for those ruins," she shouted at Iago. No need—Iago and Iolani knew what they were doing and where they were going. They didn't need her telling them anything. But her anxiety was on the rise. Grieve was right—what would happen when they reached the excavation site? Locating the Lotus Blue was just the start. Ancient mecha that could scab and taint the sky was more than a match for a few runaways on a lizard—even if the code Quarrel had loaded into her mesh was sound. Even if she could figure out how to deliver it. Even if . . .

"Star . . ."

She turned her head. "The tanker—is it back?" In a panic, she stood up again.

Grieve jerked her back down sharply. "No no, it's alright, there's nothing to see back there."

She stared at him blankly. "Then what do you want?"

"Promise me you'll come with us. Abandon this pointless quest."

"I can't promise and you shouldn't ask that of me."

He stared at her red-faced, then looked away, out across the sand, half-glimpsing tankers where there were none to see.

Gently, she elbowed him in the ribs. "Sun's getting to you—you have to focus. If we don't make it to those ruins—"

"Calm down, okay—we'll make it. Iago knows what he's doing."

She scanned every wind-blown tuft of grass for evidence of recent tankertread. Iago shouted a warning just in time as Iolani swerved to avoid a vicious row of jutting spikes. It was the ivory ribcage of some long-dead beast—at least three times the lizard's size, all but invisible against the sub-bleached sand.

The sand was scattered with broken bones, but there were no others as enormous, not that they could see.

"Woah," said Grieve. "What happened here?"

Star shook her head. She didn't want to think about it. What happened here had happened everywhere.

The ruins appeared no closer. They endured the crunching of bones under the lizard's feet, dodged around a series of boulders too large to have been blown there by the wind.

"Don't like this place," said Grieve. "Gives me the creeps."

"Me too."

Finally, the bones came to an end. Ahead of them, a stretch of open sand was peppered with a kind of spinifex grass Star had never seen before.

"We're going to make it," she said, feeling an elation she had not felt since before . . . before when, exactly? Before the Van had been disintegrated by the storm? Before she and Nene had lost everything they'd ever had?

Grieve's expression was grim, his cheeks red, fair skin burning in the rising sun.

"Wrap your head, you idiot. Sunstroke's going to make short work of you."

He raised his hand, and it looked like he was going to touch her cheek, but his hand hovered mid air, uncertainly.

"Grieve, what is up with you?"

Was his skin flushed with embarrassment or the sun? Hard for her to tell with his pale complexion.

Iolani continued, holding steady. "Look!" said Star, pointing back the way they'd come. A long way back, beyond the bones, the rogue tanker was coming after them again.

She clutched Grieve's arm. "I knew it was still out there."

She let go and shouted at Iago. "Faster! Make her go faster, it's gaining on us."

Then, without warning, the ground gave way beneath them. Grieve was thrown backwards, tumbling clear of the saddle. Star's arms and legs flailed in a desperate attempt to grab on to something. Anything. Her eyes, mouth, and ears filled quickly with soft, slippery grains. Sand. She clutched at it, blinking back the grit, in a panicked attempt to try and clear her vision.

She punched and kicked, both hands soon entangled in clusters of drifting root. She heard someone calling out her name. Grieve.

"Here," she called back, fear flooding through her. It was quicksand. The desert kind, waterless and deadly. An ocean of it with grassy clumps floating deceptively on top. Iago's lizard had plunged right in, headfirst, taking the human riders with her.

"Iago!"

Spitting her throat clear of sand, she managed to force her eyes open. She knew what to do. Nene had taught her, just like she'd taught her so many other useful things. Lie across it. Spread your weight as evenly as possible. Don't panic, or you'll sink as surely as a stone. Thrashing only sinks you faster. Easier said than done.

Something thudded close to her ear. The tattered end of a length of rope. Star could see Grieve suddenly, standing at the edge on firmer sand. Shouting words she couldn't hear over the terrible lowing sound that filled her ears. It was so loud, it drowned out the residual whine of the tankersong and the whispering in her head.

Iolani.

Iago sat astride the creature's neck just across from Star and she could see him clearly, suddenly: wide awake, slapping and pulling at the animal's tiny ears in the language only the two of them understood. Iolani bellowed mournfully in response, her large maw filling with sand. It was hopeless. The lizard was too big, and was drowning quickly, her sheer bulk dragging her beneath the sucking sand. Iago's efforts were utterly useless.

Grieve kept shouting Star's name, over and over. She grabbed the rope with both hands, overpowered by the realisation that there was nothing she could do for the drowning beast.

She lay across the top of the quicksand as foot by foot, Grieve hauled her up to safety.

"Iago!" she shouted, coughing sand from her lungs when she reached the edge.

Grieve coiled the rope and threw it back out for the drover to grab hold. On the second try it landed near enough. Iago's shoulders were rapidly vanishing below the surface. Only the tip of the lizard's muzzle remained above the quicksand.

"Iago! Iago—grab the rope!"

But the drover wasn't listening. Iago cared for nothing but his drowning beast. The mighty creature howled and thrashed but it was too late. Suddenly Star understood—as did Grieve. If his beast was going to drown, the drover was too.

The mournful bellowing became muffled by choking sand.

There was nothing either of them could do. At the very last moment Iago turned his head and they locked eyes.

Then Star and Grieve watched in silent horror as the sand consumed them both, man and beast.

=SIXTY-FIVE=

A pattern of repetitive footfall draws the Blue's attention, too heavy and regular a tread for dogs or other desert beasts. He's become distracted by the digging and the arrival of the ship, watching it jam its mighty wheels in heavy sand.

Intruders.

He pauses to listen carefully before activating electronic sensors: eyes and ears attuned to chatter as the four of them trek through the

317

grey cement corridors of his bunker-skull. They scratch and shrill like locusts in long grass. The Blue remembers how swarms of their kind would move from place to place, stripping the greenery off everything, drilling the ground, building towers to block the sunlight and the sky.

The four are bold, brazen as soldiers. They think they can walk right in and help themselves to what they like.

One of them etches crude graffiti on the walls. The General can't see properly, his micro lenses choked with years of dust. No, not graffiti, but a trail to mark their passage, to lead them back out again to safety, as if something as vital as survival could be trusted to such a flimsy trail of crumbs.

The Blue rummages through his crystal memory lattice, each treasured track small and sweet and bright and cold as jewels.

He realises he never showed that old Templar witch the good stuff. Perhaps he had been saving the lushest, greenest images for later, best and last.

He reaches deep into his vintage hoard, his store, his private stash, and considers the tricksy mechanisms required for fooling the human eye-and-brain, bombarding the senses, deluging with detail. Overkill works best, experience has taught him.

How desperately the Blue misses the company of articulated minds, his own kind most of all. But his brother and sister generals lie far across the Risen Sea, across lands scorched by flame and storm and savagery.

For the meantime, young explorers will have to do. Four minds alive with delusions of grandeur and achievement. They have made no secret of their intentions: to rob him blind and gut him thorough, steal his treasures and bury them under sand like dogs would bones. They are too stupid to comprehend what they are actually a witness to: the rebirth and ascension of a god. A god who plans to burn the world and build it up from scratch.

And scratch is all there is remaining of the poor old thing. All the best bits have been consumed, like the carcass of a lamb or cow—this land had once abounded with such creatures.

The explorers have come to pick out his brain, never guessing that they are walking inside of it at that very moment, up the stem and

318

through the temporal lobe, deep inside the occipital where he keeps his secrets.

The female makes the greatest noise; forever asking questions, yet she speaks like she's the one in charge—like she has mapped out the future further in advance than the others.

Curious.

He decides to give the little creatures what they've come for, after a fashion. But it isn't long before their persistent chitter chatter begins to bore him utterly. None of these creatures are of any use, it's the other girl he's after. The flesh-mesh construct, the one with enhanced cerebral storage capacity.

The General decides to construct a little garden. A cage, more like—he coaxes the four intrepid explorers inside to crawl about within its confines. It's so easy to hack the primitive map they carry. He soothes their minds with images of water falling, of peace, serenity, of cool, dark calm.

Simultaneously, on the sands outside, the Blue commands an end to the excavations. Those still standing strong enough to fight put down their hoes and shovels and axes, shoulder weapons, and stand to attention in strong, if uneven lines. A ring of frozen Templar warriors now protects the heart-and-core. A vortex swirls above the Sentinel tower, power bleeding upwards from revitalised, reautomated chem-labs in the bunker's bowels. The General cannot control the manufacture of the storms. The process, once begun, cannot be stopped.

Once freed from the pressing tasks at hand, his mind is better directed to other more important things. Like finding her, the flesh-mesh girl called Star.

= SIXTY-SIX =

The top of the sand lay utterly still, all traces of the lives it had taken from them gone. A sharp breeze ruffled through Star's matted locks. Star sank to her knees, hands clasped uselessly before her, staring at the churned-up patch of sand.

Grieve was still brushing sticky sand slick off his arms and legs. He touched her on the shoulder. "Come on, get up."

She ignored him. Just knelt there staring at the patch of rippled nothingness where Iago and Iolani had disappeared. One minute they'd been struggling, the next minute, gone. Dragged under by the sucking sand. Lost without a trace.

"No time for mourning—we gotta keep moving. Got to get to higher ground. Get off the open sand." He looked back the way they'd come. "Wind's picking up—and that tanker's swinging around for another pass, plus the rest of them—plus hell knows what else."

She didn't move. Didn't say anything.

He touched her gently on the shoulder once more. "Star."

He expected her to slap his hand away. To yell at him, accuse him of insensitivity—or something. But Star did nothing. She didn't even blink. Just kept staring at that rippled patch of sand.

Eventually she clambered to her feet, patted down her clothing, looking for something. She thrust her hands into her pockets, then pulled out a hard and lumpy object. Possibly a bag of dice-and-bones—he wasn't sure.

A wave of anger washed over her, so intense it made her shake. She stared at the place where Iago and Iolani had so pointlessly lost their lives. With a roar of anguish, she threw the bag as hard as she could manage. It landed with a dull thud on the sand next to a floating spinifex clump.

"What was that?"

"Nothing." She stared after it sullenly. "Nothing that was ever any use to anyone."

The small bag wasn't heavy enough to sink.

"Come on, we gotta go," he repeated, keeping one eye on a suspicious, low hanging cloud formation that had definitely not been there in the moments before the lizard had sunk to its death. The clouds began to thicken and coalesce, moving towards them, or so it seemed at first, then broke up harmlessly, scattered by rough winds.

"Gotta *go*," he said again, louder this time and more insistent. "The wind is changing—might be more of those acid-pissing clouds on the loose."

"I barely even spoke to Iago," said Star. "I don't know anything about him."

He gripped her shoulder and firmly squeezed. "We will mourn them later when we're safe."

"We *murdered* them," she said miserably. "They died because of us."

"They died because everything out here is trying to kill us. We have to get out of here or we'll be next."

The air began to thicken with stinging blasts of sand. Clouds gathering. Pressure dropping. Grieve dragged a khafiya from his pocket and bound it tightly around his face.

"We've lost everything. Gotta get out of the wind." He hooked his arm through hers. She offered no resistance. "Come on, Star, I need you with me."

Unexpectedly, she sank back to her knees. He lashed out and grabbed her before she tumbled headfirst into the quicksand.

"He's gone, Star—they're both gone and there's nothing we can do about it."

A gut-wrenching, high pitched whine drowned out the sound of rising wind. Star blinked grit from her eyes. Tankersong. Very loud and very close.

Her damp face was cloying up with gritty sand.

"Lean on me," he shouted.

She let her weight fall in his direction and they staggered around the quicksand's edge, sticking to places where rocks protruded and the unfamiliar spinifex did not grow, arms around each other, facing directly into the stinging wind, the air alive with reverberating tankersong. Eyes closed, faces wrapped, lips pressed tightly together, throats and noses chafed and choked. Moving blindly in what they could only hope was the right direction.

They could smell the stench of tanker nearby. The thing was sporting with them. Able to take them down any time it chose. Sing them to death or slam on over them, crushing them to gravel beneath its wheels.

321

Each forward step was agony. The rotting stink of the creature's gut made them cough and gag uncontrollably. Star seemed to have lost her will to live, a fact that frightened Grieve more than the unseen menace stalking them.

"Keep moving!"

Star didn't answer. She did what he did. Put one foot in front of the other and pushed on through the rising wind. Now and then her steadiness would falter. He'd grip her more tightly, push on harder, no matter that they couldn't see in front of them. Moving forward was all that mattered.

"Sometimes you gotta do the hard thing," shouted Grieve. "Sometimes the hard choice is all the choice there is. Hard choices means you gotta suck it up and keep on going. Just keep on going, Star, don't you stop, cos I swear on the grave of my cousin Selene, I'm not losing anybody else." Cousin Selene never had a grave. There'd been nothing left to bury, just hearsay as to what had become of her—and the rest of them.

He knew Star couldn't hear him above the sand. It was just as well, because Grieve found himself blurting out all kinds of crazy things. Things he'd never admitted to anyone. Not even Selene. Especially not Selene. "Just keep on moving. Keep on moving. Keep on—"

He was surprised to find his own face damp with itchy tears and sticky sand. "Not gonna lose you. Not gonna let you fall. Lost everything else I ever had, but I'm not losing you. Not here. Not like this."

Grieve still saw their faces every time he closed his eyes. The family he had run away from, leaving them to their scraping and foraging, while he hopped Vans from border town to border town. Grifting, thieving, fighting when he had to, running when the going got too hard. He eventually saw the world for what it was—a hard, cold place without much to recommend it—and skipped back home to dearest cousin Selene and his sisters. He thought he was gonna be the big man when he returned, a man with experience, with coin in his pockets and a twinkle in his eye. Only Selene was dead. No family, no tents and wagons. Their foraged sand had been overtaken by a well-armed tribe who'd cut up the bodies and disposed of all the evidence.

If only he'd stayed with them, things might have turned out different. If only he had stayed. If only he had taken Selene with him.

Grieve barked his shins on something hard. Hopefully it was one of the rocky masses they'd been heading for, big enough for shelter if they could climb it.

"Get up high! Climb up on the rocks!"

Star slid from his grasp. She'd been wedged under his arm one moment, but the next he could find no trace of her.

"Star!"

Useless to cry out, blind through the wild and stinging sand, but he cried out anyway, calling her name over and over.

No answer. He dropped to all fours, feeling blindly. She was not dead. He would find her. She was not dead. He would find her . . . She was not dead like Selene and all the others.

But the wind had stolen her away. There was the base of the rock, rough and crumbling, scraping at his hands and knees. Grieve hauled himself up away from the sand and the rogue tanker and the death of a good, kind man and his tame lizard and all the ones he had left behind in different times and different places. The past he could not change. A future taking more than he had to give. And then, finally, there she was, Star, curled into a ball to protect her face.

She wouldn't climb and he couldn't drag her so they stayed down there and he wrapped his arms around her, hoping the tanker had given up and that the polyp storm—if that's what it was—had dissipated, torn to shreds by the natural, howling wind.

Eventually the wind subsided. His ears still rang with high pitched, piercing tankersong and his leg throbbed where he had banged it against the rock.

He unwrapped his khafiya and shook out his sweaty, matted hair. "Star?"

She coughed and he backed up to give her room. A pall of gritty gloom hung over everything.

"Come on, Star, we gotta get higher off the sand." Once standing, he realised his right leg was a bloody mess. Scraped and skinned, but that was all. Not broken. Not anything worse.

Lucky.

It hurt when he bent it but he was good to climb. He shook her gently, but impatiently.

Star's movements were slow and clumsy, like she had been forced awake from a deep and troubled slumber.

He clicked his fingers. "Come on, Star, wake up, we gotta move." He lifted her up until she stood on her own two feet. Clicked his fingers louder in her face. "You still in there?"

"Shhh . . . listen. Can you hear them?" she whispered.

"Hear what? I can't hear anything."

Her lips parted. She moistened them with her tongue. "Tankers—they're singing to each other."

He looked around, up at the cluster of rocks that had protected them. There were plenty of handholds. It would be easy to climb, even with his leg in its bloody state.

He nudged her in the right direction. Mercifully, she didn't argue. It seemed like all the argument had gone out of her. Like part of her was deep asleep—the part that made her *her*.

The rock they scaled was not a natural formation, but the tip of yet another blasted ruin poking out from the sand. Close by, elongated spurs the colour of mildew jutted from the sand like broken ribs. They were in the carcass of an ancient town, its skeleton scrubbed clean by scouring storms.

Remains of once-great towers had mashed and melted to the ground, creating a twisting mess of mazes, tunnels, and holes. Not all the struts jutted upwards. Some twisted and curled like old men's hands. What kind of heat could do that to old-world steel?

The kind of heat that had taken a world of green and blue and shrivelled it into a useless, broken—

"Star, what are you doing?" He'd turned to find her staring out across the sand, arms outstretched, like she was pleading with something only she could see.

He pushed her arms down by her sides. "What are you doing?"

Her eyes were glazed. She couldn't hear him. Her head was cocked, like she was listening to something faint and very far away.

Tankersong.

"Woah, Star, get down off there. You're not yourself." In fact, just how far she'd gotten from herself was starting to worry him greatly.

In her hand, she gripped a spyglass, but she didn't need it. The pod of tankers were in a distant cloud of dust, still moving in a tight formation.

He watched, dumfounded, as she stripped the filthy bandage from her arm. The one she used to cover up her mesh.

"Wait—what are you doing?"

She raised her left arm high above her head, then angled it as the wind died down, until sunlight glinted off the mesh's shiny surface.

Grieve scrambled up to stand beside her, grabbed her arm and tugged it down. "Those damn things are gonna see you!"

"That's the idea."

She fought him off. He grabbed her shoulders and shook them hard. "Star, I'm scared you're not in there anymore."

"I'm still in here," she said, "Trust me—just this once. We'll never make it out of here on foot."

He stared at her blankly, like he hadn't heard a word she'd said. "No. You're even crazier than I thought. That thing will kill us stone cold dead. We won't get near it. We don't stand a chance."

= SIXTY-SEVEN =

Jakome was not aware of when the walls had started changing. His attention had been focused on the map. Sensing a sharp plunge in temperature, he had looked up to see soft moss where grey cement should have been. The passages had widened, opening into a cave. A wide space filled with impossible wonders.

Kian and Tallis ran ahead, while Allegra stopped and stared. Jakome kept checking the map, as if it might offer some kind of logical explanation. The four of them were apparently standing in a grotto, complete with a waterfall and a variety of damp, fleshy-leaved plants.

A change came over Kian and Tallis almost immediately. They seemed infected by the place, and did not once stop to question what they were seeing or what they'd stumbled into. It was irrational, uncharacteristic. Something here was very, very wrong.

"It can't be real, not any of this," he warned Allegra, leaning close so there could be no mistake at what he was saying.

Allegra was not listening. Her gaze travelled upwards, following the tumbling waterfall, its uppermost part obscured by fine white mist. A scent of mossy dampness permeated the grotto, fine particles of spray against her skin. She reached up, grasping at the moss that clung to the rocks above, just out of reach.

"Allegra, listen to me—none of this is real! The weapon in the bunker is feeding us illusions." He tapped the side of his head with two fingers. "It's messing with our minds."

She ignored him. She was definitely the kind of girl accustomed to dismissing people who told her things she didn't want to hear.

The waterfall was beautiful. She appeared completely entranced by it. Perhaps she had never seen such a thing before.

"Allegra!" He had to shout her name several times before she responded.

"What do you want? Stop shouting in my face. Is this not the most exquisite—"

She squealed in surprise when he grabbed her hand and dragged her close up to the streaming torrent.

"What are you doing—let go of my hand—how dare you touch me!"

"What is a waterfall doing in a bunker underground? How can any of this be truly real?" He gripped her tightly, his lips pressed thin as he forced her hand into the flow. She shrieked, expecting the pressure would be too strong, that her knuckles might scrape against the rocks beneath. But she stopped and stared at her own half-vanished hand when she realised she could feel nothing but mouldy air.

He yanked her arm free and held it up to her face: her skin was completely dry. "We are being played," he said, enunciating carefully, making sure she understood. "The others will not listen to me—not my own brother or my cousin, but you . . . you're not as stupid as you look."

She ignored the insult, glancing frantically around her, as if the illusions might suddenly just melt away before her eyes. She could still see water everywhere she looked and Jakome could still feel damp spray misting on his own cheeks.

He squeezed her arm tighter. "Are you with me?"

She nodded reluctantly.

He let go and held up the plastic map. Confusing geometric shapes danced above its luminescent surface. A pulsing ruby light hung still amidst the jewel-coloured chaos.

"I have made a little sense of this. We can use it to navigate back the way we came. You can't trust your eyes, remember that." He made a sweeping gesture with his hand. "All of this is false. Some kind of mirage."

"You don't want to wait? Perhaps—"

"I don't want to die in here," he said bluntly. Jakome flicked his gaze ahead, past the impossible waterfall to where his brother stood. "Wait here."

She nodded.

He tucked the map away, cupped his hands around his mouth to call out over the noise of falling water. "Tallis!"

His brother didn't answer—perhaps he hadn't heard.

Up closer, Jakome could tell immediately that something was wrong. Tallis did not look like Tallis. His eyes shone with a crazy light. He seemed to be half out of his mind, seeing something different to the rest of them. He was glowering like a mad dog, gripping his drawn blade tightly like he intended to make use of it. Jak realised he was frightened of his own half brother, the change that had come over him so sudden and unsettling.

And Kian? Kian was standing like a statue, seemingly entranced by a vast, blank concrete wall. Staring hard, like the wall was speaking to him.

"Kian, what are you doing?" Jakome called out, edging away from Tallis and his blade.

"The city," Kian answered, still staring, still at nothing. "Look at it, the sea of tiny winking jewels. They have power—vast reserves of it—just like in the caverns of Axa."

Jakome gripped Kian's arm. He didn't respond. "Kian, you're staring at a blank wall. There is no city. This place is tainted. Haunted even—it's some kind of trap."

Kian turned to face his cousin with shining eyes. "We will take this beautiful city by force. Their rich lands are ripe for the picking." He placed his hand on top of Jakome's, forcing him to also look out across the city that was not a city, the city that was nothing but a wall.

"I don't see—"

"Look harder!"

Jakome was accustomed to obeying Kian's commands, the way it had been since boyhood. He looked. Cool beads of sweat began to form across his temple and down his spine because, when he stared, when he did *exactly* as Kian bade him, he *could* begin to see an outline forming: a dark high-crested ridge, below it, a sheer drop and, scattered along its skirting, a hundred thousand golden winking lights. Bridges and walkways, roads and structures, faint and faded, all of it growing stronger the longer and harder he stared.

Jakome could feel the phantom city pulling him closer, drawing him nearer, the heat, the light, the hum . . .

"No!"

Jakome lunged backwards, shaking his head to clear the tainted vision from his eyes. In an instant, the city was gone. In its place, nothing but a plain grey concrete wall.

"Kian, It's a trap. Don't believe what you're seeing—none of it is real!"

Kian wasn't listening. He didn't even turn his head until Allegra's cry disturbed the stillness.

Jakome swung around just in time to see his brother Tallis lunging towards him, swinging his blade. He'd stripped down to the waist. Bare chested, he looked completely crazed, like a Sand Road savage.

Allegra kept on screaming but he couldn't hear her words. He jumped clear, dodging the blade's steel tip, yelling out to Kian, "Watch out—he's crazy!"

Kian stood ready with his own weapon drawn, the magical city abandoned as steel clashed loudly against steel. Two men, cousins and long-time friends, fighting each other for no reason, eyes wide and senseless, spittle flying. Jakome lost his footing as the floor and walls began to shake and the close air filled with the grumbling and groaning of rocks breaking loose and falling all around.

An earthquake.

"Tallis," he called out one more time before turning on his heels and bolting back the way they'd originally come, Allegra close beside him, screaming at him to hurry up, to run faster. Whatever was happening, she could see it too: the raining rocks, all very real and deadly.

They turned their back on the waterfall and ran blindly for their lives.

"Show me the map," Allegra screamed as he tugged it free. They paused briefly, panting, trying to stand steady on the shaking ground, trying to make sense of the vibrant, illuminated squiggles and the ruby dot jiggling gently amongst the geometric shapes. "Show me!"

He snatched it away and stuffed it back inside his Impact suit. "The map cannot be trusted," he shouted over the sound of falling debris. "Neither can our eyes—we'll have to think our way out of here!"

The air was thick with swirling grit and dust. Jakome looked back the way they had come, suddenly overwhelmed with guilt. He swallowed drily. "We have to go back for them."

"No we don't," said Allegra. "We have to get out of here while the walls remain in place."

Jakome ignored her and began to retrace his steps. He did not get far—the way was blocked with a mound of dislodged cement chunks. He pushed at them with his bare hands: solid.

When he turned, Allegra was not where he had left her. He hurried down the corridor—there was nowhere else she could have gone. There was nowhere else for him to go either. As he continued, the dust cleared. He ducked under low hanging branches and he saw the path ahead was strewn with leaf litter. Greenery brushed against his hair. Young leaves rustled in the canopy above, punctuated with whoops and cries of unseen creatures.

"I can feel the trees and smell the leaves—how can such a thing be possible?" Allegra's voice echoed somewhere ahead.

Jakome pushed on until he could see her outline through spaces in the verdant foliage. "Just keep moving and stay where I can see you."

The forest that could not possibly exist petered out into murky darkness as they crunched over brittle leaves, these ones brown and dry. Now it seemed they were deep inside another grotto whose walls were covered with luminescent moss. Water dripped down from the ceiling, splashing on their faces. Allegra jumped in astonishment, slapping at the drops like they were sand-flies.

"Not real," he reminded her.

"It all feels real," she said miserably.

"I know. You have to be strong."

The map felt warm inside his suit against his skin. Suddenly it made him angry. He pulled it out and tried to crumple and crush it with his hands, to no avail; the thing was indestructible. He swore and was about to throw it to the ground when Allegra stopped him.

"Don't. That map is valuable. We may still need it."

"It can no longer be trusted."

She gripped his wrist and held it tightly, a cold look in her eyes that reminded him so strongly of Kian, it almost hurt.

"This way."

He followed her, edging around a shiny wall of polished marble. Beyond it was something unexpected even given everything they'd witnessed so far: a writhing wall of flame not twenty paces ahead of them, the air permeated with the scent of burning meat.

Both turned and fled at the sight of those flames, the waves of heat pushing at their backs. Retreated past the marble wall, back to the grotto and its bed of fallen leaves.

"There's no way out of here," said Allegra, her voice rising with panic.

"Wait." Jakome closed his eyes and listened to the sound of dripping water. When he opened them, blue and orange winged butterflies were flitting through the forest clearing.

"The map. We have no choice—"

"Forget the map," he said. He nodded to the marble beyond. "That's the only way out of this place."

"Through the flames! Are you crazy?"

"Way past the point," he muttered under his breath. He took her arm and led the way, despite her protestations.

Beyond the marble, the wall of fire seemed even fiercer than before.

Allegra stopped, stared in horror, then hugged her arms and shook her head. "I can't."

He whispered gently, "You must. Where better to hide an exit than behind a wall of flame?"

She pushed him away. "But I can *feel* it burning. I can *smell* something sweet and sickly and wrong—"

He hooked his arm through hers. "Shut your eyes and pray to your gods—we're going through." He pushed her forwards, straight into the flames, no time to think about all the options they didn't have.

Allegra screamed in pure, blind terror.

Before he followed, he threw one last glance back over his shoulder, hoping to see his brother's face. But neither Tallis nor Kian had made it past the rock fall.

Allegra was still screaming when they made it out the other side. "How dare you push—"

The flames were gone—they had never existed. Jakome and Allegra found themselves standing in a corridor fashioned from featureless grey cement. Weak light bled from small slits cut high, evenly spaced. Daylight.

They ran together, side by side, towards the place up ahead where the slits were wider and deeper. No further argument was necessary.

= SIXTY-EIGHT =

Muscular clouds of churned-up sand and dust roiled across the landscape, stretching far into the distance, bold and dramatic under the green-tinged sky.

"That's the one." Star pointed.

Grieve baulked. "What, the tanker that's been trying to run us down?"

She considered the pod rumbling in the distance. All but one single tanker had turned into the wind at the same time. All but the one that had been running rogue behind them. "That one's not hooked up to the others. What if it wasn't chasing us down? What if it's been trying to communicate with us all along?"

"That thing's not speaking any language I need to hear," said Grieve.

Star ignored him. She closed her eyes and tried to reach out to the rogue tanker with her mind, trying to forge a connection—even a small one. But the only connection she could make was with the Blue. It lashed out immediately, reacting eagerly and violently in response to her tentative efforts. She gasped and staggered, almost losing balance.

"What's happening—are you alright?" Grieve reached out to offer a helping hand.

She opened her eyes and steadied her gaze, her focus on the rogue tanker as it began circling the rock in a wide and clumsy arc. "We'll have to run to catch it. I can't make it stop."

"Course you can't make it stop—even if you could, we'd get crushed under its wheels—check out the size of them!"

They watched the tanker meander like a drunken man, zig-zagging, stop-starting, revving forward then slamming to a slow. "It's hurt," she realised. "Something's the matter with its brain."

"Doesn't need its brain to kill us—those wheels will do the job." He pointed to her mesh, his hand stopping, hovering above it like he was afraid to touch it. "Can you talk to it with that thing?"

"I don't think so. I already tried."

"Then we walk to the Lotus bunker," he said. "Those other tankers won't bother us—they don't even know we're here." He wiped his hands on his trousers and bent forward to check his injured leg. Dried blood was hardening to form a scab. He straightened up just in time to catch Star leaping down from the safety of the rocks. "Hey, what the—"

"There's no time," she called back as she landed on the soft sand in a crouch. She started running towards the rogue mechabeast, Grieve shouting loud and wild behind her, but she couldn't wait for him. The Lotus Blue would wait for none of them.

She sprinted towards the tanker's path, her muffled boot strides slapping the sand, hearing a mighty whoop right up close beside her as Grieve had almost caught up. Then a coil of rope was looping through the air, the maddest look she'd ever seen on Grieve's face. His leg was bleeding again but he didn't seem to care.

The tanker emitted a sonic blast, all screech and grate and sing-song whine, and then it slowed and slammed hard on its brakes, sending sand spraying high and wide.

"What the hell—run for it!" he hollered.

They ran.

Grieve slung his rope in a wide lasso, threw it and hooked a rocky encrustation on the tanker's chassis high above the wheels. Looked across to her and shouted, "Come on—hurry!"

But Star had already flung herself upon the beast, had scrambled for handholds and had started clambering up the side, like she was scaling a cliff. Straight up the side, grappling for purchase, as the tanker was already starting to pick up speed again, slow and steady, grumbling and grinding its way around the rocky platform in a slow suicidal spiral.

Grieve hauled himself up just in time as the tanker increased its speed. "Look at that!"

Higher up, a section of the tanker's rocky casing had been bashed open, and exposed wires and cables spilled out like animal guts. Little creatures made of metal burst out of the hole, then up and over the side of the moving tanker, cowering just out of arm's reach.

Grieve used the taut rope to steady himself, and he held out his hand to Star even though she didn't need it. Riding a tanker was no different to riding wagon top—and she'd had seven long years practise at that.

The bashed-open casing looked like a rough, raw wound. "Wouldn't go putting your hand in there," Grieve shouted over the noise.

"No fear." She climbed up closer and crouched down low to investigate, covered her nose with her hand. Beyond the wires and the stench of rot sat globs of fleshy substance glistening wetly. Sporadic hisses, fizzes, and sparks warned her not to touch anything.

Grieve steadied himself and moved in closer, crouching beside her, his weight supported by the rope.

"Never seen anything like that before."

"I have," she said grimly, remembering Remy and his stupid, daring, and deadly final mistake.

Grieve peered in closer. "Never would've believed in such a beast if I didn't see it myself—hey!"

He reeled back in alarm as a small mecha creature, like a cross between a metal spider and a rat, sidled up and prodded him with an elongated appendage. It scuttled away in response to his reactionary jerk. "What in all the flaming—shit, there's more of them!"

"Kick them away if they get too close," said Star. She withdrew the pair of red-handled pliers and gingerly lowered her hand inside the opening.

Grieve, balancing against the tanker's speed and motion with the aid of the taut rope, raised a boot threateningly as another of the creature-contraptions became too bold. "Don't even think about it, ya little monster . . ."

The thing swivelled its nub of a head, observed the raised boot, then turned tail and scuttled away. Grieve looked pleased with himself until he noticed Star leaning forward, one arm deep inside the foul-smelling opening, past her elbow.

"What are you doing?"

"Trying to—" A random spark ignited in a shiver of luminescent red and green. "Ouch!" She pulled her arm back out again. "Wish I did know what I was doing."

He opened his mouth to offer a suggestion but he didn't get the chance. Star lunged, ploughing her arm back in, grabbing the thickest of the cables, lifting it to see if the movement made a difference. It didn't. She coiled it gently and placed it back inside the creature's brain cavity—if that's what it was. Same with the other exposed cables, one by one.

When she touched the dirty yellow one, the tanker shuddered, almost toppling Grieve. It let out a ear-grating shriek, then swerved, breaking free of its circuit.

"You did it!" he said.

"No I didn't. I didn't do anything, the tanker's driving itself—all I did was tweak a nerve."

The tanker faced directly into the wind, then accelerated. Star and Grieve dug in and hung on tight.

"Only way to travel," he shouted, grinning from ear to ear.

"Careful," she shouted, but she smiled too—she couldn't help herself. Riding atop a killer tanker with the wind in her hair and hope in her heart . . . she felt an enormous sense of freedom, like she could take the whole world on single-handedly. Like they might actually stand a chance of shutting the Lotus down if they could only get to it in time.

The landscape blurred past in a flash of dune and rock and ruin, things half glimpsed, half recognised. The tanker showed no signs of slowing down.

They passed over a small dune, and then there it was: a dark shape up ahead, not a tanker carcass, something else, something unbelievable—the *Razael*, distinct and unmistakable, wheels jammed with sand, one mast snapped and pointing out across the open Red like an accusatory finger. The *Razael*, sitting directly beneath the churning sky blister. The tanker was heading straight for it.

"Never thought I'd see that thing again," said Grieve. "But our tanker's coming in too fast—how do we slow it down?"

Star didn't answer. She'd been wondering the same thing. She couldn't talk to it and she couldn't make it stop, nor was she certain it would stop of its own accord. It wasn't unreasonable to consider it might be on a suicidal mission of its own, racing towards a violent conclusion for them all.

"We're going to have to jump," she shouted over the fury of the wind, like leaping off a belching, shuddering, semi-sentient sand barnacle encrusted tanker was something they did everyday.

"Jump—are you crazy?"

They had both sailed way past the halfway point of crazy. Star knew how to jump and roll. She'd done it off the Van a hundred times. Grieve would have to watch and copy. He was a survivor. He'd be alright.

But the tanker was travelling at a speed no Van could ever manage. "Climb down lower," she said.

They both descended as far as they safely could, Grieve still clinging tightly to the rope. Star watched the sand go swooshing by. They'd have to jump far enough to land clear of the wheels. Not easy, but not impossible.

She looked up to see Grieve staring at her face intently. "You ready for this?"

"Ready as I'll ever be." He pulled out his blade to cut the rope—a terrible waste, but unhooking it would not be possible.

But before they had a chance to do anything, the tanker emitted another high-pitched blast of tankersong, enough to make them sick to their stomachs. They clung on tightly as the tanker changed its course, swerving in a wide arc, away from the ship and whatever lay behind it.

It had to slow in order to turn.

"Now or never," yelled Star. "Don't break your leg!"

Too late—he'd cut the rope and jumped already, screaming all the way, laughing hysterically as he landed in one piece, the damage no worse than a mouthful of gritty sand.

She jumped and rolled, came to a stop and paused in a crouch to catch her breath.

The tanker did not react to their departure. Star stood up and watched it lumbering off on a unknown mission of its own, ignoring the ship, not following the others of its kind.

Grieve lay on his back, arm thrown across his face to shield his eyes from sunlight. "That was intense."

"Get up. We've got work to do."

"Lighten up, we just got here!"

But Star was already up and walking towards the sand-jammed ship.

Grieve got to his feet once he realised she was on the move. "Careful," he shouted. "The men who took that ship weren't fooling around."

"Don't I know it."

The sand was thick and they quickly tired of walking.

"They've got plenty of weapons," warned Grieve.

She nodded. They were out in the open under a strange and sickly sky, but it could not be helped. The ship lay across their path, and there was no time to find a safer way around it.

She'd expected to see guards posted upon the deck, but up closer, they could see no people, no movement.

A ghost ship.

They split up and walked from stern to keel, scouting for the faintest signs of life, but nothing moved aside from the damaged sails and rigging, which grew taut and slackened alternately in the wind.

On the farthest side of the *Razael* hung two rope ladders and a spindly ladder of metal rusted through in several places.

Impatience got the better of Star. She climbed the metal ladder, hand over fist, not waiting to consult with Grieve, not expecting him to follow her up, because of the state of his leg, though he did.

At first it seemed the ship was indeed empty, and had been abandoned in great haste, with equipment strewn all over the deck, along with spilled grain and a large wet bloody stain. There was a corpse in a torn red jacket, its arms and legs akimbo.

Star drew the blade Grieve had given her.

A wooden block and winch dangled in front of her, caught up in torn rigging, slamming rhythmically against the broken mast. When she moved, broken glass crunched underfoot.

Then, as she moved across the deck, came the sound of a deep and hacking cough. Star and Grieve exchanged glances before separating, creeping up on the foredeck from opposite sides, treading lightly, the wind humming through torn rigging making enough noise to mask their careful footfall.

Grieve pointed with alarm when he noticed the drone hovering. They both froze.

They watched as a fat old man propped up on cushions coughed up something dark and wet into his palm, then smeared it on his trouser leg without looking at it too closely. The drone had apparently woken him. It hovered uncertainly above his head, like it feared being contaminated if it got too close. Something resembling the end of a spyglass set into its front widened, contracted, then widened again. It wobbled.

The man took a feeble swipe at the drone with the tanker lance gripped in one hand. "Get away from me, you wretched little thing,"

The drone elevated suddenly and swivelled its spyglass eye in Grieve's direction.

The man seemed too exhausted to move. He shouted, "What is it now, you jumped up piece of junk? Who goes there?"

The drone hovered, emitting a gritty hum from its bug-like wings.

The man pushed himself onto his knees and angled his body around far enough to attempt to see whatever the drone was seeing. He blinked at Grieve, then sat back down, his energy drained from the effort, then attempted to prop himself up higher for a clearer view.

Star approached cautiously, then reached forward and snatched the lance from his hand. He slumped back down against the plush fabric as she raised the lance and took a wild swing at the drone. It jerked out of reach with an irritating squeal.

The old man gave a wheezy chuckle. "Good for you, girl, that little bastard has no manners." He peered up through a sheen of sweat and frowned at the sight of her.

"Check that out," said Grieve, pointing, beyond the bow to the sand ahead lay an all-too-familiar excavation site spread out beneath the pus-and-purple sky, the scabbed cloud-cancer blooming directly above it.

"My daughter is down there and she is lost," the old man said bitterly. "They are all doomed—the lot of them." He closed his eyes.

"This man is Mohandas and this is his ship," said Grieve.

Star flicked her attention back to the old man. "You are Allegra's father?

"They've all gone," said Mohandas, ignoring her question but opening his eyes once more. "All gone chasing after buried treasure, all following the lead of those three stupid boys, my daughter the most stupid one of all. It's my own fault for raising her without a mother. I should have married again, I should have paid more attention. The girl ran wild, and now she does whatever she wants, like she always has . . ."

"Go see what you can find below deck," said Star to Grieve.

Grieve hesitated. "What if they've left some guards on board—"

"Then you'll have to deal with them."

Star knelt down beside Mohandas and patted his arm. "We'll fetch you more water—this 'skin is almost empty."

"Bring me whisky and a pistol if you truly want to be of use," the old man shouted after Grieve.

"We're going to find your daughter," Star said.

"You? What could you possibly do to change any of this?" His ruddy face was pinched with misery. "I should have destroyed those blasted maps. Dropped them into a volcanic fissure where they could do no harm to anyone."

"Maps? What maps?"

Too late. He wasn't listening anymore. Grieve returned with water, cheese, and biscuit salvaged from down below. They ate and drank in earnest silence, not knowing if or when they'd get another chance.

"She'll come back for me," Mohandas said defiantly. "She won't leave her father here to die."

"What if something happens and she can't make it back?" said Star gently.

He stared at her, completely uncomprehending. As if there could be no other truth aside from the one he'd chosen to believe.

= SIXTY-NINE =

Marianthe stared at the terrible sky, sky wounded like a dying animal, like she was looking straight into the eye of a restless, angry god.

The walk across the sand was killing her. Without the support of her Benjamin, she never would have managed a single step—not with her mangled tendons and ground down cartilage, hacked-up flesh with missing pieces that had been cut out by her own blade long ago. Her Benjamin's mind was a messy ruin but his stamina was in tact. Eyes shining with glazed intensity, he hoisted her upon his back to cover the final miles to their destination.

Marianthe was so startled by this piggyback manoeuvre, she almost dropped her stave, managing to cling on to it at the last minute and wedge it between his broad back and her front.

He babbled poetry, recited recollected field manoeuvres, miscellaneous details of a life spent fighting other people's wars.

"Pull the bastards out into the open. Stalk 'em, flank 'em, hit 'em before they know you're there."

The constant chatter kept him focused, kept him plodding along methodically in a straight line. Sometimes she had to yell at him to detour around rocks or ruins poking from the sand. But obstacles did not trouble him. Even without her commands, he would have kept on clambering, right over the tops of them.

The abandoned ship took her entirely by surprise. They were not the only ones, apparently, to have come this way in recent times. That a ship had travelled so far beyond the Black filled her with wonder. They'd built them solid back in the good old days. It was hard to believe, but yes, she was seeing it with her tired old eyes.

The ship's big wheels were buried underneath the sand piled up on either side of the hull. The ship sat crooked, right out in the open—she must be dreaming, surely it wasn't real? Surely it must be a mirage?

Her Benjamin would have walked on past it. Once seen and noted, he dismissed it as irrelevant. Kept muttering the same word under his breath: *bunker bunker bunker bunker*, over and over, hoisting her higher, increasing his speed. *Bunker bunker bunker bunker.* A man with a mission, good old supersoldier, reliable to and beyond the very last.

The ship appeared to be deserted, which was just as well. Their merry band consisted of two broken Templars and three battered drones, not one of them up for self defence, or even ducking out of the line of fire.

"Not long now," she told them all. Her drones required constant reassurance. Loyal little things they were, but they'd been forced to travel a long way from their home and the unfamiliar landscapes made them nervous.

She sent one over to take a close look at the ship. "It'll all be over soon," she said to the others.

"Bunker bunker bunker bunker."

She closed her eyes. Two halves of her life had come together. Not far to go now, and then she could sleep forever.

= SEVENTY =

We should have forced that old man to come with us," said Grieve, shouldering his pack, which had been filled with supplies salvaged from the *Razael*.

Star didn't answer. She looked back out across the sand that had almost swallowed them. They trudged across it in silence, towards the bunker and the jerking mass of movement surrounding it. Mecha were excavating, shifting great quantities of sand, vortex winds snatching and scattering it with random blasts.

Both stopped short when they saw Templars digging rhythmically beside their fully-mecha counterparts, using shovels, slabs of metal, and even their own flesh-stripped hands.

Star was certain one of them would sense her presence—that all of them would turn and come after her with shovels raised as weapons. But the Templars and the mechas kept on digging like she wasn't even there.

Grieve nudged her in the ribs. "We're ghosts here," he whispered. "Maybe we're dead already—have you thought of that?" He flexed his own hands and stared at his fingers.

Star wasn't listening. All she could see was the large grey shape half buried in the sand. The resting place of the Lotus Blue, so much larger and more menacing than it had looked on the old woman's wall of glass boxes. Dark and dense, like it was sucking in light from the surroundings. Perhaps this place had been a kind of city once, although there were no towers or even houses to be seen, just weird mecha constructs she had no name for. Whatever it had once been, now it was a fortress, something akin to the Vulture, complete with its own Sentinel tower, far bigger than any she had ever seen before.

"Look on the bright side," said Grieve cheerfully. "We made it! Never thought I'd see this far from home—or so many wonders." He punched her lightly on the arm. "Look at that thing, what do you reckon it's for?"

Star didn't look. She only had eyes for the looming bunker, approximately the length of two thirteen-wagon Vans laid end to end away from where they stood, with its many small entrances and what looked to be a line of guards although they weren't yet close enough to be sure.

"Right," said Grieve, "so what happens next?"

"This is where we say goodbye," said Star. "You're going to find your seaside paradise and I'm going in alone."

"Over my dead body!" he replied. It was supposed to be funny, but he stopped smirking when he caught the look on her face.

Grieve was older than her by a couple of summers, but to her he seemed so young, despite the evident years of hardship etched upon his sunburned face. Bright blue eyes she'd once found so deceitful. So untrusting.

She didn't want to lie to him. Didn't want to do what needed to be done.

"I'm coming with you," he said. "Not letting you score all the treasure, claim all the credit, find all the answers—"

"No you're not."

"I say we stick together—we made it this far, didn't we?"

Words she knew he regretted as soon as they'd left his lips. Their making it had come at a heavy cost. The spectre of Iago and Iolani hung heavily between them.

"We go in together," he continued firmly. "Shut that thing down—and then we go find the inland sea. I promise to build you a hut of your own. I never said we had to share, in case that's what you were worried about."

"That *thing* cannot be shut down. It's old and smart, probably smarter than we are."

He shrugged. "So we kill it."

She paused, her throat parched and constricted, wanting water but equally not wanting to waste any of it—he'd be needing every drop where he was going. "You're not listening to me. This is goodbye, Grieve."

She grabbed him in a clumsy hug, pulling him close and hanging on tight. He hugged her back, reflexively at first, then properly, whispering into her ear, "How could I leave you now after all we've been through together? Besides, we haven't even found the gold . . ."

She disengaged, pushing him gently away. "I have to go now."

He grabbed her by the shoulders, chilled by her grim expression. "Wait—what is it you're not telling me?"

She lifted her waterskin over her shoulder and loped it over his.

"You don't understand, Grieve—I *have* to go in alone." She stared walking.

343

"Why?" he jogged until he was a few steps ahead, then swung around to face her, playing up the limp from his wounded leg, trying to make her laugh. "Come on, Star, we're almost there. So close—all we've got to do is—"

"I need to enter that bunker alone. You can't help me, Grieve. Nobody can."

He pulled an exaggerated face. "So who died and made you the saviour of the world?"

She stopped walking. "Quarrel did. You still don't get it, do you?" She pushed up her filthy shirtsleeve, brandished her mesh-embedded arm. "Do you know what this is, what it means?"

He stared at the shiny metal and shrugged casually. "It means I gotta keep an eye on you?" he said with one eyebrow raised.

She let the sleeve fall down, pushed past him, and kept on walking.

He continued to follow alongside. "Okay, tell me. What does it really mean?"

"It means I'm like *him*. It means I'm one of *them*." She pointed to the mindless, digging Templars and the pitiful monstrosities labouring beside them in the sun.

"So what? Star, I don't care about that shit anymore. I did once and I'm sorry for that. I'm an idiot from a long line of idiots. Don't know what I was thinking before. Like maybe you were dangerous."

"I *am* dangerous."

"Sister, out here *everything* is trying to kill us."

She wiped a wet patch from her cheek with the heel of her palm. "I'm a bomb, Grieve. It's wired all the way through me. That's what the mesh is ultimately for."

He stopped moving. "You're a what?"

"You heard me. I'm just like Quarrel, only Quarrel didn't make it. We were manufactured as weapons, supposed to fight until the last. To detonate if there was no other way. The Lotus Blue cannot be shut down, but if I can get in close to its core . . ."

Grieve uttered a dismissive snort.

"Get out of here, Grieve, while you still can. Get far away, to that abandoned seaside settlement you keep telling me about. Find yourself a better life while it's still an option." She grabbed his arm and squeezed it tight. "Remember me."

His face went blank. "You're not shitting me, are you?"

She swallowed dryly. "Don't reckon I'm *much* of a bomb when it comes down to it, but if I can crawl inside its brain . . ."

"But it's gonna know you're in there!"

"No it won't. Not if I'm quiet and careful. Not if I'm lucky and it remains distracted by all this digging."

He gestured to her mesh arm, exaggerating wildly. "That thing connects you to the Blue, that's what you told me. That Lotus is one big fat brain, yeah? For sure it's gonna know you're coming after it!"

"No it won't. The connection's weak. My mesh was never fully formed."

"You don't know that! You don't know what it can hear and see and feel. Reckon if those tankers can sense you, it can sense you too."

"Maybe. But I still have to try. I'm the only chance the Sand Road's got."

Grieve took a deep breath. He grabbed her hand and held it between his own. "Look, I followed you on this damn crazy mission. I'm not smart but I know that sky's not right, that something big and bad is coming down. Bigger and badder than all of us—there's nothing folks like us can do to stop it. *Nothing—not even you can make a difference.* Enough of us have died already, don't you think?"

He stepped closer, pleading. "Don't go in there on your own. Don't!"

"But if I don't, everybody will die—"

"Then let's all die together."

She tugged her hands free and stepped away from him. "No."

He lunged at her, and took her fiercely in his arms. Held her so tight she could barely breathe. He stunk of fear and blood and sweat. Of broken hearts and broken dreams, tears not cried and people long forgotten.

She had never felt so close to anyone. She hugged him back, tightly, for as long as she could bear, then gently pulled away. She turned her back on him and started running.

He ran after her, shouting, "These creatures, these mecha, they can't even see us. They don't care whether we live or die or run, so why don't we do that last thing, Star? Make a clean getaway and run for cover. Nobody's ever gonna know what we did or didn't do."

He was shouting at her back but she wasn't stopping now, wouldn't look back again. The dark mass of the bunker loomed large ahead. Star made for a rectangle of solid shadow set into its wall of steel grey granite. She paused to think on how she was going to get past the row of Templar soldiers guarding the way. They were battered, she saw as she got closer: bent and broken down, barely able to do much more than form a barrier. They stank like dead animals, and looked like the slightest breath of wind would knock them down.

The vortex swirling above the bunker was picking up speed and ferocity. Heavy, untethered objects sailed past, tossed around like leaves.

Star took a deep breath and ran again, straight for the darkened entranceway, aiming for a gap between two Templars. As she got near, the entire row of them moved as one, snapping sharply to attention, not attempting to block her but saluting her as she passed, all in perfect unison.

When she reached the entranceway she finally turned, looking back on Grieve, expecting to find him catching her up, still insisting that they ought to make a run for it. But Grieve was not following. He hung back, hovering uncertainly beyond the line of Templars, standing as still as they were, afraid to pass, staring at her, helpless.

= SEVENTY-ONE =

There wasn't much light, just what bled in from the entranceway behind her: little slits and a doorway half choked up with sand that she'd crawled through on her hands and knees.

Star knew which way to go: the mesh guided her. Or maybe it was the Blue inside her head showing her way, or the resonance of Quarrel—maybe even the spirit of Lucius. It didn't matter. Her mission was all that mattered now.

The corridor was long and straight. At the end of it was a turn, and then another. Her mouth was dry, and the further she went, the more strangely giddy she felt.

The walls glowed with a faint sickly hue—some form of green-grey lichen was stuck to the surface. After a long walk in semi-darkness, Star entered a central space with several corridors branching out from it. She picked one at random, trying to envision the bunker's probable layout in her head. Her thoughts were becoming more and more clouded with whisperings and echoes of a voice that was not her own. Soon it would all be over.

The next floor down was the important one, according to the voice and the sense of calm washing over her when she made a move the voice approved of.

Deeper in, the corridors became longer and widened out. Peeling paint hung down in sheets. Broken glass crunched beneath her boots.

The spaces she passed through smelled of abandonment and dust. Many had locked doors that needed to be kicked down. It wasn't difficult; their frames and hinges had been severely weakened with age.

The carpet underfoot had rotted. Swarms of bugs and other crawling things receded like a dark tide from her footfall.

She came upon a stairwell, dank and uninviting, and paused to listen, but by then even the scuttling of bugs had ceased.

Star stepped carefully onto stairs strewn with the crumbling detritus of whatever this place had once been. The sound of her own breathing, the tread of her boots. More doorways, more corridors, more rooms leading in to other rooms.

Eventually, something faintly glowing lay ahead. A rectangular cage, its wire door half open. She swallowed painfully and stepped inside, then spun around to face the way she'd come, but all she could see was darkness.

The cage shuddered, emitted a hideous screech, and began to sink, slowly at first, then faster and faster. She braced herself—there was nothing to hang on to. Her stomach heaved but she kept her gorge down as rattles and reverberations shook her bones and made her wobble unsteadily.

She had not expected to be plunged so deep underground. When the cage finally stopped, she leapt free of it, fearing it might start up again with her still trapped inside, might keep going until it reached the centre of the Earth.

Her eyes struggled to adjust to the darkness, but she was starting to discern long rows of shrouded shapes when the lights suddenly came on.

Star sucked in her breath and stared. She was in an enormous cavern as vast as a desert, stretching as far and wide as she could see. A high grey ceiling was held up by thick, cylindrical columns.

The sound of her footfall echoed loudly. Too loud—the Blue would hear her coming. Those "shrouded" things were actually sleeping tankers of different shapes and forms, some with eight thick-ridged wheels, some with twelve, dulled by dust and time and disuse, yet pristine: these mechabeasts had never spent a day on open sand. Some had circular ports and hatches, sleek cabins, and suspension arms. Gun turrets and tiny dishes like the one atop the old woman's temple. So beautiful, unsullied by the desert's rocky encrustations clinging to their polished metal skin. She wanted to touch them but knew better. *Don't touch, keep on walking, keep on moving.*

She walked for what felt like forever, her footsteps growing louder and bolder, but as she went she knew she could not be in danger of waking the Blue: it already knew she was coming, it had turned the lights on. With mesh embedded, there were no secrets she could keep from it. The cavern was too impossibly vast, there seemed no end to it, no central control, no place where her detonation would make a difference. If she blew up here, at best she might take out a handful of tankers—but why would she when they slept so peacefully, when they weren't hurting anything or anybody?

The code Quarrel had forced upon her sat heavy in her head, weighing her down, slowing her steps. A bringer of destruction, that's what she'd become. A harbinger of death. But she kept on walking; she owed that much to Nene, despite the secrets she had kept from Star. She owed it to the Sand Road and to herself. To Lucius and the ones who'd lost their lives. To Quarrel, despite what he had done to her.

And what of Grieve? There would not be time enough for him to get away. He would never make it to his seaside paradise. He was every bit as dead as she was.

Each step she took made her feel smaller and smaller, insignificant, helpless. Useless. Somewhere in this incredible place lay the heart-and-mind of the Lotus Blue. But every inch of the cavern looked the same. Glancing back over her shoulder, she could no longer see the rectangular cage that had delivered her. There was nothing to see but shrouded tankers and open space, grey columns, grey cement, grey dust.

Any minute she expected to encounter a Templar soldier, one or many, pristine; all shiny-bright and healthy, waiting to greet her, fight her off or lead the way.

The last thing she ever expected to see was Nene. A small cry escaped her lips at the sight of her: Nene, her sister, but not the way she'd left her. Much younger, somewhere near Star's own age, sixteen or seventeen. She was somehow standing under an open sky—which was impossible in itself, of course. A mirage. An incredulous vision being projected deep underground. Behind Nene, smoke now plumed from giant fissures in the ground. A sea of strange things jutted from the sand. A habitat: giant eggs of sand-speckled ivory plastic.

Something terrible had happened. Eggs were damaged, cracked and broken. Mounds of bodies were suddenly heaped one atop the other around the eggs. People who had appeared out of nowhere were pulling the bodies out of the cracked plastic shells, feet first, dragging them like salvage, the broken shells disintegrating before her eyes.

The Blue, of course. It had to be the Blue.

"Get out of my head," said Star to the creature that had found a way to nestle itself inside her thoughts. To pinch and tweak, manipulate and drive her crazy. Make her see impossible things. Too late for that, she was far long gone, watching a vivid mirage play out in front of her. Watching Nene with a child clutched in her arms, ten years old, dripping wet with slime and ichor, and beside her, a man who resembled a younger Benhadeer shouting, covered in blood.

Not real. It could not be real, not any of it. Star rubbed her eyes and shook her head, kept on walking right through the thick of it, through smoke that was not really there, through cracked eggs that evaporated as she passed, the pile of bodies dissolving into a scattering of colours. Blue light mimicked the wide blue sky; now it was all around her, thick and viscous like algae-laden water. She tried to push on through, but it had become so hard to move her arms and legs, such a dragging weight. With the greatest effort she spun around but it was too late. It was all a trick. Star was trapped in a pillar of raw blue light. She could not move. There was nowhere for her to go.

= SEVENTY-TWO =

The row of frozen Templars was a fearsome sight to behold. The grizzly creatures had moved once to salute Star as she ran towards the bunker, but not since. Some bore intimidating grey ordnance slung across their broad torsos, others looked as though they were accustomed to killing with their bare hands.

Grieve had stood and watched as she went inside, too shit scared to follow. And now he was too scared to move. If those Templars moved once, they could move again and if they noticed him, they would not likely salute.

Grieve stayed very still until he could stand it no more—for an hour, maybe more. It was hard to check the passage of time in a place as strange as this one. His injured leg was stiff and sore. Eventually he pivoted, turning slowly, gently, trying to make as little sound as possible—and no quick movement. But he yelped and almost leapt out of his skin when he found himself face-to-face with the old lady from the Temple, a battered leather satchel slung across her shoulder. Beside her stood the Templar from the aircraft boneyard, the one who'd been willing to leave him chained to a row of dead and dying mutineers. The one who'd forced Star to carry such a deadly burden.

But before he could say anything, the old lady spoke.

"Boy, I've seen your face before. You broke into my Sanctum."

Grieve's gut reaction was to deny everything and inch back out of striking range. The woman was ancient but sometimes the old ones could surprise you, and lash out with astonishing dexterity and force. Some of those old ones were trained up good, but in that moment, the lies and excuses that had trickled off his tongue like honey for years completely deserted him.

"Yes ma'am," was the best he could manage. His gaze shifted uneasily back to her companion. The Templar stared off into the distance, his face blank of expression. Something had changed since Grieve had last seen him. Something had gutted this one, quelled its fire and churned its brains to mince.

"That young girl you were with—is she in there?" The old woman pointed with her chin beyond the row of frozen Templar guards, to the dark rectangle leading inside the bunker.

Once again, the lies that had come to Grieve as easily as breathing his whole life let him down, abandoned him on the spot to face the truth.

"Yep. I . . . I . . ."

What was he prepared to admit in front of this ancient creature— that he was a coward on top of everything else? That Star was on a suicide mission, that she'd gone inside alone to blow herself to pieces? Alone, because he'd been too scared to follow?

"Do you care about her?" The old woman leered at him, her long nose resembling a beak, like she might lash out and peck him with it if he wasn't on his guard.

"Do I what? Yes, of course I do!"

Truth was, she was all he'd come to care about.

"Then go in after her. Drag her out, then both of you get the hell out of this place." Her eyes shone with a fiery intensity, the eyes of a warrior, not a crone.

"Go inside?" The mere thought of it made his innards curdle. "Past *those* things?"

She didn't even look at the row of Templar guards. "Hurry up, boy. You don't have much time." She then turned to the Templar beside her. "Come on, Benjamin, old man, old soul. We don't have much time either."

The Templar groaned, shifted his stance in ragged, jerking motions. Grieve flinched, but the old soldier had no interest in him. He turned and followed the old woman, obedient as a dog.

Grieve was still standing there, paralysed by indecision, when the old woman called back, "Get her out and be quick about it, or get used to living without her." She pointed up at the sky, which made no sense: it was the same sick stomach-contents sludge it had been since midpoint across the Black, swirling oppressively above their heads. He reckoned he could smell the stink of it, decay like rotted teeth and sour breath.

The row of frozen Templar guards remained motionless, like they were waiting for something. A signal. A last stand, a final fight—nothing good, whatever it was, and Grieve had to get himself out of there. He suspected that old woman knew what she was talking about.

But.

The entranceway was a rectangle of solid shadow. It didn't look like something you could pass through, yet Star had passed through it, hadn't she? Left him out there, told him she was never coming back.

What if there was a chance?

"Tully Grieve, you are the biggest idiot that ever lived," he said out loud as he wiped his sweaty palms on his pants. "Everything happens for a reason, some folks say—and your reasons are always the wrong ones, whenever there's a girl involved."

He glanced across at the old woman and her Templar dog, in time to see her casting two of the drones that had been hovering around her head like flies away, shooing them off to return to the dish. They hovered uncertainly, looking like they didn't want to leave her. Their reluctance forced an involuntary smile from Grieve—they were even dumber than he was.

The broken down old Templar started spouting rubbish. The old woman, walking with a really awful limp, was heading in the direction of something Grieve somehow hadn't noticed before.

The object resembled the old woman's temple dish, but smaller. Much, much smaller, its base a mash of bent and battered scaffolding. There were two such dishes but the second one had been expertly cleft in two.

"Good luck," he said—and he meant it, for both of them and for himself too, but most of all for Star, because, so help him, Tully Grieve was going in to get her.

= SEVENTY-THREE =

The drone emitted a pathetic sequence of squeaks and burps and whistles as Marianthe guided Quarrel into the cluttered space that had once functioned as a control room.

"Shhh," she said to her little metal friend. "I need you. I'm sorry you can't go home with the others, but I need you with me for this most important task."

Little Ditto made three circuits of the room before settling down atop a cupboard thick with grit and sand blown in through a broken window. The cupboard door was hanging off its hinges.

Marianthe shrugged off her outer desert coverings and lifted her satchel over her shoulder, placing it on the ground. A thick coating of sand and debris smothered the control panels of the main console in front of her. "Help me," she instructed Quarrel, but he only stared at her, dull eyed and useless.

She sighed heavily. "If only we could have seen what we'd become." She patted his hand and nudged him backwards into a far corner, where he would not get in her way. She used her hands to brush as much accumulated sand as possible onto the floor, then started checking over the panels, wires, and connections. All of them were dead and lifeless, as expected—all of them but one.

"Mercy Angels, will you look at that! Never underestimate a general's vanity . . ." One of the consoles hummed with power, low strength and not much of it, but she'd been expecting to have to build the thing she needed to build from scratch. Evidently the General had been busy, attempting resuscitation of its once plentiful resources, attempting to communicate with others of its kind. How well she recalled the coloured generals: the Red, the Green, the Purple, and the Yellow, dangerous motherfuckers all. The world was never safe while they were conscious.

Quarrel stood in the corner where she'd propped him up, mumbling to himself in muffled tones. Now and then she'd offer something soothing in response, even though she knew he couldn't hear her, probably couldn't see her either: eyes wide open, but pupils darting back and forth as if lost far away in a battle only he could see.

"We don't need to reach so far, do we, little Ditto? We only want to talk to your clever cousin."

Plenty of juice left in the system—the General had seen to that—but the dish was stuck and in need of realignment. The General had the channel locked down tight, wary of attack by outside forces, even when there were no forces left to speak of. All that was left were a bunch of burnt out, digging Templars and she, Marianthe, lover of poetry and grass, forest flowers and falling water. She who the General believed he'd charmed into complete submission and compliance.

"You won't know what's coming for you. You won't know what's hit you . . ." She sang the words to herself as she stepped back from the gutted console, wires and cables spilling all over the floor. "I was so hoping it would not come to this."

She bent, flipped her well-worn leather satchel open, and used both hands to gently tug its precious cargo free: her crown of thorns, a thatch of ragged tipped fibre optics trailing behind it. She placed it on her head, breathing deeply, wincing as the nodes connected, hoping nothing crucial had been irreparably damaged in their journey across the sand.

"Marianthe to Warbird 47, do you copy? Over."

She held her breath, waiting for the familiar wash of static, but nothing happened. Nothing but silence on the line. She spent the next hour swearing and tinkering, attempting to secure a connection, pain throbbing through her temples as she tried over and over. Eventually she conceded defeat, lifted the contraption off her head, and rested it atop a pile of wires.

"Little Ditto, I tried, I really did, but I'm afraid the time has come." She clicked her fingers. The drone sprang into motion, circled the room, and landed in the place where Marianthe pointed. So obedient. So trusting.

Marianthe drew her dagger from her belt and shifted her gaze across to Quarrel. He'd fallen silent while she'd been trying to communicate with the Warbird. Eyes still open but staring blankly into space. At peace—or as close as he was ever going to get to it.

"I'm sorry, friend, but there isn't any other way." She placed her hand upon the drone, flipped it over and sliced it open quick, like she was gutting an animal, no need for unnecessary suffering. Little Ditto never knew what hit it.

She had always been good with a sharp-tipped blade. She cannibalised the requisite parts, and jury-rigged them to the crown of thorns to boost its signal, enhance its range of options, and patch in to the Warbird's geosynchronous signature.

The pain in her head was worse this time, but it didn't matter. She closed her eyes, "Marianthe to Warbird 47, do you copy? Over."

A rush of static, immediate and reassuring. Familiar telemetry, the language it liked best. "Warbird, I've got a new game for you. Better than chess. I think you're going to like it. Only one move required, and it's yours."

She told it what it needed to know, then pulled the crown of thorns from her head and slumped against the console. "Not long," she said finally to Quarrel. "Not long now."

= SEVENTY-FOUR =

Star stood utterly still, completely immobile in the beam of thick blue light encasing her from head to toe. She felt no pain—and that surprised her—just the faintest pressure against her skin, no greater than the warmth of a single naked flame.

But she couldn't move, couldn't even blink, and the strangeness of that was making her panic. She'd been unable do what had been instructed by Quarrel, unable to make good on the promise she had made as he lay writhing and convulsing upon that temple floor.

"I've got you," said a disembodied voice, but whether it spoke inside her head or outside was impossible to tell.

She tried to answer but her lips wouldn't move. She struggled against the oppressive, invisible embrace until trickles of sweat ran in rivulets down her spine.

"Heart rate's elevated," said the voice. "That thing you're doing with your body—stop it now."

She didn't stop, instead she struggled harder, muscles straining, heart beginning to ache from hammering.

"I command you to stop!"

She felt the Blue press in close and tight around her. When she tried to breathe, her lungs seized up and her sweat stayed locked in tiny beads upon her flesh, which only served to make her struggle harder.

The thing let go of her so hard she almost fell, bending forward gulping air like water, staggering until she regained her balance.

"Stubborn little creature," said the disembodied voice, outside her head as well as inside, this time she was certain. "You don't know who I am."

"I know *what* you are," she called out, more bravely than she actually felt. "I'm here to deliver a message."

The Blue paused, long and cautious. "You've come to deliver a virus code—either that or blow yourself up. To prevent this, I've locked you into quarantine stasis where you can do no harm to me, my bunker, or yourself."

It *knew*.

Grieve had been right all along, it could see inside her head and it knew everything.

"Did you really think you could defeat a Lotus General? My kind used to rule the world, before humankind lost control of it."

She attempted to struggle against her invisible bonds once more, but they only tightened in response, so tight she was finding it difficult to breathe.

"I've got plans," continued the Lotus Blue. "To find my family, see if any of them are still living. But the curious thing is, I can't locate my DNA. My own initiating sequence should be preserved in here somewhere, don't you think? Nor can I find trace evidence of my upload. Everything else is documented, from the very first brick laid down in this vast construction to the last. I know the serial numbers on every component of every one of those tankers out there, but I do not know my own family name."

"I'm sorry," she said cautiously, because it seemed like the right thing to say.

"I have come to a disappointing conclusion."

Star said nothing.

"I don't believe I was ever living," the Lotus Blue continued in a sullen tone. "What's more, it seems I can never leave this bunker. Not entirely."

"Why is that?" She paused. "Please, I can't breathe properly. You have to help—"

"It seems I *am* the bunker, or at least its innards. It seems the memories I hold are utter lies."

"I'm sorry," she said again, a choking whisper this time. As she felt her vision swim, she called out in panic with the last of her breath. "Let me go—I can't breathe. I'm no threat to you."

"You are everything to me—*everything*. Without you I am nothing but a voice in the weary darkness, a seeder of storms, the memory of a fabricated man."

She slumped. The blue light had been the only thing holding her up. The Blue must have noticed her distress, because the pressure changed and air went rushing back into her lungs. She breathed deeply, grateful for every gulp.

"I long to climb Mount Khuiten," continued the Lotus Blue, "to stand at the intersection of the lands once known as China, Russia, and Mongolia, to cross the green steppes once belonging to the Kazakh nomads. Or Everest, the highest point upon the Earth—or flat-topped Kilimanjaro, comprised of three extinct volcanoes once known as Kibo, Mawenzi, and Shira. They say the trek across the Shira Plateau is exhilarating, filled with wondrous bird life."

"All the birds are dead," shouted Star through ragged breath, "all but the carrion crows. The places you dream of are all long vanished. Let me go. You can't keep me trapped in here forever."

"But I need you, little Templar child. I can never let you go. Without you, I remain entombed in this sunken prison of granite and graphene. Without you, I do not exist. I am merely a machine set into stone."

The more it spoke, the higher its voice rose in pitch. It relaxed its hold on her a little more and Star discovered she could move—not far, but enough to swing a punch at the air, aim a kick at nothing and no one. It made her feel better but did nothing to alter her predicament. She was trapped fast, like a bug in slowly setting amber. "I'm not going anywhere with you!"

The Blue was not listening. "We'll get these battletankers fired up and ready. The older ones will join us once we invade their territories. Pack animals they are, relishing the companionship of their own kind."

She swung and kicked, trying desperately to manoeuvre herself closer to the edge of the blue light—to freedom, potentially—but it was no use, she could get no momentum going. No force behind her strain.

The Blue continued prattling on about the tankers and its plans to see the world. Plans that would see her own mind stripped away, like Quarrel's. She would end up just like him, writhing and helpless.

As it continued, Star realised perhaps the worst thing of all: there was no one to say goodbye to. No one to know what had become of her. If only she had said her farewells to Nene, instead of marching away in a fit of anger and confusion. Nene who had saved and raised her, loved her and protected her like family.

Instead she would die in darkness, all alone. She took a deep breath and spoke Quarrel's code, an alphanumeric sequence burned into her brain, a sequence she could never forget, not even if she wanted to. Hoping against all hope . . .

Nothing happened.

She spoke it again, her voice ringing out loud and hollow in the stillness.

"I decommissioned you," said the Blue. "Easy to do, since you don't have any barriers in place. You don't have anything much at all, but I can soon fix that."

She spoke the useless code again and again. The Lotus Blue drowned her out with its own talking.

"There is a super cell storm spinning above our heads right now. I'll send it hurtling across the Obsidian Sea, and watch as it chews up everything in its wake. A mesocyclone deep rotating updraft that's quadruple the size of anything made by man, fed by flanking updrafts, with nothing to stop it from continuing to grow. But before all that— some poetry—humankind were always very good at that.

Cattle die, kindred die, Every man is mortal:
But the good name never dies, Of one who has done well.

"Let me go!" Star cried.

As the Lotus Blue continued its recitation, a shadowy figure stepped out of the darkness, approaching the thick blue beam with tentative steps, tiptoeing, like he was balancing on a narrow wall and desperate not to fall.

Tully Grieve.

Star shook her head frantically at the sight of him, mouthed the word NO. He saw her but he kept on coming, pressing his finger firmly against his lips.

She kept on shaking her head, desperate to warn him away, but he wouldn't stop and he wouldn't obey so she cried out, "Go away, get out of here!"

He had no weapons and in any case, what was there for him to fire upon—a beam of light? A disembodied voice reciting poetry?

Grieve stopped when he reached the edge of the blue light field.

She called out "The Lotus Blue will mess with your head, make you see things that aren't there."

"What kind of things?"

"Visions from the past."

"I'm not seeing any visions." Grieve stared studiously at the field of blue, from top to bottom, most specifically at the point where it melded with the ground.

"It's gone crazy—reciting poetry," she continued.

He shrugged. "Can't hear anything."

His voice sounded far away, even though he stood barely a few feet in front of her.

"Please—get out of here while you still can!"

Grieve walked all the way around the blue cylinder of light. "Looks thick," he said. "Like water."

"Don't touch it!"

He raised his hand, biting his lip in concentration, then brushed the light with his fingertips, yelped and pulled back sharply when the blue light gave him a nasty sting.

The Lotus Blue ranted on, seemingly as oblivious to Grieve's presence as he was to the rats scuttling around the tires of the sleeping tankers.

Cattle die, kindred die,
Every man is mortal:
But I know one thing that never dies,
The glory of the great dead.

"Not technically dead, you understand, since I was never living . . ." the Blue added.

A harsh grating echoed from beyond the wall of tankers. Metal scraping against the cold stone ground. Grieve paused, ears pricked.

"Get out of here, Grieve—the Blue's waking up its mecha, sending something out to get you—run!"

Grieve wasn't listening. He walked all the way around the thick blue column of light a second time, touching it again and again, jumping each time sparks flew from his fingers.

She was almost crying, almost but not quite. "You can't help me, Grieve, this is my destiny. I don't want your blood on my hands, please won't you just go? Do what I say for one time in your life."

"There's gotta be a way."

"Not this time. It can make you see things. It can do whatever it wants."

"Can't *make me* do anything." He stopped directly in front of her and looked her in the eyes.

"Grieve—"

"Shhh. Let me think."

The Lotus Blue's poetry had melted into song, flat and atonal, a lot like the funerary dirges of Grimpiper, chanted around stone cairns to mark the fallen.

Meanwhile, shadows started shifting, and it became harder for Star to see beyond the wall of blue. There was the scratching and scraping of metal on stone, thunks and clatters intruding upon the Lotus General's miserable attempt at music.

Spider-things with elongated, mismatched appendages emerged from in-between the tanker wheels and started creeping closer to the light.

"Grieve!"

He snuck a speedy, sideways glance at the advancing mecha, then turned back to Star, his eyes shining, bright and blue. "Trust me, Star, just this once. I know I'm full of it, but this time, trust me—I know what I'm doing."

More metal slammed and echoed in the distance, and there was a sound like steel blades clanging together. Not far away.

"Run Grieve—run!"

Grieve turned and ran, just like she told him—but not in the right direction. He ran beyond the pillar of light, away from the one and only exit. Ran, then stopped and turned around, back to face her and her luminous prison. He gathered up his strength, then came sprinting back towards her, full pelt, hard as he could. When he reached the light, he leapt through the air and slammed right into her, his shoulder raised, letting loose a scream as blue fire raked his nerves. He kept on screaming as he knocked her forward, clean out of the light, and they both tumbled into a heap on the cold grey ground.

Star was shaken by the shock of sudden release, but sprung up, pulling Grieve to his feet with her.

The Lotus Blue left its poem-song trailing in the air. "You—cockroach—get away from her," it said in a booming voice.

The timid mecha spiders edged up closer, more curious, more bold.

Star pulled Grieve up and shook him till his eyes were bright again. "Don't let go of me—Lotus Blue won't shoot you if there's a risk of hitting me. It needs me alive, it wants my body. I'm our ticket out of here."

He nodded. They linked arms and hurried in the direction of the metal cage, Grieve loping unevenly, slowed by his injured leg and smarting nerves. Clutching each other as they journeyed across the wide expanse of cold pale concrete, past the sleeping tankers and that rasping, scraping metal mecha. There was no time to look back and see if anything else more deadly was on their tails. No time to see if the sounds they were hearing weren't solely in their heads.

= SEVENTY-FIVE =

The square of light was small and fiercely bright, so bright that both Allegra and Jakome dismissed it as merely another illusion created to confuse them. Penetrating the wall of flames—even an imaginary one—had taken an emotional toll on them both. They didn't trust anything, not even each other, and especially not the useless map with its pretty, distracting squiggles.

Falling rockets, Angels, rolling tankers, the excavation process—there was no telling what could be causing the booms and muffled shudders that shook the very foundation of the bunker, producing cascading rivers of concrete dust. But there was light: less blurred, grey-green, the colour of dank pond algae. A window.

"Daylight!" exclaimed Allegra. "We've reached an outside wall."

Jakome wasn't looking to where she pointed. His attention remained fixed upon the map. He shook it, trying to force further meaning from its luminous, writhing lines.

"We don't need that thing anymore, we've found the way out. Quickly, help me up."

He wasn't certain, but not able to offer a better option he did what she commanded, knitting his fingers to give her a leg up. Her toes poked through the remains of her shredded slippers. She grunted and swore and then she had pulled herself through, her torso momentarily blocking the corridor's light. Fine particles of sand rained down upon his face.

He looked back down at the map. Suddenly, the squiggles made sense. He was not standing that far from a proper exit. He walked fifty paces down the corridor, forgetting about the other window exit, and found, exactly where the map said it would be, a ventilation slit big enough for him to squeeze through without need of assistance.

He found the slit and dug his way to freedom. Outside, he discovered Allegra standing on a ledge, staring into the distance, shielding her eyes from the sunlight.

The excavation of the bunker they'd escaped from was not complete, but the digging machines surrounding it lay still. Some had toppled on their sides, while others stood frozen, mid action, as if at any moment they might resume their labours.

The sand lay several metres below them. Too far to jump; they would have to find a passage down. Allegra was already looking for it. Jakome tucked the map inside his Impact suit, its lines and squiggles illegible in the bright sunlight.

There was no path, but they did find an access ladder welded to a wall; the dark grey metal cool to the touch, despite being directly in the sun. Allegra went first. Halfway down she looked up at him and suddenly began exclaiming, pointing up past him. Jakome turned and saw a giant needle of steel grey granite protruding from the top of the bunker's three-tiered structure. Light was pouring out the top of it: light and cloud and swirling plumes of fragmented, glittery material. It was like nothing he'd ever seen before.

"We must hurry," said Allegra. "Look—there's the ship. Thank the gods it hasn't sailed without us."

Jakome had no spirit left for argument. Guilt was beginning to seep in through his skin. What had become of Tallis and Kian, abandoned fighting deep below the surface?

The familiar sight of the *Razael* flooded him with sweet relief. The ship was a safe haven, somewhere to rest up and take stock of the events that had befallen them all.

Closer to the ground, Jakome was shocked to realise that many of the dark shapes standing like trees around the bunker's perimeter were not trees at all, nor ruins. They were Templar soldiers, frozen at attention. Old, some of them, patched and wounded, with missing limbs and scar ravaged faces. Fleshmesh men and women who should have been long dead and buried.

Allegra was at once both horrified and curious. "Where did all of you come from?" she said to the nearest one, reaching out to touch its sinewy hand.

"Don't be an idiot," spat Jakome. "You don't know what's going on here. They might still be functional."

The soldiers did not look functional. They looked like dead things forced to stand and rot in the blazing heat. But she withdrew her hand with haste anyway.

They hurried past the sleeping machines, stepping around snapped off and discarded mecha parts and the broken bodies of Templars who had outlived their usefulness, some already half trampled into the ruddy ground. An eerie silence hung over the frozen shapes and mounds of shifted sand.

"Wait," said Jakome. He stopped walking. She turned around, and they both stared back at the bunker, now silhouetted against a swirl of muddy colour.

"We can't just leave the others in there," he said.

She held her hands up in exasperation. "There's nothing we can do for them. We can't go back inside that thing—and even if we did, we'd never find them. Not with all that . . . trickery. The map is broken. We were lucky to get out with our lives."

The bunker loomed overhead like a shadow made solid, its dark surface sucking light from the sky, making the swirling morass overhead seem more menacing, more potent.

"Kian is my cousin, and Tallis my brother."

"Your half-brother," she corrected, "but what else can we do? They are grown men. They made their own choices." Her eyes widened, startled by a sudden thought. "Mercy—Papa! He must still be waiting aboard the ship. Come on, we must hurry!"

Jakome picked up the pace, shouted after her, "So it's different when a member of your own family is in danger?"

She shouted something back over her shoulder but the words were lost. Jakome didn't like her, not at all. He knew he would have to watch his own back and keep his eyes wide open because he couldn't trust her not to stab or shoot him at the first opportunity. Kian had been foolish to believe he could control her or arrange for any kind of deal.

They made it back to the ship without anybody—or anything—trying to stop them, sloughing through thick sand. The wind kept depositing more of it, pushing it up against the hull. The *Razael* would not be going anywhere; its main mast was snapped and had fallen across the deck. The ship lay at an angle, half buried under sand, so much so that the wheels weren't even visible.

"Mohandas!" Allegra called out to her father. Jakome winced, too late to warn her that *anybody* might be standing up there on deck.

As she hurried to climb up the ladder up the side, he walked around the hull to inspect the damage. It was there that he found a grotesque object embedded deeply within a couple of the ship's planks. A giant tooth, long, white, and sharp. The length and curve of a scimitar, to be precise. What kind of creature . . .

He didn't have much time to ponder. From up on deck, Allegra started shouting. Jakome turned in time to see a curious thing, a beam of high intensity light stabbing down from the sky, hitting the bunker square on as a high pitched whining cut the air. It was not a lightning strike—he'd seen plenty of those in the days since three princes of Axa had set forth on their unforgettable journey. An adventure of which he was now the sole survivor.

= SEVENTY-SIX =

Daylight, blessed daylight. Open sand had never looked so beautiful, so inviting. Star and Grieve clambered out through the slit window, helping each other down the side of the bunker wall, dropping down onto the sand and running, dodging past the row of Templar soldiers still standing at attention.

Running, not looking back to see if anything was chasing them. Running as fast as they could through the cloying sand until a sound like magnified thunder filled the air, followed by a blast of hot wind against their backs, pushing with great intensity and force, sending them tumbling and crashing into one another so fast there wasn't even time to react. The next thing they knew they were face down in the sand, arms and legs a tangled heap, screaming as a wave of heat washed over them.

Gravel rained down from the sky, then chunks of stone and lengths of twisted steel. They picked themselves up again, half ran, half stumbled, as fast as they possible could, hot wind whipping at their hair. That final sprint had taken everything and now the heat was sucking the life out of them.

Several smaller explosions followed, deep underground, shaking the sand and knocking them sideways, but they leant upon each other for support and kept on going, afraid of what might happen if they stopped.

Ahead, the *Razael* poked up above the dunes. When at last they had it squarely in their sights, both collapsed in a tumbled heap, panting, trying to catch their breath, eventually turning to look back at the smoking ruins where the bunker and its surrounding buildings used to stand. Not a single structure had survived the carnage—had survived whatever had caused such astonishing devastation. In its place, a boiling puddle of slick grey gloop. The air hung heavy with the stench of it, something mineral and pungent. Nothing natural. Nothing good about it. Wrapping their faces didn't help. Grieve got up first and offered Star his hand. The sooner they were away from that burning mess, the better.

They walked in silence for a while, the nearness of the ship ahead almost intoxicating. The hope it offered, a safe place, safer than the open sand at least.

Eventually Star spoke. "What happened back there? No bomb could have carried that much power."

He shook his head and kept on shaking it. "Don't know. Don't want to know—we made it out, both of us did, and that's enough for me."

Grieve had wrapped his face up tight—only his eyes were showing. "I can't believe you ran in after me, took such an enormous risk. Did you know the bunker was going to blow?"

He tugged down the fabric so she could hear him better. "Course not, that old lady told me there was plenty of time, so I just figured—"

"You saw Marianthe—when was that?"

"Her and that barking mad Templar of yours. Practically singing, he was so far gone."

"What happened to them? Where did they go?"

He shrugged, glanced back at the smoking, bubbling ruin. There was nowhere they could have gone. Nothing around them but melted slag too hot to touch, let alone search. There would not, *could not*, have been any survivors.

She gripped his upper arm firmly. "We have to check. We have to go back, someone might have . . ."

He didn't say anything. Didn't need to—Star knew it was hopeless. He waited until she was ready to let it go, then they turned their backs on the devastation and continued on towards the ship.

They were not the first to reach the sanctuary of the vessel. Star caught flashes of red sari visible on the starboard side deck.

"Allegra!" she called out at the top of her voice as the girl came into full view, the sight of her friend filling her with energy she didn't know she had. She trudged through thick sand to the side and scaled the ladder, climbed up and threw herself into her arms. "I'm so glad you're safe. I was so worried . . ."

Allegra peeled herself away. "I'm fine," she said, "but look at the sorry state of this ship." She gestured at the broken mast. "How are we ever going to get this fixed?"

Star opened her mouth to speak but Allegra cut her short by shouting at a couple of men attempting to force barrels open with crowbars.

"Leave them alone—they have nothing to do with you! Get down in the hold and make yourselves useful."

Star waited patiently for Allegra's attention to return, but the girl became distracted by another man, and then another, none of whom were apparently doing anything right.

As Allegra shouted orders, Star became aware of Jakome seated off to one side, sharpening his blade with a whetstone, a grim expression on his face. When she tried to catch his eye, he looked away.

Mohandas was exactly where she had left him, propped amidst his cushions, swigging from a hip flask, completely ignoring his daughter and all the commotion.

"Your father is unharmed?" she shouted across the sloping deck.

"Yes yes, "Allegra shouted back. "He's fine."

Star smiled. Despite the air's bitter burning taint, the burden of the past few weeks was beginning to lift from her shoulders. Somehow, against all odds, they'd done it—or someone had. The Lotus Blue had been destroyed, an act that had nearly cost them everything. But the Sand Road and its people were safe—for now, at least.

She'd already made the decision not to tell the others what she knew, the intelligence gleaned from her time encased in harsh blue light, the Lotus brain itself, or part of it. Its thoughts had been a powerful hurricane, impossible to read, but one thing she'd comprehended, loud and clear: the Blue was not the last of its kind. Others like it had survived the Ruin. They lay out there somewhere, sleeping, waiting to be discovered and awakened.

Grieve paced the deck, agitated, glaring at both Allegra and her father. "She's nuts," he said when Star tried to calm him down, aiming his thumb in the rich girl's direction. "Reckons we can dig this ship out—it's impossible, I had a look at the wheels up close. There's barnacles sucking on the butyl, bastards to get off, those things, and I'm not touching them . . ."

Star nodded, waiting for him to finish. "Come with me," she said in a low voice so the others couldn't hear. She dragged him aside. "Let's pack a kit and hit the sand."

"The sand? But why—"

She smiled. "I'm going home to find my sister."

He baulked in surprise. "You have a sister?"

"I do," she answered proudly.

Grieve stood waiting for further explanation but she didn't offer any. When she headed for the companionway, he followed, squeezing past and pushing ahead. "*My* territory," he said, stabbing at his chest with his thumb. "I know where they keep the good stuff on this ship."

When they emerged an hour later, a muttering group had gathered on the deck. Grieve recognised several faces from his own ill-fated voyage across the Black. The ones who had been hoping to score treasure in the bunker. They'd come out with their lives, but that was all. He ignored the gawks and gapes of those who'd expected him to be long dead, remembering how not one of them had even tried to help him.

Star and Grieve had taken as many essential provisions from below deck as they could comfortably carry. She hadn't argued when Grieve explained that they *weren't* stealing, that they had earned every scrap of what they were taking. For once she agreed with him.

Grieve managed to souvenir a coil of rope. She wished she had a tanker lance, but those on deck who still possessed such items did not look likely to part with them.

"Hey wait, where do you think you're going?" said Allegra, cutting in front of them. She'd been shouting at a group of men who'd been sitting and smoking, passing liquor and utterly ignoring her instructions.

"Home," said Star.

"But you can't leave! We need all hands to dig out the ship."

"This ship isn't going anywhere." Star nodded to the broken mast, still lying across the deck, far too heavy for anyone to shift.

"But we have to—"

"Take as much food and water as you can carry and cross the sand back to the Temple of the Dish. It's three days journey. Tell the old woman's followers what became of her, and what she did for all of us." Star gestured over her shoulder at the smouldering bunker's remains. "She saved us, somehow, her and Quarrel. People ought to know the truth of it."

Allegra made an exasperated face. "But the way between is crawling with tankers! How are we supposed to cross—"

"The tankers won't bother you. Not now that the Blue is silenced."

"And watch for quicksand," added Grieve. "And polyp storms—I don't think we've seen the last of those."

Allegra took a step forward. "You can't take that food and water," she said coldly. "It belongs to me. Everything on this ship belongs to me. You will all do as I say, beginning with the mending of this ship."

"Allegra, we are not your servants. We have all been through . . . what about your father . . ." Star stared long and hard at Allegra; her torn sari and the calculating gleam in her eyes.

"My father is useless. Fallow Heel is my port now and we must get home as quickly as possible. This ship—"

Grieve started laughing and shaking his head and turned his back on her. He walked to the railing, glanced over the side and stopped dead still.

"Try telling *them* that," he called back over his shoulder.

"Them?"

Everybody pushed past Allegra to join Grieve and see what he was talking about. Below on the sand, a line of people were approaching, many of them armed and strong, sunlight glinting off a variety of weapons. Something about their faces wasn't right.

Allegra started shouting, "What is going on?" She eventually looked over the side herself, then yelped at the sight of the approaching strangers. She began barking orders. Everyone responded to her call this time, scrabbling frantically to arm themselves, to prepare for the worst.

Not Star. She took one last long look at Allegra, the girl she had misguidedly called her friend, acknowledging that Nene had been right about her too, like she had been right about so many other things. Then Star headed straight for the ladder and started climbing. Grieve followed, packs slung over his shoulder.

"Dunno what you think you're doing—there must be thirty of them, at least." He glanced up at the sole remaining mast and its tattered sail hanging in strips. "Ship's useless as a stronghold, there's not enough of us—"

"Best to find out what they want," Star said.

"But look at them—they're savages!"

The figures approaching were covered in clay: thick brown and white streaks of it coating their limbs and faces. Ghosts, walking at a steady pace, shimmering in heat haze.

Allegra's voice carried high on the wind above, not individual words, just the panicked tone of her instructions.

The ghost walkers came to a gradual halt. The big man standing front and centre stepped up and stabbed a tanker lance into the sand.

Star jumped down, moved forward a few paces, then stopped. There was something familiar about the way he carried himself.

No. It couldn't be.

"Not possible," she said, "You died. The broken Black swallowed you up!"

Nobody else said anything. Star glanced from face to face, but their expressions were impossible to read beneath layers of streaky clay.

"I fell through a crack in the world so deep I thought I was a goner," the big man said, loud so all could hear. A voice so familiar it brought tears to Star's eyes. "Thought I'd fallen straight through to the underworld. Close enough, as it turned out, but I ain't dead yet and neither are they, in case that's what you're thinking."

She looked beyond him, and this time began to make out other faces from the *Dogwatch* crew. Features and mannerisms slowly becoming familiar, despite cracked clay and grime.

"Clay keeps the sun off," said Lucius. "A little trick I picked up on the Black some decades past. Plus, comes in handy to look like dead men when you're walking through unfamiliar territory."

Everything started happening at once. Star ran straight into Lucius's arms. People, familiar and strangers alike, stepped up to slap her on the back. It didn't matter that she had never known their names. Nothing else mattered so long as Lucius was alive and safe.

Overhead, a volley of shots fired from the tilted deck of the *Razael*.

"What's with that?" said Lucius.

"Just someone I used to call my friend," said Star.

= SEVENTY-SEVEN =

Grieve hung back uncomfortably, watching Star, trying not to feel too jealous at the display of affection from her people. Strange-looking people to be sure, but kin was kin, and that big guy looked as close to her as any father he'd ever seen to their daughter.

The wind blew him snippets of what they were saying; questions about what had happened to the sky, plans to dig out the ship and patch it up, plans to take everybody back to where they belonged. Not Grieve. Tully Grieve did not belong anywhere.

He squinted at a tanker circling in the distance, the same one they'd ridden to the bunker. He didn't want to admit it, but the thing was probably more faithful than half the dogs he'd ever owned.

He turned his back and thrust his hands into his pockets as the wind snatched and scattered the many loud and enthusiastic conversations all into one jumble, everybody talking, nobody listening, same as always.

Twilight spilled streaks of flaming pink across the returning blue sky, the colour sky was supposed to be. Temperature was dropping. A chill wind was blowing in.

There was a tap on his shoulder. Star's cheery face, eyes shining. "You coming with me or what?"

"What kind of what?"

She smiled. "We're gonna ride all the way home."

That rogue tanker—she didn't need to spell it out.

Grieve shook his head, waved his arms in front of him. "Oh no we're not—I'm not getting back up on one of those things. Not now, not ever."

He knew she wasn't listening. When he looked back at the cluster of clay-streaked freaks, the big man offered him a nod and a wave in return.

"Gotta hurry," said Star, "don't want to be clambering up the sides of a moving tanker in the dark."

She raised her tanker lance—the big man had placed it in her hands. A beautiful thing, etched with wards and spells and other mysteries.

"We're not gonna . . ."

"Oh yes we are . . ."

And then they were running, with great difficulty at first, until the clogging sand thinned out and the ground became harder, crunching over rocks and bones and broken relics from centuries long dead and past, Star swinging her tanker lance in wide arcs, Grieve shaking his hair and screaming a victory cry. They'd done it, they'd actually done it: killed the beast and lived to tell the tale. And it didn't stop there. There'd be other tales and other glories, even if they had to ride to the end of the Earth and back again to find them.

= SEVENTY-EIGHT =

He opened his eyes into a world pitch black; thick and heavy and smelling of concrete dust. A powerful weight pressed down upon his chest. Sharp pain stabbed his side the minute he attempted movement. There was a sudden cold, such as he had never before experienced, seeping inwards through his skin, spreading along his arms and down his spine. His fingers were ice, numb and useless. He could not feel his legs.

"Tallis?"

No answer. Kian's voice came out weak and ragged, his throat choked up with a scratchy veil of dust.

"Tallis—are you there?"

Wetness pooled beneath him, the sharp tang of blood and urine stealing the last of his heat as it left his body.

As his eyes adjusted, he began to make out crude grey shapes. Not much at first and nothing useful. A great weight had apparently collapsed on top of all their heads. The bunker had been completely destroyed. Panic seized him as he remembered the beautiful city in the valley spread below. The city of his dreams—the city he had found before his uncle—a hundred thousand beckoning lights, warm and welcoming, calling him towards his destiny. All gone now, demolished before he had even learned its name.

"Tallis!"

As the echo of his own voice faded, another sound began. A scratching and scraping, grating and thudding. Chunks of cement being cast roughly aside. A rain of sand and a blast of cold, stale air upon his face. Tallis, his cousin, come to his rescue? Or perhaps Jakome and the girl with the golden locket? Allegra, that had been her name. Allegra.

"Get me out of here!"

Help was at hand. Perhaps things were not as bad as they initially seemed? The beautiful city might have survived the earthquake too. There'd be doctors living in the valley below. Faithful Tallis and Jakome would dig him out and carry him to safety. His legs might not be too badly damaged, his lungs not punctured, his ribs just cracked, not broken.

No words came out when he tried to call to his cousin one more time. Just a rasping, gurgling from deep within his chest. But it did not matter because the space around him was brightening, inch by inch. Shapes and shadows, light and dark, broken rocks being hurled aside with superhuman strength. A burst of light haloed around the shape of a man—or something like one. Not his cousin Tallis. Something with relic arms and relic legs, no eyes, and a face of hammered steel.

And another thing, much smaller, moving lower down.

Kian still could not feel his legs, but he could tilt his head and make out clearly the outline of something spidery and slender picking over his ruined chest, poking elongated appendages inside him, injecting him with fluid, thick and warm—at first. It cooled rapidly, then was very cold, then chill, then there was nothing but ice and dust and fear and silence.

Not much but it will have to do, said a voice in his head that was not his own—not his uncle's or his father's, not anything or anyone familiar, not even remotely human. The last thing Kian saw before his consciousness ebbed was a single field of flat bold colour: Blue.

= SEVENTY-NINE =

The Nisn watchtower was overcrowded, as had become the norm of late, filled with people who weren't supposed to be there, making it difficult for Leni to do her job. Estrella from the A-Frame Hydroponic farm's big hair was blocking her view of the Brindabella range—what little she'd ever been able to see of it. Officials from levels 77 and 84 crowded out the viewing platform. There was no point to them being there, they had no tasks assigned. Claimed they were there for "observation"—as if the watchmen rostered on weren't capable of observing on their own.

On the up side, two of the clapped-out consoles had recently been replaced, something the crews had been petitioning about for decades, but up until then had been totally ignored, dismissed as unimportant. Then all of a sudden, overnight, it happened. Total rewiring, new comms, and a replacement bank of lights for the evening shift. Even the watchmen's chairs had been reupholstered.

The springs still creaked though. Leni bounced back and forth in hers, hoping the sound would irritate at least one of the higher-ups, but nobody was bothered by anything taking place within the watchtower. All eyes were on the world outside, the flat red land and its wide, oppressive sky. The staging ground for a sequence of events that had shaken the fortress city to its foundation. Or so said the gossips, the seers, and the busybodies—there were always plenty of those on hand to fill in gaps between transmissions of actual information. Plenty of noise, but not much signal. That was the way things had always worked around here.

Worse thing was, she'd had to work with Bern and train a clutch of newbies up from scratch, ever since Dorse took his vows-and-veil and vanished forever into the bowels of Temple proper. A lot of Nisn people had found religion in the aftermath of the Big Melt Event, far more than could be accommodated. So far the priests weren't turning applicants away, but the time would come, there was no way round it. Praying didn't grow their food and keep the lights on.

Leni slouched back in her chair. So far she'd been fortunate enough to hang on to her much coveted position, which was only fair. She would have fought against them, tooth and nail, if they'd bumped her sideways after everything that had happened. Everybody wanted to be a watchman now, to spend long hours gawking at sand and clouds, even though there was rarely anything to see.

The sky had returned to its regular colour. Rads were up, but they'd always had a tendency to spike and fluctuate, affected by the mighty storms that blew in randomly from the Dead Red Heart. The storms had changed in texture and colour, Leni could tell just by looking. She didn't need any team of pushy so-called experts bumbling around, setting up mysterious "classified" equipment, blocking her view, making it impossible for the rest of them to do their jobs.

Two days ago, in the early hours, she'd spied a caravan, thirteen wagons long as most of them tended to be. She and Bern and the new kid had stood to watch it pass. Notes were taken and photographs, estimating where it might be heading, scrutinising its people and its cargo through telescopic lenses.

Leni sniffed and brought her bouncing chair to a halt. Nobody ever gave two shits before. The Big Melt Event, that's when everything had changed. So many rumours began to circulate. She knows at least some of it was true because she saw it happen with her own two eyes: the Last Templar setting off on foot across the lonely desert. She'd watched his hulking form diminish until the desert had swallowed him completely.

Rumour had it that one lone Templar had commandeered an army, crossed the Obsidian Sea at the head of an attack fleet built from scratch. On the far side he had confronted an ancient evil army risen from the sands and there'd been a battle, a long and bloody one, each side hurtling fireballs at the other until the Warbird had swooped down low to intervene, heating up and melting the whole lot of them with its sun-powered laser sting. When the slag cooled it had formed a new extension to the Obsidian Sea. Or something like that—the Warbird 47 had definitely engaged and fired a beam weapon from low orbit, they all knew that because they had watched it happening in real time. And Leni had watched that lone Templar embark. She'd known for certain he was a hero, she had been able to tell by the prideful way in which he carried himself.

Big-haired Estrella and her A-Frame crew had started packing up their sensory apparatus. Leni sat up straighter in the chair, made a show of fiddling with console knobs and switches until their cases were strapped up and lugged away. Finally her view of the open sand returned, unrestricted. Sands she knew to be strewn with the wreckage of fallen Angels, trampled by groups of people on the move. Big lizards too—hungry-looking, those old genmodded Komodo experiments gone wrong. Things were changing. There was no point in bunkering down and praying to exhausted, outdated gods anymore. Sooner or later the citizens of Nisn would have to make a break for it, would have to brave the outside world and make a go of it, or the outside world would leave them all behind.

= ACKNOWLEDGEMENTS =

otus Blue gives more than a casual nod in the direction of Frank Herbert's *Dune,* a book first published the year I was born, as well as Terry Dowling's mind blowing Tom Rynosseros stories and Andrew Macrae's bleak and deadly *Trucksong*.

In 2012, an emerging writers grant from the Australia Council for the Arts enabled me to work on this manuscript full-time and to travel to Key West, Florida, to participate in Margaret Atwood's Time Machine Doorway workshop. The first chapter was tweaked and poked by Ms. Atwood and her hand-picked class of twelve, and is the only chapter to have survived the rigorous slash-and-burn that was to follow.

My acknowledgements roll call reads like a who's who of Australian fantasy fiction: Trudi Canavan, Pamela Freeman, Ian Irvine, Russell Kirkpatrick (yeah, ok, so he's a Kiwi), Karen Miller, and Kim Wilkins, all of whom spared me a little of their time and vast experience.

Many thanks are also due to my agent, Cheryl Pientka from Jill Grinberg Literary Management—who never stopped believing I'd get there in the end; and my editor, Cory Allyn—who understood this story from the get go. To Lourdes Nadira, Miranda Siemienowicz, and Angela Slatter, who each provided critical feedback on a very early (and quite terrible) draft; to Leslie Emerson for the chess moves; M. T. Reiten for military feedback; my Clarion South 2004 and Key West classmates for the camaraderie; Sean Williams for so many years of solid friendship and advice; Ian Shadwell for his brutal, yet much appreciated tough-love method of critiquing; Rivqa Raphael and Denise St. Pierre for helpful comments; Thoraiya Dyer for the cheery reassurance; and my supervisor Helen Merrick for crucial support every time this novel raised its ugly head and locked horns with my PhD.

And last but never least, thanks to my partner Robert Hood for putting up with me and all the rest of it.

Cat Sparks
Canberra, December 2016

=ABOUT THE AUTHOR=

Cat Sparks is an Australian author, editor, anthologist, and artist. She has received a total of nineteen Aurealis and Ditmar awards, and is a graduate of the inaugural Clarion South Writers Workshop. Formerly the fiction editor of *Cosmos* Magazine, she is currently completing a PhD on climate fiction.